# dreaming to live

Embracing Life Series

Davis T. Gerencer

# Table of Contents

# Telepathy Chapter 1

Monday, May 15th Telepathy

Sixth-hour Science was only half over, but I needed the day to be done. Mr. Smit had just finished lecturing about Mohs Hardness Scale, leaving the remainder of the period for scratching a bunch of rocks together. I pretended to be doing the given task, but my thoughts were consumed with the teen suicide prevention topic we covered in Health class today. I didn't participate in the discussion; instead, my mind was busy thinking about last Christmas Eve when my first suicide attempt had failed miserably.

My memory of the day was incredibly detailed. It was as if I was sitting in my bedroom, bleeding to death at this very moment. I could hear a snowstorm brewing outside with sleet pelting my window relentlessly. Dad was in China taking care of some business for my grandpa; the rest of my family members were in their bedrooms getting ready for church, which was what I was supposed to be doing.

The event started to unfold when I returned to my room with a razor blade. I decided not to write a suicide note; it seemed a bit cliché since my charismatic personality usually led me to the outer fringes of where I firmly planted my flag. That's the thing about suicide; the survivors never get to find out why you had done it, especially if you arbitrarily choose not to leave a note.

With my knees bent, sitting on the floor, back resting against the bed, I placed my bare feet firmly in front of me. I started to feel anxious as I picked up the razor blade, holding it between my right thumb and index finger. My left hand was shaking so hard, I had to brace it between my knees.

Each beat of my pounding heart could be felt in my wrist as I searched for the correct spot. When I touched my skin with the blade, I immediately started feeling dizzy. The sharp edge went in deeper with minimal effort as I continued to ease it up toward my hand. The pain was excruciating. A thin line of blood trickled down my arm, which quickly developed into a massive flow until I felt my whole body begin to heat up. I started to sweat profusely, and my vision became blurry before passing out.

I finally regained consciousness, finding myself lying over on my left side, with my arm tucked under my limp body. I had no idea how long I'd been out, but I was able to sit up so I could assess the damage. When I realized the razor blade was no longer in my hand, I searched frantically, finally finding it lying in a pool of blood on my carpet. I quickly fished the blade out of the large clots with my trembling hand; I knew it was time to make a second decision. Should I finish the job or try to find a less painful way to die?

While pausing for a few seconds to consider other alternatives, something clicked in my brain. I wasn't sure how or why it happened, but the moment had passed. I no longer wanted to take my own life. I needed to stop worrying about what others thought of me and focus on what was important in life; besides, there was nothing wrong with being gay. Suicide shouldn't be the way my life ended.

I needed to hit pause on my depressing trip down memory lane so I could get everything together before the end of class. As I shoved my tablet into my backpack, my mind started to wander again, thinking about someone who wasn't depressing. He was who I thought about whenever my mind had a spare minute. I couldn't stop thinking about him. Especially after the unfortunate altercation he and I had last Thursday. Kevin Larson was easily the cutest kid in my…

*"Hey, Zach, what time is your game tonight?"*

Who the hell said that? The loud, nearby voice caused me to quickly spin my head around to see who had snuck up on me while I was lost in my thoughts about Kevin.

The sudden movement toward the voice almost sent me flying off my stool, causing my knees to thump the underside of the table, creating an awkward ruckus. The fact that someone approached me without my notice had left me in a tizzy.

There was no one near me except for Abby, who was sitting across the high-rise table. She looked at me as if I had lost my mind. I checked in the other direction two more times, entirely baffled by the unexplained phenomenon. It was then, I realized I had made a scene. I quickly made eye contact with Mr. Smit, who was sitting at his desk. Oh no, I must have had evidence of panic in my expression. "Robert, is everything all right?" my teacher asked with concern.

Barely having time to figure out what, or who, I had heard, I quickly responded with a "Sorry, I'm fine." My mind began running through all the possibilities of what had just happened. Clearly, I had heard a male voice ask Zach what time his game was tonight, but who was Zach, and from whom did the message come? The only Zach I knew was Kevin's friend, neither of whom were in this classroom with me. While retracing the steps to help explain the voice, I heard it again.

*"I'll be there to watch you pitch a no-hitter after my practice lets out."* I knew this as a familiar voice, but I couldn't pinpoint the owner in my state of shock. What was I thinking–'Pinpoint the owner?'

At last, the end-of-period tone sounded. I returned the sample minerals to the front, handed in an unfinished assignment, and left the room with one hell of a headache. I began to wander down the crowded hallway, making my way toward the exit. I was beyond ready to leave this place for the day.

Almost to the doorway, someone body checked my left shoulder with so much force, I nearly lost balance, finding myself facing the opposite direction.

*Come on, Van Stark, watch where you're going!* Kevin Larson said with a booming voice as he looked back at me. After the shove, I began composing myself but stopped dead in my tracks as everyone continued to push past me. Oh no! This wasn't good. Kevin never actually opened his mouth when he spoke. Could it have been my overactive imagination? Nope, it was the same voice I heard in sixth-hour. I accidentally tapped into Kevin Larson's mind while listening to what he was thinking.

At least, now, it was confirmed. Something had gone terribly wrong with my mind. If I could only figure out why I envisioned a gray-colored corridor in Kevin's mind when I intercepted his thought, it may help me figure out why this was happening. "Oh, sorry," I told some kid who just bumped into the back of me.

As I pushed through the doors to exit the school, I wasn't surprised to find my mom parked in the fire lane. The signs clearly said, 'Fire Lane. No Parking.' My mom taught at a local Christian school and had left her job early to drive me to a doctor's appointment. I've had a cold for two weeks that I haven't been able to shake. Apparently, she believed my security detail was incapable of ensuring that I showed up at the doctor's office, so I gave Gary a wave goodbye as I climb into my mom's SUV.

Last fall, after my dad left us, Gary was assigned to protect me. Gary kept me safe–Monday through Wednesday–and I had Andy Thursday through Saturday. You may think it would be cool to have someone who was protecting you wherever you went, but from the perspective of a fourteen-year-old kid who was trying his best to fit in, I could say with certainty that it really sucked.

The truck was quiet, so I pulled my phone from my pocket and brought up Google search. I needed to figure out why I could hear what Kevin was thinking. 'What is it called when I hear voices in my head?' I entered into the search engine.

'Hearing voices is an auditory hallucination that may be associated with mental health problems.'

Nice! The search also offered another comforting possibility that said a 'psychotic disorder' might cause the voices. Great!

Next, my fingers punched in, 'What is it called when I can read someone's mind?'

'Telepathy is communication between minds.'

That sounded more accurate. Telepathy was much better than a 'psychotic disorder.' Searching for the correct phrase in Google may mean the difference between a 'communication' or a 'hallucination.'

"What are you looking at, honey?" my mom asked as I continued to surf for answers.

"Just doing some research," I told her without bothering to look up from my screen.

"Did you have a good day at school?" Yeah, some stupid dumbass stuck a hate note in my locker this morning, and then during sixth-hour, I started hearing Kevin Larson's voice even though he was nowhere to be seen. To top it all off, Kevin body-checked me on my way out of school. Oh! By the way, there's a strong possibility I'm going crazy. So, overall, I'd say my day was effing awesome, I facetiously thought to myself.

"It was fine, I guess," I mumbled instead.

"Seems like something may be bothering you. Do you want to talk about it?" When did you notice that, Mom? My life has been in a downward spiral for the last six months. You want to talk about it now? Are you serious?

"No, I'm fine," I said flatly, instead, slouching down in the shotgun seat. Thankfully, my mom didn't ask me any other stupid-ass questions. I just didn't want to talk anymore, but there was no polite way to verbalize it. At least our conversation didn't turn into an argument like it usually did.

The road noise was mesmerizing, causing me to go into a trance, thinking about how messed up my life has been since my dad left us in November. The memory was etched in my brain as if it were engraved by ancient Egyptian's taking hallucinogens.

My dad was packing his office when I walked in and plopped down in a chair opposite his desk.

"What's on your mind, Slugger?" he asked without turning toward me.

"It just sucks that you can't live here with us anymore," I told him while looking down, fiddling with the drawstrings on my sweatpants.

"We'll still be able to spend time together when I come home for Recess. Of course, the holidays will allow for some time together," my dad calmly said as he pulled some books from a shelf behind his desk.

"I know; it's just that you've always been there for me when I need someone to talk with. Nobody here understands me as you do," I explained, trying to keep the whining from seeping into my tone.

"You'll be fine here with your Mother," he said, picking up a picture of me from his desk and placing it in a box. "I think you'd be surprised how well she understands you. If you'd only let her in," he said, turning toward me, patting his chest over his heart. "Besides, I'll be home next month for a few days."

I could feel my dad's close presence as I sat there silently, sulking. He cleared his throat, apparently waiting for me to look up. When I did, he reached down to move my hair from my eyes. "Don't worry. Everything will work out fine. I promise."

The day my dad left home, things weren't 'fine' as he had promised. His job took him to Washington, DC, where he worked and lived most of the time. Both Mom and Dad decided to keep us here where we could live 'normal lives' away from politic's hectic state of being. Having a detail follow me everywhere sure didn't feel like a 'normal life.' The way I saw it, Dad abandoned us—he left me—for his political career.

I started to withdraw from everyone and everything. Not a day went by without Mom and I fighting about something. Sometimes, the fighting would make my anxiety unbearable. It made me feel as if I wanted to crawl out of my skin so I could escape from my body. I couldn't seem to dig myself out of the hole I was metaphorically stuck in. Our constant bickering wasn't helping either.

After signing me in at the doctor's office, my mom asked if I wanted her to join me in the exam room. I'm almost fifteen years old; I think I can handle this, I thought about saying.

"No, I'll be fine," I said instead, so we could avoid any confrontation while we were in public.

"Very well then," she said, patting my leg softly. I looked down at her hand, where it was still resting on my thigh, and doing my best not to show my high level of annoyance. How could she feel comfortable with displaying public affection like that? Didn't she know how uncomfortable it made me feel when she touched me in public? Quit being a dick; at least she's trying; I told my own sucky attitude. My attitude is much better now than last year during the holidays when I attempted to kill myself.

After deciding that I wanted to live, I knew it was time to put together an aggressive cover-up plan that included bleeding control. The mess would be impossible to conceal, but I was confident I'd be able to cover up the suicide attempt. There was so much blood, I remember thinking as I looked at my surroundings. Slowly I stood up, staggering toward my bathroom, leaving a trail of blood that continued to leak from my human container. After I had wrapped the blade in some toilet paper, I dropped it in the toilet before flushing. I started to feel faint, so I sat down on the cold bathroom tile.

The next time I woke up, I knew my thought process was compromised. It took me a few minutes to realize I was lying next to the toilet. The cobwebs were clouding my vision, making it difficult to focus. I knew I needed to get the bleeding under control, or my grand cover-up would never work. I'd only be able to lose a third of my 4.7 liters before my body started to shut down permanently. I crawled on all fours over to the closet, pulled a towel from the bottom shelf, and wrapped it tightly around my wrist.

After returning to the place where it looked like someone had been murdered, I smashed a ceramic lamp into several pieces with my stapler before pitching the stapler under my bed. It was the perfect cover-up. All I needed to do was find a bandage that would inconspicuously conceal my wound. While standing by my bathroom vanity, trying to apply the dressing, I started to feel nauseous before collapsing again, hitting the floor with all the force gravity could inflict. It didn't even hurt when my head hit the hard tile floor.

"Robert Van Stark," a younger woman announced, pulling my brain back into the doctor's waiting room where I was sitting beside my mom, who still has her hand resting on my leg. I jumped up from the chair, gladly following the medical personnel into the exam room.

I think my mom could tell I was pissed off after leaving the doctor's office. While I was in the doctor's office, the doctor asked me to pull my briefs down and cough. "I want to do a quick sports physical while I have you in the office," he told me. His reasoning was absurd since I wasn't even interested in sports.

"You seem angry," my mom said, stating the obvious as she approached a red traffic light. Oh? Do you think? I thought about saying. "Did something happen?" she asked, continuing to pressure me. If you recognize that I look angry, maybe you should leave me the hell alone, I thought to myself. I needed some time to defuse the bomb that was just about to go off.

"I don't really want to talk about it," I told her emphatically. I was sure she couldn't have sighed any louder if she tried.

"For the love of God, Robert, why won't you talk to me? How am I supposed to help you if you won't communicate?" she said with frustration in her voice. I took a deep breath, trying to calm myself before I exploded. She was looking at me with a deep stare when someone from behind us honked their horn. "Oh darn, sorry!" she called out as if the impatient driver from behind us could hear her apology. Mom pushed on the accelerator sending the truck forward, proceeding through the turn arrow that only allowed enough time for our vehicle to pass.

I was hoping the horn honking may have been enough of a distraction to make her forget I was sitting next to her until she said, "I'm still waiting for an answer."

You might be waiting for a long time, I thought to myself as she pulled into a parking spot at the pharmacy. I slouched down in the seat, looking out the passenger side window, hoping it would be enough of a hint that I didn't want to go in with her.

"Here," she said, pushing the prescription in my face. "I guess, if you think you're mature enough to handle everything on your own, you'll have no trouble filling your own prescription." If my loathing looks could kill, she'd spontaneously combust. I grabbed the script and left the truck without saying a word.

The smell of chemicals turned my stomach as I approach the pharmacy window. Standing at the service counter waiting to greet us was a guy wearing a lab coat, who I'd guess was around eighteen or nineteen. His name tag said 'Drew–Pharmacy Tech.' He was a smaller, thin guy with dark hair. I would guess Drew must've added a generous amount of hair product to make it stand up like it was on Viagra.

"Hello!" Drew said with a warm, welcoming smile. I felt as if Drew's dark brown eyes were dancing with excitement as he looked directly into mine. I couldn't imagine what he must be thinking. His facial expression was one you may see on a child who was ready to ask another if they'd like to play on the playground.

"Hey," I answered nonchalantly with an uncaring nod. "Could I get this filled, please?" I asked, deciding to change my attitude, so I didn't come off as a total dick. I handed Drew the folded piece of paper, offering a genuine smile. I was surprised my doctor didn't have the technological capabilities of sending the prescription electronically.

"Sure. Would you like to wait in the store, or will you be returning to pick it up?" I stood there staring at Drew as if he had asked me to solve a complicated calculus problem.

"We'll be waiting in the store. I have a few things to pick up," my mom said from behind me. Like he cared that she had a few things to pick up. When I tried to roll my eyes discreetly, Drew tried to stifle a smile after catching me in the act.

My mom was the kind of person who didn't care what others thought about her, which may seem surprising since my dad was a politician who cared what everyone thought about him; us too, unfortunately. Now that I think about it, I wasn't sure how a person with her liberal views could hook someone with ultra-conservative views like my dad. Oh well, I guess it's like they say—opposites attract.

"Very well, it should only be a few minutes," Drew said as he glanced back in my direction with a wink. Did he just wink at me? Easy there, fella, I'm only fourteen. But I understood how my height could be misleading since I could easily pass for a sixteen-year-old. I appreciated the attention, but if he could refrain from doing that shit in front of my mom, it would be great.

Drew left Mom and me standing at the counter with heated tension between us. A thermal imager would max out at two thousand degrees if pointed in our direction. "I'll be right back," she finally said. Oh boy, I'll be waiting with every bated breath for that one, I thought to myself. I could tell she was still angry, but it wasn't like I was trying to piss her off. She just needed to trust me when I didn't want to talk about embarrassing shit like the doctor fondling my nut sack.

A few minutes passed before Drew returned to the window holding a bag of drugs, just as my mom reappeared with an arm full of items. Drew was looking at me again with those big brown eyes until, suddenly, his eyes widened when he saw what my mom had just placed on the counter in front of us. Oh my God, it was a pinkish, purple box of KY warming gel. Printed on the box in big, bold letters, it said 'Intense Pleasure Gel!'

I looked back at her to see if it was a joke or an attempt to embarrass me for refusing to talk with her when we were in the truck. But she looked at me with confusion, as if she were asking, 'What's the big deal? I can't buy a huge bottle of sexual warming gel when my teenage son is standing here in front of me? Oh! And the nineteen-year-old pharmacy tech's cheeks shouldn't flush when he noticed how embarrassed my son was?' Why didn't she just throw a cock ring or a giant purple dildo up there on the counter while she was on a roll?

Drew didn't miss a beat; he started picking up each item, scanning them one at a time, all the while pretending that my face wasn't on fire. I could feel the heat as if it were a three-alarm fire with flames breaching the upper floors. If they had a bucket of ice water on the counter, I'd be dunking my whole head until I had to come up for air.

The Kotex and Fleets enema scanned with ease, but Drew had some issues with the price tag covering the barcode on the 'intense pleasure gel.' "Sometimes they put these in the wrong spot," Drew said as he squinted one eye and sticking the point of his cute little tongue out the corner of his mouth as he took the time to carefully peel the sticker off. I bit my upper lip, almost hard enough to make it bleed. I needed to stand here to endure the punishment. I thought it would be way too obvious if I just walked away at this point, –making more of a scene–so, I decided to stick it out.

"This is for you," Drew said as he looked into my eyes again. *Wow! Look at those beautiful green eyes!* I heard Drew add as he handed me the bag containing my prescription. Everything went from bad to worse within a split second. As if it could get any worse. I clearly heard Drew say that my eyes were beautiful, but I didn't take the time to realize that I had seen flashes of a gray corridor in his mind just as I had in Kevin's when I was at school.

Drew hadn't even opened his mouth to speak, but I didn't pause for a few seconds to process the information before I blurted out, "excuse me?" I had so much shock in my voice. Drew jumped backward at *least* two feet.

My jaw was resting on the shiny countertop where my mom's 'intense pleasure gel' was still sitting out in the open for everyone to see.

I was sure my eyes were still bulging from my head when Drew bravely stepped forward. "I'm sorry! Is there something wrong?" Drew had a surprised, nervous expression on his face, which was now as white as his lab coat. His deceitful brown eyes were all telling. Drew was trying to figure out if he had just let something slip.

"Are you all right, Robert?" my mom quickly asked with a perplexed expression. I looked down at the floor, shaking my head in hopes that the pounding in my brain would soon subside.

"Yeah, I'm fine. I just thought I heard someone say something," I explained, pointing at Drew.

"No, I'm sorry I didn't say anything," he repeated, pulling my eyes back to his frantic expression.

"I didn't hear him say anything, honey," my mom said, placing her hand on my shoulder. No, I'm sure you wouldn't have noticed, Mom, since all you can think about is going home to try out your new warming gel, I thought to myself. Drew's posture relaxed a bit as he took a big cleansing breath, but he glanced up at me before placing each of my mom's 'personal items' in a bag. It was as if Drew was afraid to look away in case he needed to dive under the counter if I made a wrong move. I read Drew's thoughts, so that was the only explanation for this unfortunate encounter.

After my mom's third attempt at getting her chip to work in the credit card reader, Drew tried to offer some direction. "Pull it out. Stick it back in. Nope pull it out. You need to hit the yellow button for credit," he said. Drew sounded as if he was giving her instructions on using her 'intense pleasure gel.' I just held my hand out so I could do it for her. She reluctantly handed me her card so I could complete the transaction within five seconds. I needed to get the hell out of here to start sorting through everything that was going on in my messed-up mind.

The house was filled with the smell of dinner cooking as we walked in, so I headed straight for the kitchen to see how Mrs. Wells was doing.

"Hey, Mrs. Wells," I announced before taking a seat at the kitchen island.

"Hello, Robert; I'm making your favorite for dinner this evening." I didn't have the heart to tell her I wasn't hungry for a large meal.

"Thank you. How was your day?" I asked while scooping some guacamole dip with a corn chip.

"Oh, it was lovely. Petey and I went grocery shopping. He loves to go for a ride in the car," she said as she slid a pan in the oven.

My parents hired Mrs. Wells last fall when school started so she could help around the house. Petey was her cute little Shih Tzu dog; they both lived in our home with us. "What did the doctor say about that darn cold?"

"He thought it may be a sinus infection, so he gave me some pills." Regrettably, he did some unnecessary touching of my genitalia as well, I thought to myself.

"Oh my, those infections can be dreadful. Would you be a darling and let Petey in, please?" she asked, pointing at the glass door where Petey was peering in with big puppy dog eyes. "I forgot he was out there," she said with a smirk. When I opened the door, Petey ran in, taking three laps around my feet as I retrieved a treat from a glass container that sat by the door. "If you'll, by chance, be going upstairs, would you please let your sister and mother know dinner will be ready in ten minutes?" Mrs. Wells asked as she continued to scurry around the kitchen at high speed.

"Yeah, sure," I answered before heading for the third floor with Petey close behind.

"Hey, Kate, dinner will be ready in ten," I said as I glanced through her open bedroom door. I wasn't surprised to see her playing Row Blocks on her computer since that was where she spent most of her time.

"Thanks," she said with a non-hostile tone. My thirteen-year-old sister Kate was hardly ever civil with me, so I was surprised when she didn't make any snide comments. Before knocking on my mom's office door, I stopped for a second to think about what I could be interrupting. After witnessing her purchase at the pharmacy, one could never be too careful.

"I don't know; he's been acting strange. Maybe somewhat distant," I heard my mom say through her office door. "He won't tell me what's bothering him… I know, I know, but he's been sick for two weeks; he seems almost despondent at times." I assumed she was having a phone conversation with my dad.

"Yes, you're right; I'm probably just overreacting." *My* mom overreact? When has that ever happened? I thought facetiously.

"Mom, dinner is ready," I said, knocking on the door lightly.

"Hang on for a second," she whispers to whoever she was talking with. "Okay, honey, I'll be down in a minute." Mental note to Rob: The doors in this house didn't offer an adequate sound barrier when I spent time alone in my room. 'Strange, distant, despondent?' Really? Just wait until she found out I was a freak who was hearing voices.

It was my mom who found me bleeding in my room on Christmas eve. I woke up lying near the bathroom vanity when I heard her frantically pounding on my locked bedroom door. I examined my wrist, finding that the bleeding had stopped. Either I had run out of blood or I stayed conscious long enough to secure a bandage. When I tried to sit up, I felt weak, and I could feel blood leaking from my head as well. I immediately laid back down to combat the dizziness. Who knew how many times my head could bounce off a tile floor before the trauma caused irreversible brain damage?

There was more urgent knocking at my door; it sounded like someone was trying to unlock it from the outside. I heard the door finally open with screams erupting from my bedroom.

"Robert!" my mom screamed with panic in her voice. "Where are you?" I wasn't hard to find; all she had to do was follow the blood trail. "What happened?" my mom asked, trying to control her hysteria as she appeared by my side.

"My lamp broke. When I was trying to clean it up, I must've fallen on a sharp piece," I lied with a groggy voice.

"Where are you cut?" she asked, frantically searching my blood-covered body.

"It's just a tiny cut on my wrist," I told her as I turned my hand over, so she could see for herself.

"You're so clumsy. Why didn't you call for help?" Oh, believe me, I was hoping for some, but it didn't arrive until after I had changed my mind, I said to myself.

"I couldn't find my phone," I told her, lying through my teeth again.

"Let's see if you'll need stitches," she said as she carefully pulled back the bandage. "Yes, we need to get you into the emergency room." That-was-that. My first suicide attempt failed. No one even suspected the cut was intentional.

After we finished dinner, I sat down in front of my computer to research telepathy. There was a lot more information online than I thought there would be. 'Ten Steps to Master Telepathy.' There was nothing about the gray corridors.

'Telepathy is used so we can speak to someone else without verbal exchange.'

I know I saw a glimpse of a gray hallway when Drew told me I had beautiful eyes. He really was kind of cute. Especially the way Drew pretended to not be embarrassed for me while he scanned my mom's 'personal items.'

An article on the second page claimed most people didn't believe in telepathy, so non-believers may work to my advantage. Tomorrow, I needed to figure out the corridors' significance and how they correspond with the gray color while telepathy was occurring. Solving the mystery of the gray hallway thing may be the key to finding the cause of my new clairvoyant issues. My eyes were getting heavy as I continued to surf the net.

I was jolted awake when I heard my mom say my name through my closed bedroom door. While still in a confused state, I lifted my face from my desk, grabbed my mouse, and quickly clicked out of the screen, so she wouldn't see what I had been surfing. Unfortunately, there was a long string of drool still hanging from the corner of my mouth attached to the keyboard as she approached my desk.

"It's late; how come you're not in bed?" my mom asked. Since the Christmas Eve incident, she invited herself into my room every night to make sure I still had a pulse. Maybe my mom had a maternal instinct that told her I shouldn't be trusted alone in my bedroom. One of these times, I was afraid my mom would catch me doing something she wouldn't want to see her teenage son doing.

"I must've fallen asleep while I was doing my homework," I explained, grabbing a tissue from my desk to sop up the gooey substance from the keyboard.

"All right, get off to bed please. Are you sure you're okay?" Mom asked with a noticeable 'ew expression.'

"Just kinda tired," I answered with a fake smile.

“Okay, goodnight, honey,” my mom said as she closed my door.

My mind was racing a million miles an hour, bouncing around like a tennis ball from one question to the next as I climbed into bed. How was it that I could hear Kevin’s voice? He didn’t even like me. The cute pharmacy tech thought I had beautiful eyes. I know it was Orin who stuck the hate note in my locker this morning. As soon as I read the short, poorly written love letter, my theory was confirmed. Orin had misspelled faggot. But his request for me to ‘do the right thing and just end it all’ has been denied. If he was going to be an effective bully, he should learn to spell.

*****

A warm, gentle breeze blowing on my face woke me from a deep sleep. Had I left my window open? I felt as light as a feather when I reached out to close the window. I was surprised to find that the window was missing. I floated through the opening and continued to drift out into the warm spring air. Suddenly I found myself hovering four feet off the sandy beach until I came across Kevin sitting by himself near the water’s edge. I quickly started to ascend, so I could stay out of sight. I didn’t want Kevin to think I was stalking him.

A bright flash of lightning struck out over the water, drawing my attention away for a split second. As I anticipated the crash of thunder, I looked back to check on Kevin. He was gone. Instead, I saw Drew from the pharmacy sitting where Kevin was only seconds ago. It seemed odd that Drew was wearing only gray underwear with ‘FLEETS’ printed in green on the waistband of the briefs. My eyes opened wide when I realized he was holding a tube of KY warming gel. The cold rain on my bare skin woke me up as an opening in the clouds appeared.

*****

I grabbed my phone from the nightstand. Damn, it was only 03:35. That was messed up.

# Coming to Terms Chapter 2

Tuesday, May 16th Coming to Terms

The time on my phone said 05:23 when I woke up to the sound of waves crashing on the beach. My annoying alarm would be chirping at me in less than seven minutes, so I decided to drag my ass out of bed and head for the pool. It was early February when Mr. Smit recommended I start exercising to help cope with my anxiety and depression, but I had been skipping my routine a lot over the last couple of weeks. Maybe my mom was right. I guess I could be somewhat 'despondent.'

When I finally made it down to the pool room, which was located on our lower level, I could see that I would be working out alone this morning. Most mornings, I was accompanied by my seventeen-year-old brother Sam, but his new girlfriend has been controlling his morning schedule lately.

Sam and I had another big fight a few weeks ago, which had put a strain on our–already–failing relationship. Mom and I had our daily argument about spending too much time in my bedroom and not wanting to go to a church activity. Anyway, she left my room crying, so Sam thought it was his God-given right as the firstborn to step in for our absent father and immediately laid into me.

"You're a self-centered, entitled little jerk," he said as he stood towering over me. "What's your problem this time?"

"She wants me to go to youth group," I answered defensively.

"So, what's wrong with that? Would it kill you to go?" he asked with attitude in his tone.

"The kids at youth group are mean to me," I told him, crossing my arms over my chest and trying not to let my lower lip droop in a visible sulk.

"Dad's not going to be happy, you know. You need to stop messing with Mom and do what you're told. His being gone isn't easy for any of us, especially Mom. So, suck it up, get your ass dressed, and ask Andy to drive you to church." Speechless, I threw my arms in the air with a wild gesture and leaned back in my chair dramatically.

Sam left the room without another word. I didn't waste the opportunity to flip him off as soon as my door closed. I reached for my remote, queued up YouTube on my TV, and blasted it loud enough for Sam to hear from his room. I started to get ahold of my anger as I sat on my bed watching Sergei Polunin dance to Hozier's song, "Take Me to Church." What pissed me off the most was, I knew Sam was right. Dad was going to be ticked off when he found out I was acting like an immature prick. I went to youth group that night but was sent home within an hour when I refused to participate in a stupid-ass game.

The fifty-meter pool was kicking my ass this morning. I started to feel the burn in my arms and legs only about ten minutes into my forty-minute workout. But swimming gave me a feeling that I was the only one in absolute control of my mind and body. The muscle burn reminded me of why it was important not to skip any more workouts.

We arrived at school early, as usual. My detail insisted on having me at school before the halls filled up with fellow students. I didn't mind getting there early; it gave me enough time to get to first-hour without any unwanted confrontation. When I walked into first-hour, I saw a new kid talking with Mr. Kave. The tall, wiry kid had long, blonde, surfer hair that was almost as long as mine.

"Hey," the new kid said as he strolled past me with a stride that resembled a male model walking down a runway.

"Hey," I said in return as the new kid sat down at a desk behind me. I just couldn't fight the urge to turn around to take another look. I slowly turned, but unfortunately, I was caught when he looked up. His soft blue eyes meet mine for a moment before I turned back around. I couldn't believe I had just done that. What an idiot.

Of course, he was going to look up when he saw me turn to gawk. The new kid and I were the only students in the classroom, so I decided to work on my telepathy mystery. Yesterday, when Drew's voice broke into my mind, I saw a gray corridor. I was wigging out when Kevin's voice surprised me during sixth-hour too, but I was still able to get a glimpse of a gray passageway of some sort. Maybe if I focused on the new kid's mind, I would find a corridor that would allow entry.

I closed my eyes, concentrating on the visualization of the kid's passages. Several doors were lining his gray entry area. It felt as though I could reach out to open any of the doors if I tried. Hey! Where did they go? The corridors were gone! I knew I needed to focus, but it was difficult when there was so much excitement flooding my brain cells. I tried to convince myself to settle down, clear my mind, and attempt to visualize his corridors again. All right, good, other colored entrances were in full view as well.

I was immediately capable of entering his brain without opposition, if my sub-conscience was subdued. Using my frontal cortex to connect our energy, I targeted both corridors. It was creepy as I started to slowly venture down the same empty, gray-colored passage before stopping to open the first gray door.

*He seems nice. I think that's actually him;* I heard the new kid think. Yes, yes, yes! I did it! Who was he thinking about? What the hell does 'that's actually him' mean? I was struggling to stay calm as I started to process everything. I needed to keep reminding myself to not freak out like I did when I heard Kevin and Drew yesterday. Slow your breathing down, I told myself calmly. There was no way of knowing how long I had been in the new kid's mind, so I found the closest exit.

When I left the cute kid's brain, reality hit. The entire class was full of fellow students. I must have been in the new kid's mind for at least five minutes. I wondered what the rest of my body was doing while I was in his mind? I turned to look at David, who sat to my left. He was smiling at me as if I had missed something. All year, I've been trying to figure him out, but my "gaydar" wouldn't ping. It was a shame, considering how cute David was.

During the rest of first-hour, I practiced entering new brains throughout the classroom. Finding the right doors to use was getting more comfortable for me as I efficiently opened different doors to hear others' thoughts. Even though I could only enter the gray corridor, I noticed three other various colored passages. The gray one was lined up perfectly with the green, yellow, and red hallways.

It was time for lunch, so I slowly meandered toward the cafeteria. After I got my food, I headed for my table at the very back of the cafeteria. I had taken ownership of the table because I was the only one who occupied it during the 'A' lunch period. I only had one earbud in, working on the other when I had a feeling that someone was looking at me.

"Hey, you mind if I join you?" I heard someone ask. I was caught totally off guard when I saw the new kid standing in front of me with his tray of food.

"Sure, have a seat. There's plenty of room," I answered as I pointed at seven other empty chairs at my table.

"My name is Cameron. I sit behind you in first-hour," he said as if I would forget the cute new kid with mesmerizing eyes. I quickly entered his gray corridor to open the first door. *Why am I so nervous? Just cool it, take a deep breath, and sit down;* I heard him think.

"Hey, Cameron," I said with a delayed response, trying to refrain from sounding like a complete idiot. "My name is Robert. Are you new here at our school?" I asked, revealing my lack of social skills.

"Yeah, I just moved from South Dakota." Cameron looked at me kind of funny as I continued to listen in on his thoughts. *Why is he looking at me like that?* I read. I couldn't apologize for staring; he never said anything out loud. Why did it have to be so awkward when I talked to other kids my age? He was nervous, but I was even more nervous.

"Welcome to Michigan, land of the lake effect snowstorms," I told him, wishing I wouldn't have said anything at all. I just needed to calm myself down.

Cameron grinned as he picked up his overcooked chicken strips to take a bite. *Damn, this chicken is tough,* he thought as I listened in.

"It's always tough," I said emphatically as he was taking a drink of water to wash the chicken down. Unfortunately, Cameron choked on his drink, causing it to reach his sinus cavity and shooting the liquid out through his nostrils. He quickly used his napkin to catch any other escaping secretions.

"You, okay?" I quickly asked, handing him my napkin for backup. Cameron looked at me with confusion and embarrassment.

"Yeah," he squeaked out as he tried to recover. "Did you just read my mind?" he asked while still covering his mouth with a napkin. I laughed as if he was joking.

"No, the chicken is always tough. I had it yesterday; it's always overcooked. What you're eating is probably leftover from last week. The lunch lady microwaved it, hoping you wouldn't notice," I told him quickly, realizing my newly found clairvoyant abilities could get me into some trouble.

There was silence between us for a few seconds, which seemed more like an eternity. Cameron probably thought I was some effed-up science project. Nope. He was thinking about his dad. His dad was gone too? But where? His thoughts were becoming more explicit. I was able to hear almost everything he thought if I stood just inside the doorway.

"So, when did you move here?" I asked, trying to break the awkward silence.

"Two weeks ago. My mom and I are staying with my aunt and uncle for a year or two." Cameron's explanation sounded more like a canned speech that I helped my dad memorize during his campaign last summer. I knew what a well-prepared spiel sounded like. Cameron had practiced that one a few times.

"What grade are you in?" I asked.

"Ninth," he said before picking up his glass of water, carefully drinking more water to replenish enough moisture to allow for safe passage of the dry chicken.

"You're kinda tall for a freshman," I said, stating the obvious again.

"Yeah, I just turned sixteen; I missed out on a lot of my classes when I was in third grade. My dad was deployed to South Korea, so we lived there with him. I didn't start back at school until the following year, so they decided to hold me back," he explained with a hint of embarrassment.

"Where's your dad now?" I asked, hoping I wasn't too forward with my questioning.

"I don't know. My dad works for the Government, so he travels a lot." Cameron's answer was vague, so I wasn't sure if I should press for more information regarding his father's current disposition.

"Yeah, my dad works for the Federal Government; he travels a lot as well. But he stays in Washington DC most of the time," I explained as he looked at me with suspicion.

"What branch?" he asked as he looked into my eyes for a hint of untruth.

"He's a United States Congressman."

"So, it would be my best assumption; the guy standing over there is here for you," he said as he pointed in Gary's direction.

"Wow, you're intuitive, Cameron. What gave him away?" I ask with a hint of sarcasm.

"Umm, the suit?" he said, with an exaggerated squint of one eye. "Your bodyguard is dressed like he's guarding the president." I just smiled. Cameron was right; Andy and Gary would blend in a lot better if they didn't wear a suit. They wore black pants, a white shirt, a black tie, and a black jacket to match. The shoes they wore were so shiny I could see my own reflection.

"Ah, yeah, he doesn't blend very well, does he?" Cameron smiled as I tried to hide my embarrassment.

"My friends back home call me Cam." Wait, what? Did he just hint that he wanted to be my friend? I tried to keep myself calm as I contemplated the possibility of a new friend prospect.

"You can call me Rob," I said after finishing off my orange juice. "My friends would call me Rob as well, if I had any," I professed with a nervous laugh.

"Come on, you must have a ton of friends," Cam said as if he was convinced that I was lying.

"Yup! I have so many friends, I had to ask one of them to leave so you'd have a place to sit down," I said as I pointed at the other empty chairs. We both started to laugh until other kids sitting near us began to look in our direction. I was amazed when the end-of-the-period alarm chimed. It was hard to believe how fast lunch had flown by.

"See you around, Cam."

"See ya, Rob. Same place tomorrow?"

"Sounds good!" I answered with excitement.

*He's cool, but why doesn't he have any friends?* Cam thought as he left the table. I could stay in his brain as he walked away, but I lost the signal when I could no longer see him.

I wouldn't mind having a couple of friends. Especially someone like him, I thought to myself as I walked my untouched fries over to the trash.

*If Robert thinks I'm going to cover for him while he skips PE again today, he's sorely mistaken.* I heard Gary think from an open gray door as I walked past him.

I felt sorry for Gary and Andy. I couldn't imagine how annoying it would be to babysit a 14-year-old three days per week. It was probably worse yet for Jennifer and Kasi, who were responsible for my sister Kate's safety. Sam wasn't required to have a detail follow him around. Somehow, he lucked out; it didn't seem fair.

Cautiously–and reluctantly–I entered the locker room to get dressed for PE. I saw Kevin Larson sitting on a concrete bench by his locker, so I took a quick read on him.

*What's he looking at?* I heard Kevin think with annoyance in his thoughts as I walked past him. I tried to ignore what I had heard and continued to look straight ahead.

In my opinion, Kevin was, by far, the cutest kid in my freshman class. He had a difficult time taming his ultra-fine, blondish, light-brown, messy hair. But it was Kevin's blue eyes that made him irresistible. His thin, ripped body was one I could only dream of having. I wondered if my obsessive attraction was causing our wired connection.

Unfortunately, Kevin caught me glancing in his direction while we were in the shower last Thursday. Most of my PE classmates didn't bother taking a shower after sweating, but I couldn't even stand the smell of myself after perspiring for forty minutes, let alone, some poor sap who had to sit by me in fifth-hour. Anyway, Kevin kind of lost his cool.

I haven't ever had any problems with Kevin until the shower incident when he came unglued, throwing his shoulder into mine, causing me to lose my balance, ultimately ending up with my bare ass sitting on the shower floor. I looked up at him to see what would be coming next, like maybe a foot in the gut. What I saw instead was his regretful expression.

Even though my shoulder and ass hurt after the incident, what bothered me the most was acknowledging that Kevin didn't like me. Anyway, that was why I skipped PE last Friday and again yesterday. I was so embarrassed; I just couldn't bring myself to face Kevin. I think Andy must've told on me. When I was leaving for school today, my mom told me to attend all my classes.

*Hey man, how's it going?* I read Kevin asking someone. I peeked around my locker door to find Kevin talking to his friend Zach.

I'd like to apologize to Kevin, but I didn't have the guts to confront him. If I ever did find the courage, I wasn't sure how it would sound.

Maybe I'd say, *"Hey, Kevin, sorry if you thought I was checking you out..."* I paused when I saw a yellow corridor in Kevin's mind. I wondered if he just heard what I thought? I was curious how I was able to connect. It was as if my mind automatically went for the yellow corridor. I needed to try that again.

*"I'm really sorry about what happened in the shower last week."* I could clearly visualize the yellow corridor lined with yellow open doors, so I could effortlessly connect our energy.

*Why do I hear voices in my head?* I read from Kevin's gray corridor as I physically peeked around the locker door again. I could barely keep myself calm, so I sat down to tie my shoes, hoping the distraction would reduce my anxiety. Kevin was still talking with Zach as they dress out, but Kevin was looking directly at me. I quickly tucked behind the locker door as if I were playing hide and seek. What was I, four? I could plainly see five corridors in Kevin's mind. I had used the gray to read him and now the yellow to talk to him telepathically, but what were the green, red, and orange corridors used for? I didn't remember seeing an orange passage in Cam's mind today.

Kevin and Zach stood to leave the locker room, so I followed at a safe distance. Most of my classmates were lining up for dodgeball when we arrived in the gym. I sucked at dodgeball, primarily because I throw like a girl. At least that was what Sam told me a few years back when he was trying to teach me how to throw a ball. I was hoping I wouldn't be picked last again today. But they wanted their team to win, so who could blame them?

Mr. Dewey chose Kevin and Trae as team captains; they were up in front of the group, ready to select their teams. Before Kevin made his first choice, I looked directly at him; my mind automatically entered a green corridor in his brain, as if it knew instantly where to go. *Please don't pick me last,* I thought to myself. I stood in line for a few seconds trying to figure out how I ended up in Kevin's green corridor. Suddenly, Zach gave me a push, causing me to stumble out of the lineup.

"He called your name, Robert," Zach said.

"Wait, what? Who?" I stammered with confusion. I never even heard my name get called. Gary looked up with a surprised expression from where he was sitting on the bleachers across the gym. Mr. Dewey looked perplexed as he stood at the sidelines, scratching his head.

"Kevin picked you to be on his team," Zach said with disbelief in his tone.

I slowly made my way over to Kevin, wondering what the hell just happened. Kevin shook his head from side to side as if he were trying to clear some cobwebs. He picked Zach for his second choice. I was amazed that Kevin honored my request. Oh man, this was getting weird.

"Dude, what's wrong with you?" Zach asked Kevin as I quickly entered Zach's gray corridor. *Why would Kevin pick Robert first?* I heard Zach think. Zach had some jealousy boiling up in his brain, as well. Wait! I can read emotion? Hmm, Zach didn't have an orange corridor either.

"Shut up!" Kevin whispered to Zach. I must have sent Kevin a request because there was no way he would have ever picked me first on his own. I wondered if Kevin could hear me when I used the green corridor to make my plea.

I was careful to keep my eyes from wandering when we were in the shower today. I entered Kevin's yellow corridor to ask him not to reveal anything to anyone about my wandering eyes. I was surprised when he answered back, 'okay.' So, now I knew that we had a two-way connection with the ability to communicate telepathically from the same yellow corridor.

Mr. Smit started sixth-hour by introducing Cam to the rest of the students. I didn't care about science that much, but I did like my teacher. When I say 'like,' I mean, I had a schoolboy crush on him. Mr. Smit had helped me through a lot of personal crap this year after he figured out I was having emotional issues. Somehow, he was able to connect with me in a way that made me feel as if I were someone special. Mr. Smit became a person I could trust. He taught me the importance of having a purpose in life.

As Mr. Smit started to lecture, my habitual mind began to go through its routine, thinking about Kevin. I had no trouble accessing his gray corridor, simultaneously opening a few doors. *When I finish practice, I need to pick up groceries. Oh, yeah, I'll need to make the house payment too,* I heard Kevin think. What the hell? Why would a fourteen-year-old be expected to juggle all of these responsibilities?

Oh no, Mr. Smit was walking through the class handing back our Mohs Hardness Scale worksheets that I was expected to complete yesterday. *I hope this doesn't count toward my grade,* I thought to myself, just as a green passageway showed up in Mr. Smit's mind. Oops. That may have leaked.

"These won't be counted against your grade, but you guys need to start taking these class assignments more seriously. By the way, remember you have a homework assignment tonight. You'll be expected to turn it in tomorrow," Mr. Smit said as he handed me my blank worksheet and giving me 'the eye.' I needed to get a handle on this shit.

I could hear Petey's tiny nails clicking behind me as I ascended the stairs to my bedroom. I wasn't sure if Petey liked to hang with me because he loved my music or if it was the snacks I had in my possession. My science assignment needed to be finished before dinner, so I got started immediately.

"Come in," I said as I reached for my phone to turn Shawn Mendes down. Just for the record, if asked, I'd never 'turn Shawn down.'

"Robert, are you hungry?" Mrs. Wells asked as she stuck her head in the door.

"Yeah, I'm starving." This was highly unusual, given the fact that I hadn't had much of an appetite lately.

"Petey. What are you doing up here?" She said to him as if he were capable of answering. He gave a little bark before sitting back down on my sockless feet. "I have a lasagna in the oven; it will be ready in 30 minutes," she said kindly.

"Thank you," I answered as she started to leave. "Ah… Mrs. Wells?"

"Yes?" she said, sticking her head back in the doorway.

"Do you think I'm weird? I mean, do you think I'm too weird for someone to like me as a friend?"

"No. Why would you ask such a silly thing? You're the most wonderful boy I've ever met. You would make someone a delightful friend." Man, I loved her.

"Thank you," I said, smiling, as she turned to leave again.

When I ventured downstairs to eat dinner, I only saw two places set at the kitchen island. So, I guessed it would be just the two of us tonight. We were usually required to eat dinner at the dining room table when the family was together. Apparently, Mom had a meeting at school, Sam was working at his job with a local sporting goods store, and Kate must have been at her friend's house.

"Is everything all right?" Mrs. Wells asked with genuine concern as we ate together.

"Just some stuff going on at school."

"Do you want to talk about it?" she offered kindly.

"Not really; I think I'll be able to figure everything out on my own," I replied as I pushed my glasses up the bridge of my nose with my index finger. Yup, it wasn't bad enough that Sam stole all of the good looks and athletic genes. I ended up farsighted, having to wear glasses or contacts. "I met a new kid at school today; he's really cool," I blurted out. What the hell made me just say that?

"That's exciting. What's the boy's name?" Mrs. Wells asked as she attempted to pile the second helping of lasagna on my plate.

"No, thank you, I'm stuffed. The kid's name is Cameron. He just moved here from South Dakota."

"This is wonderful news, Robert," she said as I stood to take our plates to the sink. "I'll get those," Mrs. Wells insisted as I started to load the dishwasher.

"Nope, you made the delicious lasagna. I'm doing dishes."

"Thank you, sweetie," she said with a proud grin. All the while, Petey sat at my feet, hoping I'd drop some food.

After dinner, I took off hiking through the woods toward my new quiet spot that I discovered up in the dunes last week. After my detail left, I could sneak out on my own to reclaim some of my freedom. The secluded spot was in the northwest corner of our undeveloped one-hundred-eighty-five acres. I could think there without any distractions. Today, I needed some space to sort through all the confusing shit that was messing with my mind.

My cell didn't have reception out here for some reason, but it wasn't like my phone was blowing up with messages anyway. When I sat down on a smooth black boulder that was large enough to seat two, I saw a freighter moving like a snail out on the flat surface of Lake Michigan. I could see a lot from my elevated position on top of the steep two-hundred-foot dune. The sky was a beautiful orange color as the sun started its final descent toward the horizon.

The sky's color reminded me of Kevin's orange-colored corridor that I hadn't explored yet. I was curious about the orange passage because everyone else only had gray, yellow, green, and red, but Kevin's orange corridor must have meant something. Though intrigued, I needed to be careful; he already resented me as it was.

Kevin and I haven't had a genuine conversation since fourth grade. He was way out of my league on the popularity scale. But I did remember him being kind to me when we were in the same third-grade class. Kevin became friends with Zach sometime during the fourth grade. Since then, it has been just the two of them. I wondered why I was able to connect telepathically with Kevin so easily? It was as if he were required to do what I was requesting when he chose me first for his team.

The cool breeze coming in off the lake helped me focus as I categorized the facts I was faced with. Telepathy was in a subcategory alongside the exceptional memory category. My parents had always been adamant about concealing my intellectual capacity. Unfortunately, I have never forgotten anything, not even my dreams. When I was eight years old, I overheard my mom telling my dad that she didn't want me to be 'one of those prodigy kids who ended up imploding by the time they were seventeen.'

As I ran my hand over the rock I was sitting on, I felt something I hadn't noticed before. There were fine grooves that didn't seem to have any pattern or design. Sometime when I had more light, I planned to take a closer look. Wait. What happened to the sun? It was completely gone already. The steep trail was challenging to navigate with only the light that was offered by dusk. I heard my phone chirp, which meant my dad was texting me or had texted me when I didn't have service:

Hey slugger.

A smile automatically developed on my face. I wasn't sure why my dad always called me slugger. I couldn't hit a ball with a bat, even if it were perched on one of those t-ball stands. It was as if I couldn't stay mad at my dad when he called or texted, and I couldn't seem to ignore any attention he was willing to offer.

Hey, Dad!!!

Did you have a good day at school? Dad texted back immediately.

Yeah, it was fine.

Your Mother is worried about you. My dad was always expected to do the dirty work for my mom. She knew we had a close connection, so I guess she was playing it smart.

I know she is... I'm fine: )

Do you want to fly out here and spend this weekend with me?

Wow, that would be great!!!

I'll have Brad find you a flight tomorrow morning.

Thanks, Dad!

Can't wait to see you! Sorry to cut this short, but I have another meeting:-(

K see ya, Dad.

It was going to be a bit awkward when I visited him. Our relationship has been strained. At some point, we needed to discuss how his leaving has changed things between us. I was afraid our relationship would never go back to how it was, but hopefully, we could patch things up a bit.

*****

I wasn't sure why, but I was already on my way back out to my thinking spot in the dunes. The trail was lined with candles burning every ten feet; the open flame seemed to be a fire hazard, burning so close to the beach grass. When I finally reached my spot, I found Cam sitting on my rock, holding a KFC box while eating some chicken strips.

Kevin was standing directly behind Cam, bouncing a dodgeball on the rock. When I tried to ask them what they were both doing out there, I couldn't make any words come out of my mouth, so I sent them a telepathic message. *"Why are you here?"* Neither answered; they stared at me as if I was a zombie. Oh no, they may be the zombies. Now they were coming right at me. I lifted off the ground, trying to get away, but they were holding my feet. Finally, I was able to break free, leaving them both standing on the dune.

*****

When I opened my eyes, I felt myself start to fall, but it was short-lived, only dropping a few feet, landing flat, back onto my king-sized mattress. I must've been standing on my bed during my dream. No, that couldn't be right; my sweat-drenched sheets and blankets were still covering me. Man, that was weird. It was only 02:22; I needed to figure everything out after I had more sleep.

# Colored Corridors Chapter 3

Wednesday, May 17th Colored Corridors

I heard the water moving as Sam sliced through the water with minimal effort; his body was designed for swimming. Sam had been on the school swim team since he was in sixth grade and the water polo team throughout high school. This year he was offered a scholarship to swim for Michigan State University. He turned their offer down after he was accepted into the United States Naval Academy.

Swimming was mind-numbing for me, but it seemed to help me feel better about myself. Mr. Smit told me that an exercise routine would help me with personal accountability, which would allow me to develop self-respect. According to Mr. Smit, those who respect themselves were more resilient, and I needed resilience in my life more than ever.

Once I got into my rhythm, my mind was tasked with figuring out how to cope with my newly acquired gifts. More importantly, how I got the abilities in the first place. Today, I needed to carefully experiment with the different colored corridors. The gray passageways were getting more comfortable to navigate, but I needed to work on the yellow and green.

Somehow, I lost track of my lap count but decided to keep going until I hit my forty minutes. Having someone to eat lunch with yesterday helped build my confidence. If I could pull off this new friendship with Cam, it would prove that I was, at least, capable of making new friends. Yesterday, my life seemed more meaningful than it did the day before.

While reaching for the side of the pool, I saw Sam standing on the deck, waiting for me to finish.

"Hey," Sam said with a nod.

"Hey," I answered awkwardly, shaking the water out of my ears.

"How are you feeling? Mom told me you've been sick," he said while drying his hair with a towel.

"It was just a sinus infection. I'll be fine." I wasn't sure how it was with other kids my age, but having a non-confrontational conversation with my brother wasn't familiar. So, this atypical conversation we were having was a bit unnerving.

"Cool. Have a good day at school," he said abruptly as he turned to leave.

"I will. Thanks, you too..." I said before trailing off as I watched him leave the room. What the hell was that all about? Was this how brothers communicated when they became more mature?

As Gary escaped into the teacher's prep area for his morning coffee, I entered first-hour hoping to find Cam, but no such luck.

"Good morning, Robert; how are you?" Mr. Kave asked. Sometimes I wondered if my teachers treated me kind only because of who my dad was.

"Fine, thanks. And you, Sir?" I asked as I sat at my desk.

"Very well," he answered with a warm expression. *I can't believe Kathy asked me to go tonight. She knows I hate that shit,* I heard Mr. Kave think. Apparently, he wasn't 'very well' as he had said. I wondered why people lied so often. Maybe it was a defense mechanism they use to ignore reality.

"Hey, Rob," Cam said, interrupting my thoughts. I turned to look at him and could tell he was reading my facial expression as it lit up like an LED headlight.

"Hey, Cam!" I said with way too much enthusiasm in my voice.

"Did you get your science homework done last night?" Cam asked. I shook my head, yes. "I didn't. Fell asleep at eight and didn't wake up until this morning," he said as he plopped down in his seat, looking kind of stressed out and tired.

"It's no problem. I'll help you at lunch; it'll only take us ten minutes."

"Cool, thanks," he said. I smiled when I looked into his sparkling eyes. Man, you are so damn cute, I thought to myself. Cam smiled back. I freaked for a second when it occurred to me that I may have accidentally sent the message through his yellow corridor. Nope, I hadn't seen any hallways.

Other students started to trickle in one or two at a time, so I decided to read the next random person who came through the door. Dan Schrade trudged through the door as if he were walking through two feet of snow. Dan was a bigger kid who dressed kind of frumpy. I wasn't saying he wore dirty or crappy clothes; they just look like they should be worn by a lumberjack. I entered his brain to navigate his gray corridor. Dan was thinking about what he would be doing with his friend Tim immediately after school. Wait, what? I couldn't believe they were planning to hunt down some poor, helpless squirrel.

I had to quickly refocus when David waved at me as he passed my desk. I just nodded and smiled. There was something about David that made me want to search around in his brain. He was thinking about my hair. *Man, I wish my hair was more like Robert's.* The irony was, I wanted to have hair like David's. His sleek-dark, almost black, straight hair laid perfectly against his zit-free, olive skin. His deep-red lips nicely contrasted with the other two colors. And those dimples were to die for. If he wore black clothing, he wouldn't have any trouble pulling off the whole Emo thing.

By the time first-hour was over, I successfully walked through the corridors of five different fellow classmates, finding something new. Some of the gray passages had random blue doors mixed in. Memories inside the blue doors played like videos. The most disturbing information I learned was from reading 'Ryan Bigot.' Ryan's last name was actually Hanes, but damn, how can anyone be so hateful?

I was walking so fast that I was almost running while on my way down to the cafeteria. Cam gave me a wave as I lined up for food. The line was moving slowly as usual, so I elected to use my time wisely by opening and closing a few doors. I saw the kid in front of me wink at a lunch lady who was twice his age. I believed he was a senior, and apparently, they must have known each other.

After I carefully traveled down a short gray corridor in the kid's mind, I noticed a colorful door. It had every color in the rainbow. Curiosity won over, so I opened the door to see what was inside. Oh no! They didn't only know each other; they were participating in some extracurricular activities.

He had an X-rated memory of the lunch lady lying totally naked on a brown sofa. I quickly closed the door just as he touched her in a place on her body, I didn't want to mention. My face heated up like an oven. Even as disturbing as his memory was, I was intrigued. Was the colorful door a sign of his past, or was it a fantasy he was having? Maybe if I checked her thoughts.

When I entered the lunch lady's corridor, I ignored the blue doors and automatically reached for the colorful one calling my name. I believed I would find her room and contents much cleaner than his. After all, women weren't a bunch of pigs like guys were. Without exercising any caution, I rapidly opened the door. When I looked inside, my assumptions were squashed. Her thoughts were worse yet.

I immediately tried to pull the door shut, but it hadn't closed before seeing a memory that looked more like a streaming video. The kid's muscular, bare ass was bouncing up and down between her naked legs. Mayday! Mayday! Mayday! Slam the door shut! Evacuate! Evacuate! Evacuate! Get the hell out of her mind! I was finally able to close the door, but it was already too late. The damage had been done.

Alarms were still sounding in my brain as I watched the teen student grin at the lunch lady. A deep burgundy blush appeared on her face as she scooped some potato salad on his plate. I stood there looking at his clothed backside, trying to edit the video that would be etched in my brain forever. Some things could never be unseen.

"Would you like some potato salad, Hun?" the lunch lady asked, snapping me out of my trance.

"Oh, ah… No, I… Umm, I'm all set, thank you," I was finally able to say after my vocal cords started working again.

During lunch, my brain searched for a delete key to erase the porn video I had witnessed. I've looked at porn online, but what I saw in the rainbow video was different. Every time I saw either one of the lovebirds, I would have an unpleasant memory of their secret love affair. Unfortunately, my search for the deletion capability was unsuccessful.

"Hey, you wanna go catch a movie this weekend?" Cam asked as I helped him with his homework.

"I, ah, I'm going to DC this weekend to visit my dad," I told him, wishing there was a way I could do both. Damn, he looked disappointed.

"It's okay, we can go next weekend," he quickly replied before changing his frown to a fake smile. "Hey, can I get your cell?" he asked, after grabbing his cell from the table. As we exchange information, I couldn't keep the excitement from bubbling out of my entire body.

"See ya in science. Thanks for the help," Cam said as he left the table.

"Okay, see ya," I respond as I tried to get ahold of my giddy mood.

Kevin had been paired up with me in PE for wrestling today. I was going to get my ass kicked. I was an inch taller than he was, but he had at least ten pounds on me. Not to mention, he had twice the muscle mass compared to my body. I had my contacts in, so at least I would be able to see while he threw me around like a ragdoll. I had come to the realization that Mr. Dewey was on drugs if he thought we were close to a fair match.

The whistle blew, and I was lying on my back with Kevin lying on top of me within seconds. Oddly enough, I noticed how good he smelled. Kevin pushed into my chest with his shoulder, attempting to pin me to the mat. Out of my peripheral vision, I could see Mr. Dewey's head on the mat, trying to determine if the end of the match were near. I wasn't going to let Kevin pin me without putting up a good fight; besides, if I let him pin me, we wouldn't be touching anymore. Somehow, an explosion of strength helped me turn him, and now I was lying on top of Kevin.

Where the hell did that eruption of energy come from? Kevin's face had a surprised expression, but it quickly changed into a look of pure determination as he put the death grip on my nuts and turned me within seconds. My back smashed into the mat first, with Kevin's body hitting my diaphragm, causing all available air to escape me. I was doing everything I could to catch my breath as I planned my next move. Thankfully, Mr. Dewey blew the whistle, saving me. A wave of confusion hit my brain when Kevin stood up and extended his hand to pull me to my feet.

"Great job, dude, your reversal was outstanding," he said with a quiet voice. The little bitch wasn't even breathing hard, unlike me. I felt as if I may die any second, but I was still able to say thanks.

"Well done, Robert," Mr. Dewey said after giving me a slap on the back. I didn't even know what a reversal was. *Thanks for not killing me,* I sent Kevin through a green corridor.

The showers were uneventful today until someone slapped me on the back while I was rinsing the body wash out of my hair. I turned quickly, ready to protect myself, but Kevin stood there smiling. The slap wasn't malicious; it was a slap of acceptance. I was emotionally moved to the point of almost crying. This was something I had wished for since I was ten. I needed to reel in my emotions before anyone noticed.

"You're just a little sleeper cell, aren't you?" Kevin said, still smiling.

*"You have no idea,"* I told his mind emphatically through a yellow hallway. Kevin's facial expression quickly turned to obvious concern. He laughed nervously and walked out of the shower.

*Why can I hear Robert's voice in my mind? He isn't even talking. I need to hold it together. My dad really needs me now, more than ever,* I heard Kevin think.

As Kevin left the locker room, I found a yellow passage again and transmitted, *"See ya, Kevin."*

Kevin quickly turned to look at me with a perplexed expression and answered with a meek, "Bye."

"Bye, Kevin," I answered, pretending that I hadn't sent him anything.

I had to stay late today to work on my chemistry project, but I was finally on my way home. Gary was quietly driving as I stared at my phone screen, searching for wrestling videos that would show me what a reversal was. Wow! Those singlets didn't leave a lot to the imagination. I could see the guy's bulging muscles through the skin-tight uniform. How come I hadn't been attending the wrestling meets?

"You did well today," Gary said, pulling my mind out of the gutter.

"Thanks. Are you referring to when I was wrestling?"

"Yeah, you put him in his place."

"He's a lot faster and stronger than I am."

"I don't know about that, he seemed surprised when you pulled off that amazing reversal. You have the athletic ability necessary; you just need to believe in yourself," Gary said, looking over at me where I was sitting shotgun.

“Nothing like Sam’s athletic ability,” I said, trying to determine if Gary was willing to be honest about the vast differences between my brother and me.

“You and Sam share a lot of the same DNA, so you have what it takes! You just need more time and self-assurance.”

“You mean like the self-assurance I have when I try to throw a dodgeball. Right?” We both started to laugh. I liked Gary’s laugh. It came from the bottom of his gut.

When I arrived home, everyone but my dad was there. Sam was self-tasked with devouring a large pizza while Kate watched a movie in the second-floor family room. So, I grabbed some snacks and headed upstairs to get started on my homework. As I walked past my mom’s office, I heard her call for me.

“Hey, Robert, please come in here for a minute. I need to talk with you about something.” About something? That didn’t sound good.

“What is it?” I asked as I stood in the doorway.

“I just wanted to let you know I made an appointment for you to see a doctor tomorrow.”

“I’m over my cold; I won’t need to go,” I reassured her as I turned to leave.

“Why don’t you come in and sit down for a few minutes?” she suggested with a non-confrontational tone.

“I’m fine standing,” I told her defiantly, remaining in the doorway. Other than the porn video I saw in the cafeteria, I’ve had a good day. I just didn’t want to ruin it by having another fight with my mom.

“The appointment isn’t for your cold. The doctor will be able to help you learn to cope with the depression you’ve been having.”

“What depression?” I asked calmly as anger started to rear its ugly head. *Let me see, how do I explain this? Don’t screw this up, Suzanne,* I heard my mom think. She didn’t want to fight either. It didn’t matter. I wasn’t going to a shrink unless she physically drug me there against my will.

“You seem to be under a lot of stress lately. Your Father and I would like you to see this doctor who specializes in teen therapy.” I was getting more pissed off by the second.

“I just don’t see what would make you think I need to see a therapist.”

“Honey, I’m worried about you. Please just go see this doctor. I think you’ll like him.”

"You haven't answered my question," I demanded with a hint of disrespect in my tone.

"I've already explained that I'm worried about you."

"Why?" I snap back with an antagonistic attack.

"Because lately, you've seemed depressed." We were just going around in circles, so I needed to try a different tactic.

"Please don't make me do this," I said with a bit of a whine, trying to play the begging angle. Nope, my mom has had enough. Her mind was made up, and there was nothing I could say that would change her decision.

"Andy will take you to your appointment tomorrow at three." I was so angry; I just turned and walk away. "Robert, come back here. I'm not finished talking with you," I heard her say as I slammed my bedroom door so hard that a picture of Leonardo Da Vinci fell off the wall. I threw my backpack at my desk, and it hit the chair before dropping to the floor as well.

A wave of tears glazed over my eyes until my vision became utterly clouded. I tried to fight through the feeling, but audible sobs escaped my lips before I dropped face down into my pillow, screaming the f-word at the top of my lungs.

My abs were sore when I was finished with my wrenching and sobbing, but I felt better. How could she do this to me? It was stupid and unfair. I should have tried changing her mind through her green corridor, but I was so pissed I couldn't stay focused.

"Samuel, will you please talk to your brother? I need him to understand how important it is for him to see this doctor tomorrow," I heard my mom say with a barely audible voice from Sam's room.

"No way! What am I supposed to tell him?" I heard Sam ask, with dread in his voice.

"Just be kind to him, and maybe he'll talk to you," my mom answered with a muffled tone.

"I'll give it a try, but I doubt it will do any good," Sam said, finally giving in.

I reached over to pick up a picture of Sam and me from my nightstand. We were close back then. Dad took the picture almost two years ago when we were camping up north. The fun we had on that trip made me yearn for those days to return. Since then, a division had developed between Sam and me. I wasn't sure why; it just happened over time. In the picture, Sam's blonde hair and blue eyes sparkle in the sun. My curly brown hair was pressed up against the side of his tanned chest as he pulled me in tight. It was hard to believe we were siblings; we didn't look that much alike.

Life was much better back then when Dad had time to spend with Sam and me. He took us camping in the dunes near Ludington. Our dad wanted us to have firsthand experience sleeping in a tent and eating meals prepared over an open fire. My dad wanted to teach his sons what it was like to 'go without.' Apparently, starving half to death and sleeping on the rock-hard ground helped us to better understand what it was like to go without—something the wealthy wasn't accustomed to.

"Hey, little brother, can I come in?" I heard Sam say with a muffled voice through my closed door. I didn't answer, hoping he'd go away. Why the hell couldn't they just leave me alone?

"What do you want? Are you here to F with me too?" I asked as Sam entered uninvited.

"Nope, Mom asked me to come in here to talk with you. So, I'm doing what I've been asked to do." At least he was honest. Sam does everything asked of him. Unlike me, he was a rule follower, for the most part. I could follow the rules if required to do so, but I was more likely to follow my own rules as I made them up.

"I don't want to talk right now," I said adamantly as he stood beside my bed, looking down at me.

"Believe me, this is not my favorite place to be either, but Mom is worried about you," he said as he picked up the picture of us that I had just sat back in its place.

"She can go get screwed," I mumbled as I buried my face in my pillow again. "I'll be fine. You can leave now."

"I'm worried about you too," he said with a kind, tender, atypical tone. I picked my head up from my pillow and slowly looked up at him with confusion. I usually felt intimidated by his six-foot-two stature, which was framed with solid muscle. But now, he sounded and looked different, maybe even concerned.

"Why would you give two shits about me?" I replied as I looked away.

"Come on, look at me for a second. Would you?" Sam asked kindly, apparently trying to take the high road. I would've gotten pissed and left by now if our roles were reversed. I slowly turned toward him again to find him sitting beside me. He was honestly worried. Uh-oh! I could easily read that Sam knew what happened to my wrist during the holiday break. I couldn't believe he was worried about almost losing me. I never knew he even cared.

"What are you worried about?" I asked, trying to figure out how much Sam knew. He grabbed my left arm and pulled it up toward his face.

"This," he said as he ran his fingers across the scar on my wrist.

"What?"

"Come on. I'm not as smart as you are, but I'm not stupid either. You cut yourself on purpose."

"It was an accident," I quickly responded defensively.

"Don't try to sell me on that line of shit. I know you broke the lamp so you could make it look like an accident," Sam said as he pointed at my matching lamp on the other side of my bed. My brother surprised me; he knew I staged the whole thing. I really wish I could have talked with him about what I was planning to do that fateful night. I even paused for a bit, hoping he'd knock on my door. Maybe he could've tried to talk me out of it, but we didn't have that kind of relationship anymore.

I thought I had fooled everyone, but not Sam, apparently. I couldn't imagine how I would've told him what was going through my mind at that fleeting moment. I couldn't fathom how the conversation would've sounded to Sam had I explained that it might be okay to not be alive anymore. At that moment, I felt trapped as if there was no hope, and I had no one who could help me find that hope.

"Please don't tell Mom and Dad," I begged him. We sat there on my bed, staring at each other for a few uncomfortable seconds until I literally saw an idea pop into Sam's brain.

"If you'll willingly go see this doctor tomorrow, I'll keep it our secret." I was impressed with Sam's blackmail tactics.

"Thank you," I uttered with relief. "Do you think Mom and Dad know the truth?"

Sam shook his head no and said, "I don't think so, but while you're visiting Dad, I would recommend you tell him what's going on with your life." *It may be a good time for Robert to tell Dad about the gay thing too.*

*His secret life could add complications to Dad's re-election. But how do I broach that subject?* I heard Sam think.

"How long have you known?" I quickly asked Sam. I hadn't taken the time to realize that Sam had never said anything out loud about me not being straight.

"Known about what? You mean cutting yourself?"

"No. About me being… um, gay."

"You're gay?" he asked, with an intentional gasp as he dramatically brought his hands to his chest. I tipped my head and stared at Sam above my glasses.

"How long have you known?" I asked again.

"About a year," he said with a slight smile. "You tend to check the guys out when we're down at the beach, and you don't pay much attention to the girls. Not to mention the way you decorate your spotless bedroom," he said, pointing at my wall that was plastered with large pictures of my heroes and cute guys.

"Are you referring to Albert Einstein or the shirtless Cameron Dallas?" Now it was Sam's turn to give me a 'don't be stupid look. "What can I say? Cameron is gorgeous. Don't you agree?" I asked, knowing that I would make Sam feel a tad bit uncomfortable.

"He's talented, but I'm really not sexually interested in his gender," he said with his face scrunched up. "Is that why you did it?"

"Did what?" I asked.

"Cut yourself. Did you cut yourself because you were having trouble coming out?" Sam asked with some gloom in his tone.

"That was most of it," I admitted.

"You know, there's nothing wrong with being gay," Sam said with a supportive voice.

"I know," I answered, looking down at my bare feet that were touching the spot on the carpet where my own blood pooled a few months back.

"I just need you to promise me something," Sam said as I redirected my gaze and looked into his sad eyes. "Don't-ever-hurt-yourself-again," he said slowly and methodically. "If you ever find yourself in that situation again, please come and talk to me."

"Sure, I can live with that," I answered with a half-smile, not knowing if Sam got the pun. "Thanks."

"You're welcome. You little twerp; I love you." The L-word just kind of hung in the air for a few seconds until I realized I needed to say something to reciprocate my feelings for him. Anything that came out of my mouth would sound corny.

"You're not going to hug me now, are you?" I asked Sam, with my left eye squinted half shut.

"Not in this lifetime," he said with a shake of his head.

"Good. I don't want to start believing you actually care about me."

"Shut up, you little cock bite," Sam said, giving me a slight shove and grinning.

"That's more like it. Now get the hell out of my room." Sam left, but not before flipping me off.

*****

Someone shook me awake, and I was surprised to find Kevin standing beside my bed, only wearing shorts and a white tank top. "Hey, let's go for a walk on the beach; we need to talk," he whispered. I quietly slid out of my bed and slipped into some shorts. "Come on, let's go," he whispered anxiously. We were able to leave the house undetected without security alarms going off. I was surprised at how warm and humid the air was. The weather seemed more typical for July than May.

"Give me your hand," I told Kevin as we approached the trailhead that led down to the beach. He put his hand in mine, and we both lifted off the ground together. Kevin didn't seem surprised that I could fly as we hovered about five feet off the sandy earth. The wet sand felt cool on our bare feet when we touch down on the beach. No words were spoken. Kevin said he wanted to talk, but we weren't talking. The way Kevin looked at me invited me in closer and closer until our faces were almost touching. Just as our lips softly touched, a bright light flashed and...

*****

Fireworks woke me, and I realized it had only been a dream, but it was a dream I wouldn't mind having again. I could hear a thunderstorm brewing outside. That would explain the bright flash of light. I rolled toward my phone to check the time and... oh, gross. I just rolled over something wet and sticky. Getting my sheets down to the laundry in the morning without anyone noticing would be a bit tricky. My phone displayed 03:03.

# Relationships Chapter 4

Thursday, May 18th Relationships

I woke up believing I must've dreamed the whole Sam conversation, but I was quickly reminded by my hunger pains that I missed dinner last night. I was still too pissed off to leave my room for dinner. So, it wasn't a dream. Sam knew I was gay, and he knew I attempted suicide. His knowing the truth would complicate my life even more. Oh yeah, speaking of complicated, I kissed Kevin last night during a hot dream.

After I finished up with my forty-minute swim, I took a quick shower before stripping my bed. I was able to sneak the dirty sheets into the laundry room and hid the linens under some other unlaundered clothing. I paused for a second, wondering if I should leave a note to warn Mrs. Wells of the potential hazmat situation.

I was on edge, knowing I should apologize to my mom this morning when I went down for breakfast, but I was relieved when I found out she had already left for work.

"Good morning, Robert!" Mrs. Wells said with a warm, reassuring smile. Have I mentioned I love her? "Sit down; I made you some breakfast."

"Thank you. It smells terrific," I said as I watched Petey position himself at the best vantage point to retrieve food that would inadvertently be dropped.

"Your mother wanted me to remind you about your appointment at three," Mrs. Wells said as she placed a glass of orange juice in front of me.

"Yeah, how can I forget that one?" I mumbled, with my mouth half full of scrambled eggs.

"After my Charlie died, I went to a counselor, and she helped me get through some tough spots," Mrs. Wells said just as Kate entered the kitchen.

"I'll be fine," I promised Mrs. Wells.

"I heard you had another fight with Mom last night," Kate said as she sat down. I turned to give her the stink eye but refrained from engaging her with a vindictive response.

"Let's keep our comments to ourselves, please," Mrs. Wells warned Kate as she placed a plate of eggs in front of her.

"Good morning, Sir Robert. How are you?" Andy asked as I climbed into the back seat.

"Fine, thanks," I lied. I was required to ride in the back seat when Andy drove me. His rules had something to do with safety and tinted glass in the rear of the truck.

"I have the address of the doctor you'll be seeing today at three." Wow! Could I get just one more reminder that I have to see the damn doctor today? I thought to myself.

"Do you know the name of the doctor?" I asked with as much respect as I could muster.

"Kelly, I think," Andy answered, without taking his eyes off the road. I did a quick search for 'Dr. Kelly, Holland, Michigan' and there he was on my screen. What a doof. Was that a comb-over or a toupee? He looked a bit younger than my grandpa.

Anger struck my brain again, only this time, in the form of a tantrum. I threw my head back against the headrest, quickly realizing the headrest wasn't as soft as it looked. Andy glanced in the mirror, noticing my childish behavior, but he didn't offer any words of encouragement like Mrs. Wells had.

I closed my eyes and started thinking about the dream I had–kissing Kevin. Just as my eyes shut, I began envisioning something new, but this time I didn't know if it was past-tense or pretense. I could sense everything Kevin saw and felt through his orange corridor as he rode his bike to school. Hell yes! Kevin was thinking about me.

*Why can I hear Robert's voice? It's some wild shit. Why did I pick him first for dodgeball? It's like he suggested it to my mind, and I honored his request? What am I thinking? In reality, he didn't ask me anything.*

*"If you use your turn signal, dumbass, I'd know you were turning right,"* I heard Kevin tell the driver of a bright blue car who appeared to be talking on his phone. *Wow! Those trees are beautiful.* Kevin was right, the pink flowering trees were gorgeous, but I never would've taken him for someone who noticed the beauty of nature. *The pollen must be messing with my allergies,* he thought immediately after he sneezed. *Damn. There aren't any spots left on the bike rack again.*

"Robert, we're here," I heard Andy say as he shook my arm. "Did you fall asleep?"

"Oh… umm… no… I'm fine. Sorry, maybe I did," I lied as I bailed out of the truck. What the hell was going on? Why was I able to see and hear everything Kevin was experiencing? I could even smell the beautiful flowering trees he had been riding under as he pedaled down the bike path. Kevin hit the nail on the head. 'It was really wild shit.'

"Hey, Robert," David said as he walked past my desk in first-hour. I was kind of surprised since he had never spoken to me before. Yesterday it was a wave, and today there were words.

"Hey David," I said shyly, returning his greeting. The remainder of first-hour was consumed with working through algorithms to figure out how the orange corridor worked in Kevin's mind. The fact that Kevin had an orange corridor I could traverse through was an incredible addition, but maybe a smidge unethical to use.

Every time I walked into second-hour psychology, I felt anxious. I was the only freshman in the class, and having upperclassmen look down their noses at me for having the audacity to enroll in the course was a bit intimidating, yet I didn't have a choice. My mom insisted I sign up for the advanced placement class as an elective to 'challenge me intellectually.' The course was easy, and there wasn't much homework, so there was a silver lining.

I had a psychology paper due next week, and today, Ms. Manning instructed everyone to share the outline of their paper with the class. Luckily, I finished my draft last evening after Sam left my room. "Go ahead and read us your outline, Robert," Ms. Manning said. I took a deep breath. Everyone was watching me, which made me even more anxious.

"So, you think you know him?" I began reading. Ms. Manning gave me a reassuring head nod as if she were impressed with my title. "But what do you really know about him for sure? Even if he tells you who he is. Do you really know him? The fact is, people withhold the truth from others. Everyone lies at some point for various reasons. So, how do we know for sure if he's telling the truth about who he is? Why would someone lie about who they are anyway?"

"Because he's still in the closet," someone said as if he were covering a cough, but the words happened to be recognizable as he did so. Someone from behind me giggled, apparently not able to ignore the humor.

"Jake! That will be enough," Ms. Manning said, scolding Jake with a furious expression. I looked at Jake's malicious smirk while making eye contact with him. I had a typical reaction of flaring anger, but Jake squinted his eyes closed, reached up with both hands, and placed them over his ears. Jake started to moan loudly, rocking back and forth in his desk chair, acting as if he was in excruciating pain. "Jake! What's wrong?" Ms. Manning asked with a frantic tone as she rushed to his side.

"It's getting better," he muttered, lifting his head from his desk. I could see actual tears rolling down his cheeks as a low murmur filled the classroom.

"Do you want to go lie down," Ms. Manning asked, placing her hand on his shoulder.

"No, I'll be fine," he said, drying his tears with the back of his hand.

My mom guilted me into attending a girls' varsity basketball game with her last winter. We ended up staying to watch the boy's game as well. The way Jake moved his athletic body on the court was incredible. His speed and agility paid off for him as he repeatedly stole the ball from his opponent. I would guess Jake was about six-four, with a thin, sleek build. In my opinion, Jake was the best-looking senior in his class, but he didn't hold a candle to Kevin.

I had never treated Jake poorly, so I was surprised he chose to publicly humiliate me.

"Very well then, if you're sure," Ms. Manning said, bending down close to Jake's ear. He shook his head, yes, to whatever she had whispered. "Were you finished, Robert?" she asked. I gave her a nod, still trying to figure out the unexplainable event that just played out. Jake was acting all cocky, and one second later, he was experiencing excruciating pain. "Well done, Robert. Your outline has left me intrigued. I can't wait to read your finished paper," she said, looking at Jake, then back at me. She was obviously still concerned about Jake's wellbeing.

Second-hour had finished, and while stuffing my tablet into my backpack, I sensed someone's close presence. When I cautiously looked to my left, I saw Jake standing beside me with a humble posture. He seemed nervous. I could tell he wanted to talk with me. "Hey, ah..." He tapped his forehead with two fingers as if he were trying to remember something.

"It's Robert," I told him after reading his memory lapse. I couldn't blame him. For what reason would a guy like Jake have to remember the name of a random freshman?

"Yeah, Robert," he said, starting over. "I'm sorry about that…"

I gave him a wave and interrupted, saying, "It's fine. Forget it."

"Cool," he said, raising his fist to give me knucks before walking toward the door. I sat in amazement, watching him walk away. He could crush concrete with those muscles.

By the time third-hour was finished, I was so hungry. It was hard to imagine Mrs. Wells had made me a full course meal not more than four hours earlier. When I entered the cafeteria, I saw Cam standing in line, waving me over. I caught a glimpse of Kevin, who had joined the back of the line. *Looks like Robert has found himself a new friend,* I heard Kevin think. I wasn't sure why Kevin would care about who I was friends with.

"Hey, my mom said you can stay over at my house next weekend after we go to the movie. If it's okay with your parents?" Cam quickly added.

"Hell yeah! That would be awesome!" I said with too much excitement.

"Would you like some stuffing with your turkey, Hun?" I heard the X-rated lunch lady ask.

"Yes, please," I replied timidly. The turkey was as perfectly round as her teen lover's bubble butt.

"What time do you think you'll be able to come over on Friday night?" Cam asked as the lunch lady served him some dried-out stuffing.

"Andy can drop me off on the way home from school. If that'll work?"

"Sounds good. Does that mean you'll be able to stay at my house without..." he intentionally stopped mid-sentence to point at Andy, who was standing only ten feet away? I gave Cam a shrug. I hadn't really thought about how all of that would work. I hadn't stayed over at anyone's house since the third grade. Why did everything have to be so complicated?

*I need to talk to Robert today; this can't wait any longer,* I heard Kevin think from the other side of the cafeteria.

*If you want to talk, let's talk,* I sent Kevin through a green hallway as he looked directly at me. I couldn't seem to shut his voice off when we were in the same room.

As I approached the locker room, I saw Kevin standing by the entrance. *Oh good! Here he comes,* I heard him think. Hell yes! Kevin was waiting for me!

"Hey, Robert?" he said with a subtle nod as if he were expecting me to stop. "Could I have a word?" Kevin asked, pointing at the weight room across the hall. I gave him a quick nod in return.

"Dude, I know this is going to sound weird, but…" Kevin said, turning toward me, pausing for a few seconds as if he wasn't sure he wanted to continue. "I ah… I started hearing voices, I mean not voices, but the voice sounds like yours." How could that be possible? I had no idea my voice would be recognizable since it wasn't passing through my vocal cords. Kevin was clearly terrified about what he was telling me.

My brain started to sort through what was going on. I was standing in a room—alone—with the hottest guy in my grade. Kevin seemed intimidated by me, or maybe he was just freaking about my telepathy.

"Voices? Are you okay, Kevin?" I asked out of genuine concern. "You don't look so well." He shook his head, no.

"I haven't been getting enough sleep. I think something's going wrong with my mind. I've been hearing you talk to me while we're at school, but you aren't even saying anything out loud." I knew I shouldn't be basking in the moment, but it was difficult not to take the opportunity to gloat in my own mind for a few seconds.

"I don't know what or who you've been hearing, but it's not me." I didn't want to get my ass kicked, so I thought it would be best to deny everything. Kevin looked as if he were a scared little kid who was lost and confused. How could I make him believe he wasn't going insane without revealing my newfound gifts?

My stomach wouldn't stop fluttering with excitement as I talked with Kevin. The effort it took to stay calm was honestly exhausting. I tried to keep from smiling as I thought about the dream I had last night. Kevin's body language was vulnerable as if he were willing to ask for help. At the same time, his mind kept telling him to walk out of the weight room and forget it.

"Look, I don't know what's going on, but I'm sure everything will be fine," I told him with confidence.

"Dude, I don't think so," he said as he shook his head, no again. "I think I'm having a nervous breakdown. I've been under a lot of pressure and…"

"Tell you what, let's meet at Mary's coffee shop at four-thirty. We can talk there. I'll try to help you figure this thing out." I needed to interrupt him; we had been alone together way too long. Soon, someone would notice we were missing. Or worse, we would be late. I couldn't be tardy or absent from PE class one more time, which would cost me a passing grade.

"That's fine, but I don't get out of track practice until four-thirty, so it'll have to be five," Kevin explained as he rubbed his handsome face. I gave Kevin a subtle nod of agreement.

"Let me see your phone for a second," I said, reaching out. Kevin's fingers grazed my hand, sending my pulse rate into a rage. "Text me if you can't make it," I told him after handing his phone back. Andy gave me a funny look when Kevin and I walked out of the weight room together. *What the hell is going on with those two?* I heard Andy think.

"Good afternoon, Robert, would you please come with me?" a tall thin man asked, holding the waiting room door open. Yup, it was definitely a toupee.

"Have a seat, please," Doctor Kelly said, pointing at a comfy-looking chair covered in a large plaid print. The walls of his office were dark wood panels from ceiling to floor. The burgundy carpet that covered the floor was almost completely worn through heavily trafficked areas. There was only one large picture hanging on the wall with a few framed certificates and a diploma from the University of Michigan. If his patients weren't depressed before they stepped into this room, they surely would be by the time they left.

"So... welcome. What can I help you with today?" Doctor Kelly asked, starting off with a friendly hand gesture. He sounded more like a Home Depot associate who was trying to help me find some bolts.

"I'm not sure. Maybe you could tell me. You've talked with my mother. She's the one who sent me here." *The patient starts off with a sarcastic tone.* I couldn't see what he was writing, but I could clearly hear what he was thinking.

"Yes, I've conferred with your mother, but there are always two sides to every story. Maybe you'd like to share your side of the story."

That was smooth, dumbass, but I'm not some stupid kid you can manipulate, I thought to myself. *The patient seems withdrawn and is unwilling to communicate his feelings.*

*Withdrawn? Are you serious?* Wait! What was that? Something new just happened to cause the good doctor to rub his head where his toupee was loosely attached. When I entered his green hallway, I tried the second door on the left to inconspicuously plant the message. In doing so, I accidentally turned the handle in the wrong direction. I saw the effects of pain written in his facial expression when I applied a small amount of pressure on the door handle. His eyes closed as if he had 'Brain Freeze.' When I turned the handle back, I could see the relief on his face. I did it a couple more times just to make sure it was me who was causing his pain.

"Are you okay, Doctor?" I asked with a hint of sarcasm.

"Yes, I'm quite fine, thank you," he said as he started to rub his temples again as if there were some lingering effects. Have I ever mentioned that I could be a horrible human being when I was angry? Oh no! It just occurred to me; I may have caused Jake's head pain today. His reaction was exactly like Doctor Kelly's. How the hell was I able to create misery for Jake without turning any door handles? I hoped Jake was all right.

My moral compass finally decided to kick in, and now I was feeling guilty for experimenting with the doctor's brain.

"My parents believe I have some depression that I need help with," I admitted.

"I'm wondering if you may not agree with your parents." I shook my head, yes. "Do you feel you're not being affected by depression?"

"Sure, maybe a little, but it's not anything I need to talk with you about." *The patient has a high intellectual aptitude; he's a bright boy.* Maybe he wasn't such a bad guy, after all, I thought to myself. *The patient does not hold any contempt or moral depravity,* the doctor wrote on his tablet. *I need to remember to do some testing on Robert's photographic memory,* I heard the doctor think. If he tried to test me, my mom would have an effing cow.

"So, is there anything you wish to share with me, Robert?"

"I'm not sure I can trust you. We only met less than ten minutes ago." *The patient has a unique sense of humor and answers questions with a condescending tone.* I smiled, thinking about how condescending I could be at times. Last week, my mom warned me to watch my sharp tongue. She said, 'people don't like to be talked down to. Yes, you're capable of outwitting most people you encounter, but you should ask yourself if that's kind.'

"You can trust I won't share anything we've discussed here today with anyone."

"Unless what I tell you is criminal, violent, or life-threatening to me or someone else." He shook his head, yes, in agreement.

"That's correct. Have you ever had any professional counseling before today?" the doctor asked. I shook my head, no.

"If you wouldn't mind sharing some advice..." I trailed off with apprehension, interrupting the rest of my request.

"Yes?" he said as he looked up from his tablet. I almost started to laugh when his toupee flipped up. At the same time, his eyes lit up. I needed to get him to do that again before I left today.

"I'm meeting with a kid from school after I leave here. His name is Kevin. For some reason, unbeknownst to me, he doesn't like me. Kevin may even hate me, but I kinda like him and wouldn't mind becoming his friend. How do I get him to like me?"

"Do you have trouble making friends?" the doctor asked as he looked down at his screen, probably thinking it would help me open up if he wasn't looking directly at me.

"Yeah, I'm not great with social interaction. So, how do I do it?" *The patient seems vulnerable when he explains his social inadequacies.*

"What qualities would you look for in a friend?" he asked with a serious tone.

"Um, I don't know, maybe honesty and trustworthiness. Someone I could count on to be nice, understanding, and nonjudgmental. It wouldn't hurt if the person were cute like Kevin," I said just before delivering a nervous laugh.

"Well, if I were you, I'd try to be honest with Kevin, just as you would expect from him. Be yourself, don't try to impress him. You seem to be a charming boy who is open and inviting." Yeah, right. So charming that I had no problem with giving you a killer headache ten minutes into our session, I thought to myself. "If Kevin's core values are similar to yours, I believe he will be enticed to learn more about you. If he's able to recognize the same qualities I see in you, I believe you'll be encouraged when your relationship starts to develop." I scrunched up my face. It was difficult to believe that making friends with Kevin would be that easy. Sometimes, I try too hard, making things much more complicated than they needed to be.

"Okay, and if I blow it?"

"I would keep trying; persistence almost always pays off when you're attempting to build a lasting relationship."

"Thank you, Doctor. How much time do I have left?"

"Twenty minutes," he said as he looked at the clock behind me.

"I'm sure there won't be enough time today, but maybe you could help me with coming out to my parents. *The patient is willing to open up about his sexual orientation and has asked for help.*

"Yes, I would be delighted to help you with the process. Thank you for putting your trust in me with this big step," the doctor said.

"Before I get started, I just want to mention how unfair it is that straight kids aren't required to come out to their parents about being straight." The doctor smiled. "I'm flying out to DC to visit my father this weekend. My older brother Sam recommended I tell my father that I'm gay."

"And you're apprehensive about talking with your father about sexual orientation?"

"Ah… yeah... I'm sure you're aware that we live in an extremely conservative community. Unfortunately, the LGBTQ community is not greeted with open arms around here. My family attends a rather conservative church, and my father is a Republican Congressman. Need I explain more?"

"I know who your father is, Robert. I also agree with you about the conservative views of many who live in this community. Your mother and father love you, and they want what is best for you. I suspect honesty will be your best approach. Just lay it out there, let them deal with it in their own way. Homosexuality is nothing anyone should be ashamed of." I shook my head in agreement. "You mentioned church, Robert. Is going to church important to you?"

"Have you ever heard the song, 'Take Me to Church'?" The doctor's smile told me yes, so I continued. "I believe Hozier's song identifies how the church will often use religion to manipulate their followers into believing that loving the same gender is wrong. How can being in love with someone ever be wrong?" Doctor Kelly was still smiling and gave me a nod when I looked up. "The church allows ignorance to breed hate. Acceptance of all beliefs should be celebrated. If the church stuck to teaching about loving each other unconditionally, they would be less likely to push their followers away."

Everything in the room was silent except the big clock behind me, clicking off every second that went by. "My parents taught me to embrace free will. They believe critical thinking skills are imperative. Still, they're insistent on me believing things about their faith that I just can't buy into." The doctor gave me an inquisitive look as if he were asking for an example. "Science has proven that our planet is over 4.5 billion years old. Leaders at my church want me to believe God created earth only ten thousand years ago. How can I buy into that?"

"That's an excellent example, Robert. We should talk more about this on your next visit. It looks as if we're out of time."

"Thank you," I said with sincere appreciation.

"You're welcome. I'll see you next week, then?"

"Yes, I have a few other things to run by you next week."

"That sounds promising," he said as he stood to shake my hand.

*I'm sorry for giving you a headache,* I sent him as a peace offering through his green corridor.

I didn't see Kevin anywhere when I entered the stuffy coffee shop, so I sent him a quick text:

Just arrived

On my way, b there in 3, Kevin sent back.

K

I took a seat in an open booth by the window so I could see when Kevin arrived. I had three minutes, so I tried to focus on Kevin's orange corridor, but nothing happened as it did this morning. I wondered what I was doing wrong.

I was sweating by the gallons. My deodorant stopped working an hour ago. I would definitely stink by the time Kevin arrived. The temperature was seventy-five degrees today with the sun shining bright, but it must have been at least eighty in the small coffee shop. They had the doors propped open, probably hoping for a cool breeze.

I quickly jumped out of my seat when I saw Kevin ride his bike through the parking lot. As I approached the service counter to meet Kevin, he didn't look too hot. Well, I mean, Kevin always looked hot. He just seemed to be stressed out.

"Hey, thanks for meeting me, man," he said, sounding winded as if he had been riding hard.

After settling into a corner booth, Kevin looked into my eyes before starting our conversation. "Robert, you have special powers, right?"

"Ah... no, I don't think so," I answered. I guess this honesty thing I had discussed with my doctor less than an hour ago wasn't going so well for me.

"I heard you ask me something in my brain on Tuesday when we were in the locker room and again on Wednesday. You didn't say anything out loud, but I still heard it in my mind," he said before pausing to take a drink of his iced coffee. "Sometimes, it seems like you have me under a magical spell." Join the club. Shawn Mendes has me under a spell twenty-four-seven, I thought to myself.

"Yeah, you mentioned that when we were talking in the weight room," I said as I squirmed in my seat.

"When my mom died last December, I went through a lot of emotional issues and ended up having to see a therapist. Now things are getting worse at home again," Kevin said as he dropped his sad gaze to the table. I felt horrible for making matters worse.

"I'm sorry you lost your Mom. I can't imagine how hard it must have been for you and your dad," I told him, hoping he would detect my genuine tone. Kevin looked at me as if he were waiting for me to come clean. "Is there something I did or said that would cause you to hate me so much?" I finally asked with a meek voice as I dabbed my forehead with a napkin.

"Who said that I hate you?" Kevin answered.

"Come on, admit it, you resent me."

"I don't hate or resent you. I'm just dealing with a lot of shit in my life. My dad started drinking when my mom died, and he lost his job in late January. I think we may lose our house if he doesn't get help. I've been taking care of everything at home while my dad continues to drink himself to death. I'm worried my mom's life insurance funds will run out within the next few months," Kevin explained as he took another drink of coffee to keep himself from crying. "My life sucks. There's nothing I can do about it." Kevin paused while looking into my eyes for a few seconds. I wished he'd stop doing that; he was making me blush.

Fear and anger were festering in Kevin's thoughts. I wish I could reassure him that everything would work in his favor, but I wasn't sure that was true, so I stayed quiet. "This is stupid. Why am I even telling you all this? You don't give a shit anyway," Kevin said with a defeated tone.

"I do give a shit, and it's not stupid. It just sounds like you need help with all the bad shit that you're dealing with."

"Like I said, why would you care? You've got it all," he said with disgust in his tone.

"What do you mean, I've got it all?" I asked defensively.

"Your family is rich. You live in the high rent district. Both of your parents are alive, you have a cool older brother, a dad who's a Congressman, and you're good-looking. Hell, you even have your own bodyguard!" he said, pointing at Andy, who was sitting across the shop sipping his iced drink.

Wow, I didn't even have to read Kevin. He told me exactly how he felt. Wait, what? Did he just casually mention that I was 'good-looking?' Kevin was trying to be honest with me. I needed to work harder to reciprocate.

"Listen, my parents are always gone from home, my brother thinks I'm annoying to be around, and my younger sister hates my guts. By the way, it sucks to have a detail following me around every step I take. I can't even take a piss without being watched. But none of what you said explains why you hate me."

"I don't hate you!" he said with a tinge of anger.

"You must resent me. Otherwise, you wouldn't be body-checking me."

"Dude, you're always walking with your head down. I'm surprised it doesn't happen more often." I looked at Kevin, waiting for him to answer my question. "Maybe some," he finally admitted with a soft voice.

"I can live with that, but did you just say I was good-looking?"

"Yeah, of course, you are," he said with confusion.

"I'm a nerd who doesn't have any friends. Compared to you, I'm the ugliest guy in our school." Kevin shook his head, no.

"You don't see it, do you? When you look in the mirror every morning, you don't see a brilliant, attractive, privileged kid, do you?" Wow! Now I was attractive?

"So, you're envious of me as well?" I asked with surprise in my tone.

"Yeah, I guess you could say that," he agreed.

"It doesn't make any sense why you'd be envious. You're the most popular guy in our grade, and you have a ton of friends. You have athletic abilities that I could only dream of having. Girls scratch each other's eyes out just to have a chance to sit by you at lunch. By the way, things are tough all over," I said as I pulled my wet shirt away from my sticky back and chest.

"Oh, poor little rich kid," he said with a mocking voice. "How could life be rough for a kid like you?"

"Money isn't everything, Kevin. My life sucks too; it just sucks differently," I said, trying to make my point. "So, I guess we have something in common." I still regretted making things worse for Kevin, but now I knew why he has been struggling. I needed to be honest, as the doctor recommended. If I wanted to be friends with Kevin, I needed to come clean and convince him he wasn't the one going crazy, but I couldn't tell him here in a public place. He might freak out. Wait, if I told him the truth, he might never want to have anything to do with me again. I guess that was the chance I would have to take.

"We have nothing in common," Kevin finally said with anger. "Why is it so damn hot in here?" Kevin asked, lifting his shirt from the bottom, so he could wipe the sweat from his face. What the hell was wrong with me? It was as if I couldn't resist the temptation to catch a glimpse of his abs whenever I had an opportunity.

"I think their air must be broken. Are you hungry?"

"Starving," Kevin responded, lowering his shirt.

"You want to come to my house for dinner?" Kevin looked at me as if I were on drugs.

"I don't think that's a good idea," he finally said, scrunching up his face and pursing his lips as he pulled them to one side. It was the second time today I've seen him make that face. Maybe it was something he did when he became nervous. I didn't care; it was damn cute.

"Will your dad be expecting you home for dinner? We could call him."

"Haha," Kevin said with a sinister laugh. "When my dad drinks, he could care less whether I'm dead or alive." Kevin reached up with his forearm, this time to wipe the sweat from his brow.

"What is it, then? Oh, I get it, you don't want to be seen with me. You're afraid I'll tarnish your popularity." I was trying to read Kevin, but all I got was anger, anger, and more anger as he glared at me. I must've gotten the tone wrong.

"You're an asshole, Robert!" Kevin said with fury as his eyes bored a hole through my brain. I was trying to come up with a quick apology, but it was too late. Kevin abruptly started to slide out of the booth as if he was planning to leave. "I'm out of here!" he said. I quickly grabbed Kevin's wrist before he could stand up.

"Wait! Wait, a second, please just let me apologize." *Please sit back down,* I sent him through a green corridor. "I'm really sorry, sometimes I can have a sharp tongue, and you're right, I can be a bit of an asshole, especially when I'm hungry." Kevin pulled his arm free from my grip as he started to relax his posture. "Please, just explain to me why you think it's a bad idea to come over to my house for dinner?" *Come on, please, just this once,* I sent through a green door that I had to open first. Kevin sat back against the booth and tilted his head back as if he were stressed to the max.

"I don't take handouts from anyone, especially wealthy people!"

"It's not a handout. It's a genuine invitation to have dinner at my house." Kevin blew out a heavy breath through his pursed lips.

"I guess I wouldn't mind having a home-cooked meal," he said as he nodded.

Andy seemed surprised when Kevin pushed his bike up to the truck so we could load it into the back. "Am I driving you home, Kevin?" Andy asked as he jumped into the driver's seat.

"How do you know my name?" Kevin asked as he tilted his head to look at Andy.

"Oh, trust me, he knows a lot more about you than just your name," I told Kevin while watching Andy smile in the rearview mirror. "He's joining me for dinner at home," I told Andy.

"As you wish," Andy said with a smirk as I texted my mom:

Hey Mom, is it okay if I bring a friend home for dinner?

Sure, honey, how did your appointment go?

It was fine, I'll be home in 10 min.

Kevin gasped as we drove up to our house that sat high on a dune overlooking Lake Michigan. “Holy shit, dude, you live in a mansion!”

“Um... Ah... yeah,” I muttered with a hint of embarrassment mixed in with my acknowledgment.

“This view is gorgeous,” he said as he looked out over the water. “What’s it like to live in a palace?”

“It’s nice, but I guess you get used to it, and it doesn’t really seem that special,” I said while giving him a shrug.

When we walked into the mudroom, I bent down to untie my shoes. Before I had one shoe untied, I noticed Kevin had already slipped both of his shoes off without untying them. I follow suit, slipping out of my other untied shoe before kicking it to the wall. Luckily, Kevin didn’t seem to notice my obsessive-compulsive tendencies. I was surprised my parents never had me tested to determine if I was on the spectrum or not. Now that I think of it, maybe they have.

I could tell Kevin felt uncomfortable in his surroundings when we left the mudroom to enter the main foyer. *And he doesn’t think he’s privileged? Give me a break,* I heard Kevin think as he looked up at the thirty-foot ceiling.

“Dinner smells great, Mrs. Wells,” I announced with a raised voice from the foyer.

“Hello, Robert. I’m making spaghetti and meatballs. It will be ready at six-thirty. Oh. Who do we have here?” Mrs. Wells asked after noticing Kevin standing beside me. A big smile stretched across her face while wiping her hands on a towel.

“Mrs. Wells, this is Kevin. I’ve invited him to dinner if that’s all right.”

“Sure, there’s always room for one more. It’s a pleasure to meet you, Kevin.” I couldn’t believe the hottest guy in our school was standing in my kitchen, but I shouldn’t get too excited. He would probably jet as soon as I told him the truth about my special gift.

“See you in thirty minutes,” I told Mrs. Wells as I turned to leave the room. “Come on, I’ll show you my room,” I said to Kevin with a motion indicating he should follow me to the stairs. *This place is amazing!* I heard his brain think as we made our way up the open marble staircase that led to the next two floors. “How big is this place?” Kevin asked.

"It's around twenty thousand square feet. There are twelve guest bedrooms." I knew that the house was twenty-two thousand, three hundred sixty-six square feet, but I was trying to hide my overly capable memory.

"Have you lived here your whole life?" Kevin asked as we topped the second-floor landing.

"Yeah, my grandparents bought it for my parents the year before Sam was born."

"Holy shit, dude!" Kevin said when I opened my bedroom door.

"What!" I asked quickly, realizing maybe I should have de-gay-ifyed my room a bit before I brought Kevin here. After what Sam told me last night, I figured I needed to make some changes if I planned to stay in the closet.

"Damn, you could fit my entire house into your bedroom. I've never been in a guy's room that's as clean as yours," he said as he walked through my room, taking a quick survey of his surroundings. Oh good, he was referring to the room's size and cleanliness, not the gayness.

"Who is this, Robert?" Kevin asked as he pointed at a large framed poster on my wall. I've always figured you could tell a lot about a person by looking at their bedroom. A guy's space was usually a reflection of their personality and dreams, but I only had pictures hanging in my room of my heroes and posters of cute guys. So, there should be no doubt in Kevin's mind what my interests consist of.

"He's my favorite singer. His name is Shawn Mendes."

"Yeah, I know his music. Is he your boyfriend?" Kevin teased, still looking at the poster of Shawn, who was holding his guitar.

"Shut up," I mumbled as I carefully placed my backpack on my desk.

"It's a valid question," Kevin teased. I pretended to ignore him as I removed my tablet from my backpack before plugging it in. "Man, I could get used to a view like this," Kevin said as he stood with his back to me, looking out over the lake. Me too, I thought to myself while looking at the back of his Billabong shorts.

"Seriously, Robert? You have a four-seat jacuzzi in your own private bathroom," he said with a raised voice. "We should set up some hoops in here. It's big enough to play full-court!" he continued as he returned to my room and picked up a small Michelangelo statue on his way.

"It's Rob."

"What?" Kevin asked as he quickly turned toward me, still holding the statue of David. I hoped he wouldn't drop it. Grandma bought the figure for me last year when she was in Italy. It must have been expensive.

"You can call me Rob," I offered again. Come on, just do it, I told myself, trying to propel my brain into the inevitable. I needed to tell Kevin the truth, so he could freak out and leave.

"Rob, it is then," he said, returning the statue to its place.

"By the way, you're not having a mental breakdown," I finally admitted.

"What are you talking about?" Kevin asked with a tucked chin and a raised eyebrow. Man, he is so gorgeous! Come on, stop being a coward, just spill it, I told myself.

"Can I trust you? You know, if I tell you something about me, that's really private?"

"Ah, yeah, I guess." *He's going to tell me he's gay. Like I didn't already know that,* I heard him think. I entered Kevin's yellow corridor and opened a door. Here goes nothing.

*"I'm telepathic, Kevin. I can read your mind and talk to you without saying anything verbally."*

"What the hell was that!" Kevin shouted as he jumped back away from me. "You just did it again! You just did that thing! You… ah… You said something to my mind!" Kevin stammered while continuing to back away slowly as if I was planning to kill him. I quickly put my left index finger up to my lips, hoping he wouldn't alert everyone in the house.

"You won't tell anyone, will you?" I whispered in a panicked tone as I held my hands up, surrendering.

"Okay, I have to admit, I'm freaked," he said with a shaky voice as he got closer and closer to my closed bedroom door. He was probably getting ready to bolt. "But at the same time, I'm relieved to know I'm not going crazy. Yesterday, I Googled hearing voices. It said I was having a hallucination or had a psychotic disorder. Whatever the hell that is."

"I'm sorry, that's why I wanted to bring you here. So, I could tell you all of this in private. I didn't want you to think you were going insane," I said, feeling defeated as I flopped onto my bed and stared at the ceiling.

"You lied to me when we were in the weight room today. Why didn't you just come clean when I confronted you?"

"I'm a coward. Now that you know the truth, don't feel like you have to stay. I'll ask Andy to drive you home," I told Kevin in a sulky voice.

"Are you out of your freaking mind, dude? And miss out on Mrs. Wells's spaghetti? The smell from your kitchen reminded me of when my mom used to cook us dinner," Kevin explained as he moved away from my door. He sounded as if he was starting to chill just a bit.

"It was an accident. You know, the first time I talked to your mind. I didn't even know I could do it at the time."

"You talked to me in the locker room and in the shower. I think I answered you," Kevin said as he started to look around my room again.

"Yeah, I can hear you when you answer me. I just have to use the yellow corridor," I explained as Kevin looked toward me with apparent confusion. "You have several different corridors in your mind that I can navigate." Kevin still seemed confused as he stood next to a picture of Leonardo Da Vinci, pointing at it as if he wanted to know why I would have a photograph like this hanging on my wall. "He's been my hero since I was six."

"You're so weird, dude," Kevin said with a big grin.

"Robert, it's time for dinner," my mom announced through my closed door.

"We'll be down in a second," I answered with a raised voice.

*"So, like, you can hear me now?"* Kevin asked from his yellow hallway.

*"Yeah, I can read your feelings and emotions too."*

"That's so creepy, dude," he said with a shaky voice. "How long have you been able to… you know... do this stuff?"

"Three days. But it's like I'm learning something new every day."

"Wow," he said as he rubbed his forehead. I hoped I wasn't giving him a headache.

"Let's head downstairs. We can talk more after dinner. Can I trust you to keep my secret?" I asked Kevin as he shook his head, yes.

When we walked into the dining room, the place went silent. Mom, Kate, and Mrs. Wells were sitting at the table waiting for us. Mom had a look of astonishment. I wasn't sure why she'd be surprised; I told her I was bringing someone to dinner. "Mom and Kate, this is Kevin. Kevin, this is my mom and sister."

"Hey, Kate, Mrs. Van Stark," Kevin said kindly with a nod as my mom stood to shake Kevin's hand.

"It's so nice to meet you, Kevin. Welcome to our home," Mom said.

*Oh my God, he is so hot! I can't believe Kevin Larson is at my house! Wait until I tell Sara. She's going to flip out,* I heard Kate think.

*Take it easy, Kate, you're only thirteen;* I sent her through a green corridor as she broke the dinnertime rules by texting under the table.

We started to chow down after Mrs. Wells and Mom served our food. Kevin looked as if he hasn't eaten in weeks. "This is the best spaghetti I've ever eaten, Mrs. Wells," Kevin said.

"Thank you, Kevin," Mrs. Wells answered.

*"You're so charming,"* I sent Kevin, hoping I wouldn't offend him.

*"Shut up, dude! I almost choked when you broke into my brain."*

"So, Kevin, how long have you been friends with Robert?"

*"What should I tell her?"* Kevin sent me through my yellow corridor as he looked into my eyes.

*"Tell her we've known each other since the third grade."*

"We've known each other since third grade, Mrs. Van Stark," he answered just before he chewed off another bite of garlic bread. I was effectively able to help Kevin sidestep the friend question. After all, I wasn't sure Kevin wanted to be friends with me.

"Kevin, you can call me Suzanne," Mom offered.

*"Man, that was cool,"* Kevin sent me as he continued to grin. Oops, Mom noticed our secretive looks; we needed to be more careful.

"Do you boys have any classes together?" I could tell that my mom was still fishing to confirm her suspicions about me having a crush on Kevin. Was there anyone in this family who wasn't suspicious about my attraction to guys?

"Gym class," I answered after swallowing my mouthful of chocolate cake.

"It's nice to see your appetite return," Mom said, looking at me. "How did your doc...?" Mom stopped mid-sentence and bit her bottom lip when she saw me shake my head, no.

*"Does anyone else know about... you know? Your gifts?"* Kevin sent me.

*"Just you,"* I sent him, hoping he would believe our connection was something special that only he and I shared.

*"Why me?"* Kevin sent with a questioning eye.

*"I don't know. I'm still working on that one."*

"Why are you boys so quiet?" Mom asked.

"Busy stuffing our faces," I lied. *"You wanna go back up to my room?"*

*"Sure, if you're done,"* Kevin answered through his yellow corridor.

*"Yup, I'm all set,"* I told him just before we slid our chairs out to leave the table.

"What's wrong?" my mom asked. "Where are you two going?" It suddenly occurred to me why she was surprised when we both got up to leave the table simultaneously without mentioning anything to each other. I had better get my act together.

"Oh, nothing's wrong. We're just heading back up," I responded, pointing at the ceiling, referring to my room two stories up.

"Thank you for the wonderful home-cooked meal, Mrs. Wells," Kevin said, revealing one of his suave personality traits.

Kevin flashed me a mischievous look as I locked my bedroom door behind us. His expression led me to believe that he could be troublesome if given the opportunity. "Do we have to be in the same room to do this telepathy stuff?" Kevin asked as he sat at my desk, turning the chair toward me.

"No. I could hear you in sixth-hour, four classrooms away."

"Hey! Maybe you could help me with my quizzes." I smiled as silence filled the room. "We're connected," Kevin said as more of a statement, pointing at me, then back at himself.

He was correct; for some reason, our minds were tethered. I wondered if this connection with Kevin was coincidental or if my brain was subconsciously creating a trap for him to fall into. "Are you okay?" Kevin asked as he sat down on my bed beside me.

"Ah… yeah. Sorry, I got kinda lost in thought about what you just said. You know, about our connection. This is a lot to process," I told him before glancing up at his beautiful eyes.

"Why do you think this stuff with your brain started? Were you struck by lightning, or did you have a head injury?" he asked with a smirk. We both chuckled, knowing that only happened fictitiously.

"I'm not sure," I answered, telling the absolute truth.

"And why me? Why did you connect with me first?" There it was again, he was asking for honesty, but I didn't know if I should tell him what I believed to be true.

"I'm still trying to figure that out, too," I lied as I looked down at the floor, so he wouldn't notice the deception in my eyes.

"Are you planning to tell anyone else? I mean about your gifts."

"No way! People already shun me as it is."

"So, what's your deal?" Kevin asked bluntly.

"Deal?" I asked with confusion.

"You know, like, why don't you hang out with friends?" I shrugged as I folded my left leg under me, turning slightly toward him. "Until today, I've always taken you for some stuck-up rich kid who thinks he's too good for everyone," Kevin added.

"I'm shy and not that much fun to be around," I tried to explain with a bit of humility as I dropped my gaze to the floor again.

"I saw you hangin' with the new kid today. What's his story?"

"His name is Cam. He just moved here from South Dakota with his Mom."

"It's been fun hangin' with you today," Kevin said with a convincing tone while rubbing the back of his neck. "Please don't take offense, but you're really much cooler than I thought you'd be."

"Thanks, I think," I said with an awkward laugh. "I don't want to come across as a miserable, antisocial nerd, but I've had more fun in the last two hours than I've had in years."

"So, that's it. You just need to make some friends," he said as if it was as simple as that.

"Yeah, but what do you need?" I asked before realizing I should have asked the question with more finesse.

"What do you mean by that?" Kevin asked in a defensive tone.

"You miss your Mom. You're afraid you'll lose your dad as well. You feel abandoned and have no idea how to fix any of it. At the coffee shop, you were worried about having to live with your grandparents in Florida, but here you are, trying to help me with my problems and asking for nothing in return."

I could see pain as I looked into Kevin's watery eyes. "I can read your feelings. I can literally sense your fear, confusion, anger, grief, and profound sadness," I explained, holding my arms crossed over my chest, trying to deal with the pain I was experiencing as well.

I couldn't control my tears anymore; they were flowing freely. "I can even see memories of you and your Mom," I said as I choked up a bit. "You used to love every second of your life, but now that it's spiraling out of control, you won't ask anyone for help." Kevin lowered his head before shaking it in agreement. “I had you all wrong, too,” I admitted. “Zach is fortunate to have you as a friend.”

“I’m afraid, dude; you’re right about the grief too. Sometimes it makes me wanna puke,” he said as he took the last few tissues remaining from my frequently used stash. “Can you keep my secret?” he asked, trying to hide his raw emotion as he sat down next to me again.

“Are you serious? Before dinner, I asked you to keep my secret; you didn’t hesitate for a second. I don’t know why, but I feel like I can trust you with anything,” I told Kevin with confidence.

“Robert?” Mom said with a muffled voice through my locked door.

“What is it, Mom.”

“It’s almost eight. Andy will be going off shift soon. If you want to give Kevin a ride home, you’ll need to leave soon.”

“Okay, thanks.”

“Dude, I can ride my bike,” Kevin whispered.

“Where do you live?”

“One Hundred Thirty-Sixth and Quincy.”

“That’s like six miles from here. It’ll be dark before you get home.”

“It’s warm tonight; I’ll be fine,” Kevin assured me.

“No, I’ll ask Andy to drive us. Hey, let’s see if Andy knows where you live without telling him.” We both chuckled as we bumped our knuckles together.

Andy dropped Kevin off without any location instructions. It was kind of scary how much these guys knew about other people. Kevin lived in a modest, two-story house in a well-kept neighborhood. “See you tomorrow.” “Thanks, Andy,” Kevin said as he opened the truck door. I felt closer to Kevin than I had ever felt to anyone my age. When I closed my eyes to focus on Kevin. I could see his orange corridor. *“Hey, Dad, I’m home,”* Kevin said as he entered.

*“Where the hell have you been?”* I heard his dad ask as Kevin walked into the messy living room.

*“I had track practice until four-thirty, I went to a coffee shop with my new friend. Then he invited me over to his house for a hot, home-cooked meal.”* New friend? Hell yes!

*“You should’ve called to tell me you’d be late.”*

*"Why would I call? You never answer when I text or call anyway,"* Kevin answered with a sassy tone.

*"Kevin, you'll address me with respect!"*

*"I'll give respect when it's deserved, Dad. You didn't come home until two this morning. You never bothered to call me. Do you understand how nervous I get when you do that?"*

*"I don't report to you, young man; you report to me."* Kevin's dad sounded scary when he was angry.

*"Oh, you want a report? Here's your report from yesterday and today since I haven't seen you at all."* Kevin said with sarcasm. *"I went to the bank to make the house payment yesterday. Betty asked how you were doing, by the way. So, I lied and told her you were doing fine. I also stopped at Meijer to buy some cereal, toilet paper, and milk. This morning, I did three loads of laundry before I left for school. Just in case you were looking for some clean underwear, I left your clothes in the dryer. You're welcome, and goodnight!"* I could see Kevin walking through his messy house. His vision was blurry as I looked through his tears.

*"Hey! I'm not finished discussing this, Kevin. Get your ass back down here."* Hearing Kevin's door slam reminded me of the conversation I had with my mom last night. Kevin locked his door before he started to strip down. Shut it off! Shut it off!

"Robert, you're home, wake up," I heard Andy say from the front seat. When I opened my eyes, I realized that we were already parked in the security apparatus garage. I must have looked like I was sleeping while in Kevin's orange corridor. I didn't remember the ride home.

Mom was waiting for me when I entered the mudroom. Her arms were crossed as she stood on one leg with the other foot resting against the wall. She had a grin pasted on her face as I slipped my shoes off without untying them.

"Kevin seems nice," she said with a wink. "You haven't had any friends over since, Annie."

Annie was my best friend when we were in seventh grade. Annie and I were joined at the hip (so my mom claimed). Annie's family moved to Colorado after her mother started a new medical practice in Denver. I never rebounded after losing her. I was like, what's the use of making friends? Whenever I get close to someone, they end up leaving me.

"Yeah," I said nonchalantly, hoping to hide my excitement about having Kevin over.

"I overheard you and Kevin laughing. It's been years since I've heard you laugh like that," my mom said. She was referring to when Annie and I used to sit in my bedroom laughing our asses off at stupid shit, like me trying to braid her hair. "How did your appointment go this afternoon?" she asked as she brushed the curls out of my eyes.

"He's nice. We talked about stuff," I said, trying to keep the conversation from becoming another counseling session.

"I hope you'll be able to connect with Doctor Kelly." I wasn't used to having a conversation like this with my mom, so it was making me feel uncomfortable. "I don't need to know any details, honey. I'm proud of you," she said as she wrapped her arms around me, squeezing me hard enough to make my eyes bulge. "You better get off to bed." I smiled, thinking about the phrase she frequently uses. If you replaced 'to' with an 'in.' It would have an entirely different meaning.

"Okay, love you," I told her as I started for the stairs.

*"Goodnight, Kevin,"* I sent after connecting with his yellow hallway.

*"Goodnight, Rob."* I was so surprised when he answered, I almost spat a mouth full of toothpaste at my mirror.

*"Did you just hear me?"* I asked.

*"Yeah, I did. Could we just text like normal kids?"* he asked.

*"If I was normal."* I liked to hear Kevin laugh, so I was taking every opportunity I could to add humor.

*"Thanks for inviting me to dinner."*

*"No problem, you're welcome any time. You seem sad?"* I said with genuine empathy.

*"I'll be fine. I just need some sleep."*

*"Goodnight, man."*

As I laid on my bed trying to fall asleep, I couldn't stop thinking about Kevin. Even though we came from significantly different socioeconomic lifestyles, we both dealt with pressures. We were tasked with learning new coping skills while we muddled our way through adolescence.

*****

The iced coffee I sipped on was surprisingly refreshing as I sat on the top deck of my grandparent's one-hundred-fifty-foot yacht in Grand Haven. The boat was docked near the boardwalk so I could people-watch while waiting for Kevin. Finally, I heard someone climb aboard, but it wasn't Kevin's voice calling out my name.

"I'm up on the top deck," I shouted down below.

"Hey," David said with a nervous tone as he topped the stairway.

"Hey, David, sorry, I wasn't expecting you."

"Umm... Kevin asked me to come in his place. That's cool, isn't it?" he said as he sat at the foot of my reclining deck chair.

"Sure, why wasn't Kevin able to come?" I asked with confusion.

"He told me he was grounded. I figured this would give us some time to have a serious discussion.

"Umm, okay," I told him with bravery, even though I was incredibly nervous.

"Will you marry me?" David asked.

*****

I sat up in my bed, and David was gone. My phone displayed 04:26. Wow! That was weird.

# Friendship Chapter 5

Friday, May 19th Friendship

At mid-stroke, on my last lap, I literally bumped into Sam, who had been standing chest-deep in my lane.

"Hey, dill rod," Sam said.

"Hey, what's up?" I asked as I stood in neck-deep water.

"Heard you invited a boyfriend over to meet the parent last night," he said, teasing me.

"He's not my boyfriend. We were hanging out," I tried to explain as Sam closed one eye, still looking at me through the other as if he didn't believe me. "Who told you about Kevin coming over?"

"Mom mentioned it when I got home from work last night. Kevin Larson is popular, isn't he?"

"Why would it matter if Kevin is popular or not?" I was instantly pissed off and in desperate need of something to punch. Maybe even Sam.

"What I mean is you normally don't hang with…"

"Are you implying that a nerd shouldn't hang out with a popular guy?" I asked, interrupting him. I could tell Sam's brain was in overdrive, trying to dig himself out of his self-imposed predicament. I almost felt bad for getting angry.

Everything in the pool room was silent, except for the water sloshing against the poolside. "I'm just messing with you, Sam. It's fine," I told him, willing to give him a free pass. "I haven't hung out with any friends since Annie."

"Ah… So, do you like Kevin?" Sam asked. Was he stupid? Why would he dig himself another hole?

"I like hangin with him. He's a lot of fun," I claimed, trying to ignore the fact that Sam believed Kevin and I were together.

"No, I mean, do you like him?" The pool water wasn't cold enough to keep my face from burning up with embarrassment. All I wanted to do was leave this awkward conversation so I could take a shower. What I was about to say next was going to cut deep enough to piss him off so he'd leave me alone.

"Look, I know what you're asking, but Kevin isn't into me. By the way, thanks for pretending to be interested in my life, but you don't have to try so hard," I told Sam with a nasty, self-righteous tone. I should have left that last part out about him trying too hard. Sam's anger was easy to read. Mission accomplished.

"Why do you always have to be a dick?" Sam asked with an aggressive tone as he pulled his goggles off. After hoisting himself out of the water, Sam stood with his back to me, drying his body. There was still time to apologize. When Sam turned to look at me, I could see the frustration in his expression. Sam opened his mouth to say something, but nothing came out.

"Sorry, my blood sugar could be low," I quickly told him, trying to repair the damage I had undoubtedly caused. Sam turned to leave the deck without saying another word. Damn, I needed to get a handle on my mood swings. No wonder people didn't want to hang out with me.

When I finally made it out to the truck with my suitcase and carry-on in hand, I found Andy opening his vehicle's rear gate, anticipating my arrival.

"Here, you want me to get that?" Andy asked, reaching for my bag.

"Nope, I'm fine," I told him as I quickly threw the luggage in the back.

"So, how long have you known Kevin Larson?" Andy asked as any accomplished Gitmo interrogator would. Andy worked for government intelligence before he went to work for my grandpa.

"Since the third grade. Why do you ask?"

"Gary told me you were having some confrontation with Kevin last week. I guess I was surprised when you two met for coffee yesterday."

"Yeah, we have a newfound respect for each other; I'm kinda hoping we can be friends." Kevin would probably blow me off at school when he was around Zach. But that was no big deal. I would take any time Kevin was willing to give, even if it ended up only happening in private.

"Keep us in the loop; let us know if you have any problems," Andy said.

"I will. Do you know what time my flight leaves?" I asked, hoping to move the conversation away from Kevin.

"Around three, as soon as you arrive at the airport," Andy explained as he pulled out onto Lakeshore Drive.

"Wait, what? Your time schedule isn't making any sense; I don't get out of school until two forty-five. There's no way we can make it to Grand Rapids in fifteen minutes."

"Your father's chief wasn't able to find tickets on a commercial flight that would accommodate your tight schedule. You'll be flying in one of your grandfather's corporate jets."

"Oh," I said instead of screaming, hell, yes!

"You're a lucky boy."

"Ah yeah, I am." I couldn't help but recall what Kevin said about my privilege. Last week, in my AP class, we talked about racial inequality and white privilege. Anyone who didn't believe that it still existed was living in another dimension. I realize that I was privileged, but there was nothing I could do about my birthright. I didn't choose to be born into a wealthy family. Sometimes, I wished I could trade out with someone from a less privileged family.

Cam was waiting for me when I made my way into first-hour. "Hey, how's it going? You look distracted this morning," he said with a troubled expression.

"Oh, I'm fine; I just have a lot going on in my brain, I guess."

"What time do you leave for DC?"

"Three or so. Hang on, my dad is texting me:"

Good morning Robert.

Hey Dad!!!

I have a big surprise for you this evening.

I heard. I get to fly on one of grandpa's jets.

Yes, but this surprise is bigger yet. We'll be dining in the White House this evening.

Oh, man! I can't believe it!!!

See you around 7.

Can't wait!!! Love you!

"Find your seats, all electronics away, please," Mr. Kave announced before handing out our quizzes. It would be difficult to focus on an examination. The excitement created by hanging out with Kevin last night, along with having the opportunity to see my dad tonight, had my brain buzzing. I would be lucky to make it through the day without pissing myself.

Before class ended, Mr. Kave announced that he had teamed me up with Cam and David to do a project that was due next week. David was grinning at me when I turn to look at him. My face warmed up when I started to think about David proposing marriage last night in my dream. I wasn't even sure what David's last name was; he moved to Holland last June at the end of eighth grade. He seemed even shyer than I was. The dream last night was a bit weird but flattering at the same time.

When I walked into the cafeteria for lunch, I saw Cam sitting with someone at our table. Oh, it was Kevin. Wow, that was a daring move for his reputation. While standing in line for food, well, food gave the stuff too much credit. I instantly connected with Kevin's yellow corridor to search for the reason behind his venue change.

*"Hey, man,"* I sent, so I could get Kevin to look in my direction.

*"Is it okay if Zach and I join you and the new kid?"* Kevin sent back.

*"Sure, that will be great!"* I answered from the other side of the room.

"Hey, guys, how's it going?" I asked as I sat down at the awkwardly silent table.

*"What happened between you two?"* I sent to Kevin's yellow corridor.

*"I don't trust him. He's not who he says he is. The lire told me he's sixteen. That dude looks at least seventeen, maybe eighteen,"* Kevin sent back.

"What's up? Why do you look so pissed off?" I finally asked Cam as I dug into my dried-out mac and cheese.

"He's a jerk," Cam said, pointing at Kevin.

"Wow, you guys got off to a good start." It suddenly occurred to me that there was a lot less confrontation in my life when I didn't have any friends.

"Oh, I'm a jerk? Well, you're a liar," Kevin said, pointing back at Cam.

"What the hell did I do to you?" Cam said, throwing his hands out in front of him, displaying a what-the-F gesture.

"Okay, guys, come on," I said, attempting to mediate their differences.

"Dude, you're like eighteen; why are you trying to convince us that you're sixteen?" I kind of disagreed; I thought Cam had a baby-face.

Cam pulled his wallet from his pocket to produce a Michigan ID. "Here, see for yourself," Cam said, handing the ID to Kevin. 'Cameron Jonathan Haas, under 21,' was clearly printed across the front.

"It looks fake. If this is you, what's your birthday?" Kevin shot back, testing the document's validity.

"February 26, 2004," Cam said defensively.

"Sorry, I guess I have some trust issues," Kevin said before handing the ID back to Cam.

*"And yet you trust me,"* I sent Kevin, trying to lighten the mood.

*"Get out of my brain,"* Kevin sent with agitation, oozing from his yellow corridor.

"Can we all be friends now, or maybe just start over?" I suggested trying to insert a sarcastic tone, so I didn't sound uncool.

"Hey, Kevin, my name is Cameron. My friends back home call me Cam; I turned sixteen three months ago. I just moved here from South Dakota," Cam said as he reached across the table with his hand extended.

Kevin tilted his head back, closed his eyes, took a deep breath, opened his eyes again, and reached across the table to shake Cam's hand. Suddenly I noticed Zach sitting next to Kevin.

"Hey, I'm Zach," he said with a perky voice as Zach fist-bumped Cam.

"Hey, Zach, I'm Cam," he answered with a broad smile.

"What grade are you in, dude?" Zach asked. Before Cam could answer, Kevin interrupted without warning.

"He's a freshman. He's sixteen, and he's from South Dakota," Kevin said with a sarcastic tone as he looked down at his dried-out pasta. *"Even though he looks eighteen,"* Kevin sent to my mind to exercise his defiance.

*"Please give him a chance; he seems like a nice guy."*

*"I don't trust him; I have a feeling he's hiding something!"* Kevin warned.

"You're kind of tall for a sixteen-year-old," Zach said with a mouthful of food.

"Yeah, I hear that a lot. My dad is six foot eight, and my mom is six foot one," Cam said with a smile.

"So, do you play basketball?" Zach asked, taking the conversation immediately to sports. I wasn't entirely naive. I knew that most guys my age had a narrow focus span, but did it always have to be sports? Why not talk about something interesting like the vastness of our solar system or the possibility of other life forms on planets in different galaxies.

“I had to drop when we moved here,” Cam said with convincing disappointment in his tone.

Mr. Dewey instructed our PE class to work in teams of three, so we could be introduced to one field event per day over the next two weeks. It took everything in me to hold my emotions in check when Kevin asked me to work with him and Zach. All I could do was nod my head as if I were one of those stupid bobblehead statues. *“Are you sure Zach won’t mind hanging out with me?”* I asked with apprehension.

*“Just shut up, stop worrying; Zach is cool with you.”*

“Have you ever done the long jump before?” Zach asked me when we arrived at the giant sandbox.

“No, this is all new for me. Maybe one of you could show me how it’s done first before I make a fool of myself.”

“I’ll show you the basics,” Kevin said as he placed his foot on the white launch board. “Look, this is where you place your foot when you push off. Your lead foot can’t step over the edge of this board,” Kevin explained. “Running in a straight line is easy but running and jumping at the same time is kinda messing with my mind,” I told them both.

“Just give it a try; I’m sure you’ll do fine,” Kevin said, kindly trying to encourage me.

I could feel a stiff breeze behind me, so I assumed it would help my forward launch trajectory. I took a deep breath, thinking about Kevin waiting for me to jump. I didn’t want to fail or look stupid. ‘Don’t try to impress him,’ my doctor had told me yesterday.

*“Well, come on, just get it over with.”* Last night and now again today, I heard Kevin first without me being in his corridor. My ability to listen to him first must have something to do with him standing nearby.

*“I’m coming. Will you promise not to laugh?”* I pled.

*“No promises from me. If it’s funny, I’ll be laughing.”*

*“You know? It’s all right not to be a dick sometimes,”* I said, trying to insert a small amount of trash talk, attempting to fit in with the guys. I’ve often heard other guys interject trash talk to create a competitive male atmosphere. Perhaps, competitiveness was a biological trait that co-evolved with the basic need for human survival.

*"Haha, just shut up and jump already,"* Kevin sent from where he stood by the sandbox.

I took off at top speed, trying to mimic what Kevin had done. Still, it felt as if everything was moving in slow motion while making my best attempt to claim a higher rank in the male dominance scale. When I planted my right foot on the whiteboard, it was as if the rest of my body knew precisely what to do. After landing in the big sandbox, I expected the laughter to begin, but when I turned to look at Kevin, his mouth was hanging wide open.

"Dude!" Zach yelled. "We're going to measure that one."

"You continue to surprise me, you, little sleeper cell!" Kevin said as he slapped me on the ass. "That was outstanding; you never told me you were fast."

"I'm not," I said, trying to convince them that I had no athletic ability.

"Dude! You jumped 17 feet, 5 inches."

"Umm... is that good?" I asked, hoping my measurement would at least place me on an average dominance scale.

"Ah… yeah... dork! You could blow away most of the guys on our track team!" I know one of them I wouldn't mind... Just be happy to have him as a friend, I reminded myself. I needed to control my raging teenage hormones.

"Thanks, man, you know how to boost my confidence," I said instead.

"You jumped almost as far as I can." I didn't know what to say, so I just shrugged my shoulders. As we left the field event area, I felt an excitement that I hadn't felt in years. Was making friends really this easy? If it was, why haven't I tried sooner?

"Hey, do you want to come to a movie tonight with Zach and me?" Kevin asked as he slipped his shirt off over his head. I knew I should answer honestly, but I was so tongue-tied from looking at Kevin's torso glistening in the sun that I couldn't seem to utter a word. It all just got worse when Zach took his off too. What was I supposed to do here? Should I take my shirt off, so I would fit in? Zach kicked off his shoes and plopped down in the freshly cut grass to take his socks off. Kevin finally looked at me to see what was taking me so long to answer.

"I'd ah, umm, I'd love to join you, but I'm going to see my dad in DC today. I'll be flying out at three this afternoon," I told him, thinking that I just sounded like a nerd again.

"That's cool; I've never flown before. Do you think I could come along?" "Sorry, Zach, you'll have to go to the movie by yourself." Zach smiled as he showed Kevin one of his selected fingers before grabbing his shoes and socks. What the hell. I'm taking it off. When I pulled the sweat-soaked shirt over my head, no one seemed to take notice.

Why would something so simple seem so foreign to me socially? Kevin and Zach were able to comfortably remove their shirts while out in public without a second thought. The sun was warm on my back, and the breeze felt unbelievable, blowing against my moist skin. Zach drug his toes through the grass as if he enjoyed the feeling. I did my best to stall our conversation while I figured out where Kevin would stay tonight when I was at the White House.

"Umm... I'll have to check with my dad, but I don't think he'd mind if you came along."

"Dude, I'm joking." Damn, I needed to learn how to search for social humor. *"I can't go; I have a track meet tomorrow, but maybe we could talk like this while you're DC. I've always wanted to go there."* I looked directly at Kevin reading his facial expression to confirm he wasn't messing with me again.

*"That would be fun! If we can transmit that far."*

"Are you two in love? You're looking at one another like you want to bone each other!" Zach said. Kevin and I didn't need to look at each other when we used telepathy, but those blue eyes. I felt a shiver just thinking about what they did to me.

"Shut up, Zach. You're just jealous?" Kevin said as he opened the door to the school.

"Maybe, a little," he said as we all started to laugh.

Andy drove onto the tarmac at Tulip City Airport, where I saw one of Grandpa's corporate jets waiting. I was going to have a hard time ever flying coach on a commercial flight again. Andy handed my luggage to a guy standing next to the plane as I got out of the truck. After climbing the steps, I gave Andy a wave as he talked to the pilots who were already sitting in the cockpit. I kind of chuckled as I chose from one of the eight empty seats. Cockpit. Who named it a cockpit? I thought to myself as an immature giggle slipped from my lips. Apparently, we were on a tight schedule, so I quickly buckled up.

Before I knew it, we were forty minutes into our flight. It was difficult to believe how fast time had slipped away while surfing Kevin's Instagram posts. Oh yeah, Kevin. I figured it would be an excellent time to learn if long-distance telepathy worked.

*"Hey, we're in the air; you can fly vicariously with me if you wish,"* I sent to Kevin as I looked at a picture of him on his Instagram.

*"What does vicariously mean?"* Kevin sent back. I usually tried to hide my vocabulary when I communicated with other kids my age, but excitement sometimes caused me to forget. Once I had visualized a word, my memory would never forget it. I used to win all the spelling bees in school until kids started teasing me when I'd win. After that, I intentionally messed up the spelling of the word so I could be immediately disqualified.

*"Um, sorry, I mean, you can imagine what it would be like if you were flying with me."*

*"That's cool,"* Kevin said, trying to pretend it didn't bother him that he didn't know the word.

*"What airline are you flying with?"*

*"I'm on one of my grandpa's corporate jets."*

*"That's sick, dude! Please take me with you next time."* It sounded kind of funny when I heard someone use the word sick for something excellent or outstanding.

*"For real this time, or are you just kidding again?"* I didn't want a repeat of me looking as if I were a gullible idiot.

*"No, I'm serious,"* he sent back.

*"Hell yeah! Traveling alone is kinda intimidating,"* I told Kevin with the absolute truth.

*"That sounds great!"*

*"Hey, it feels like we're coming in for a landing already,"* I sent to Kevin as the aircraft went into a steep left bank and the landing gear doors opened.

*"Holy shit, that was fast,"* Kevin said with surprise.

*"We're on a tight schedule. My dad and I are eating dinner at the White House tonight."*

*"Wait, what? You're messing with me, right?"*

*"Nope. We have to be at the gate by seven."*

*"Yes!"* he shouted through my yellow passage. *"I'm going to the White House with my friend!"* I felt both sides of my smile, almost touching my ears.

When the aircraft sat down on the runway, I barely felt the tires hit. I doubted that I was flying with amateurs today. The landing was, by far, the smoothest I've ever felt. As we taxied up to a large hanger where some huge FedEx planes were parked, I saw Brad standing by a truck waving at me, so I waved out the small window of the aircraft. Brad was my dad's Chief of Staff, and during the campaign, he was my dad's manager. I really liked Brad, even though he was a bit pushy and bossy.

"Hey, Robert!" Brad yelled with excitement as I disembarked. I could hardly hear him over the sound of the jet engines that were revving back up. "Jump in; we're on a tight schedule this afternoon. It's great to see you! How've you been?" Well, right up until three days ago, my life really sucked; I wanted to tell him.

"I'm fine, I guess," I told Brad instead. "I'm excited to be spending the weekend with my dad."

"Yes, your mother was kind for giving up her opportunity to spend the weekend with your father and missing her first state dinner."

"Wait, what! My mom was planning on being here this weekend?" I asked as I looked at Brad with astonishment.

"Oh yeah, they've been planning this weekend for the last two months," Brad told me without taking his eyes off the road. I was so ashamed of myself; I felt as if I was about to be sick.

*"Fuck!"* I thought to myself.

"Robert!" Brad said as he gasped, nearly causing me to jump out of my skin.

"What?" I asked.

"You just said the F word?" Damn, it must have transmitted telepathically by mistake. I didn't even see any corridors open.

"I did? I'm sorry, it won't happen again," I quickly promised, hoping Brad wouldn't tell my dad.

"Why are you so upset?" I shook my head, trying to get my thoughts together so I could figure out why my mind let the F word slip. "Shaking your head, no, isn't going to make me forget about what I just asked." Brad was like a mad dog with his teeth sunk into my ass cheek.

"I've been treating my mom like shit lately. I mean, like crap lately." Brad looked over at me with a bit of a scowl. "I've been a whiny little bitc... brat."

After Brad gave me the news about my mom missing the trip, it started to hit home. All I've done lately was think about poor, little, unfortunate me and how unfair my life was—what a jerk.

"You're an adolescent male with testosterone dripping from your adrenal cortex," Brad said. No wonder I talk the way I do. Hanging out with Brad was always a learning experience. "So, I'm going to give you a free pass on this one, but when you're in public with your father, you'll need to keep that testosterone in check."

"Thanks," I muttered so he could barely hear me. "I feel awful about my mom missing this opportunity," I told Brad.

"She could've come along as well. However, she knew that you needed some time alone with your father." The truck stopped at a large store with male mannequins dressed in formal wear in the front window. "Why are we stopping here?" I asked.

"We need to get you something to wear for this evening. Your Mother told me that you wouldn't fit into the suit you wore during the election."

"Okay... I suppose jeans and a t-shirt won't do. I kinda feel like Cinderella getting ready for the ball." Brad smiled as we got out of his truck.

"I think we have time to stop for a haircut, too, if you wish," my 'Fairy Godfather' said as I gave him the evil eye. "I'll take that as a definite no then," Brad said with a smile.

"Is there something on your mind?" Brad asked as we got back into the truck with my new kick-ass suit.

"Oh. Ah, no, I'm sorry, I was just thinking about my new friend."

"Please do tell," Brad said with a big smile. "Who is he?"

"Who said he was a he?" I asked defensively.

"Um, I just assumed your new friend would be a boy. At your age, most boys hang out with other boys; besides, it's a fifty-fifty chance of getting it right," he said, trying to cover. *Man, I messed that up!* I heard Brad think.

"His name is Kevin, and he's a freshman as well."

"Great! How long have you two been friends?"

"Three days."

"Okay…," Brad said as if things were getting awkward. "Oh look, here we are," Brad quickly announced as we pulled up to the front of the townhouse. "We're going to hurry and get you into the shower. One of your father's trucks will be here to collect you in thirty-seven minutes." I lifted my arm and took a sniff, trying to get him to laugh. Brad did chuckle a bit as I got out of the truck, but he was right. I needed another shower.

I rushed into the townhouse, and I gotta tell ya, it wasn't what I was expecting. I thought it would be a lot nicer. The house looked more like an old-style apartment with new paint and carpet.

I was out of the shower within ten minutes, getting dressed, when I heard Brad's voice through the closed door. "How's it going in there?" he asked.

"I'm almost set," I announced as I ran some gel through my hair.

"Whoa... look at you! I need to send a picture to your Mother," Brad said as if he were a proud father. Brad didn't have any children of his own. His girlfriend dumped him last November during the general election. She said he was married to his work, and she couldn't compete.

"Um, would you mind if I sent it to her?" I asked as I handed him my phone.

"Sure, it would mean more coming from you anyway," Brad said as he took three pictures.

I headed out the door and jump into one of dad's trucks. The driver sped off into traffic as I sent my mom a text picture:

Hey, Mom, thank you so much for allowing me the opportunity to spend the weekend with Dad. Love you XOXO

Within ten minutes, we pulled up to a side street near the White House, where I saw my dad standing near three of his hovering security. "Hey, Dad," I announced with excitement after jumping out of the truck and throwing my arms around him.

"Let me take a look at you," my dad said as he held me at arm's length. "You've grown at least a foot since Christmas, and look how handsome you are in that new suit." I grinned at him, remembering the last conversation we had during Christmas break. He lectured me about why I needed to stay awake in church. I hadn't been sleeping; I was closing my eyes, trying to escape the ridiculous sermon our pastor was giving about how being homosexual was sinful. The pastor was trying to convince the congregation that anyone 'partaking in homosexual activity was heading straight to hell.' While sitting there in the church, I knew there was a good chance I was already in hell, so it couldn't get much worse.

"We'll need to enter the grounds through the East entrance," my dad advised. We were walking toward the gate when I remembered Kevin shouldn't be missing any of this.

*"We're entering through the East Gate of the White House grounds,"* I sent Kevin.

*"How cool is it?"* Kevin asked.

*"Extremely. I just sent you a pic of me wearing my new suit and another of the East entrance. Are you and Zach at the movie yet?"*

*"Yeah, the movie sucks. I'll check the pics when I get out of here,"* Kevin said."

"So, how have you been? I heard you made a couple of new friends," my dad said as we stood in a long line waiting to enter through the gate.

"I've been fine. It's kinda cool having friends," I answered without being able to control the excitement in my voice.

"Congressman Van Stark, right this way, please," I heard someone announce, pulling us out of line to take us through another gate. "You must be Robert Thomas Van Stark," the man said while shuffling through some paperwork.

"Yes, Sir," I answered respectfully.

"We're all set, Mr. Congressman; you have a fine evening."

*"We made it through the gate. The Secret Service agents are treating me as if I'm someone important."*

*"News flash, dumbass, you are someone important!"* Kevin sent back with sarcasm.

*"Haha, whatever. We're inside now, waiting in line again. Nope, we're getting pulled from another line, going through security."*

*"I googled White House State Dinners; it's first-class, dude. By the way, they're going to take your phone away,"* Kevin sent me.

*"Thanks for the heads up." "Hey! That was my D, you just touched!"*

*"What?"* Kevin asked.

*"Oh, sorry, that wasn't supposed to transmit. The secret service guy, who's doing the whole stranger danger thing, just touched me. Like it's any*

*different if he touches my D with the back of his hand."* I heard Kevin laughing. *"Shut up! You were correct; they just took my phone before sealing it in an envelope."*

*"You don't have anything private on there, do you?"*

*"Everything on my phone is private."*

*"I mean, like sexting pictures and things like that,"* he said.

*"Who would I be sexing with?"* I asked, trying to send some humor with the message.

*"Don't be so salty. You seem fond of the Troye guy you have hanging on your bedroom wall."*

*"Troye Sivan is a famous singer and actor."* And just happens to be gorgeous.

*"Just tell me what you see, dude."*

*"We're climbing a wide staircase, and my dad is shaking hands with some people who I don't know." "It's nice to meet you too, ma'am." "Oops, sorry. I'm getting mixed up on what I'm supposed to be saying to whom."*

*"I'm surprised you can even walk and talk at the same time,"* Kevin said with sarcasm.

*"Shut up, this is a lot harder than... Hang on. I need to focus for a minute. I'm in a receiving line to shake the President's hand. Hey, his son is in the greeting line. I thought he went to school in Vermont, so I didn't expect him to be here."*

*"Oh yeah, I think he's around our age,"* Kevin said.

*"Hey, would you please google something for me?"* I asked with desperation in my request.

*"What am I, your secretary?"* Kevin sent back with a humorous emotion in his mind.

*"Come on, please! I'm just about to him. Check to see if he goes by Luke or Lukas."*

*"It says here, the First Son goes by Lukas. He turned fifteen last month on the third. In this pic, he's almost as tall as his dad."*

*"Thanks, man, I owe you one."* I peeked around my dad to get a better look at Lukas. The gorgeous kid wore a dark blue suit that complimented his blondish hair with a hint of red. Oh man, look at those hazel-colored eyes. When I say handsome, it doesn't even begin to describe his beautiful features.

We were about the same height. Our bodies were similar in size and mass. Lukas had cute, hardly noticeable freckles perched at the top of his high cheekbones. His clearly defined jawline made me shiver. Even if he were gay, which I didn't believe he was, he'd be way out of my league.

"Hello, how are you this evening?" Lukas asked, shaking my hand with a firm grip. His voice was so effing sexy.

I was sure this must be a daunting task for Lukas to stand here, on display, pretending to care about who he was meeting. But for me, the experience was intoxicating. The excitement and apprehensive effect Lukas Barnes was having on me from holding the hand had flooded my mind with something reckless and dangerous. I felt myself floating higher and higher as if I could fly away, taking him with me, of course.

*"You owe me a lot more than one,"* Kevin said through an open yellow corridor that I carelessly left open. Kevin's voice gave me a jolt that I needed to firmly plant my feet back on the floor.

"Very well, thank you," I finally said to Lukas, doing my best to recover from my transfixed state. "I'm Robert."

"It's nice to meet you, Robert; I hope you enjoy the party," Lukas said as a muscle in his jaw moved to cause a tug at the corner of his mouth, creating an irresistible, almost naughty grin. Before releasing my hand, Lukas squeezed it three times at the same rate as my own beating heart. Holy shit! I stood corrected; he was attracted to me. I guess there was a good chance Lukas wasn't totally straight. The surprised look on my face brought a bright white, immaculate smile to his. I was able to pull my mesmerized eyes away from Lukas and move on to the next person in line. I didn't even hear a word the lady was saying. I think the woman may have been the First Lady, but my mind was in free fall, so I wouldn't have known.

*"My dad is talking to the President of the United States, as if they were best buddies,"* I sent to Kevin so I could occupy my thoughts with someone other than Lukas.

*"They're politicians from the same party. Of course, they're best buddies." Oh no, there's no way he survived that fall. Hmm, he's tougher than he looks,* I heard Kevin think about the movie he was watching. Ew, the President's hand was all sweaty; I needed to find the restrooms to wash my hands.

*"We're being seated at a large round table with several other people. I recognize some of them from the news. Just a minute, my dad is introducing me,"* I sent to Kevin, hoping that I wasn't interrupting anything important.

"Ladies and gentlemen, this is my son Robert." All the people were standing to shake my hand as if I were someone special. Meeting people like this made me feel anxious and edgy.

"Where do you attend school, Robert?" Congressman Marshall asked.

"Public Schools in Holland, Michigan, Sir."

*Wow! I can't believe Cal allows his kid to attend public schools,* I heard Congressman Marshall think. "I'm sorry, Robert. Did you say you attend a public school?" Congressman Marshall asked, bringing me back to the conversation.

"Ah… yeah, why?" I asked as a guy stepped up beside Congressman Marshall, who was now bending over, whispering into Congressman Marshall's ear. The unknown guy who looked as if he could be from the Secret Service was whispering something into my dad's ear now, as well. I wondered if a National emergency was going down. My dad was the Chairman of a Strategic Forces subcommittee and a member of the Armed Forces Committee.

"Where were we? Oh yes, you were saying that you attended public schools?" the Congressman said.

"Yes, Sir," I answered.

"Public schools in Michigan are some of the best," my dad confirmed, coming to my aid. I just smiled, shaking my head in agreement. But let's be honest. I attended public school, so my dad could prove to everyone that if the public schools were good enough for his constituent's kids, they were good enough for his own. Besides, conservative politicians like people to believe they're paupers, but everyone knew that being wealthy was the only way to get elected to office.

"How would you like to live here in this house someday, Robert?" Congressman Marshall asked with a big grin.

"I think it would be outstanding, Sir," I lied. It would suck ass to live here. Having one detail following me around was bad enough. My dad had a 'shut your big trap' expression as he glared at Congressman Marshall.

*"Are you still in the movie?"* I asked Kevin.

*"No, we're at McDonald's having a Big Mac while you're basking in the good life. I just looked at the text with your picture. That suit probably*

*set someone back a few grand."* There it was again. Kevin thought of me as a privileged, little rich bitch. That kind of backfired on me. I was hoping he'd think I looked hot. Or I'd have even settled for handsome.

*"Ah, yeah. A Congressman at our table randomly suggested that my dad may become President someday,"* I said, trying to change the subject.

*"So. That would be kind of cool. Wouldn't it?"*

*"That would be a colossal failure for me."*

*"You're so cute, thinking it should always be about you,"* Kevin said archly.

*"You're so funny,"* I retorted, contemplating what Kevin just said. Did he really believe I was so self-absorbed that I only thought of myself, or was he only joking? Being narcissistic wasn't a trait I cared to be associated with.

A large pillar was blocking my view of Lukas, so I had to lean way back in my chair to get a better look at him. Why was I so smitten over this guy? Was I envious of the confidence he exhibited or the way he held his posture while on display for the whole world to see? I wasn't sure how a fifteen-year-old kid could become so polished and perfect? What the hell would someone like Lukas Barnes see in someone like me?

There weren't many pictures posted online of Lukas, but the ones I've seen don't do him justice. There was something… I don't know… maybe something elegant about Lukas. I was attracted to him, but I thought it must be his confidence that intrigued me.

Lukas wasn't talking to anyone at his table. Instead, he was thinking about hiking in the mountains, somewhere. I also found some common thoughts of his that I frequently had. Lukas was thinking about how pissed off he was at one of his details for being a nark about something that happened at school this week.

I continued to watch as Lukas reached up to rub his forehead. Suddenly he turned to look in my direction before I had a chance to look away. It was as if he knew I was staring at him. Damn it, caught in the act. At first, his facial expression was devious but seemed to short-circuit, changing into the same flirtatious grin he had displayed in the reception line. I was so embarrassed, I wanted nothing more than to borrow Harry Potter's wand and magically disappear.

I needed to break our eye contact, so I took a quick bite of my delicious chocolate truffle dessert that immediately melted in my mouth. When I glanced back up at Lukas to see if the distraction had broken the spell, he was holding his long-stemmed dessert goblet in one hand as he stuck his right index finger into the chocolate truffle. Lukas glanced around to ensure he wasn't being watched before using his finger to lusciously taste the desert. He left his finger in his mouth for a second or two before removing it seductively.

*"Kevin?"* I said, anticipating a conversation that would help distract me before my entire body ignited.

*"Yeah?"*

*"Are you there?"* I asked, not knowing what to say next.

*"Umm yeah. Is everything all right?"* I needed to get my shit together. I nearly panicked and told Kevin that I had a crush on the President's son.

*"Oh yeah. I was just checking in to see what's going on."*

*"Are you sure? You seem panicked."* Wow! I must have been transmitting emotion without knowing.

*"We're just finishing dinner,"* I sent, trying to run for cover.

*"What's next? Will you be waltzing with the first boy?"*

*"Haha. No, I don't dance."* Oops, that almost sounded as if I wouldn't mind dancing with Lukas if the occasion presented itself. This telepathy stuff was tricky.

*"Are you able to walk around and check things out?"* Kevin asked.

*"I'm not sure; I'll check with my dad,"* I answered as I tried to find an opportunity to break into my dad's conversation.

Several minutes went by before I heard a female's voice say, "Hello, Robert."

"Oh… hey," I answered, noticing a young woman standing behind me who was wearing a red dress that showed more cleavage than most.

"My name is Stacey. I'm an intern here in the White House. Your father told me you were asking about a tour." I don't know why, but a presidential scandal immediately came to mind as soon as she said White House intern. First Family scandals have been a prominent subject matter since the very first President. I wondered how a gay sex scandal between the first son and the son of a conservative congressman from Michigan would go down in history?

"Yes, I would," I said as I slid my chair back. *"Hell yeah! My dad just set me up with this nice lady who's going to take us on a short tour."*

*"Who's us?"* Kevin asked.

*"You and me, of course. We're walking down a long hallway. Now we've entered the west wing."*

*"I wonder if we'll be able to see the Oval Office?"* Kevin asked with hope in his thought.

*"No, our tour guide said we had to stay away from that area. It's mostly offices. Now we've entered a small red movie theater near the First Family's residence. Everything in the room is red, including the chairs and walls."*

*"Anything playing?"* Kevin asked.

*"Nope."*

While rounding the corner to exit the red theater, I literally ran into Lukas. Lukas quickly reached out to grab my shoulder to save me from falling backward. "Whoa, whoa, whoa. Are you okay, Robert?" Lukas asked in a calm, caring tone. I couldn't believe he remembered my name. After all, he met over two hundred people tonight.

"I... ah... I'm sorry... So clumsy of me," I stammered stupidly in my star-struck response.

"See ya, Robert," he said with a wink before continuing to walk in his original direction of travel. All I could get out of my mouth was 'bye.' When I turned to look back at the First Son, I was surprised to see him walking backward in a playful manner, looking comfortably handsome, with his tie in one hand and waving with the other. Reading Lukas now would be a big mistake since I couldn't control my burning desire to follow him wherever he led me. So, all I did was grin uncontrollably.

"Do you think we could see the Lincoln Bedroom?" I asked Stacey, hoping the answer would be yes.

The Lincoln bedroom was located in the First Family's residence, so I was a bit surprised we could see the room. I was flooded with excitement, knowing that we were close to where Lukas lives. *"We're in the Lincoln Bedroom. It has a plush-connected sitting room,"* I reported to Kevin. *"This is the highlight of my trip so far,"* I said untruthfully since meeting Lukas was secretly the highlight.

"President Lincoln turned this room into his office during the Civil War, and it remained the office of the president until 1961," she said with a forced smile.

*"Why would a bedroom be a highlight?"* Kevin asked.

*"There have been reports from White House guests who have seen a ghost in this room, and there are some rumors that someone saw the ghost of Lincoln a few times."*

*"Apparently someone with an excellent imagination,"* Kevin said with doubt in his thought.

"Do you know Lukas at all?" I asked Stacey as we left Lincoln's bedroom.

"Not very well," she answered. "Lukas stays to himself for the most part, but I think he likes you."

"Wait, what?" I asked with surprise as I turned toward Stacey.

"I saw you two flirting with each other in the hallway by the theater," she said with a broad smile.

"Is he? Erm…" I start to ask before realizing that I should refrain since Lukas was the First Son.

"Last, I knew he had a girlfriend, but you never know, right?" she finished for me as if she knew what I was going to ask.

"Oh... Sorry for asking."

"No need to apologize. You were simply curious. Are you out?" Stacey asked as we continued to walk.

"Only to some of my family and now, you, I guess," I said with an awkward, nervous laugh.

"Thank you," I told Stacy after returning to the party.

"You're welcome, Robert. Your secret is safe with me," Stacey whispered as she leaned in close.

"Are you ready to get out of here?" my dad asked, slapping me lightly on the back.

"I thought we could spend the night in the Lincoln bedroom," I recommended.

"Anywhere but there, Son, I've heard the room is haunted."

Our next stop was in the security area to claim our phones and other belongings. "Did you enjoy yourself?" my dad asked as we used the South Gate to exit, where a truck was waiting for us.

"It was a great experience. You don't know how much this means to me," I said.

"I believe I do; I've missed you as well. Especially our late-night talks and watching scary movies." Our late-night talks would usually turn into fun, high-spirited debates that we would take turns winning.

"I'll be fine; you and Mom don't need to worry about me," I said with a convincing tone. "What was the deal about you running for President?" I asked, trying to change the subject.

"Congressman Marshall was just messing around, don't worry about politics. It will rot your brain," he said with a smile. "Tell me about these new friends of yours," he said, taking his turn at changing the subject. I knew that a conversation about my friends would be a good segue into what Sam recommended I discuss with Dad. I would leave Kevin for last.

"Cam is cool; he recently moved from South Dakota. He and his mother are living with his aunt and uncle for a couple of years. Apparently, Cam's father travels a lot for work."

"And this boy named Kevin?" he asked.

"Yeah, he's athletic, nice, and we have this special connection."

"What kind of connection?" Dad asked with worry in his voice. I don't think my dad knew I was gay; nevertheless, he seemed worried.

"It's like this trust thing. You know, like we can trust each other with anything."

"Those sound like some good friends. You better try to hang on to them. Any potential girlfriends?"

"No, Dad," I said with embarrassment oozing from my tone. I don't even know why I'd feel embarrassed, but I could feel it in my face.

"You're a handsome young man, and you have one of the kindest hearts I've ever known a person to have. You must have girls breaking down your door." No, I'm breaking down their doors, so I can search through their corridors, I thought to myself.

"I'm just not really interested in girls," I told him, trying to test the waters before I dropped the bombshell.

"Well, there is nothing wrong with waiting until you're ready." I wished that I had more courage to come right out and tell him. But there would be no turning back once I've decided to peek my head out of the closet door. Oh well, here it goes.

"What if I'm never ready for a girlfriend?" There. I finally said it.

"Oh, trust me, the day will come when girls are all you'll be able to think about."

This was my big chance to clear the air. The way I figured it, this could end up going one of two ways. Number one, my dad may give me a hug, reassuring me that he loved me regardless of who I was attracted to. Or number two, it could go badly when he sent me away to an all-girls military boarding school.

"I don't know; I just can't see myself ever being sexually attracted to girls." Come on, Rob, just come out with it, I told myself.

"What are you trying to say?" Dad asked. I think you know what I'm trying to say. I'm struggling with the most challenging discussion I've ever had with you. You're not making it any easier by pretending that you're stupid, I wanted to say.

My dad was the smartest man I knew. He finished at the top of his class at the Naval Academy. At Harvard, my dad graduated with honors. He just needed to come to terms with what he didn't want to hear.

"What I'm trying to tell you is, I'm attracted to guys." *Oh no, my worst nightmare has come true. I have a gay son, just like Keith.* My heart sunk deeper and deeper as my dad contemplated the reality of me being gay. Wait, what! My uncle Keith was gay? I never met my dad's only sibling.

Uncle Keith was killed in a helicopter crash in Afghanistan when I was a newborn. My grandparents were still struggling with my uncle's death. But gay? The tall, buff, handsome, special ops marine was gay? I don't get it. Why was I never told about this? Why so many family secrets? Why do we always have to worry about what others think? Listen to me. The hypocritical kid who has his closet packed full of secrets was asking why. That was funny.

"Robert," my dad said with a whisper, so the driver wouldn't hear him. "I'm sure you're simply confused about your attraction to boys. Soon you'll have a better understanding of who you're attracted to sexually. You'll get through this temporary phase." Oh great, I was getting the typical, infamous, 'it's only a phase' speech.

"Dad, I'm gay. Alright?" I said loud enough for the driver to hear. At that point in our conversation, I didn't give a shit who listened to me. I looked at my dad in the eyes as he swallowed so loudly that I could hear it over the road noise. An eerie chill found my skin, causing me to shiver as I folded my arms and then turned away to stare out into the dark.

"I think I need some time to digest this. Does your Mother know?" my dad asked quietly again. I don't know. Do mothers have a sixth sense? I believe their intuition allows them to know things about their children that no one else will ever know.

"No, just, Sam," I said instead.

"Let's just keep a lid on this until your mother and I have a chance to sit down with you to talk about everything in private."

"Thank you for understanding," I muttered.

"I never said that I understood. I'm having a tough time with your choices." There it was. My dad thought it was my choice to be gay. Anger had moved into every part of my body, including my clenched fists and grinding teeth. My dad had been listening to our pastor's propaganda again. I needed to share some scientific facts with my dad rather than making matters worse when I said something I would regret.

"I haven't chosen anything; I was born gay," I told him with too much anger in my tone. "A person doesn't get to choose what gender they're attracted to." I took a deep breath and continued. "I've been stressing about telling you I was gay for a long time," I admitted. "I practiced by telling the lamp beside my bed fifty times last week."

*I can't believe I said choices. Why did I say 'choices'? Come on, Calvin, think before you talk. I wonder if Robert is sexually active?* I heard my dad think.

"So, this Kevin boy, are you and he...?"

"Just friends," I interrupted as if I knew what he was going to ask. Besides, I should be careful, so he didn't detect my disappointment. "Kevin is going through some rough times at home." I didn't think Kevin would mind if I filled my dad in on his personal life. Maybe I'd be able to take our conversation in a different direction.

"Oh, how's that?"

"Kevin's mother lost her battle with cancer last winter. His father has been drinking excessively since his mother died. Recently, Kevin's father lost his job related to his drinking problem."

"Does Kevin have any siblings?"

"He's an only child." Good, our conversation was moving away from me being gay, but my dad still wasn't okay with it.

"And this boy named Cameron?" he asked.

"He's an only child as well."

"No, I'm asking if he's straight?" he said bluntly. I don't know why it would matter what gender Cam was attracted to, but his question kind of set me off.

"As an arrow, Dad," I replied with sarcasm dripping from my tongue. Our confrontational conversation was back on track.

"Okay," he said with relief. *I hope I didn't mess this up,* I heard him think.

*Don't worry, Dad, I'm getting your message loud and clear. You haven't accepted that I'm gay,* I sent him through his green corridor that only had a few open doors.

After arriving at the townhouse, I headed upstairs, but I couldn't resist the urge to eavesdrop through my dad's closed-door during his phone conversation with my mom. He didn't discuss the conversation we had on the way home. Instead, he mentioned something about a security breach during dinner tonight.

A Secret Service agent told him a guest at the White House allegedly used telepathy to read people's minds. I laid there in bed, freaking out for a few minutes until I realized they didn't know who was using telepathy. If so, they would've confronted me while I was there. My dad finished his conversation without mentioning anything about me being gay.

*"Are you still awake?"* I asked Kevin.

*"Yeah, I've been waiting up for your goodnight wishes,"* he sent, playfully teasing me. *"Is something wrong?"* Kevin asked as if he could since I was stressed out.

*"They had someone at the White House trying to figure out who was communicating with telepathy."*

*"They knew we were talking?"* Kevin sent with worry in his thought.

*"Yeah, but they couldn't figure out who it was."*

*"Damn, dude. What are we gonna do?"* Kevin asked. I had been asking myself the same thing.

*"Nothing. There's no way for them to know it was us."*

*"If you say so."*

We laid in bed, talking with each other until Kevin's words started running together.

*"Thank you for being my friend, Kevin."* He didn't answer, so he must have dozed off.

*****

"Hello, Mr. President, does it bother you that people don't like you?" I asked as I shook his hand. Why did I keep shaking his sweaty hand? Yuk.

"I think there are more who like me than those who don't," he answered. I wondered if being narcissistic was a prerequisite if you want to become president of the United States? "Go ahead, have a seat, Robert," the President offered as he sat behind his desk in the Oval Office. "What can I help you with?"

"I was wondering if you could help me understand why you hate the LGBTQ community."

"I don't hate anyone, Robert. My constituents expect me to act like a bigot, so if I want to get re-elected, I'll have to pretend."

"I have an idea. You could just love everyone equally, and then you'd be all set," I recommend as an easy fix. "Or maybe you should ask your son Lukas what gender he's attracted to."

"Excuse me?" the President asked as three red horns grew out of his skull.

*****

When I woke up, it was already 0630. Wow! Those horns were disturbing.

# Telekinesis Chapter 6

Saturday, May 20 Telekinesis

I was starving when I woke up again at 07:30. *"Hey, are you up yet?"* I asked, hoping that I wasn't waking Kevin too early.

*"Yeah, I'm awake,"* he answered with anger in his thoughts.

*"What's wrong? You seem upset."* I could sense fear, and he had been crying or still was.

*"My dad didn't come home from the bar last night. He didn't call or text me."*

*"I'll do some searching around if you want."*

*"Sure,"* is all Kevin sent back. His dad's first name is… that was it, Devon. Not in jail. Not in the hospital either. A knock on my door startled me a bit.

"Good morning, Robert," my dad said as he peeked in. "I know a nice breakfast place not too far from here; let's go grab something to eat."

"That's music to my ears," I said, putting my search on hold for a few seconds.

"Okay, meet me downstairs after you shower. I'll have a truck ready."

"Cool, give me twenty minutes," I told my dad.

*"He's not in jail or any of the hospitals,"* I told Kevin when my dad left the room.

*"Thanks, man, I couldn't bring myself to check,"* Kevin sent with relief.

*"Does he have any friends or a girlfriend he could have stayed with overnight?"*

*"Gross, Dude! Don't even say that shit."* Kevin was starting to sound better as I stepped into the shower.

*"I'm just checking all of the possibilities,"* I replied with empathy.

*"Just a minute, he's calling me."* I quickly close my eyes, entering Kevin's orange corridor. *"What the hell do you mean you fell asleep at Mark's? I've been freaking out here. Do you get that?"* Kevin stood up and walked over to the window. *"Sorry, isn't doing it for me, Dad. Just come home, please!"* Their conversation sounded as if the parental roles were reversed, and Kevin was the parent, disciplining his poorly behaved adolescent. Kevin started to cry again as he threw his cell at his bed. He reached up, grabbed his hair, and pulled with both hands while screaming.

As we traveled to the restaurant, I figured that I better check in on Kevin. While I was in the shower, I quickly exited Kevin's orange corridor when I felt myself falling to the shower floor. Note to Robert: Sit your ass down before entering Kevin's orange hallway.

*"Is your dad home yet?"* I asked Kevin.

*"I just heard him come in five minutes ago. I'm gonna wait so I can cool down before I confront him."*

*"That sounds like a good plan."*

Speaking of a good plan, I needed to develop an exit plan to stop thinking about Lukas Barnes. He and I lived a thousand miles from each other, and I needed to somehow convince my mind that we would never see each other again. Besides, Lukas was probably just toying with me last night. Still, I couldn't keep his sexy voice from entering my mind. 'I hope you enjoy the party,' Lukas had said when I first met him in the receiving line. Every time I had a spare second, my mind struggled with the prospect of our mutual attraction. If only I could text him. How would I even go about getting his number?

Dad and I were dropped off at the front entrance of a vintage-looking restaurant. After entering, we were greeted by a tall guy who looked like a thirty-year-old version of Asa Butterfield. "Congressman Van Stark! Right this way, please," he said with a thick British accent. "And what can I get for you, gentlemen, to drink?" he asked as he placed some menus in front of us.

"Coffee, please," I told him with a hand-covered yawn.

"Blimey, mate, we'll add a shot of espresso to yours," he said with a grin.

"George, this is my youngest son Robert," Dad told the handsome man proudly.

"Are you here on holiday with your father?" George asked.

"Just for the weekend," I answered with a smile. I wasn't sure yet, but I believed that George was attracted to my dad. I sensed something, and I definitely needed to take a read on him.

"Here you go, guys," George said as he served our coffee. "Have you decided yet, or would you like a minute or two?" When George looked over at my dad, I was able to read him like a book. A door in his mind was left wide open, with colors flooding into the corridor. He liked the way my dad looked in his blue shirt this morning. George didn't care if anyone else knew that he was attracted to guys. I've been finding that some people would lock their doors if they didn't want anyone to know their secrets; others would leave their doors ajar if they didn't care. Not me. My closet doors were heavily fortified.

The confrontation I had with my dad last evening had left me with several unanswered questions about how he honestly felt about gay people. Maybe it was acceptable for others to be gay if it wasn't his own son. I needed to delve into my dad's brain today, so I could find some answers. I wanted to know if he would accept me for who I am. If he didn't… well, I just hoped he would.

After George took our order, I couldn't keep a grin from forming. My poor dad had absolutely no idea George was crushing on him. It was so damn cute.

"What are you smiling about?" my dad finally asked.

"I'd rather not say."

"Come on, level with me. Obviously, you have found something quite amusing," my dad said as he put his cup down before wiping his mouth with his linen napkin.

"I think George likes you," I said as I allowed a giggle to escape and then quickly realized how immature it must have sounded. Dad looked out the corner of his eye as if he wasn't buying into my speculation.

"What do you mean?" he asked.

"You know what I'm talking about," I said as I picked up my cup and took a sip to check the temperature.

"What has he done to deserve an accusation like that?" my dad asked, tipping his head forward as if he was interested in hearing about my speculative reasons.

"I sense he's attracted to you," I tried to explain, referring to my gaydar that has started to develop. Not to mention the telepathy I was using to cheat a bit. "George just kinda seemed to be hitting on you, is all. Does he know you're married?" I asked as I picked up my cup and took in a giant slug of much-needed caffeine.

"I think so," my dad said, pointing at his wedding band. "Should I mention something to him about your speculations?"

"No, please don't do it. That's not fair to George." My dad smiled but didn't contest my plea.

As our mouthwatering food was placed on the table, George asked if he could bring us anything else. My dad cleared his throat.

*Please don't say it!* I sent my dad.

"George, I'd like to ask you a question," my dad said, ignoring my request. My face was as red as a burner on a stovetop, so I covered my eyes with my hands peeking between my fingers as if I were six years old. I could hardly bear to watch the disaster unfold, but I didn't want to miss my dad's reaction when George told him. It was like watching a train wreck. You don't really want to witness the horrific event, but your eyes won't let you look away.

"Yes, Sir?" George replied with a nervous voice.

*You're really going to blow this, Dad. But don't say I didn't warn you,* I sent him through a green corridor as a last-ditch effort.

"Robert believes you may be attracted to me." Dad started to laugh, then George followed suit. I was so embarrassed, I considered crawling under the table. But George abruptly stopped laughing when his expression became serious. Come to find out, George's laughter was all part of a plan to help me embarrass my dad.

"Well, aren't you an observant young man," George said, looking in my direction. My dad was mortified as his eyes lifted from his hot plate of food.

George looked over at my dad and said, "Please don't be offended, Sir, but Robert is correct. I've been deeply attracted to you for ages. It's not like we can choose who we're attracted to, can we?"

"Umm, no, I guess not," my dad mumbled, looking at me with a slight grimace.

"I understand you're already taken, however," George said as he pointed at my dad's ring finger. "But a mate can always dream, right?" I started to laugh when my dad's face turned beet red. George gave me a high five as he turned to leave our table. Somehow, George was able to sense my orientation. There was no doubt in his thoughts that I was gay.

"That kinda backfired on you, didn't it?" I teased as I tried to get my laughter under control. When I grabbed my napkin to wipe the tears, my fork slid off the table, dropping to the floor. I quickly tied to retrieve my silverware that was just out of reach. I stretch further until suddenly, a shock wave shot through my arm. It took a second to register in my mind what had just happened, but I saw it with my own two eyes. The fork had slid across the floor and was seated firmly in my hand.

*"What the hell was that?"* my brain asked itself, responding to the shock of the self-moving fork.

*"What?"* Kevin asked. Damn it! For some reason, when I got upset or excited, my message spilled over into Kevin's mind without me knowing. I needed to learn what was causing the information to leave my mind without permission.

*"Sorry, I'll explain as soon as I figure out what the hell just happened."*

"What's wrong?" Dad asked as I sat up, holding my fork. "You look like you just saw a ghost," he added as he slid another set of wrapped silverware toward me.

"Um, I was just trying to reach this fork; I must've cut off my circulation," I replied, lying to his face.

"Are you sure?" he said with concern written all over his expression.

"Wow, this looks great!" I announced, referring to my breakfast while trying to hide my psychogenic shock.

*"Sorry, I freaked out, but something new just happened to my brain. I moved a fork with my mind,"* I tried to explain to Kevin.

*"Wait, what? You just moved what with what?"* Kevin sent back with confusion.

*"My silverware! It was just like Jedi shit. My mind moved the fork from six inches away, right into my hand. This is really starting to scare me."*

*"Settle down; everything will be fine, dude."*

"So, tell me more about this boy named Kevin," Dad ironically said.

"Ah… Kevin has brownish blonde hair, blue eyes, I'm about an inch taller than him, but he has at least ten pounds on me." My dad asked to know more about Kevin. Instead, like a dumbass, I was describing Kevin's hot features. I didn't think he cared to know about my lustful description.

"What's his last name?" my dad asked to be more specific.

"Larsen," I answered just before I shoveled some French toast in my mouth and accidentally dripped some syrup on my shorts.

"Oh yes, I know his family; I went to high school with his mother; she was a beautiful woman. So, I'm sure her son is good-looking as well," he said. Wow, that was a leap for my dad. He made a reference to my attraction to guys.

After finishing our breakfast, we headed over to Dad's office. Apparently, he needed to pick up some work he planned to complete over the weekend. As we entered his office, Kristi greeted us with a warm smile, giving us a wave as she continued to talk on the phone. "Just a minute, Sir, let me check the Congressman's calendar to see when he'll be returning." Kristi put her hand over the receiver and whispered, "It's the FBI. They need to speak with you at your earliest convenience."

"Put them through to my office," my dad said with annoyance in his voice.

"Oh, hold just a minute, Sir. Congressman Van Stark just walked in unexpectedly; I'll transfer you."

"Good morning, this is Congressman Van Stark," my dad said as he sat at his desk. "What can I help you with, Special Agent Clone?" There was something wrong; my dad's smile was fake for my benefit. Ah, there it is. He had fear boiling in his brain. I was finding that fear was one of the strongest emotions and the easiest for me to read. "Yes, we've taken appropriate safety measures. My son Robert and daughter Kate both have a security detail with them wherever they're out on their own. Yes, at school as well. Yes, I do have an older son. Sam is seventeen, soon to be eighteen; he'll be fine on his own."

I gave my dad a confused look as I sat opposite his large desk. Dad's conversation continued while I studied a picture of him and me sitting on his credenza's far side. "Yes," my dad said with a chuckle, winking at me. I needed to start working on my deception skills if this shit was going to be part of my life. "Very well, thank you, Sir; you have a good morning too."

During my dad's phone conversation with the agent, I learned the FBI had reason to believe that some of the family members from Congress may be at risk of abduction; therefore, the FBI wanted to make sure all necessary precautions were taken. "So, the FBI?" I asked after climbing into the truck.

"It's really nothing to worry about," my dad said while he tried to determine the best approach when he explained the FBI warning to Mom without freaking her out. "We get these warnings all the time," my dad said, looking up at me over the top of his reading glasses.

"Warnings? What kind of warnings?" I asked, playing dumb.

"Don't worry about it," my dad said as he gave me an all-knowing Jedi wave as if he was trying to make me forget. I decided to drop the subject since he didn't seem to want to talk about the warning.

*"Kevin?"*

*"Hang on, I'm setting my blocks for the one-hundred meters,"* he answered as if he didn't have time to talk.

*"Sorry. I'll check in later."*

My mind had a free second, so I started to think about Lukas Barnes again. I knew the first son was way out of my league. What was it about him? Could it be that he's unobtainable? My chances of hooking up with Lukas Barnes were as likely as a snowflake making it to the ground in July. But damn. That perfect smile and irresistible body and those freckles. Just stop already. Good luck with that exit plan, I told myself.

I immediately headed into the restroom when we arrived at the townhouse. My toothbrush would work as a movable object, so I placed my hand about five inches above the toothbrush, and it started to move toward me without touching it. Okay, I wasn't going crazy, I reassured myself. I could move shit with my mind. Hell yeah! 'What's it called when I can move things with my mind?' I asked Google. 'Telekinesis.' Hmm. Most people believe it's a magic trick. It must be a thing; otherwise, it wouldn't be listed on google, right?

*"Are you there?"* I asked Kevin.

*"Dude! Shut up for two seconds. I'm trying to focus. Hell yes! Seventeen feet eight inches, my new personal record. Now, what was so important that it couldn't wait until the end of my track meet?"* Kevin asked.

*"I just moved my toothbrush without touching it."*

*"Snap it to me; I can't wait to see it."* Even hanging out with Kevin telepathically made me feel giddy inside.

After snapping my new telekinetic awesomeness to Kevin, I headed out with Dad for dinner. Just before entering the restaurant, Cam texted me:

Hey Rob, how is your weekend going with your dad?

It's way cool! Dinner at the White House was outstanding.

Did you see the president there?

Yeah...

Visiting the White House is one of my dreams. Your profile says it's your birthday tomorrow.

Yeah, 15th.

If I don't see you tomorrow... Happy Birthday!

Thanks, man!

We had just finished eating our dinner when my dad started to devise a plan to segue into a complicated discussion about Doctor Kelly. *Let me see. How should I approach this?* I heard my dad think.

"I promised your mother that I'd talk with you about the depression she believes you're having." Well, that was typical; just throw Mom right under the bus since she wasn't here.

"We don't need to talk about this; we already covered it last night; besides, I've agreed to continue seeing Doctor Kelly."

"There's more to discuss, but I'll let you have the floor first."

"Have the floor, really?" Dad rolled his eyes. "Yes, I've had a hard time with you being gone. And yes, I've had some depression. But what kid doesn't have depression from time to time?" Dad took a long look at me.

"Have you ever thought about hurting yourself?" he asked pointedly.

"Just because I've been sad, lonely, and under a lot of pressure doesn't mean I want to hurt myself," I lied. "Having new friends is helping me cope," I added, trying to change the direction of the conversation.

"Last night, after you went to bed, I did some research. I learned that kids who identify as gay or bisexual are five times more likely to attempt suicide than heterosexual teens. Boys are at twice the risk of taking their own life. My research also mentioned that teens who live in conservative communities are at a higher risk as well," he said before finishing off his glass of wine. That was three strikes against me. It would have been four strikes if he had mentioned that rich kids are at higher risk too. "So, I would like you to talk with the doctor about the depression you've been experiencing. We're not going to just blow this off. You're way too important to your mother and me. We won't let anyone or anything take you from us, especially something preventable."

*You could try to be more accepting of my sexual orientation,* I sent through his green corridor.

"Just a minute, I better take this," my dad said as he reached for his phone that was sitting on the table.

"Hello, this is Congressman Van Stark. Yes, what can I help you with?" My dad was silent for a few minutes as he listened. "No, Sir, I can assure you that my son is not telepathic," he said with a chuckle and then winked. I sat quietly, trying to stay calm while working on my deception plan. "I think that will be fine; I'll talk to Robert and give you a callback."

"What was that all about?" I asked, trying not to panic as my dad laid his phone on the table.

"I just spoke with an agent from the Secret Service. The agent told me they're investigating a communications breach that apparently occurred at the White House last evening. He has asked to talk with you to confirm that it wasn't you who allegedly used telepathy to communicate with someone last night." We both started to laugh.

"I could only wish to have special powers. Is that really a thing?" I asked with an inquisitive look.

"Apparently, it is a thing," he said.

"Why would they think it was me? There must have been three hundred people there last night."

"I don't know, but he wants to talk with you," my dad said, looking moderately annoyed.

"That will be fine, I guess, but I'm kinda nervous. Can you stay with me if I agree to talk with the agent?"

"No one is talking with you unless I accompany you."

"Where do they want to meet?"

"They'll be waiting for us when we exit the restaurant," Dad said, pointing at the front door. Them knowing where I was located was kind of creepy.

"This won't get me on the 'no-fly list,' will it?" I joked, trying to pretend that I wasn't scared out of my wits.

When Special Agent Daniels introduced himself to my dad and me, I tried to search around in his brain. Regrettably, I wasted my time exploring. Every single corridor was locked down. The twenty-something buff guy dressed in a suit looked a lot like a taller version of Mr. Smit.

"Robert, we're trying to rule out some of the suspects who attended the State Dinner last evening."

"Am I a suspect, Sir? I promise I didn't take a drink from that wine glass last night. I took it off the tray. But I could smell alcohol, so I put it right back before I took a drink." My dad kind of chuckled at my attempted humor, but the agent didn't seem to appreciate me joking around.

"We are investigating a telepathy breach, Robert," he said with a professional tone. Oh, I see, that's how it's gonna be, I thought to myself.

"I'm sorry, Sir, what exactly is a telepathy breach?" I asked, trying to sound as ignorant as possible.

"Telepathy is a communication between two people that may occur without any actual conversation being verbalized. We have reason to believe the person who was communicating telepathically last evening was a child." Oh… that narrowed it down. I was probably one of only five kids there last night.

With a sense of urgency, every corridor and door slammed shut in my mind. It reminded me of the way doors slammed in my school when there was a lockdown drill. However, when I searched inside the agent's mind again, I found an open door in his gray passage. He was planning to use telepathy on me. Wait. If the agent were telepathic, he'd still be able to communicate with me even if I weren't telepathic.

"I believe I've heard of telepathy before, Sir. But if a child were using telepathy, they wouldn't be much of a threat, would they? Why is it so important to find this person?"

*"I want you to know that you are not in any trouble. Your gift is so unique that I have never met anyone who has the same gift we have,"* the agent sent me after completely ignoring my ligament question.

It suddenly dawned on me that this guy couldn't read me when I was locked down. If he could, he'd know what I was currently thinking. He could only hear me when I talked to others. Agent Daniels had nowhere near the level of abilities I have.

"That was really wild, Sir, but other than my atypical memory, I don't have any gifts," I respond, as my dad looked at me with surprise. Bingo! Found it! Kipton was Agent Daniels's first name. Kipton had a perplexed expression as he looked at me. I could tell my dad was starting to get a bit pissed.

*"Robert, please talk to me; I know you're curious about your gift. I can teach you so much, and we could learn from each other."* The agent wasn't giving up, so I needed to take some drastic actions. Let's see if I can make him forget about this whole telepathy thing. But if I messed it up, he would know it was me. Oh well, here it goes. When I tried to enter the agent's green corridor, I was immediately sucked into his red passage. It was as if my mind didn't have a choice. *"Kipton, you will report back to your superiors and tell them you have found nothing in your investigation.*

"Thank you, Robert, and you as well, Mr. Congressman; I apologize for any inconvenience this may have caused. It was a pleasure meeting you both."

"It was a pleasure meeting you as well, Kipton," I told him with a hint of superiority. Kipton's facial expression was priceless as he turned to leave. Every door in his brain had opened as he searched his memory banks, trying to figure out how I knew his first name.

Suddenly, and without warning, I was forced back into Kipton's red corridor. I couldn't escape, and I was unable to find a way out! Several red doors had automatically opened before I was thrust into a red room. An unfamiliar memory started to play like a video. I felt as if I was no longer in my own body. Instead, I was a twelve-year-old boy riding on a school bus, and two older boys were sitting behind me. They kept hitting me in the back of the head, and it hurt. "Oh, poor baby." "Look, Scott, the little baby is crying," the boys teased. "She'll never like you, Kippy; you're nothing but a loser," one of the boys said as he hit me in the back of the head again…

"Robert, what's wrong?" I heard my dad ask as I floated back into my own body. Oh no, I was sitting down on the sidewalk in front of the restaurant.

"Sorry, Dad, I just got kinda dizzy," I lied. As I tried to stand. I did indeed become dizzy and sat my ass back down. Dad was down on one knee, looking at me with obvious concern.

"Is he sick, Sir?" my dad's bodyguard asked as she knelt. Several people started to gather around us, so I wanted nothing more than to stand up and get the hell out of there.

"I'm fine; I just got dizzy," I said again, trying to convince them both that EMS wouldn't be necessary.

"Are you able to stand?" the bodyguard asked.

"Sure, no problem," I lied again. With my developing headache, walking back to the truck could be problematic.

"Let's get you back to the truck," Dad said, with concern in his tone.

Traffic was moving slowly as we headed back to the townhouse. It was so weird to leave my own body and experience Kipton's memory. Somehow his messed-up recall transferred into my mind. The red corridor in Kipton's mind pulled me in as if a tractor beam had been installed. The instructions I gave Kipton to call off the investigation must have had consequences. Well, at least I knew what the red corridor was used for now.

I desperately needed to watch my attitude. I may have come across as an arrogant jerk. I knew there was a fine line between confidence and arrogance, both of which I have never had much of. Tonight, when I learned my gifts were not only scarce but superior as well, I became someone who I didn't care to be. Yeah, I've treated others like crap before, but only after they had treated me like crap. Kipton did nothing wrong. He was just doing his job.

"How are you feeling?" my dad asked.

"Better," I lied. My head was still pounding as if someone had a jackhammer in there, trying to crack my skull open.

"I don't recall Agent Daniels telling us his first name, but apparently you did," my dad said.

"It's like a steel trap, Dad," is all I told him while hitting the side of my head with my hand a few times.

After returning to the townhouse, I quickly climbed into bed. *"Hey, are you still awake?"* I asked Kevin.

*"Yeah, I'm awake,"* he answered.

*"Someone from the Secret Service interrogated me tonight,"* I told Kevin.

*"They know it was you, don't they?"* Kevin asked, with worry mixed into his message.

*"We've done nothing wrong. It's not like we were trading national secrets with terrorists or anything; besides, I made the agent forget why he was questioning me."*

*"Wait, what? Can you force people to forget things too? How'd you do that?"*

*"I'm not sure how it all works yet, but I found a way into a part of the agent's brain where I could open a door, pull out what I needed, and then planted new information. I closed the door behind me and locked it before hiding the key."*

*"That's some scary shit, dude. Hey! That's it!*

*"What's it?"* I asked.

*"You could come over to my house and encourage my dad to stop drinking."*

*"I'll give it a try,"* I said boldly as if I was willing to try anything for Kevin.

*"How about Monday right after school?"* Kevin recommended.

*"Brilliant. What if it doesn't work like it did on Kipton, and I fail? Stand by for a second; my dad is knocking on my door,"* I sent Kevin.

"Come in, Dad," I announced as I grabbed my phone off the nightstand and pretend to be talking to Kevin. "Okay, Kevin, I gotta go; my dad just came in. See ya," I said out loud into the blank screen.

"I just wanted to tell you goodnight," my dad said with a warm smile. "It's nice you've made some new friends. Get some sleep, birthday boy." I looked down at my phone, and it was one in the morning. Wow, Saturday was a long day.

"Love you, Dad. Thank you for the awesome weekend."

"You're welcome; I love you too."

*"I better get some sleep, man,"* Kevin sent.

*"Okay, goodnight."*

*****

I was all pissed off when some stupid ass woke me up. There was no way I've had enough sleep. "Why can't I see anything?" I asked just before someone took a blindfold off my face. I found myself in a small office with

Kipton standing in front of me, holding the blindfold. Kipton removed his suit jacket before continuing to undress. He was only wearing briefs and socks by the time he was finished.

"Where am I?" I asked with hostility.

"You're in the Pentagon," Kipton answered. I always thought the Pentagon would be a lot more impressive, to be honest. The small room was nothing to write home about. It had bare white walls and a painted concrete floor. There was a small desk in the corner where Kipton had thrown his clothes.

"Why are you undressed, Kipton?"

"I thought you may be more comfortable if I was wearing less clothing, you know, since you're totally naked." I looked down to find that Kipton was correct. I quickly cover my front with my cupped hands.

"Umm... you thought wrong; it just makes things creepier. What the hell am I doing here, anyway?" I asked, demanding an answer.

"I've brought you here for more questioning," Kipton told me as he scratched his bare thigh.

"Where's my dad? And where are my damn clothes?" I asked with a hint of urgency in my tone.

"Your father is at home, probably sleeping. You weren't wearing any clothes when I took you from your bed. Apparently, you must sleep nude." Kipton said with sarcasm.

"Do you have something I can slip into?" I asked.

"How did you learn my first name, Robert? I don't recall ever telling you," he said, ignoring my request to regain my dignity.

"I don't know; maybe it was a good guess." Kipton looked at me with a confident smile.

"Well, George, I think he's lying. What do you think?" Kipton asked, looking over my left shoulder. I turned around to see the British guy from the restaurant who had a crush on my dad. He was sitting in a chair behind me, dressed in a clown costume with a big red nose.

"It doesn't bother me if Robert chooses to lie," he said with a creepy voice. I removed one hand from my front, trying to cover my backside as well.

"Guys, I'm only fifteen..." My plea was cut short when the office door flew open with a crash. Kevin stepped in and pointed a gun at Kipton.

"Don't move, creepers!" Kevin shouted as he threw me a pair of shorts. "Come on, we're out of here!" Kevin yelled with a commanding voice as I made my way to the door.

Bright lights started to flash, accompanied by loud alarms sounding as we ran down a long skinny hallway that resembled a school bus.

"Come on, this way!" Lukas said, holding an open door. After we entered the room, Lukas closed the door behind us.

"Damn, this is the Lincoln bedroom. How did we get here? It's several miles from the Pentagon," I whispered into Lukas's ear. Lukas didn't waste the opportunity of my closeness. He leaned in to kiss me on the lips just as Kevin let out a blood-curdling scream. When we turned to see what was wrong with Kevin, we saw the ghost of Lincoln floating above the bed. All three of us screamed bloody murder when the legless spirit started to move toward us. I couldn't seem to make my legs move.

*****

"Robert? Wake up, you had a dream," I heard my dad say.

"What? Where am I?"

"You're in the guest bedroom."

"Oh yeah, sorry. B.. ba... d… dream," I stammered as I wiped my eyes. "Did I scream?"

"Yes, you did. You woke me from a dead sleep. Do you want to tell me about your dream?" my dad asked kindly. Absolutely not, especially about Lukas kissing me! I thought to myself.

"No, I'll be fine now. Sorry, I woke you," I said instead.

"No problem, slugger, get some sleep." I picked up my phone to check the time, and it was 03:20. It would be the last time I ever went to bed without wearing shorts.

# Fifteen Chapter 7

Sunday, May 21 Fifteen

My dad woke me up at six. I've only had four hours of sleep, but I drug my half-dead ass into the shower anyway. As I stood in the shower stall, I kept revisiting my messed-up dream. I started to laugh when I thought about the creepy clown costume George was wearing. And the kiss from Lukas was amazing.

My phone was buzzing when I came out of the bathroom. Grandma Zysk was calling from Florida. I needed to put some underwear on before I answered. It would be too awkward talking with her before I dressed.

"Hello, Grandma."

"Happy Birthday Robert Thomas," my Grandma said with excessive morning energy. Grandma Zysk was the only person I knew who called me by my first and middle name. I was named after her late husband. Grandma loved that his name lived on through me. My mom's father died when she was fifteen. Apparently, a drunk driver fell asleep and crossed the centerline, hitting him head-on. My grandma raised my mom and her younger sister in Holland all by herself and never remarried.

"Thank you, Grandma." How are you feeling?"

"Oh, I'm doing well for an old lady; thank you, honey. Your mother told me you're visiting your father this weekend."

"Yes, it's been fun. When will you be visiting Michigan?"

"I'll be there in three weeks so I can kiss those soft little cheeks of yours," she said with excitement in her voice. Grandma stayed with us for a few weeks every summer. I expected she would hit it off with Mrs. Wells during her visit this summer.

“Thanks for calling, Grandma; I have a plane to catch. Can’t wait to see you in June.”

“Love you too, sweaty, have a great birthday.”

We were on our way to the airport when my dad handed me a wrapped gift. “Here you go. I’ve been planning to give you this for quite some time. Now that you’re fifteen, I think you’ll understand the significance of the gift,” my dad said.

“Thank you,” I told him as I ripped into the package. There was a small white box inside, only large enough to fit a small piece of jewelry. I breathed in deep when I opened the top. I was excited when I first saw the contents of the box and quickly become disappointed. I knew there must’ve been a mix-up; there was no way my dad would’ve knowingly given me a gift like this. I’ve always believed his dog tags would be reserved for Sam at some point, but never me. *I thought you’d save them for Sam;* I sent through my dad’s green corridor.

“Sam will get a set for his birthday in June. I have split the tags. One tag is mine, and the other is Uncle Keith’s. I looked up at him with astonishment. I couldn’t believe he would trust me with such a valuable possession. “I wore this during a hectic time of my life when I was struggling with several life changes and trying to find my place in this world.

I was able to navigate some troubled waters. I believe you may be trying to travel through some rough waters in your life as well. You know, it’s all right to talk to your parents about these challenges you’re experiencing.” I shook my head, yes, as he reached out to help me place my gift around my neck.

I couldn’t say anything now without becoming emotional, so I settled for a simple “thank you.”

“I know these tags weren’t responsible for my successful navigation, but I thought they’d be a reminder that you aren’t on this journey alone as you contend with rough, dangerous seas,” he said with a wink.

“Thank you, this gift means more to me than you can imagine,” I said as I clutched the tags tightly.

“You’re welcome,” he answered.

"Was Uncle Keith gay?" I asked in a quiet voice so only my dad could hear. His head snapped toward me as if it had a rubber band attached. My dad's facial expression answered my blunt question without him having to say a word. He gave me a nod, swallowed deeply, turned his head away, and looked out his side window. *Robert didn't even know Keith. How did he learn this information?* I heard my dad think. I was immediately frustrated and confused. Why did the sexual orientation subject affect his behavior like this? It was as if he would rather jump off an aircraft carrier in the middle of the South Pacific than talk about a family member who was gay. "Why is this so difficult for you," I finally asked when I couldn't take the silence anymore.

"You must never share that information with anyone," he said, altogether, avoiding an official answer to my question. My dad was still looking out his window as if he didn't want to miss something.

"Dad?" I said, trying to get him to look in my direction. When he finally did, I was so caught off guard, I was speechless. I had never seen my dad cry. I must have really struck a chord or maybe a bad memory. Yes, that was it. A memory of Uncle Keith's funeral had leaked some unwanted emotions into our conversation.

"It's a complicated subject," he said as he wiped away a tear. I'll need some time to sort through what Uncle Kieth would have wanted me to share with you."

"I can live with that," I agreed.

My dad turned toward me and smiled weakly as our vehicle passed under the Ronald Reagan International Departures sign.

"Your Mother and I love you very much. Talk to her and let her help you when you're struggling. She's smart, you know." I felt as if there was so much unresolved tension between my dad and me that I hated to end our conversation.

"Yes, I know she is," I told him as I reached over to give his hand a squeeze. "I can make it to the gate on my own," I said with confidence.

"Yes, I'm sure you're fully capable, but I want to spend every minute I can with you. Brad called ahead to arrange everything with the TSA. They'll allow us to stay with you until you board your flight." When he said 'us,' he meant his driver, who was also his bodyguard. My dad was apparently afraid to let me out of his sight since he had received a warning from the FBI yesterday.

As I got ready to board the aircraft, my dad gave me a hug. Even though it was great to spend time with my dad, it seemed as if something had changed between us. Our relationship was different somehow. His weak hug felt unconvincing. The kiss he gave me on the forehead seemed forced, as well. I didn't like it.

I found my seat in coach before putting my buds in. Kevin must still be sleeping because everything was dark when I checked in on him. The plane taxied and sat in line for fifteen minutes before we took off. I was kind of spoiled after flying on one of grandpa's jets.

It should be a short ride; my ticket said 1.4 hours. An older guy was sleeping by the window with an empty seat between us. He smelled like stale cigarette smoke, so I was thankful for the separation. I sat my phone on my lap before lifting it about six inches into mid-air. Sliding objects was much easier than lifting. My focus needed to be spot on.

Just as I telekinetically lifted my phone for the third time, I caught a glimpse of someone moving to my right. I lost focus, causing my phone to softly drop back into my lap. I carefully looked to my right, where I found a wide-eyed little boy standing beside me, pointing at my hands that were covering my phone. I put my finger up to my lips, giving him the 'not a peep' sign. The kid wasn't leaving; instead, he quickly slid in past my knees before sitting in the empty seat between the smoky guy and me.

"Can I try?" I heard him ask just as I took my earbuds out.

"Sure," I told the cute little guy. "How old are you?"

"Six. Show me how first," the little boy said, not taking his eyes off my phone that was still sitting on my lap. I quickly looked around to make sure no one is watching.

"You just put your hand like this; it will lift like magic," I told him. I carefully lifted the phone before letting it drop again.

"Wild! Does an app make it float?" he asked as he moved his hand over the phone...

"Oh, there you are; I'm so sorry he's bugging you," a woman said, who I would assume was his mother. "Come on, Ahmad, back to your seat."

"He's fine; I was just teaching him some magic," I told her with a smile.

"Aw, Mama, please let me stay," he begged. I was sure she wasn't thrilled with her son's hand hovering only inches above my crotch.

"We'll be landing soon, so you'll need to come back to your seat and buckle up." His face was so sad it made me feel bad. *Bye, Ahmad,* I sent as he scooched past my long legs.

While disembarking at Gerald R. Ford in Grand Rapids, I saw Andy awaiting my arrival in the jetway. I wasn't sure what arrangements were made with the TSA on this end, but I was surprised they'd let him enter a secured area with a gun. "Hey, Robert! Happy Birthday," Andy said.

"Thank you," I answered with a grin. How'd you get stuck working on a Sunday?" I asked him as we made our way out of the concourse.

"I didn't have you yesterday, so I switched out my day off," he said as we stood by the vacant baggage reclaim carousel, watching it go around in circles. "Besides, I didn't want to miss your birthday." Suddenly, I felt a small hand holding mine. I quickly looked down to find Ahmad standing right beside me, looking at the carousel as well. He was so damn cute.

"Hey, Ahmad, this is Andy."

"Is Andy your Baba?" he asked. I started to answer, but Ahmad's mother reappeared to collect him.

"I'm so sorry; I guess he really likes you," she said with a big grin. "You need to stay by me; I don't want to lose you," she added as she grabbed his other little hand.

"What's your name?" Ahmad asked, looking into my eyes.

"My name is Robert. It was nice to meet you, Ahmad," I told him as I shook his hand.

"Bye, Robert," Ahmad said as his mother gave me a wink.

"You've become quite popular," Andy teased as he grabbed my luggage from the carousel. "Did you have fun?"

"Yes, it was great." Other than the nudity incident in the Pentagon last night, I thought to myself.

"You seem to be doing much better than you were a week ago," Andy said.

"Yeah, thanks," I answered as the warm spring air hit my face. "Hey, you got a new truck," I said, stating the obvious. "Why always black?" Andy gave me a shrug before opening the driver's door.

"The gift sitting on the seat beside you is from me and the fam," he said, looking at me as he backed the truck out of the parking spot.

"Thanks, Andy, you didn't have to get me anything." I felt kind of bad. His thirty-fifth birthday was a few months ago, and I didn't get him anything.

"It's not much; go ahead and open it," he said as he put the credit card in the parking collection computer. I tore into the paper to find a bright green t-shirt that said, 'I'm So Fine!'

"Thank you." Andy must have seen my confused expression when he looked in the mirror.

"You don't get the reference?" he asked.

"Erm, I ah…"

"You say that you're fine at least five times every day."

"It's a great gift!" I reassured Andy with a chuckle. He was right; I probably say 'I'm fine,' way too often. I pulled my shirt off over my head, so I could slip my new shirt on. I knew that my mom would ask me to remove it as soon as I got home. She was always concerned about all the chemicals that reside in new, unwashed garments. I figured, if it wasn't my briefs, I'd be all set. Besides, breathing these new car chemicals was probably ten times worse.

*"Hey, are you awake yet?* I sent Kevin.

*"What is it with you jumping in the shower with me, dude?"* I was half tempted to close my eyes to see if he was telling the truth, but I refrained.

*"Sorry, I'll check back in thirty minutes."*

*"No, you're all right; I'm getting used to it. Have you landed yet?"*

*"Yeah, Andy is driving me home. We're just leaving the airport. I should be home in thirty-five minutes. What are you doing this afternoon?"*

*"Homework mostly. Why?"* Kevin asked.

*"Do you want to hang out this afternoon? Maybe we could work together on your homework."*

*"What time are you thinking?"* he asked.

*"I'll let you know as soon as I get home and check with my mom. Are you out of the shower yet?"*

*"Nope, still scrubbing."*

Before we pulled into the security garage, I saw two cars that I didn't recognize and a limo belonging to my grandparents. I wasn't sure what my mom had planned for my birthday, but I was bummed out, knowing the plans wouldn't include Kevin. Everyone yelled surprise when I stepped through the threshold of the great central room.

Even though there was a sea of people looking back at me when I scanned the room, it seemed that the only face I could see clearly was Kevin's. My mom stepped up to give me a hug. "Thank you, Mom! And thank you for giving up your weekend with Dad, as well."

"You're welcome," she said as she rubbed her fingers through my messy curls.

*"I can't believe you're here. How were you able to withhold the fact that you were coming to my party? You were in the shower less than twenty minutes ago."*

*"Maybe I've found a way to block your relentless mind probing."* Kevin teased.

*"How'd you do that?"*

*"I'm not revealing my tactics. Do you think I'm stupid? I was riding in Sam's truck while you and I were talking."*

"Hello, Grandpa; thank you for the ride to DC this weekend."

"You're welcome. Consider it a fifteenth birthday gift," Grandpa said, reaching out for a big hug. Now, that hug was for real! I could feel my eyes bulging as he squeezed the shit out of me. Over his shoulder, I could see Kevin talking with Sam as they both held their drinks. They were talking about baseball, and Sam was telling Kevin something about Zach's fastball. Leave it to Sam; he was all about the jock stuff. The last time I had a conversation with Sam was on Friday when I obviously offended him. I think he was just trying to be brotherly, and I was just a dick.

*"I'll be over to save you as soon as I thank my Grandma for coming."*

*"You don't have to hurry; your brother is cool. He's fun."*

"Hey there, Robert, happy birthday!" Uncle Aaron said as he shook my hand.

"Thank you." "And how are you, Aunt Megan?" I asked as she stepped in to offer a hug. Aunt Megan was my mom's younger sister. I don't think my parents cared for Uncle Aaron that much, but they tolerated him. "Is my favorite cousin here?" I asked, looking around for Grady, who was my only cousin.

"No, I'm sorry, Grady had a youth group trip this weekend," Aunt Megan said.

"Please send him my best, and thanks again for making the trip over here."

I heard my phone chirp while I was talking to Grandpa, so I check it as I made my way over to Kevin and Sam. The screen said, 'Restricted.' There was no number or name with it:

Happy Birthday, Robert. I didn't have time to deal with whoever 'Restricted' was. The only person I had time for right now was Kevin.

"So, Mom told me you went to the White House, you lucky bum," Sam said with a hint of jealousy in his tone.

"You went to the White House?" Kevin asked with surprise. Kevin was good at this deception stuff as well. We made an excellent secret-keeping team. I just grinned and shook my head, yes.

"Did you get to meet the President?" Sam asked.

"Saying that I 'got to meet him may be a stretch, but his son, Lukas, seemed nice."

"Did you talk with Dad about that one thing I recommended?" Sam asked, right in front of Kevin. It was probably retaliation for being a dick to him on Friday.

"Yes, Sam, he's in the know," I muttered as I felt the temperature rise twenty degrees in my cheeks.

*"What's he talking about? Why does your face have a shade of candy apple red?"* Kevin asked.

*"Sam is trying to embarrass me."*

*"About what? You have a vein on your forehead that's about ready to pop.* Kevin was fishing, trying to get me on the hook, but I wasn't biting.

*"I'll explain later."*

*"Or you could explain now since no one else can hear us."*

I could tell Sam was wondering why there was an awkward silence between us. "Robert, it's time for cake," my mom announced. Having a happy birthday song sung is, by far, the worst part of having a birthday.

Whoever invented the ridiculous tradition should have all their toenails plucked out one at a time.

After the embarrassing, off-key song was painfully completed, Kevin and I escaped to the formal dining room with our cake and ice cream.

"Thanks again for coming to my party. Hopefully, it hasn't been unpleasant." I can't believe I just used the word unpleasant in a sentence while speaking to Kevin, but he didn't seem to notice.

"Are you joking? It's been fun. What kind of business do your grandparents have?"

"They own a software company. Why?" I asked, trying not to expose my mouth full of cake.

"I was just wondering," Kevin said as I opened the gift Kevin bought for me. It was a hardcover book about Leonardo Da Vinci by Walter Isaacson. "Thanks, man, I love it!" I was impressed Kevin remembered that Da Vinci was one of my heroes.

"You're welcome," Kevin answered with a proud expression. "Are you going to tell me why you were embarrassed about what Sam said a few minutes ago?"

"I'm not ready… I really don't want to tell you."

"I think you can trust me on this one," he said, cocking his head to the side as if he was mildly annoyed.

"Okay, I'm gay," I whispered as I leaned in close so no one else would hear me.

"Dope! You didn't think I already knew that?" he whispered back. "Come on, tell me the truth. Why were you so embarrassed?"

"That is the truth. Sam recommended I come out to my dad this weekend," I contend, feeling the temperature increase in my cheeks again. "Wait. What do you mean you already knew?"

"Dude, you've been checking me out in the shower all year. If that's not a big enough clue, I don't know what is," he said, glancing in my direction. "Are you attracted to all of the guys at our school?"

"Yuck! No, of course not, only a few. So, it doesn't bother you that I'm gay?"

"Nah, I don't care about stuff like that," Kevin said before taking a bite of cake.

"If you don't have a problem with me being gay, why'd you push me on my ass in the shower that one day?"

"Yeah, sorry about that. I thought you were the one who slapped my bare ass. Zach admitted to it later." I looked at Kevin with confusion. If I had mistakenly pushed someone on their ass, I would have sought them to apologize immediately. In our conversation, a long silent period caused Kevin some discomfort as he thought about how he should have handled the pushing incident differently. I guess we all had character flaws, but he did finally apologize just now. Better late than never.

"And you?" I finally asked before I spooned in some half-melted ice cream.

"And me, what?"

"Sexual orientation?" I asked with a confident tone. Now that the truth was out about me, I felt bolder.

"Why does it always have to be about labels?" Kevin asked with a roll of his eyes. "Why can't someone just be attracted to a person without attaching labels?" I guess I had never thought about it that way, but he still hadn't answered my question. All I could think to do was shrug my shoulders. Whenever I read Kevin, I didn't find him thinking about anyone sexually, female or male. It was as if sexuality was missing from his thoughts. Kevin would make a sexual reference or a sexual joke from time to time, but we hadn't talked about the subject since we had become friends.

"People like labels; it cleans things up for them, so they don't have to think. If it's written on the label, they don't have to guess what's inside," I told him, offering an analogy with sincerity. I looked up just as Kevin leaked some melted ice cream out the corner of his mouth. He allowed the white drizzle to run down his chin and onto the plate.

*"I never swallow GMOs; the label said they're bad for me,"* he sent, apparently referring to the label on the ice cream carton. We both started to laugh out loud, and now Grandma was looking in our direction, wondering if we would recover.

"My turn to ask the next question," he said, continuing our unplanned, ruleless game of truth or dare.

*"But you haven't answered my question yet."*

*"I'm not gonna sexually label myself. It's too complicated."*

*I think I'll be able to keep up;* I sent Kevin through a green corridor, hoping he'll change his mind. Somehow, he was ready to deflect my recommendation as he continued his unfair probing.

*"How'd you get the scar on your left wrist?"* Kevin asked. I knew the question would come up at some point; the scar was still quite noticeable, but I was hoping it wouldn't have been asked so soon.

*"Um, I a... don't want to talk about any of that. It's complicated."* I said, expecting him to offer the same free pass I was willing to give him.

"Why are you boys sitting in here all by yourselves? Is everything all right?" Mom asked, suddenly appearing at my side. I kept forgetting how weird it must look when Kevin and I were communicating without verbalizing. Still, we had been doing much better, not looking at each other while we communicated telepathically.

"We're fine. We were trying to figure out what we were going to do for Kevin's birthday tomorrow."

"Oh, I didn't know your birthdays were so close," she said.

"Yeah, I asked Rob over to my house tomorrow for dinner if that's all right."

*"You did?"*

"It'll be fine with me as long as you're home at a decent hour," Mom said as she placed her hand on my shoulder and squeezed it lightly.

*"Work with me here, dude. You're coming to my house tomorrow after school, so I thought it would play nicely into your lie,"* he said, still looking at my mom.

*"Nice."*

*"Let's go up to your room so you can show me your new tricks."*

*"I'm not a dog. I don't do tricks,"* I sent as we both grinned.

"Where did you get that cute shirt?" my mom asked, facing me directly as she studied the cyanide-laced garment, wondering if it was washed before I put it on. Cancer-causing chemicals were excreting from the shirt as my skin pores absorb the chemicals, which will undoubtedly result in death.

"Andy and his family," I answered, leaving out the snide comments.

"Well, it's very fitting for you," she said, looking at me as Kevin stuck his tongue out and started to roll some melted ice cream around. I could see the whites of his eyes as he looked upward. He was acting as if he were experiencing extreme ecstasy. Kevin's tongue continued to curl and flick his vanilla delight around, apparently trying to make me lose it. The scene reminded me of Lukas sucking the chocolate truffle from his finger.

Even though Mom was standing right in front of me, I finally lost the battle and started to laugh hysterically. Kevin quickly swallowed before grabbing his napkin from the table. He dabbed some vanilla ice cream from his lips with the paper napkin as if he were in a formal dining experience.

*"I thought you said you never swallow GMOs!"*

*"But, the taste was irresistible."* Thankfully, Mom had missed Kevin's entire erotic performance. I couldn't believe how fun it was to have a friend.

After most of the company had left, Kevin and I retreated to my room. After locking my bedroom door, I turned to see Kevin grinning. "What?" I asked.

"Let's see then," he said, walking over to where I stood. Kevin was so close he nearly sent me into a gasping panic. He reached up to do his signature maneuver, running his fingers through his hair, just as Shawn Mendes often did on stage. It drove me sexually insane. There was that smell again, it was intoxicating, and it was the same smell I noticed when we were wrestling in PE.

"You smell good. What are you wearing?" I asked nervously.

"Soap?" Kevin answered flatly, apparently trying to take advantage of my vulnerability.

"Oh, I thought it was cologne."

"Erm, nope, it's Axe body wash and Old Spice deodorant."

"You sure you're ready for this?" I asked. Kevin reached up to my chest, where my dad's dog tags hung. When he lightly touched my chest, it sent little tingles down my entire body until I felt them in my toes. I tried to concentrate on keeping my respirations at a reasonable rate, so I wouldn't hyperventilate. He pulled the tags away from my chest, examining them closely.

"I've never seen you wear these before," he said inquisitively.

"They're my birthday gift from my dad," I said, looking at his handsome face.

"Your dad was in the military?" he asked, still reading the small print.

"Navy. He was a Jag attorney. The other tag belonged to my Uncle Keith. He was a Marine."

I placed my hand over Kevin's medallion that hung on a chain around his neck. When I pulled my hand away, his medallion moved away from his chest to hang in mid-air. Kevin's eyes opened wide as he swallowed profoundly. "That is so sick, dude." Kevin took my hand in his, turning it over before brushing his fingers lightly over my scar. I pulled away, took a few steps back, looking anxiously into his eyes. "What's wrong, Dude?" he asked, extending his arms, with his palms turned upward.

"I didn't… I didn't mean to... I just…" I stammered as I continued to increase the space between us.

"Do you think I have a problem with you being gay?" I flopped down on my bed and didn't answer. A million things were going through my mind at the speed of light. I honestly didn't know what to think. First off, I was confused about Kevin's sexual orientation. Second, if he was gay or bi, was he interested in me? Third, why should any of that matter? Was I a typical sex-hungry fifteen-year-old, or should I add 'sex fanatic' to my list of abnormalities? Why was I even worried about that shit?

Kevin hadn't moved from where I left him standing in the middle of the room. "Listen, I've never developed a close friendship with anyone as quickly as I have with you. If that sounds weird or demi, I don't care. I'm just telling you how I feel," Kevin added as he came over and laid down beside me.

"Dimi?" I asked.

"Yeah, you said you wanted a label," Kevin answered.

"I'm sorry, erm… What's dimi?"

"Demisexual is on the asexual spectrum," he explained. "I don't feel any sexual attraction to anyone without having a strong emotional connection first."

"So, you're not attracted to any specific gender?"

"Not really. I'm more attracted to a person's particular attributes and personality." I like the way he used the word 'person' as a non-gender-specific noun. "For example, if I look at him," he said, pointing at a large poster of Troye Sivan wearing a see-through shirt. "I have no sexual attraction; he's just another average-looking dude." I must have looked astonished as Kevin continued. "And if he were a female wearing the same thing, I'd have the same lack of attraction. So, if you need a label, I guess you can use asexual."

"So, that whole erotic, sexy, ice cream on the tongue thing was nothing more than you trying to get me to laugh?"

"Guilty," he said with a snicker. "I know how to get you going; it doesn't take much."

"Wouldn't dimi kinda put you in the bisexual category?"

Kevin shook his head no and said, "It's just asexual since I'm not attracted sexually to either gender. Like I said before, it's complicated."

"So, do you ever like…" I cupped my hand and move it in a jerking hand gesture. Kevin's grin made me laugh.

"Probably not as much as you," he said with a blush shaking his head, yes.

"Is twice a day too often?" I asked, matching his shade of red. We both giggled as if we were back in third grade. "Hey, have you ever checked out the Trevor Project website? I remember reading about some asexual information last week, so you may be interested." Kevin shook his head, no. "Mr. Smit told me about the website back in February when my future was looking bleak. Their hotline gave a lot of information about all the challenges that LGBTQ teens typically face. You know? Kids like me. They helped me get through some tough spots."

"I'll check it out sometime," Kevin said.

I knew it was my turn, to be honest, but I stalled instead by raising my hand to telekinetically lift the yellow lamp off my nightstand.

"I told my mom that I cut my wrist when I was trying to clean up the pieces of my broken lamp."

"What really happened," Kevin asked as I felt his hand rest up against my left lower leg.

"I got depressed during the holidays, and…" I started to explain before trailing off.

"Why were you depressed?" Kevin asked.

"I think it was a bunch of stuff. I'd been under a lot of pressure, and my dad had left us. But most of it was feeling hopeless about not being accepted," I explained without giving any specifics.

"Accepted as a gay kid?" Kevin asked. I shook my head, yes.

"I cut my wrist with a razor blade. After changing my mind, I panicked and staged the incident with a broken lamp," I admitted to Kevin as I returned the lamp safely to my nightstand.

"Damn, dude," he said as he pulled his arms up behind his head, causing his shirt to ride-up his irresistibly sexy torso. "What made you change your mind?"

"What?" I asked, only using one word to keep my drool from leaking.

"What made you decide not to go through with your plan to...."

"I paused for a minute, and the moment passed," I said, quickly interrupting him, so he didn't have to finish explaining.

"Huh?" he said as he turned on his side toward me. Damn, now I couldn't see his perfectly flat belly button anymore.

"You know if you take a minute to think about what you're doing, you change your mind? My suicidal moment had passed. A short time had passed, and I felt different about wanting to live." Kevin's elbow touched mine as he scooched up onto the bed to get more comfortable. Kevin's unintentional touch sent a shock wave through my body that increased my heart rate to the point where it felt as if my heart could jump out of my chest.

"Oh yeah," Kevin said as if he understood. "In health class, Mr. Dean told us that those who survived their suicide attempt after jumping off the Golden Gate Bridge. The jumpers said they wished they wouldn't have gone through with it. On their way to the water, they said; 'I want to live now.'"

"I can relate to that," I told Kevin with an uneasy worry, eating away at me.

"But you're all right now, aren't you?" Kevin asked with a caring expression.

"Erm, yeah, ever since Mr. Smit helped me feel wanted. He became my person and gave me hope."

"What do you mean, he became your person?" Kevin asked as he pulled his shirt down.

"He made me feel whole again. When I'm feeling like hope is slipping away, I can bounce things off him."

"Zach is my person," Kevin said as he sat up, slapping me on the knee so hard that it hurt. What a sissy. I was sure he didn't mean to hurt me, so I tried to hide my anguish with a fake smile that probably looked more like a grimace. "When my mom died, Zach was there for me," Kevin explained as he stood. "I better get going. My history assignment isn't gonna finish itself."

When Andy and I returned home after dropping Kevin at his house, I headed straight to Sam's room.

"Enter at your own risk," I heard Sam announce after I knocked. Given the 'all-clear,' I carefully open his door. Sam's bedroom had the same layout as mine, but they were much different considering the cleanliness. His room smelled like a locker room. He had dirty clothes strewn across his room with empty pizza boxes stacked up on his nightstand. I don't know how he could feel comfortable with having dirty, stinky socks hanging from the same chair he was sitting in. I wanted to tell him how disgusting his room smelled, but that wasn't why I was there.

"Hey, thanks for the cool shirt; it's a great birthday gift," I told him as I carefully navigated his gross room, trying not to step on the spilled cheese goldfish. There was a good chance I could contract typhoid in his room if I weren't careful.

"You're welcome." I stood in front of Sam like a dumbass, trying to figure out what to say next. "Was there something else? Cuz I gotta finish this," he said as he pointed at his computer screen.

"Ah, yeah. Erm... Sorry, I was a dickhead Friday morning."

"Forget it," he said with a hand wave. "So, you told Dad?" I shook my head, yes, assuming that he was talking about the gay thing. "How did he react when you told him?"

"Not as well as I had hoped. It's like Dad was disgusted or maybe just disappointed. I'm not really sure yet, but he wasn't happy about it."

"Sorry if I steered you wrong on that one, little bro. Does Kevin know you're gay?"

"Yeah, I told him."

"Is he into you? I mean... are you two like?" Sam paused and rolled his tongue back and forth on the inside of his cheek to make it look like he was sucking someone. What a pig.

"Just friends," I interrupted.

"Whatever," he said with a wink before turning back toward his computer.

"Okay, night. Thanks again for the shirt."

It was only nine o'clock when I finished helping Kevin with his math homework. I was kind of tired, but I knew there was a good chance I wouldn't be able to fall asleep right away. The close encounter I had with Kevin this afternoon had left me in a frenzy of uncharted emotions. When I closed my eyes to enter Kevin's orange corridor, I saw a game on his desktop screen that he seemed to be studying.

*"Hey, Zach, where are the guys?"*

*"I don't know; I'll text Carter."* Kevin was still looking at his screen, where I could see a character wearing a skeleton uniform. As Kevin glanced around the screen, I could see the name 'Fortnite' at the top. Nothing was

happening on the screen, but a school bus looked like it was being suspended in the air by a hot air balloon above the character's picture.

I've never had much interest in learning how to play video games. Most kids my age frequently play screen games, so maybe if I learned to play, I could virtually hang out with other kids my age, perhaps even make a friend or two. It would be a lot less awkward hanging in a virtual setting anyway.

*"They'll be on in two minutes,"* I heard Zach say.

*"Dude, you should see the new headset my Grandma sent me for my birthday,"* Kevin said to Zach.

*"What kind?"* Zach asked.

*"Turtle Beach Stealth 400."*

*"That's sick, dude,"* Zach replied.

*"What's up, bitches?"* a booming voice said to Kevin through a microphone.

*"Where the hell have you guys been?"* Kevin asked.

*"Doing homework,"* another person said. *"You probably didn't even do yours."*

*"Yeah, I did. Rob helped me finish mine twenty minutes ago."* Hey, Kevin mentioned my name. Hell yeah!

*"Did he blow you too?"* a voice asked. I was immediately pissed at whoever just said that. But I shouldn't take offense. It was probably just trash talk. He probably wasn't making the reference about me being gay.

*"Shut up, Carter! I'm gonna come over there and kick your ass,"* Kevin said with a high level of anger in his mind.

*"Could we just play already?"* Zach asked as I saw two other players join Kevin and Zach. He looked at his controller before pushing Y to start.

*"Lucky Landing?"* Zach said just before Kevin's guy jumped out of the bus and was flying on a glider. I could learn to play the game without too much trouble. When Kevin's guy landed, he started to pick up weapons and supplies.

*"Zach, grab those bandages over there,"* someone shouted.

*"Got Em,"* Zach said with some urgency in his voice.

*"Kevin, you have a guy coming in at South 225,"* someone said.

*"Die, you jerk,"* Kevin said as he took his ax thing and chopped at an apparent enemy. Three of the team members, including Kevin, crossed a river, now they were in a circle, but the fourth team member was missing.

*"Guys, I'm caught in the storm; I'm losing health fast!"* someone said with desperation in his voice.

*"On my way,"* Kevin said. I heard gunshots ringing out all around Kevin's guy as he moved into the storm.

*"I need bandages fast! I'm down to 24 health! Hurry guys, I'm failing fast!"* the poor guy said, who was obviously in a lot of trouble.

"Robert! Robert, can you hear me? Answer me, Robert!" I could hear someone yelling with a panicked voice. I thought it could be my mom, but it was like she was talking to me from another dimension or a realm from the unknown. "Samuel! Samuel, come quick!" I heard my mom scream as she frantically shook me.

"What's wrong, Mom? Why are you shaking me?" I tried to ask her as I started to come out of my stupor. But for some reason, everything came out garbled. My vision was blurred as if the storm was still blowing dirt into Kevin's eyes.

"Mom, is everything all right?" Sam asked as he rushed into my room. I could see Sam, but he was blurry as well.

"Samuel! Call 911! Robert just had a seizure!" she told him.

"No ambulance," I was finally able to say with some semblance of a speech pattern.

"Robert, can you hear me?" It was as if she had no idea what I was trying to tell her.

"Mom, I'm fine," I told her, hoping she wouldn't call EMS. But I knew it was nothing more than a feeble attempt when I heard Sam talking to the 911 dispatcher.

"Yes, my younger brother just had a seizure. Fourteen! No, I mean, he's fifteen! Yeah, he's awake now. I don't know." "Mom, does he seem confused?"

"Yes, tell them his eyes were rolled back in his head, his whole body was convulsing," Mom told Sam with a commanding voice.

"Mom, the dispatcher, wants you to roll him up on his left side," Sam said.

"Hey, Mom, I'm fine. I don't need EMS," I begged her.

"Robert, you weren't answering me; your arms and legs were shaking. Your father said you passed out yesterday, as well. So, you're going to the hospital." She was correct; if I did, in fact, have a seizure, I should probably be seen by a doctor. But I didn't think it was a seizure. I was only playing a game. Well, I wasn't playing the game; Kevin was.

It was good that I had a spacious bedroom. There were five cops, two firefighters, and two paramedics in my room who were all busy doing something.

"Robert, have you taken any street drugs or prescription medicine tonight?" the paramedic asked. The kind paramedic who couldn't be any older than twenty was asking all the wrong questions. She should be asking me if I stayed inside Kevin's mind for too long. That was what must have happened. There must be a limit to how long I can stay in before I start experiencing adverse ramifications? I could say with certainty that it was scary as hell to have several people trying to figure out what was wrong with me.

"Robert, are you sure you didn't take any BMG or Molly tonight?" the paramedic asked again, probably believing my answer would change if she raised the question multiple times.

I had heard guys at school talk about how Molly makes anyone who took it horny as hell; I didn't need any help with that. But I had never heard of BMG.

"Sinus Tach, at one-thirty," the older paramedic said unenthusiastically to his partner.

"Have you ever had an IV before, Robert?" the paramedic asked as she pulled a bag of fluid out of a blue backpack.

I woke up at 04:55. Damn, another messed-up dream. The last thing I remembered was watching Kevin play his Fortnite game; I must've fallen asleep. No, that's not right; I remembered coming home from the hospital. That's not right, either. The emergency room visit must have been part of my dream. Damn, I was too tired to work it out. I should sleep for another hour.

# Consequences Chapter 8

Monday, May 22 Consequences

"Honey, are you awake?" I heard my mom ask as she gently shook my shoulder.

"Hey, Mom, sorry I must've overslept," I mumbled as I blindly reach for my glasses.

"How are you feeling?" My mom asked as she sat beside me on my bed, brushing my hair to the side. I was just about ready to question why she'd be asking how I felt, but when I pulled my left arm from under the blankets, I noticed a bandage just below my bicep. Either the vampires were kind enough to apply a dressing to my arm, or I was, in fact, in the emergency room last night.

"Umm, I'm feeling fine."

"You better stay home with Mrs. Wells today," Mom said with a sympathetic tone. No way. I'm planning to go to Kevin's today after school; I won't be missing that once-in-a-lifetime invitation.

"Nope, I'm going to school," I answered, declining her recommendation.

"All right, you better jump in the shower then," Mom said before leaving my room.

While standing in the shower, I started to recall everything in the ER last night. After being asked if I had taken any street or prescription drugs at least eight more times, having a brain scan and three gallons of blood drawn from my arm. I was sent home at 02:00 with the diagnosis of a "situational syncope." The doctor thought it may have been caused by anxiety. I was going to have to respectfully disagree. It was more likely to be another consequence I would have to deal with if I chose to stay in Kevin's orange corridor for an extended period. But I wasn't offering any of my unprofessional opinions to someone who had gone to college for longer than I had been alive.

After dressing for school and on my way down for breakfast, I checked my phone. Oh, that's right. I received a birthday wish from that restricted number last night. Opening the text again made me wonder who I knew that would have a restricted number:

Happy Birthday, Robert. It said without any other hints to whom it may be.

Thank you. Who is this? I texted back.

There was still no answer from the restricted number when I checked my phone after breakfast. Oh yeah, it was Kevin's birthday today.

*"Hey, there, Birthday boy, how's it going?"*

*"Ah... I'm currently dumping my dad's alcohol down the drain. Next, I need to hide his truck keys so he can't make any party store runs. I want to make sure he's sober when we get out of school,"* Kevin answered.

*"Okay, I'll see you at lunch,"* I told Kevin.

If someone had been taking a video of Gary and me struggling to wrap Kevin's gift, it would have been YouTube-worthy or at least a Snap.

"No, it goes like this, Robert," Gary told me as he took over the project folding the paper another way. We were both laughing at our apparent ineptitude, so I was thrilled there was no one in the school parking lot to witness our fiasco. "You're such a goofball," Gary said after we finished wrapping the gift.

Cam greeted me with a big smile as I walked into first-hour. "How was your trip to the White House?" he asked loud enough for Mr. Kave to hear.

"It was really cool," I said only loud enough for Cam to hear. "The State Dinner was unbelievable."

"You went to a State Dinner at the White House?" Mr. Kave asked, startling me. Somehow, he was able to stealthily move into position behind me within a few seconds of him hearing Cam's question.

"Umm yeah, my dad took me," I answered, turning toward Mr. Kave so I could make eye contact.

"Oh my!" he said, sounding more like my grandma than a thirty-eight-year-old male.

"My dad was able to set up a personalized tour for me." Mr. Kave had a look of awestruck in his expression as he processed what I had told him. *You lucky little shit,* I heard Mr. Kave think.

"Would you mind sharing your experience with the rest of the class this morning? Most of us will never have an opportunity to experience something so rare. I'm sure there will be great interest among your classmates." I doubted that but finally caved after Mr. Kave did the puppy dog eyes thing.

During my short speaking engagement, David asked if I shook hands with the president. When I mentioned that the president's hand was sweaty and gross, everyone laughed. I was able to read TJ when he thought I should have 'taken out' the president. I don't believe TJ meant I should 'take him out' for lunch. Sandy thought I needed to take pictures to prove I was at the White House. Ryan thought I shouldn't 'dress and act like a fag.' I always made great strides trying to stay in the closet, so I never dressed flamboyantly—maybe kind of preppy, but never like a stereotypical gay kid who wanted everyone to know.

Just as I was finishing up answering questions, something new happened in my brain, causing a popping noise like gunshots. Each bang made me flinch, which didn't go unnoticed by David. David's eyes widened as Sandy's notebook went flying over into Lori's lap. At the same time, Ryan's backpack was sent flying to the floor between David and Cam. Other than David, I don't think anyone saw me flinch. A scuffle broke out when Lori accused Sandy of throwing her notebook at her.

I looked in their general direction just before I heard the pops, but how did my mind automatically and vindictively choose to cause mayhem with Sandy and Ryan? I usually tried to refrain from partaking in vindictive behavior, except when my sister deserved it.

It was finally lunchtime, so I was headed for the cafeteria when some random kid stopped me in the crowded hall.

"Hey, Robert, do you have a second?" the kid asked. Why would this extremely hot upperclassman want to talk to me? I was having a hard time staying calm as he stared into my eyes. "Could I get your phone number?" the kid asked.

"Ah… why do you want my phone number?" I asked, looking over my shoulder to see if Gary was nearby.

"Last night, Trent Dade got hit by a car and broke his leg. We need to find someone to take his place in our school play," he explained with desperation in his tone.

"I don't understand. What would Trent getting injured have to do with me?"

"Trent was a lead role in the spring play; he'll be out of commission for several weeks," the kid explained.

"Still not following you," I admitted. *What a shame, all the beauty in the world with no brains,* I heard the kid think. He continued to talk while I brushed off the mixed slam and complement.

"Robert. That's your name, right?" the gorgeous kid asked.

"Yeah, Robert," I finally responded. I knew I must have sounded like a dumbass, but it was challenging to concentrate with the adorable kid talking to me. Gary had moved into earshot of me as he tried to figure out what was going on.

"Well, let me start over... My name is Liam... we need a replacement for the play; you fit that bill," the beautiful guy said in a slow patronizing voice.

"Look, Liam, I've never been in a play, and I have absolutely no acting talent," I finally said after regaining my composure. Liam had the brightest light blue eye I had ever seen. His long blondish hair was pulled back in a small man bun.

"Please just give me your number so I can give it to Ms. Hukins," he said, holding his cell and waving his index finger over the screen. "Thanks, see ya, man," Liam said after I reluctantly gave him my number.

When I reached our table with a plate of stroganoff, which oddly enough resembled Petey's dog food, I was happy to see that Kevin and Cam were civil with each other.

*"It's good to see you two getting along. Happy birthday, by the way."*

*"Thanks,"* Kevin sent back.

"Happy fifteenth, Bruh!" Zach said as he came up behind Kevin and slapping him on the back. It was always bruh or dude. I wasn't planning on adopting their unique dialect just to fit in.

"Thanks, man," Kevin answered. I guess I do use 'man' as an alternate reference. When I handed Kevin his gift, he looked surprised. He tore into the paper as he looked at me with those irresistible blue eyes.

*"Thanks. This is a great gift, but it costs way too much,"* Kevin told me, looking in my direction.

*"It's just a freaking tablet and prepaid hotspot. It didn't cost that much,"* I assured Kevin as I looked into his eyes again.

"Hey, do you two need some alone time?" Zach asked.

"Shut up, dude," Kevin said.

"I'm just saying when you stare at each other without saying anything, it looks suspicious." Cam smiled as if he was thinking the same thing. "Are you two like ah… you know, involved?" Zach asked with a big grin as Kevin flashed him the bird. "Here," Zach said, handing Kevin a gift. Zach's present was a new set of Bluetooth earbuds.

*"We need to stop looking at each other when we talk secretly,"* I sent Kevin without looking up from my plate of stroganoff that was surprisingly good.

"Thank you, these are awesome gifts, guys." "So, what did you get me?" Kevin asked Cam sarcastically as he looked across the table at him.

"Your gift is right here," Cam said as he pointed down at his crotch with one hand, grabbing himself with his other.

"Oh, does it come with a microscope? I'm sure I'll need one," Kevin said as we all started to laugh, including Cam, who had it coming.

I wasn't sure when they showed up or how much of our inappropriate conversation they heard, but we were suddenly joined by four girls standing next to our table. I only knew two of the four. Kimberly was in my math class, and Rebecca was holding a birthday cake. Kevin was smiling as he ate up the attention.

*"I think Rebecca has the hots for you,"* I sent Kevin, hoping he didn't sense my jealousy.

*"She's just my friend,"* Kevin sent back as he took his birthday cake from Rebecca and placed it on the table in front of him.

As we all started to sing happy birthday, I realized that this may be the only birthday recognition Kevin would get today. Cam enjoyed an occasional flirtatious touch as he helped one of the girls serve the cake on small paper plates.

Just as I finished my last bite of cake, I received a text from a number that I didn't recognize. There was a new text from the 'Restricted' number as well:

Hi Robert, this is Ms. Hukins. Liam gave me a bit of good news... He said you may be interested in participating in the Spring play!

Liam must have misunderstood.

Okay... I'll take that as a maybe... Please meet me after school in the media center if you have time.

I'll be there, I texted back.

The text from the restricted number was another short message:

I can't give up my identity… Damn, who could it be? I wondered if I should show Gary the text so he could do some investigation. Second thought, bad idea. He'd make me delete it, then I'd never figure it out.

Before sixth-hour ended, Mr. Smit approached me and said, "Hey, Robert, would you mind staying after for a few minutes today?"

"Sure, no problem," I answered as I caught Cam glancing in my direction.

*What does he need to talk with Rob about? I wonder if he's onto me?* Cam thought to himself. What did 'onto me' mean? I tried to search Cam's passages, but the end of the period tone sounded, distracting me from my task.

"See ya," Cam said as he left the room. I just gave him an awkward wave as I tried to figure out what 'onto me' meant.

"Hey, Robert, have a seat; I just wanted to check in to see how things are going," Mr. Smit said with a friendly voice. I suddenly picked up on some discomfort in Mr. Smit's brain activity. He was wondering how things were going with my counseling sessions. He was trying to hide the fact that he breached our confidentiality. I hadn't told him I was seeing Doctor Kelly for depression. That son-of-a-bitch told my mom. You two-faced...

I had difficulty controlling my anger, so I stared at Mr. Smit until he had a worried expression creep in. He knew I had figured it out somehow. He told my mom, betrayed me, broke our trust, and destroyed our friendship. I stood up, look at him without uttering a single word before starting for the door.

"Robert, what's wrong," I heard Mr. Smit say as his chair kicked out from behind him. "Wait for a second," he said as he grabbed my left arm with more force than I expected. I unsuccessfully tried to pull away from his hold. I could hear Gary coming through the door just as I turn on Mr. Smit.

"Why did you do it?" I shouted. Mr. Smit was trying to calm me down by holding my arm lightly, but it was too late for him to fix this; Gary was standing right beside me when I realized I had tears in my eyes.

"Ah, you're going to want to take your hand off Robert's arm," Gary said with an authoritative voice, giving Mr. Smit a look. You know, the look someone gives just before they remove your head from your body?

"I only asked you a question. Why are you reacting like this?" Mr. Smit asked as he let go. I stared at him for a few seconds before I turned to walk away.

"What's going on? Why are you so pissed?" Kevin asked as I walked past him in the doorway.

"He told my mom that I was having depression and emotional issues. I trusted him; he broke our trust," I responded as we walked down the mostly empty hallway with Gary bringing up the rear. Kevin pulled on my shirt sleeve, trying to get me to look in his direction.

"How do you know?" Kevin asked, referring to what I had said about Mr. Smit.

"I read him. He was wondering how it was going with my shrink," I explained.

"Maybe he's just concerned about you," Kevin countered.

"I don't want to talk about it," I told Kevin as I wiped my tears with my shirt sleeve. Damn it, I was acting like a spoiled brat. "I'm sorry, I shouldn't have caused so much drama on your birthday," I said apologetically as we continue toward the exit.

"No. You have a right to be angry, but there's a strong possibility Mr. Smit was required by law to tell your Mom." Kevin was right; I didn't think it through before I reacted. Someone must've required Mr. Smit to tell her. Otherwise, he never would have broken our trust.

"You're right; I got so mad I wasn't thinking," I admitted. "Shit! I told Ms. Hukins I would meet her in the Media room for a few minutes after school."

"Can you put it off until tomorrow?" Kevin asked.

"No, it's right up here; it'll only take a second," I told Kevin as he followed me into the media room.

There were at least twenty kids in the media room who all went silent when we walked in.

"Ah, Robert, thank you for stopping by. Liam is right; you're a perfect fit for Peter Pan!" Ms. Hukins said with excitement.

*"Peter effing Pan? Is she kidding me?"*

*"I… don't think so, dude, she looks pretty serious,"* Kevin sent back

"Umm… Peter Pan, Ma'am?"

"Yes, you have the perfect build for the part. How well can you sing?" Ms. Hukins asked as she circled me like a vulture.

"I've only had two years of music lessons, Ma'am." *"Shut up, you jackass; I can hear you laughing back there,"* I sent to Kevin.

*"I would never laugh; I was just picturing you in a pair of cute little green tights."*

"I'll think about it and get back to you in the morning," I told Ms. Hukins.

"That will be fine, but I must encourage you to hurry with your decision. The play will open in two weeks."

"Two weeks? I'm not sure I'll be able to learn the lines for a lead role in two weeks." I lied.

"Pish-posh, you're a bright boy; I've talked with several of your teachers. They're confident you won't have any problem learning the script," Ms. Hukins said as she caressed my left shoulder.

*"She must be kind of touchy-feely,"* I sent Kevin when I heard him laughing again. "Okay, tomorrow morning then," I told Ms. Hukins as Liam gave me a big grin.

As we entered Kevin's house, I could see that no one had attempted to clean the house in quite some time. There were stacks of dirty dishes in the kitchen sink. My OCD immediately went into overdrive. All I could think about was folding the stack of towels that I saw piled on the dining room table.

"Hey, Dad?" Kevin said as he shook his dad's knee to wake him. Kevin's father was tall and thin, with an average build. His face was handsome; I could see where Kevin got his good looks.

“Hey, Kev, have you seen my keys? I seem to have misplaced them,” Kevin’s dad asked as he sat up in his recliner. I knew what was coming next, and I wasn’t looking forward to it. I would be introduced to Kevin’s father and then expected to delve into his brain so I could try to correct his drinking problem, but not without severe consequences.

“I think your keys are in the basket by the phone. Did you remember I was bringing my friend Robert this afternoon?” Man, I liked the sound of him referring to me as his friend.

“Oh yeah. Hey, Robert, it’s nice to meet you,” he said with a sleepy smile.

“It’s nice to meet you as well, Sir, *but we need to talk.”* Kevin’s dad shook his head as I entered his red corridor.

*“You will stop drinking today. You need to start going to AA meetings tomorrow. You will find a new job before the end of this week because a job will make your life more meaningful. You will make an appointment with a counselor tomorrow. You won’t remember why I came here today, but you will recall that it’s your son’s fifteenth birthday today. Oh, and one more thing; you want your son to have friends like Rob.”* I couldn’t resist throwing in that last part. If I was going to pay the price for this, I needed to have a little takeaway for myself.

“Are you okay, Dad?” Kevin asked.

“I’m alright. I just remembered some things I have to get done this afternoon.”

*“How’s he responding?”* I heard Kevin ask.

*“He’s doing well, but this just seems wrong.”*

*“Just stay focused. We can worry about ethics later.”*

“It was nice to meet you, Robert,” Kevin’s dad said as he stood to shake my hand and immediately walked toward the kitchen. The effects hit me as if someone just dropped a truck on my head. I started to get dizzy and fell sideways onto the sofa piled with magazines and empty potato chip bags.

“Are you okay?” Kevin whispered as I held my head. I could see and hear Kevin, but it was as if he were in a dark, blurry, muffled tunnel.

“I don’t think so,” I mumbled, sounding like I was talking into a tin can. I knew what was coming next when a red door slammed shut behind me in Kevin's father’s mind.

I was frantically trying to do CPR on a boy who was the same age as me. Blood-tinged vomit was oozing from the lifeless boy’s mouth as I leaned down to give him two breaths. I could taste vomit in my mouth and gagged a few times as I start back in on compressions. Tears were streaming down my face and were now pooling on the bare chest of the boy. Just as I got ready to give another breath, first responders came crashing through the door of the tool shed with their medical equipment. I become hysterical, screaming for them to help me. The first responder calmly asked me to continue compressions as he removed a heavy-duty, yellow extension cord from around the boy's neck. Another first responder took over chest compressions as I stepped back, looking at the horrific scene. "Don't you die on me, Eric!" I screamed at him. "Please don't die," I begged.

"Rob, can you hear me?" Kevin asked as he shook both of my shoulders with a lot of force.

"Oh... okay… I ah… I had a," I stammered without making any sense.

"Rob, what happened? Do you want me to go get my dad?"

"No!" I said with too much fear in my voice. "Don't do that. Please don't do that. Is there somewhere we can go to talk?" I asked calmly. I could still literally taste Eric's vomit in my mouth, so I reached up to check for the residual with the back of my hand. There wasn't any blood or vomit, just my own tears that had leaked down my face. I checked my knees to see if they were wet after kneeling in Eric's body fluids, but they were dry. This is a ridiculous thought process. It wasn't real, it wasn't real, it wasn't real, I kept trying to tell myself.

"Come on, let's go up to my room," Kevin said as he helped me up. Kevin still had a hold of my arm as we made our way toward the stairway until he stopped to reach into his pocket and pulled out his dad's keys. After dropping the keys into a basket that sat by their landline phone, I followed Kevin like a puppy dog up to his room. I couldn't help but watch his muscles flex as he took each step. Wait, what? Did people still use landlines?

"Now tell me, what the hell is going on?" Kevin said, closing his door behind him. I just stood in his spotless bedroom, dazed, waiting for my mind to clear. "What happened down there?" Kevin asked as if I couldn't comprehend what he had asked the first time.

"Just after I finished rewiring your dad's mind, I... a... I saw a traumatic memory of his. It flooded my brain; I couldn't seem to stop it," I tried to explain as I started to get dizzy again.

"Come over here; you need to lie down," Kevin said with concern in his voice. "Here you go," Kevin said, handing me a tissue for my tears before I laid on his bed.

"I think I'm starting to feel better," I told Kevin when I opened my eyes. "You said you saw some of my dad's memories?"

"Yeah, it was horrible. It was more than just seeing it. I felt like I took your dad's place in the memory," I explained as Kevin climbed over the top of me and laid down beside me on his queen-size bed.

Kevin sat back up when we heard the front door close. "Oh, shit!" Kevin said as he looked out his bedroom window when his dad's truck started.

"There he goes," Kevin said before lying back down beside me. "Oh well, so much for trying to get him to stop drinking. He's probably on his way to buy more alcohol, Kevin said before exhaling loudly. "What did you see in my dad's memory? Or don't you want to talk about it?" Kevin asked with a soft, kind tone.

"Do you know anything about your dad's adolescent years? You know, like around fifteen or sixteen, maybe?"

"Not much; he doesn't like to share anything about that time in his life."

"And with good reason, he went through some bad shit. Has he ever mentioned anything about Eric?"

"I don't know any, Eric, except for Eric Randolph at school."

"Well, the vision I saw was me in your dad's body doing CPR on his friend Eric after the friend had hung himself with an extension cord. I assume Eric was a close friend who he found hanging in a shed. It was one of the most disturbing things I've ever experienced."

"I'm sorry you had to see all of that. Why do you think it happened? I mean, why did his memories leak over to you?" Kevin asked as he draped his arm over my chest.

"I'm not sure, but it happened with Kipton too."

"Who's Kipton?" Kevin asked as he laid his head on my chest, not more than three inches from my face. I could hardly concentrate enough to answer his question about who Kipton was. Kevin's closeness and the smell of his hair were sending me into a frenzy.

"Kipton was the Secret Service Agent whose mind I manipulated on Saturday," I told Kevin barely, able to open my mouth without allowing leakage.

"That's some crazy shit, dude," he said without lifting his head from my chest. I could feel the vibration in Kevin's jaw when he talked, and he was causing my whole body to heat up.

"There will be a price to pay every time I try to change someone's brain. But I know one thing for sure. I don't want to ever try anything like that again."

"What did you tell my dad?" I rehearsed my response for a second to get my story straight. There were a few things I needed to leave out.

"To stop drinking, to go to AA tomorrow, find a counselor, and to find a new job." I list off on four fingers, leaving the fifth in place.

"Thanks, man; I really owe you for trying."

"You don't owe me anything; that's what friends do for friends." I could feel Kevin's face muscles tighten on my chest when he smiled. *You hugging me is payment enough,* I sent Kevin through a green corridor.

"Are you feeling better now?" he asked.

"Yeah, I'm doing fine."

"Do you feel well enough to play a game, or do you wanna go home?" he asked as he let go of me and rolled onto his back. Are you insane? I'm on the bed that belongs to the hottest boy in our school, I thought to myself.

"I won't have to be home for a couple of hours. I wouldn't mind playing with you," I told Kevin, trying to make a joke without being too obvious. Kevin jumped up off his bed to turn on his TV, obviously not getting the non-explicit fantasy request.

"I'd be happy to kick your ass in Halo," Kevin said, warning me of his superiority.

"Don't be so confident in yourself. These games don't take any athletic ability. I just might kick your ass," I told Kevin with a smirk.

After Kevin beat me two out of three games, I stood to stretch my legs. Damn, it was already time to leave. "I gotta get going," I told him as I shoved my phone back into my pocket. "I think your dad is cooking dinner. It smells delicious. Why do you look so surprised?" I asked with confusion.

"My dad hasn't cooked anything in this house since I was five," he answered with a concerned expression.

"Should we check it out?" I asked. I was anxious to see if Kevin's dad was drinking alcohol or if the mind-altering efforts worked.

"I'm almost afraid to check," Kevin said.

I couldn't believe my eyes when I saw Kevin's dad cooking in the spotless kitchen that was almost uninhabitable before we went upstairs. There was a store-bought birthday cake on the island with fifteen candles stuck in the top. "Happy birthday, Kev." Mr. Larsen said, turning toward us. Kevin's eyes were as big as car tires.

"Thanks, Dad, this is awesome," he answered with a guarded tone.

"Robert, would you like to stay for Kevin's birthday dinner? I'm afraid it won't be as good as Kevin's mother's dinner, but I thought we'd give it a try," Mr. Larsen said. Kevin appeared to be struggling with his emotions.

"Sure, I'd love to stay for dinner, Sir."

"Sounds good," Kevin's dad said as he turned his attention to the food on the stove.

*"Are you okay?"* I sent Kevin.

*"Follow me,"* Kevin sent back as he turned to walk toward the hallway. He abruptly stopped, turned toward me before throwing his arm around me, and hugging me so tight that I couldn't breathe. "Thank you!" he said.

"You're welcome?" I answered, pulling my phone from my pocket. "I better let Gary know I'll be staying later than planned."

"I'll go tell him," Kevin said as he ran out the door. I checked my phone, and there was a text from my mom:

How are you feeling, honey?

I'm fine. Having fun at Kevin's birthday party.

Very well. Don't stay too late. My mom text back immediately.

The dinner was fantastic. I never knew chili dogs and tater tots could taste so good. Mr. Larsen even had 'Happy 15th Kev' written on top of the cake. It looked like 'Birthday' wouldn't fit. When we sang happy birthday to Kevin, he couldn't stop smiling.

"Here you go," Kevin's dad said, handing him a gift bag. There were gift certificates to the movies and a restaurant called 'On the Border.'

*"You want to go get some food tomorrow night?"* I blushed bright red.

*"Sure, I'd love to."* I sent back as Mr. Larsen looked up from his half-eaten cake, apparently noticing my red face.

"Thanks, Dad, this is a great gift," Kevin said.

"You're welcome. I thought maybe you could ask a young lady out on a date," he said with a wink.

"I'm taking my friend," Kevin said with a grin as he looked at me. Mr. Larsen glanced at me and then back at Kevin.

“You can take whomever you wish; it’s your gift,” Mr. Larson said.

“Come on, I want to show you something,” Kevin said, leading me into their spacious attached garage. “There she is,” he said enthusiastically, pointing at a green Subaru Forester.

“Who’s she?”

“That’s my car. Well, it was my mom’s, but my dad said it would be mine as soon as I get my license next year.”

“Wow, it’s really nice.”

“Go ahead and get in,” he said with excitement while running around to the other side of the car before sliding into the driver's seat. “So, what do you think?” he asked as he pretended to be driving. He didn’t want to know what I was thinking. It had something to do with me leaning over to kiss him.

“I can’t wait to go for a ride,” I said with intensity in my tone.

“Hey, I’ve been wondering.” Oh good. Maybe he wants to tell me how he really feels about me, and then we would kiss.

“Yeah?” I asked without taking the time to read him.

“I was wondering if you could move a car.”

“A what?”

“You know, with telekinesis? I saw you move your lamp yesterday, maybe you could move the car. Come on, let’s give it a try,” he said, opening his door and jumping out.

“Umm… sure, I guess.” I held my hand out near the back of Kevin’s car. It was as if my brain were waiting for a command as I concentrated, so I gave it; the whole rear of his car slid over about four feet. Thankfully, no one had taken notice of the squawking noise that the tires made.

“Holy shit!” Kevin said, jumping up and down as if he didn’t know what to do with his energy. “Is it harder to do with a larger object?”

“No, but I have a hard time controlling how far something moves. I only expected it to move one foot; it moved a lot further.” The car was crooked now, so I was anxious to move it back before Kevin’s dad came out to check on us. I studied the projected movement necessary to move the car back to its original position before looking at the rear tires and gave the command. The car slid back to its original parking spot with minimal effort.

"Hey, wait!" Kevin said with excitement. "If you can move a car, you should be able to lift your own body! My car weighs more than two thousand pounds, and you're like what? A buck and a quarter?"

"What do you mean?" I asked, looking at him with a tilted head, mimicking a curious puppy.

"If you put your hands down like this." He pointed his palms toward the ground. "It seems like you'd be able to lift yourself off the ground. You know, like the way Iron Man does."

"I don't know; I'm kinda worried that I'll go too high and fall. I fly in my dreams, but I usually just kinda hover."

"I'll hold onto your waist to keep you steady in case you start to crash." I gave Kevin a worried look. "I'll catch you if you start to fall," he promised.

I did just as Kevin instructed. Pointing my hands down and… Damn! We had lift-off, but my head was only a foot from the twelve-foot ceiling. I had taken Kevin up with me. His feet were dangling at least two-foot off the floor as he held onto my waist for dear life.

"Dude, you're doing it!" Kevin yelled with excitement.

"What now?" I yelled as if he couldn't hear me.

"Just let us down slowly." I did my best to let us down as he recommended, but suddenly, we fell, crashing into a trash can. We were both sitting on the concrete floor, laughing our asses off. "Yes!" Kevin yelled out as he helped me up to my feet. He wrapped his arms around me, pulling me tight into his warm, firm body.

I'd like to tell Kevin how I felt when he hugged me, but I didn't want to scare him off. I got these butterflies in my stomach every time he touched me. I was afraid our friendship had become a one-sided romance.

"You okay? You're staring into space," Kevin asked.

"Yeah, I'm fine. I was trying to figure out how all of this could be happening to me. It's really messed up."

"I'm not sure, but it's the coolest thing I've ever seen!" he said as he tipped the garbage can back on its wheels.

"Kevin, what was that big crash?" His dad asked, after opening the door only far enough to poke his head through.

"We were just messing around, and the trash tipped," Kevin said, telling him the absolute truth.

"A man named Gary is at the front door asking for Robert."

Mom was waiting for me when I walked into the kitchen after I arrived home. It was like I couldn't get enough food in my stomach, so I needed a snack before going to bed. She must have noticed the big grin I had pasted on my face.

"Did you have fun?" my mom asked. I just shook my head, yes. "Mr. Smit called me just as I was leaving school this afternoon. He told me you, and he had some confrontation. Do you want to tell me what happened?"

"Not really; I think he and I can work it out on our own."

"Okay… I also received a call from Ms. Hukins, who is apparently the drama teacher. Would you care to tell me about the conversation you had with her?"

"Apparently, one of the lead kids in the spring play was injured last weekend, so they asked me to play his part. I told Ms. Hukins; I'd have to run it by you."

"Oh, that's exciting. You can be in the play if you wish."

"I ah... I wanted to apologize for giving you so much trouble over the last six months," I told her as I stood in front of the open refrigerator gazing in, hoping to find some food, and settling for some cold pizza.

"You've been under a great deal of pressure over the last few months; I know it hasn't been easy with your Father being gone," my mom said.

"It hasn't been easy for any of us, Mom. And somehow, you've been holding the family together." When she stepped toward me to give me a hug, a piece of pepperoni fell to the floor, allowing Petey to scarf it up. I put my finger up to my lips, telling Petty not to tattle or it will never happen again.

"How did it go at Kevin's party tonight?"

"It was a lot of fun."

"And your relationship with Kevin?" I squinted one eye closed. She was totally convinced I was going to tell her that I was gay. But nope, not gonna happen yet. After the Dad catastrophe, I was gun shy. "Is Kevin your boyfriend?" Wow! I didn't even have to tell her. Then again, she never wastes time beating around the bush on anything.

"Yes, Kevin is a boy, and he's my friend, but he's not interested in me that way."

"Well, you two would make a cute couple," she said as she tried to mess up my already messed-up hair.

"Thanks, but don't you think he's a little out of my league?"

"Absolutely not."

"Did Dad tell you what happened last weekend?"

"Yes, he's still trying to deal with what you told him, but don't worry, he'll come around. He just needs some time to process everything."

"I'm not so sure. You weren't there when I told Dad. At one point during our conversation, I thought he might vomit." She kind of half-smiled as she put her hand over her mouth to hide her amusement.

"I'm sorry, it's not funny," Mom said. "The way you described your Father's reaction is... It's almost as if I were there to see his face." She sounded as if she may be enjoying the fact that her husband was on edge.

I smiled and said, "Thank you for being so cool about all of this."

"You don't have to thank me, you're my son, and I love you," she said. "Just between you and me, I think Kevin likes you," my mom whispered.

"How can you tell?"

"I saw the way he was looking into your eyes yesterday." I scrunch up my face. "What's the matter? she asked. My mom had obviously noticed Kevin and me communicating telepathically; that was what she was referring to.

"Erm... It's just kinda awkward having this conversation with my mom," I tried to explain. "Kevin asked me to go to a movie and get some food tomorrow after he gets done with track practice."

"On a school night?" she asked with surprise.

"Yeah, we would be home early," I begged. I'd get down on my knees if I thought it would help.

"I don't know."

"Please, I've never been asked to do anything like this with a friend before."

"I guess it would be all right. If you're driven by Gary."

"Okay, it's a deal," I said in agreement as I hugged her.

"Really, a hug? Who are you, and where did you hide my son's body?" she asked with a warm smile.

"Did you know? I mean… about me being gay?"

"Mothers always know."

"Why didn't you tell Dad?" Here, it comes. I would find out if she withheld the truth from her own husband to protect her son. I've read that some mammals will kill anything or anyone to protect their offspring. Even the father of her child if necessary.

"It's not my place to out anyone, especially my own son. That would be for you to do in your own time, but I'm going to tell you the same thing I told Sam when he had his first girlfriend come over to the house. Your door must always remain open when you're in there with another boy." I didn't have the heart to tell her what Sam and his girlfriend were doing in the pool last week. They weren't wearing bathing suits, and they were close enough to be connected. If you know what I mean.

"Sounds like a rule I can live with." She didn't mention any of the other thirty places I could hide to make out with another boy in this monstrosity.

"Okay, you better get off to bed." I smirked as usual when she told me to 'get off.' "Oh, and there's a gift on your bed that came in the mail for you today."

"Thanks, Mom. Love you."

*"Good news. My mom gave me the thumbs up for tomorrow afternoon."*

*"Okay. Great! I'm dead tired,"* Kevin said with a sleepy thought.

*"Night, man."*

*"Night."*

I felt the corners of my mouth turn up when I remove the wrapped gift I took from the flat fee, priority-mailbox Grandma had sent me from Florida. It was a Shawn Mendes Illuminate CD. She was so cute, thinking that I still listened to CDs. She didn't get the memo about streaming yet, but it was the thought that counted. My grandma lived on a tight budget and had taken the time to drive somewhere to buy the gift. I don't think she'd ever order anything from Amazon. She snail-mailed it from Florida, probably costing more than the CD itself.

Before I plugged my phone into the charger, I checked for a new text message from the restricted number. I was disappointed to find none. My curiosity inspired me to send a return text:

Come on, who are you???

I'm your secret admirer. The text said, showing up immediately.

Haha, right... How about a clue? B or G?

Boy, lol... I'll text you again soon, Robert, I have to go.

Goodbye, restricted number, secret admirer.

As I laid in my bed, clutching my dog tags, I started to think about everything that had happened today. I was overwhelmed, but I didn't feel anxious like I usually did. It was nice to finally come clean with my mom about what gender I was sexually attracted to. She was cool with everything, even about the crush I had on Kevin. Damn, it was already 11:45; I gotta get some sleep.

*****

I don't know how Kevin and I ended up out here, but we were standing at a steep ledge on top of a sand dune overlooking Lake Michigan.

"Isn't it beautiful out here?" I asked Kevin.

"Beautiful," he said as he started to tie a yellow extension cord around his neck.

"No, don't do that, Kevin!" I said frantically as I tried to remove it. The other end was tied off to a tree limb about thirty feet up.

"Why not? You think it's okay to end your life. Why can't I?"

"Because I love you," I plead as I pulled him away from the edge.

"Why should that matter? It didn't matter to you when you tried to take your life."

*****

When I woke up, I was hyperventilating and drenched in sweat. I looked at my phone, and it was 03:33. I wished I didn't have to remember that one.

# Resolution Chapter 9

Tuesday, May 23rd Resolution

Mr. Smit was standing at the school's main entrance, waiting for me when we arrived.

"Good morning, Robert," Mr. Smit said with a worried expression as I approached.

"Good morning, Mr. Smit; how are you?" I asked, pretending nothing had happened yesterday. He was wondering if he should apologize after grabbing my arm. *You didn't hurt me physically;* I sent Mr. Smit after entering his green corridor. I left the part out about scarring me emotionally. Come on, cut the drama, I told myself.

"I was wondering if you have a few minutes to talk before first-hour?" Mr. Smit asked.

"Sure. Where?"

"In my classroom?" Mr. Smit suggested, looking at Gary for approval. Gary gave the nod, but his expression had some evidence of concern. Mr. Smit closed the classroom door behind him, leaving Gary in the hall looking through the window.

"Robert, I'd like to discuss what happened yesterday afternoon." Yeah, I bet you would. I'm sure you're interested in finding out how I knew.

"Yeah, I agree," I said instead. "We need to get the cards out on the table," I continued, hoping Mr. Smit would be willing to reveal his first.

"Do you want to show your cards first?" he asked, sitting down on a stool near where I usually sat.

"Not really," I said, shaking my head.

"I'll go first then," he said with a shaky voice. "Why did you get so upset with me yesterday?"

“I think you already know the answer to that question. Why are you hiding your Kings?” Mr. Smit knew that I knew, but I wanted him to admit what he did first. It was the only way he would regain my trust.

“I’m sorry. I had to share some information you had entrusted me with. I was required to tell a school counselor about the discussions we’ve been having.”

“Why?” I was trying to control the anger that began creeping back in.

“Are you?...,” Mr. Smit started to ask before trailing off, apparently deciding not to answer my question. “You seem different than you did just two weeks ago.”

“I’m fine, Sir.” I use the noun Sir rather than his name to show how our relationship had deteriorated since yesterday when I found out he couldn’t be trusted.

“Robert, I feel like we’ve developed a special bond. I can’t stand the thought of anything happening to you.”

“You mean like me killing myself?” I bluntly said, trying to use the shock factor. I wasn’t making this any easier for him than I had to. Yup, he was shocked. I could see it in his face. “What enticed you to help me in the first place? Apparently, no one else saw what you were seeing?”

The room was silent for several seconds before Mr. Smit responded. “When I was fourteen, my best friend Greg decided suicide was his only way out of the pain and rejection he experienced. So, rather than learning to cope, he chose to end his life.” Mr. Smit took a pause before continuing. “Greg’s sexual orientation wasn’t compatible with his parent’s beliefs. He swam out into Lake Michigan and drowned to make it look like an accident. I found his suicide note in my history book three days after he went missing. It was the same day they recovered his body.”

“I’m sorry,” I said softly.

“Greg’s death really messed me up. I became depressed after he was gone; no one could reach me, not even my parents. I considered suicide as well,” he said as he choked up a bit. Mr. Smit’s eyes were shiny as he tried to fight back the tears. “The horrific memories still come back to visit me at times.” I sat quietly as Mr.Smit collected himself.

“When I approached you back in January, I wasn’t sure what you had going on. You had returned from the holiday break with a fresh scar on your wrist. After meeting with you for a few weeks, I could tell you were doing better, so I decided not to tell anyone. I thought I was doing the right thing, but…"

"But what?" I asked, pushing him to continue.

"Someone here at the school started questioning me about why you and I were spending one-on-one time together. I was instructed to stop counseling you because I didn't have the proper credentials. I argued that I was only a mentor." I agreed. If it weren't for my person mentoring me, I doubted Kevin or Cam would be in the picture.

"I didn't know mentoring a student was against the rules," I said, trying to understand the school's stance on the issue.

"It's not against the rules if I have your parent's permission, but I didn't have that did I? They told me I should have encouraged you to seek professional treatment as well," he said with a sad expression as if he had failed me. "I can't bear losing you, Robert. Guilt is a powerful emotion; I've always thought that I could have done more to prevent Greg's death." I was starting to feel some guilt myself for the way I treated Mr. Smit yesterday.

"You saved my life," I told Mr. Smit bluntly. "I felt like there was no hope of things ever getting better for me. Even after my first attempt failed, things weren't improving until you became my person." Mr. Smit gave me a weak smile. "You pulled me into your circle and treated me like I was someone special. You introduced me to 'It Gets Better' and 'The Trevor Project' websites."

I needed to find out who turned Mr. Smit into the school administration, so I entered his gray corridor and found a blue door unlocked. The video showed Mr. Burns complaining to the Principal as Mr. Smit tried to defend his own actions. That jerk was going down.

*Mr. Smit, Greg's death was not your fault,* I planted in his green corridor. "Thank you for saving my life," I said before standing to leave. He smiled and tried to brush a tear from his cheek without me noticing.

Gary seemed relieved when I left Mr. Smit's room. He thought he'd be free to get his coffee, but I didn't go to first-hour; I headed straight for the counselor's office. Again, I was astounded by my newfound courage. Two weeks ago, I would've stuck my head in a hole, hoping no one would notice me. I believed that my confidence had grown two sizes over the past week.

"Hello, Mrs. Miller; I was wondering if Mr. Burns has any openings today." Mrs. Miller was a wonderful lady in her mid-fifties who had long blonde hair and a thin face. She always wore bright red lipstick and dark eyeliner.

"Ah... let me see here," she said as she clicked on her keyboard, studying her side-by-side monitors. "He has an eleven-fifteen if that works for you?"

"Okay, thank you, eleven-fifteen will work just fine," I told her with a bright smile.

"Your name?" She asked without looking up.

"Robert Van Stark." She snapped her head up and looked at me with surprise.

"Robert, you're a freshman. Am I correct?"

"Yes, Ma'am?"

"Well, Mr. Burns only counsels' seniors. I could make you an appointment with your freshman counselor." I figured there may be a snag, so I was prepared to use whatever means necessary to get my way on this one. If she didn't make the appointment for me, I would just have to insist.

"No, this is a personal matter. I'll need to speak directly with Mr. Burns."

"Okay, you're all set for an eleven fifteen with Mr. Burns. Will you need a pass for first-hour?"

"Yes, please," I answered with a forced smile.

*"Hey,"* I sent to Kevin.

*"Holy shit, don't barge in when I'm trying to take my history quiz."* I knew he was taking a test, but I couldn't get enough of his attention.

*"Sorry. How's your dad feeling?"*

*"He seemed sick this morning. He was puking in the toilet while I was in the shower."* I had checked out withdrawals online this morning; it said delirium tremens was a severe form of alcohol withdrawal. Today and tomorrow would be Devon's worst two days, but I didn't want to sound like a nerd who researched everything, so I didn't say anything.

*"When did World War 2 start?"* Kevin asked.

*"Erm..., are you asking when it started or when the US entered the war?"*

*"Yes, that."*

*"December seventh, nineteen forty-two,"* I answered.
*"Thanks,"* he said quickly.
*"Is this considered cheating?"* I asked.
*"Maybe a little. What was the end date?"*
*"May seventh, nineteen Forty-Five. See ya at lunch?"*
*"Yup. Thanks for the help,"* he said.

When I walked into Mr. Kave's room late, every head turned; it felt as if fifty-two eyes were watching me. As I handed my slip to Mr. Kave, I heard someone from the back of the room mutter a snide remark, "He was probably having breakfast with the First Boy." I ended up ignoring the rude comment, even though I wanted to find out who said it so I could confront them.

We were instructed to work with our teams again today. I loved David's voice. It was thick and raspy when he spoke. "Okay, I have this figured out," David said, just as I heard a knock at the door.

"It's for you, Robert," Mr. Kave announced. "Ms. Hukins is asking for you."

Ms. Hukins was wearing a dress with large pastel-colored flowers that screamed, I'm a hippie from the sixties. I wasn't sure what perfume she was wearing, but she smelled good. *Please say yes. Please say yes,* I heard her think.

"Have you had enough time to make your decision about the play?" Ms. Hukins asked with a twinkle in her eyes.

"Yes, and yes."

"You'll do it?" she asked with excitement as she jumped up and down, clapping her hands.

"Yes."

"Brilliant," she responded, rubbing her hands together, like let's get down to business. "I'll send a manuscript to your tablet within the hour."

"Thank you," I told her, hoping I wouldn't regret my decision.

"I'll see you at rehearsal today at two. I've arranged for you to skip your sixth-hour science class. Mr. Smit will have your homework ready for you." She must have been confident my decision would be in her favor.

"Sounds good, as long as I can leave at four; I'm going out for some food and a movie at four fifteen."

“Oh… you are, are you?” Ms. Hukins said in a lovey-dovey voice. “All right, friend, I’ll see you at two.” Friend?

“Well? What did you tell her, Robert?” David asked as I sat down with our small group.

“Erm, I said yes. By the way, you can call me Rob.” David’s gray corridor was flooding with excitement. *I love it! We’ll have more time to get to know each other,”* I heard David think. I couldn’t agree more. I thought I was starting to develop a bit of a crush on him.

The food at lunch today actually looked edible and much less terrible than usual.

*“You good, man?”* I sent Kevin as I sat down at our table.

*“Yeah. I’m just a little concerned about my dad; he isn’t answering his text.”*

“Hey, are you two planning on joining our conversation?” Zach asked.

“What do you mean by that?” Kevin snapped back.

“You’re both sitting there staring off into space,” he said, looking at both of us as if we were lost. Truthfully, we were lost in our own conversation. I gave Zach a shrug but didn’t bother answering.

“It’s fine, guys,” Cam said with a roll of his eyes. “Zach and I were just dissing you both while you were in another world.” Well said, Cam. If you only knew what the fifth dimension we were in.

“Time to come clean, guys; what do you two have going on?” Zach blurted out with frustration in his tone. Shit, he was thinking Kevin and I had a thing going. Zach was calling us out, and it was painfully clear what he was thinking.

“What do you mean?” Kevin asked Zach.

“This is like the third time I’ve caught you two staring out into space while the rest of us are carrying on a conversation. Just tell me what’s going on,” Zach demanded as he slammed both hands on the table.

*“Let me handle this,”* I sent Kevin.

*“Be careful!”*

“Okay, guys, you want us to come clean? Here it is. I can talk to people through telepathy. You caught me talking to Kevin just now. Obviously, you guys couldn’t hear me,” I explained with a sincere expression.

*“What are you doing?”* Kevin asked with concern in his thought.

*“Trust me. I can handle this.”*

*"Bruh, I don't think this is the best approach."*

"So, that's what's going on," I said before taking a quick swig of Gatorade and continuing. Zach and Cam were both staring at me with their mouths hanging open. "I can also read your mind and emotions. I'm kinda new at moving objects telekinetically, but I'm getting better. Oh, by the way, I can fly." They still weren't responding, so I continued to pile it on. "I think there's a strong possibility I'm developing superpowers." They both looked at Kevin for confirmation, so he shook his head, yes, in agreement with a stern expression. First, Zach started to laugh hysterically, and then we all joined in until our faces were red. "Yesterday, I picked up a car!" I said, continuing the assault.

"Just stop; my gut hurts," Zach said between his cute high-pitched wheezes that he made when he laughed. I couldn't believe how much fun it was to have friends.

*"Well done!"* Kevin sent.

"Hello, Master Van Stark, he hasn't returned from lunch yet, but you're welcome to wait right over there if you wish," Mrs. Miller said, pointing at an ugly orange sofa by the wall. Did she just refer to me as Master Van Stark? What would she call me if my last name were Bates?

I sat down on the smelly oversized sofa and pulled my phone out to see if anyone had tried to reach me. There was a new text from the restricted number:

Good morning Robert!

Hey RSA… is all I wrote back.

I didn't know who the author was, so I was exercising some caution. But it was kind of exhilarating and risky to have a boy texting me.

RSA?

Restricted Secret Admirer (RSA). Gotta go... I sent back when I saw a tall guy with perfect brown hair walk past us. His stride and arrogant expression set me off immediately, and he hadn't even opened his mouth yet.

Mr. Burns took a note from Mrs. Miller, read it, and looked in my direction. *What a tool,* I heard Gary think. I couldn't keep the corners of my mouth from creeping upward.

"Robert, you can come with me," Mr. Burns said with an uncaring tone as he walked along, slurping his energy drink. *I know what this kid wants. He'll be getting nothing. I don't have time for this bullshit; I have five kids to see before I can leave for my three o'clock appointment.* I could read his concern about some uncomfortable hemorrhoids. Was he serious? *Eat more fiber and drink more water, dumbass,* I sent him through a green corridor.

"Go ahead and have a seat. What can I help you with?" Mr. Burns asked, pointing at a chair that was held together with duct tape. I carefully ease my one hundred thirty-five pounds onto the poor chair, hoping it wouldn't topple under my weight.

"I'm here to talk to you about Mr. Smit."

"Why, what has he done to you?" *It's what you've done to him, you stupid twit,* I sent after slipping into his green corridor.

"Mr. Smit has been helping me, but I believe he has been unfairly accused."

"Accused of what?" he retorted with a superior expression before taking another swig of his energy drink and then leaning way back in his office chair. "What's this about, Robert?" he asked impatiently with the same kind of tone he might use to say; You're a dumbass kid, in every respect of the meaning.

"I'll just get to the point; you're obviously on a tight schedule today. As you're already aware, Mr. Smit has been mentoring me to help me get through some personal issues..."

"I'm sorry to interrupt, but I'm not at liberty to discuss any of this with you, Robert." I looked at him with surprise. If this Neanderthal had an ounce of common sense, he would stop interrupting me and listen to what I had to say.

"I mean no disrespect, Sir, but this is affecting the relationship between Mr. Smit and me; therefore, I believe I have a vested interest in the matter." Mr. Burns looked at me with a fake smile. *I've got to get this kid out of my office; he's starting to give me a headache.*

*You have no idea what a headache really feels like until I've given you one;* I sent him, hoping he would take it as a warning shot across the bow.

"I'm going to have to ask you to leave," he told me. I was getting angrier by the second, and even though I knew how important it was to control my temper, an involuntary reaction took over, causing a gunshot to go off in my brain. Mr. Burns's energy drink took off like a rocket, dumping bright red, sticky liquid on his desk and covering the crotch of his khakis. Oh man, that was going to leave a stain. The popping sound was exactly like the incident I had in first-hour yesterday. Anger and fear are strong emotions; they're both capable of causing devastation.

*Shit!* Mr. Burns thought in his mind as he grabbed some tissues off his desk, attempting to soak up the mess.

*"You okay? I heard a gunshot go off in my brain."* Kevin said. Damn, it leaked again.

*"I just caused an energy drink to spill on Mr. Burns's crotch."*

*"No way, that's awesome!"*

*"I don't think Mr. Burns thinks it's awesome."* Mr. Burns was taking a deep breath as if he were trying to get his anger under control while throwing wet, red-tinged tissues in the trash.

*"Get your ass down here; we're starting with the shot put today,"* Kevin said with excitement. Shot put? That sounds fun.

*"Okay, I'll hurry. Wait! I can't throw."*

*"Just get down here; I'll teach you."* Suddenly, the room grew dark; I was unable to see anything in Mr. Burns's office. Instead, I was experiencing a vision of Kevin standing close behind me as we lightly touched. He was instructing me on the proper shot-put form.

I was snapped out of my daydream when Mr. Burns asked why I was still in his office.

"I'm sorry, Sir, but I'm not going anywhere until we have a resolution to the problem you've created." The hell with it; we weren't getting anywhere by just talking.

As I pushed myself out of the chair, I almost cause the armrest to detach. I turn toward Mr. Burns, found his red passage, and... *"Listen up, you pompous, arrogant ass. You're going to personally apologize to Mr. Smit today before you leave for your doctor's appointment. You will confront the principal and tell him you've overreacted about this whole incident."* I started to leave his office and thought of something else he could do. *Tomorrow morning you'll bring flowers for Mr. Smit to show your appreciation for all he does for the students here in this school,"*

I was almost to Gary when it hit me. I was being forced back into Mr. Burns's red corridor. I entered the brain of a five or six-year-old Mr. Burns sitting up in a hospital emergency room bed. I was terrified as I struggle to pull each breath into my lungs. I couldn't make any words to tell the doctor that I was unable to inhale. A frantic woman who looked as if she could be my mother walked through the door, asking the doctor why my skin color was dusky. The doctor explained that I was having an asthma attack. If my condition didn't improve soon, I would need a breathing tube placed in my airway.

"Robert, can you hear me?" I barely heard Gary asking while he shook my shoulder. Damn it, I was lying on the floor just outside of Mr. Burns's office.

"I'm fine," I tried to answer.

"What happened? Are you sick?" Gary asked.

"I must've stood up too fast. I got kinda dizzy, so I just sat down."

"No, you fell face first. If I hadn't been playing catch, you would've face-planted. We need to get you to the emergency room," Gary said as he took his cell from his pocket.

"Please don't call; I'll be fine," I plead with Gary. Too late, he was already on his phone, talking to my mom.

"No, Suzanne, he's requesting I not take him to the hospital. Just a minute," Gary said as he handed me his phone. "Robert, your mother wants to speak with you." There were now three people hovering over me, including the tall, blonde resource officer.

"Hello, Mom."

"Robert. What's going on? Gary said that you passed out," she said calmly.

"No, I didn't. I just got dizzy when I stood up too fast. I'll be fine," I attempted to explain as Gary gave me an exaggerated eye roll.

"I'm not sure, Robert; I think you should get rechecked," Mom countered.

"Please, Mom, Gary will stay with me. If it happens again, I promise to have Gary take me in." Have I ever mentioned how manipulative I could be?

"All right, let me talk to Gary."

"Here he is," I told her as I handed the phone back to Gary. When I stood to leave, I still felt some after-effect. Note to Rob, stop messing with people's minds.

When I finally made it out to the track field, I found Kevin and Zach standing by the shot-put area.

"How'd it go with Burns?" Kevin asked as I came running up.

"Fine."

"What did you have to see him about? Isn't he a senior advisor?" Zach asked.

"He was mean to Mr. Smit, so I had to straighten him out."

"How did you do that? You can't even straighten yourself out," Zach teased.

"I can be persuasive," I told Zach, ignoring the fact that he may have been referring to me as not straight.

"Just throw the damn shot put so we can move on to high jump," Zach said.

"Holy shit! This thing is heavy; it's gotta weigh twenty pounds," I said while picking up the big metal ball.

"Dude, it's like twelve pounds, just throw the damn thing," Zach said as if he were becoming impatient.

"Can someone show me how to do it first?" I asked. I'd probably dislocate my shoulder if I tried to throw it like a baseball.

"Good God, bruh, do you live in a cave? Let me see that thing," Zach said impatiently while grabbing the ball from my hands and demonstrating a throw. It was actually more of a push than anything.

I ran over to retrieve the heavy steel, held it against my chin like Zach did, and shuffle across the ring. Unfortunately, the heavy ball only flew about three feet before falling to the ground. Zach and Kevin laughed while covering their mouths with their hands. Mildly humiliated, I walked over, pick the damn thing up, and brought it back to try again.

*"Come on, please help me; I'm making myself look like a sissy."*

*"Well, if the shoe fits,"* Kevin sent as he looked at me with a smirk.

"Look," Kevin said as he stepped up behind me precisely as he did in my vision. He pushed softly up against me. The reality was playing out like some deja vu shit. "No, pull your elbow out," he said as he pulled my elbow up, pushing the steel ball into my cheek. His touch was intoxicating, to the point of discomfort. "Okay, now just move faster across the ring and push off with your lead leg," he said as he reached down softly, slapping just below my left ass cheek. I took off across the ring and released the ball as I was instructed.

"Holy shit!" Zach said as he looked at me with surprise. "That was so sick!"

"Ah… What's wrong?" I asked, glancing over at Kevin, who seemed surprised as well.

"Get the tape," Zach said as he pointed over toward Kevin's feet!

"Was it good?" I asked as Zach looked at Kevin.

"Sixty-two feet," Zach announced from the other end.

*"Oh, shit! Did you use your powers?"* Kevin asked.

*"I don't think so. Why?"*

"How far are the seniors on your team throwing," Zach asked?

"I think fifty-one feet," Kevin answered.

*I only threw the steel ball thirty feet,* I sent Zach through his green corridor, hoping it will do the trick. There was no way I would attempt to use his red passage.

"Wow, thirty feet, well done," Zach repeated. "Kevin is right; you're a little sleeper cell. Let's go try the high jump." As we walked over toward the high jump, I filed away another emotion to add to the list of involuntary reactions. Sexual excitement and dick butterflies would cause problems, as well.

The rest of the school day sped by, and I found myself sitting in the media room. "Listen up, everyone," Ms. Hukins announced, "Pair up to work on your lines. Hook, you can work with Peter." Great, Liam was Captain Hook. His cuteness level would make focusing difficult.

"Peter, I guess it's you and me," Liam said with a wink. "Ms. Hukins told me she sent the transcripts to your tablet this morning. Have you had a chance to go over any of it?"

"Yeah, I've been able to memorize the fourth scene where I start, but I still need to work on where other parts fit in." He looked at me as if I were messing with him.

"Really... How far did you get?"

"The fourth scene, like I said."

"That's like twenty pages," he said with disbelief.

"Erm, what's your point?"

"I just… Never mind, let's get started." I couldn't blame Liam for thinking I was dense. I may have come across as a bit of an airhead when we met yesterday.

As we read through the fourth scene, Hook's leg kept bumping into mine under the table until he got the courage to rest it there. At that rate, his hand would be relaxing on my thigh by tomorrow. He moved his leg when Ms. Hukins stopped at our table to check our progress.

"How's it going, boys?" Ms. Hukins asked.

"We're doing great; Robert has a brilliant mind!" Liam said with excitement.

Dinner with Kevin was excellent; the movie was a C- at best, but the popcorn was extraordinary with extra heart attack drizzled on our heavily salted popcorn. The truck was quiet as we were on our way home from the movie; something seemed to be bothering Kevin. *Is everything okay?* I sent Kevin's green corridor.

"So, when you went to Mr. Burns's office today, Cam told Zach and me you were staying over at his house this Friday night," Kevin said with genuine concern in his facial expression.

"Yeah, what about it?" I kind of mumble.

"I don't know; there's just something about the guy I don't trust."

"Like what?"

*"I just get the feeling he's hiding something. Please don't take this the wrong way, but I think Cam is a spy."* I was trying to keep from giggling out loud. I looked over at Kevin with a smirk expecting to see the same, but he wasn't smiling; he was dead serious.

*"Erm... What? A spy?"* I asked, trying to encourage him to explain. Would Kevin say these things about Cam so he could keep me from spending time with him? No, he really believed Cam was a spy.

*"You know, a spy who will try to befriend you to get information from your dad."*

*"That's preposterous!"* was the first thing that came to my mind.

*"Okay, dude, I just have to tell you; that sounded nerdy,"* Kevin said.

*"Yeah, you're right, it was. But I can't imagine someone going to that much trouble to get to my dad."*

*"Your dad is a big deal. Last night I had a weird dream where Cam and some other guy kidnapped you and held you hostage."* I giggled out loud, but this time Gary looked in his mirror at us with suspicion.

The light was on in my mom's office, I could hear tapping on her keyboard, so I tiptoed, hoping to conceal my occupancy of the hallway. "Robert, is that you?" she asked, trying to terminate my escape. I didn't have time to chat. After I was done helping Kevin study, I had an urgent need to attend to.

"Yes?" I answered with dread.

"Can you come in here for a minute, please?" she asked.

"Yes," I said unenthusiastically as I walked into her office and plopped down a chair.

"How was your night out on the town, honey?"

"It was great; we had a lot of fun," I said, standing up so she would recognize my intent to retreat to my room.

"Goodnight, you better get off to bed." Yes. I was thinking the same thing!

After I finished working with Kevin on his history assignment, I laid down on my bed so I could safely close my eyes. Kevin was talking with Zach on the phone about how he did at his game tonight. Kevin was throwing a baseball in the air and catching it each time just before it hit his face. I flinched every time it came close to his face. Their conversation moved to Zach, teasing Kevin about going out on a date with me.

*"You know he's gay, right?"* Zach asked. There was a pause in the conversation before Kevin finally answered.

*"So, who cares if he's gay?"*

*"I'm just saying, I get the feeling he likes you. I mean, really likes you,"* Zach said in a convincing tone.

*"Grow up, Zach; it doesn't matter if he's gay or straight. Rob is my friend, and I'm sure he wouldn't mind being your friend too if you'd stop worrying about who he's attracted to."*

I moved out of Kevin's orange corridor and moved to his yellow so I wouldn't risk having another seizure. After lifting my lamp, I made it hover above my bed as I listen to Kevin. I was feeling more confident with my telekinetic control. I raised my stupid little piggy bank from my dresser and brought it over to where the lamp was hanging.

Kevin's side of the conversation was all I could hear, but they finally moved away from me and started talking about Britney attending Zach's game tonight. I could read some jealousy in Kevin's mind while Zach talked about Britney.

*"Dude, I'm getting tired; I better...,"* Kevin hinted. I had figured out who Kevin was in love with, and it wasn't me. Kevin told me that his attraction to others had nothing to do with gender or sex.

*****

I couldn't believe how free I felt, driving my own car. Kevin was sitting in the passenger seat as we cruised down a gravel road at turtle speed. I heard the gravel crunching under my tires as I pulled into David's driveway, where we found him and Zach playing basketball on a concrete pad near the garage.

"Hey, nice wheels," David said as he approached the driver's side window. "When did you get your license?"

"Yesterday," I said proudly. "Come on, get in, let's go."

"Dude, you're only fifteen," Zach said, leaning on the driver's side window. "How did you get a driver's license? You don't even know how to drive."

"Wait, you're right! I haven't even taken driver's training yet," I admitted.

"He did fine on the way over here," Kevin said.

"I'm not going anywhere with an unlicensed driver. My mom will throw a fit," Zach said as he threw the ball at the hoop. David climbed into the back seat and was running his fingers through my hair.

"I've always wanted hair like this," David said.

"Quit being so gay," Zach told him.

"What's wrong with being gay?" Kevin asked, confronting Zach with clenched fists.

"Come on, guys, don't fight," I told them both as I stepped between them. Kevin threw a punch in Zach's direction. Unfortunately, I became the recipient of friendly fire.

*****

I woke up rubbing my jaw where Kevin's fist had just connected, but I wasn't lying in David's driveway; I was in my own bed. It was 04:45, almost time to get up. Oh well, I got to take a pee anyway.

# Bullies Beware Chapter 10

Wednesday, May 24th Bullies Beware

Before I left the pool this morning, I wanted to practice lifting myself like I did on Monday in Kevin's garage. The water was a much safer place to crash if something went wrong. When I pushed off, I felt myself lift about six inches entirely out of the water. My arms went slack as I felt the energy flowing through my whole body. The feeling of floating in the air was exhilarating, especially when I tipped my head back and closed my eyes. I didn't want the feeling to end. Still, no one needed to witness my abilities, so I knew I would have to finish it soon.

When I opened my eyes, I noticed that my altitude had changed dramatically. I was less than a foot from the ceiling. Slowly, I start my descent, hoping for a controlled landing; unfortunately, the power shut down prematurely, allowing gravity to do its job. My landing wasn't as smooth as I had hoped. After floating back to the surface, I started laughing when I realized what I had just accomplished. "Hell, yes! I can fly!" I yelled out loud.

Gary was in rare form this morning. He must have had a good night's sleep. So it wasn't difficult to talk him into picking up Kevin on the way to school.

*"Hey, man, how are you doing today?"* I sent Kevin.

*"Great! You?"* Kevin answered.

*"Fantastic! I feel like a new person today. Have you left for school yet?"*

*"No, I'm still getting dressed."*

*"Don't get on the bus or ride your bike. I'll have Gary slide by and pick you up. He's in a good mood this morning, so he won't mind."*

When we pulled up in front of Kevin's house, he stood outside with his backpack in hand. As Kevin climbed in, I felt my phone vibrate. I slid it out of my pocket just far enough to see that it was Liam texting me. While Kevin settled into the back seat, I greeted him with an awkward wave. I started to sneak a peek at the text, but suddenly I felt conscious of my cautiousness. Was there a problem with texting Liam when I was with Kevin? I decided not to chance it and slide the phone back into my pocket. I wasn't sure why, but I was hoping it would be a text from RSA.

"How's your dad feeling this morning?" I asked as Kevin buckled his seatbelt.

"He seems to be doing better. What time is play practice tonight?" Kevin asked as Gary sent the truck into reverse.

"Rehearsal is after school, until six. Why?"

"Oh… so it's a rehearsal, is it?" Kevin said in a mocking voice, putting his pinky finger up to the corner of his mouth. "I thought we could hang out after rehearsal," Kevin said with air quotes around rehearsal.

"Sure! Where would you like to go?" I asked, turning farther in my seat to look at him directly.

"Zach has a doubleheader. I thought we could go to his game."

"That sounds fun. I'll check with my mom."

When we arrived at school, I pulled my phone out to see what Liam wanted:

Hey! The text from Liam said.

Hey, Liam, what's up?

I just wanted to say hey.

I stopped walking in the middle of the hall as I stared at the text; someone bumped into me from behind. "Sorry," I mumbled as the disgruntled student glared at me but kept going. Was this how most kids my age communicated? There wasn't much purpose in a text like that, but maybe there didn't have to be.

Okay... Just heading for first-hour

K, C, ya at rehearsal. See, I knew it was a rehearsal.

K cool

The windows were open in first-hour, allowing the smell of the flowering trees and the fresh spring air to flood the classroom. A deep breath made me realize how much I've missed the smell of spring.

I finished up with my assignment early, so I started working on our group project. I picked up my things and plopped down in the empty seat next to David, who had already started working. He was busy writing a project summary but turned briefly to offer a warm smile. I was becoming more aware of David's positive features. I loved the cute faces he made as he tried to figure something out. David and I needed to start hanging out so we could get to know each other better. Maybe even become friends. David sighed deeply while tapping the end of a pencil on his desk, which broke me out of my trance. Something was bothering him; it was time we cut the silence.

*Tell me what's bothering you*; I sent David through his green corridor.

The tapping stopped, "Hey, Rob, could you help me with this summary? I don't remember what we did for the first part."

"Sure, you can check out what I wrote if that helps." I was confused with how David avoided my mental suggestion as he said thanks and started looking over my paper. Suddenly my answer came in a strange form. The room grew dark just as it did in Burns's office yesterday. I soon found myself near David in the hallway. My arrival was in time to see David get shoved by Orin. Orin looked almost twice David's size. David's things went flying, and while trying to gather them, David was kicked by another kid. The kids around David didn't risk stepping in to contest the bullies. When the vision ended, I was back in the classroom; David was still referencing my summary. I was left wondering if what I saw will come true like it did yesterday with Kevin in the shot-put-ring.

I've seen upperclassmen and jocks tormenting other kids throughout the year, especially the kids who act or dress differently or kids who are in undesirable cliques. But other than Orin's hate letters, or an occasional push, I was left alone. Having an older brother probably helped deter some kids from picking on me. Not to mention Gary and Andy's intimidating presence. So, I considered myself one of the lucky ones. I didn't believe our school had a bullying culture as many schools had before the Columbine school massacre back in 1999, but those who say it doesn't exist should walk in David's shoes for a day.

To be sure David stayed safe, I decided to follow him to his next class; besides, I needed to know how all of this vision stuff worked. I waited until David left the classroom before I took up the rear, following him. Sure enough, we were in the sophomore hall. I saw Orin, who was with the other big kid, heading straight for David. I watched in disbelief as it started to play out exactly as I had seen in my vision. Glancing quickly behind me, I saw Gary giving me a look that said, 'What the hell are you doing, Robert?' I never traveled the sophomore hall, so there was no reason for me to be there.

Suddenly just like in my vision, Orin pushed David, his tablet and books went flying. A para-pro was standing at the opposite end of the hall, unaware of any wrongdoing. I bent over to help David pick up his books just as the other kid kicked David in the back. David fell face-first into his pile of books that were still lying on the floor.

"Hey!" I yelled at the grinning jerks. Orin, who never broke his stride, acted as if nothing had happened and didn't turn around to look. He placed his hand inside an open locker just as I heard gunshots go off in my mind. The locker door slammed shut on Orin's hand with the speed and force of a swinging hammer.

What I had seen in my vision was over, but the situation just kept playing out as Orin screamed. The oversized bully yanked his hand out of the locker, holding it and continuing to yell and cuss like it had been cut clean off. It was fitting to see karma catch up to him so soon. A few students stopped to watch Orin dance around as he tried to self-splint with his uninjured hand. The other jerk tried unsuccessfully to leave in Gary's direction.

When the para-pro finally made it over to sort out the commotion, Gary had the second bully by the back of his shirt, calmly explaining the event. David and I were occupied with collecting his things amid the shuffling feet of students. All the while, teary-eyed Orin was still holding his hand, pretending to be the victim. No such luck, idiot.

As soon as we finish gathering everything, David thanked me before disappearing into the crowd. The para-pro carried off Orin and company while Gary gave me the motion to come with him. He didn't look happy.

"What was that all about?" Gary asked.

"David told me the kids have been picking on him, and he was nervous about going to his next class."

"So, you decided on your own to use me as a para-pro."

"No, not at all; I didn't plan on getting involved until I saw everything unfold."

"Did you see who slammed the locker door on the other boy's hand?" Gary asked with a slight smile.

"No, but Orin had it coming; he's been pushing me around all year as well."

"I know he has, and you're right; karma has a way of rearing its ugly head at the most inopportune times," he said with a wink. Good, Gary didn't seem to be too angry. "What's going on with you, Robert? Why are you suddenly getting involved with this kind of confrontation?"

"I don't know; I guess it's just time for some change in my life. I'm not going to lie down and be a victim anymore. I'm not going to stand around watching my friends get bullied, either."

"Well, good for you, but remember, I'm here for you, not David. I can't be involved with distractions like this every day."

"Okay, sorry. I'll try to keep a lid on it," I promised Gary.

The algebra test was simple in third-hour; I finished it within the first ten minutes of class, so I used the rest of the period to work on my lines. I couldn't believe how hungry I was as I headed down to lunch. This is fantastic, I thought to myself when I realized they were serving burgers today! Even though they're usually like eating cardboard, I took three burgers and two orders of fries. My pornographic lunch lady was making eyes at someone, so I checked the front of the line where I saw her gazing at her young lover.

Everyone at our table was in deep conversation when I arrived with a pile of food.

"Hey, guys, what's up?" I asked.

"Did you guys hear what happened in Pod three today?" Zach asked. Cam and I both shook our heads, no. "Orin Smith and Paul Ripley got their asses kicked by some freshman just before second-hour."

"Who was it? I mean, who was the freshman?" Kevin asked after he swallowed his chocolate milk.

"I'm not sure, but apparently, Orin is in the hospital, and Paul got sent home."

"Well, they probably had it coming," I alleged as I finished off my first burger. *"I think I may have broken Orin's hand."*

*"It was you who took those guys out?"* Kevin asked as he turned toward me with surprise written all over his face.

*"The idiots were picking on David, so I think I slammed the locker door on Orin's hand."*

*"You think?"*

*"Just as I looked up at the locker, the door slammed with a tremendous amount of speed and force."*

"Using those special powers again, Rob?" Zach asked as he waved his hand between our faces. Damn it! We forgot again. I looked up at Cam's smirk. "Or maybe you two were just reminiscing about your date last night," Zach teased as Kevin flung his elbow into Zach's side. We needed to get our shit together. Being careless was idiotic, but I loved to look into his blue eyes; besides, I thought it was human nature and socially expected to look at the person you talked to. Still, we needed to be more cognizant of our actions.

"It wasn't a date; we just went out to grab some food and went to a movie. You're just jealous because I didn't ask you to go?" Kevin told Zach.

"I had a game last night, so I couldn't go even if you would have asked," Zach said defensively.

"Knock it off, guys; people are going to think you're having a lover's quarrel," Cam said, trying to defuse the confrontation.

"Anyone want some fries?" I asked as I dump some more ketchup on my tray.

"Did you eat all three of those burgers?" Cam asked me. Zach leaned in and playfully tried to kiss Kevin on his cheek as I shook my head, yes.

"Get out of here, you dick," Kevin said as he pushed Zach away.

"What? I'm just trying to give you a forgiveness kiss. It's okay if you took Rob out on a date and didn't ask me."

"Three's a crowd," Kevin said as he got up to leave.

"Wait up, dude!" Zach said as he tried to catch Kevin. There was trouble in paradise between Kevin and Zach, and the problem was probably me.

"What's up with them?" Cam asked as he grabbed some fries off my tray. I just gave a shrug.

I was heading down to rehearsal after sixth-hour when I got a text from Kevin:

Remember the game tonight???

Haha, right. I couldn't forget even if I tried.

LMAO. I forgot. Isn't that ironic? BTW it seems weird to be texting U…

LOL, this is how normal kids do it… I punched in.

Does that make us both abnormal or just you?

Nope, just me…

*"See you at the game,"* I sent Kevin through a yellow corridor as I approached the media center, where I saw Liam standing at the entrance, talking with David.

"What's up, guys?" I asked nonchalantly.

"David was just filling me in on how you saved him from some jerks today," Liam said.

"Nah, I just helped him pick up his books," I explained as I looked over at David for confirmation.

"Orin's hand is broken," David said.

"What?" I asked with surprise.

"Yeah, I heard that his mom took him to the hospital; he has two broken bones in his hand," David explained.

"Well, the dumbass should watch where he puts his hand then," I said, trying to pretend that I had nothing to do with Orin's injury. But truthfully, my gut was turning inside as I attempted to process the facts. I was, in fact, responsible for injuring another human being. I was feeling some remorse even though Orin was a bully.

Our conversation was cut short when Ms. Hukins came into the room, asking for everyone's attention. She announced that ticket sales were 'meager at best' this year, and she asked us to spread the word. I didn't think she had too much to worry about. I was sure my mom would buy her share and someone else's, hoping that everyone she knew would attend.

After Liam and I got done working on part eight, where Hook and Peter ended up sparring, I saw David looking in my direction again, so I gave him a wave. I wanted to know more about the confrontation he had with Orin and the other kid. What I needed most was to piece together why I had a vision in the first place.

“Hey,” I said as I approach David.

“Hey,” he answered with a lift of his chin and dimples in full display.

“What’s up with Orin? How come he’s been a prick to you?” I asked before sitting down next to David on the steps of a fake ship.

“I’m not sure what Orin’s deal is,” he said with a shrug of his left shoulder. “My mom told me that a kid who bullies other kids has social issues and hasn’t learned to manage their emotions,” David answered as if he was reading from a psychology textbook. “I’ve seen him push you around as well.”

“Yeah, I usually just try to ignore him; other than a few love notes he has slipped into my locker, he leaves me alone. I think he’s figured out that my detail is never too far away.”

“Let me guess,” David said with a chuckle. “Orin has spelling errors in his love notes.” We both started to laugh about Orin’s clumsy, incriminating actions.

“I have a question for you,” I blurted out before I even knew how I was going to ask the question.

“Sure,” David answered with a worried look.

“Why do you always eat alone in the hallway by the band room?” David gave a shrug while rubbing both hands on his thighs. “You should come to eat with the guys and me.”

“I don’t know; I have issues. I’m not really much fun to be around.” We were both temporarily distracted as Kimberly walked by. “See ya, Kimberly,” David said as I gave a friendly wave.

“We all have issues,” I admitted. “What kind of issues would make you want to be alone,” I asked, copying the exact phrase Kevin used on me last Thursday.

“Ever since my brother Grant died last year, I’ve been messed up,” he said as he dropped his head.

“I’m sorry, I didn’t know you had lost your brother.”

“Yeah,” he said, continuing to rub his thighs. “He crashed his motorcycle. My mother was having trouble when she drove past the tree that he hit, so my dad transferred to the Holland division.”

“That really sucks. Were you and your brother close?” That was a stupid ass question, Rob; they were brothers, of course, they were close.

"We were seven years apart, so there was a disconnect between us." David's pain was excruciating; I could feel actual pain in my chest as he told me about his brother. "But we were still close."

*Come and eat lunch in the cafeteria with us some time. It may be a good distraction;* I sent David through a green corridor. "Do you have anything to finish up before you leave?" I asked him.

"Yeah, I'm out of here as soon as I move these props backstage."

"You need some help?" I asked eagerly.

"Sure, it will only take a few minutes with two of us working at it. Thanks for being there for me this morning. Things didn't seem quite as hopeless knowing you were there for me," he said as we got started. Hmm, hopeless. I knew how that felt.

"No problem, that's what friends are for."

I enjoyed watching Zach while he performed on the baseball field tonight. He was strong, fast, and had impressive coordination. The speed that he could throw a ball was unbelievable. I guess we all had our gifts, and he was undoubtedly a gifted pitcher. After getting home from the game, I immediately crawled into bed. My stomach did a few flips when I heard my phone chime knowing it could be RSA:

Hey, are you sleeping? RSA wrote.

Not yet. How do I know you're not a dangerous stalker?

You've caught me… I've been stalking you online since we met. But I'm dull and harmless.

Where did we meet?

Can't say... It would out me.

Do we go to the same school?

Nope.

How old are you? Please don't say 30 something.

LMAO. No, I'm only 15…

Do you have any hobbies?

I like to write and play music.

What do you play?

Piano and keyboard?

Do I know any of your music?

I doubt it. I'm not a famous musician. Haha... Parent in room. Talk tomorrow.

Bye.

*****

Suddenly, I found myself standing at the top of our stadium bleachers at school. I was watching Kevin run track. As Kevin got closer, he waved for me to come down. But for some reason, my legs wouldn't move. No problem; I would just float to the bottom of the bleachers. There was a young boy who alerted his mother when he saw me drifting toward the bottom. A tall blonde kid who stood next to Kevin was now kissing him.

When the two of them broke their kiss, I couldn't believe my eyes. It was Cam locking lips with Kevin. "What are you doing, Cam! Why are you kissing Kevin? I thought you were straight," I asked him. Cam shook his head, no.

"I hate to do this, but you leave me no other choice," Cam said as if he was a robot talking in a monotone voice. A large knife materialized out of nowhere. The blade plunged into my chest, but it didn't even hurt. All I could get out of my mouth was, Why? I knew I need to flee, but my legs still wouldn't work. My only option was to fly. As I start to float upward, I saw tears begin to flow from Cam's eyes.

Was I dying? No way. I was way too young to die. I reached down and pulled the knife from my chest. Wait, I wasn't even bleeding. I was now hovering thirty feet over Kevin and Cam, looking down at them. I felt so free, but I was getting close to the power lines. I couldn't seem to control my movement away from the power lines. As I got closer, I was surprised to see David sitting on the power pole by himself, eating his sack lunch. David blew me a kiss as I started to veer away. I began my descent, which ended up being a disaster when I land on a few trash cans.

*****

I woke up in a cold sweat with difficulty breathing. I felt myself drop onto my bed again. Damn, it was 02:35. I must have been hovering above my bed while I was still asleep.

# Inclusiveness Chapter 11

Thursday, May 25th Inclusiveness

I was starving after my faster-than-usual swim this morning. Not Michael Phelps fast, but I seemed to be moving much more quickly in the water. I was tempted to sneak into the kitchen for some food before my shower, but I didn't want to chance getting caught with my dripping, wet swimwear.

When I walked past my bathroom mirror, I couldn't believe what I was seeing. Holy shit! I had abs! Remarkably defined abdominal muscles, to be precise. Where did they come from? I've always had a slim build, but never any abs that could be seen by the human eye.

The warm water felt wonderful, running down my back as I stood in the shower. I close my eyes so I could peer through the orange corridor of you know who. I found Kevin frying hamburger in his kitchen as he read a handwritten recipe. He stirred in some tomatoes, tomato sauce, and tomato paste. My friend was impressive in the kitchen.

*"Kev, have you seen my blue tie? I can't seem to find it. Wow, that smells terrific,"* Kevin's dad said as he approached Kevin.

*"Thanks, Dad. All three' of your ties are on your top shelf, just to the left of your t-shirts,"* Kevin said as he poured the hamburger tomato mixture over the pasta. *"Dad?"* Kevin said as his dad started to walk away.

*"What is it, Kev?"*

*"I'll leave a note on top of the lasagna in the fridge. It needs to go in the oven on 350 at four-thirty. Zach will be here for dinner tonight,"* Kevin said as he covered the glass dish with foil and placed it in the refrigerator.

*"Got it, 350 at four-thirty. What time will you be home?"* Devon asked.

*"Five thirty. Can we trust your memory to pick up some garlic bread on your way home, or should I send you a text?"*

*"I think I can handle that,"* Devon answered.

*"Good luck at your interview,"* Kevin said as he turned to give Devon a fist bump.

*"Thank you, I'll need it,"* Devon said as he left the room. Kevin walked to his front door, slipped his shoes on, grabbed his backpack, and out the door he went.

"Good morning!" I told Ms. Hukins as I made my way into the media room. Her office desk was piled high with books and stacks of papers that almost blocked her computer monitor.

"Robert!" she said with excitement in her tone as she turned to look at me.

"I have a doctor's appointment this afternoon, so I won't be attending rehearsal until four fifteen."

"It's not a problem; we'll make do. I plan to integrate you into some parts with Wendy today. Liam is most impressed with your quick study," Ms. Hukins said.

"Thank you, I'll see you at four fifteen," I assured her as I walked out.

I nearly ran into Cam when I rounded the corner by first-hour. "Hey, sorry, I didn't see you coming! Are we all set for tomorrow night?" Cam asked as we started to navigate our way through a sea of fellow students.

"Yeah, I have rehearsal until five, but Andy will bring me over right after it's done."

"Hey, do you want to go to the skate park in Grand Haven on Saturday morning?" Cam asked.

"Sorry, I have a special rehearsal Saturday morning, so I can't." I didn't think I'd be able to stand on a skateboard anyway, let alone ride on it while it was traveling at high speed down a steep grade.

"That's cool, no problem," he said as we stepped into Mr. Kave's class.

Cam was working on a plan as first-hour neared the end; he was trying to find a way to tell someone that a change had occurred in his plans. I could sense fear. Cam was worried about his mom as well. What was wrong with his mom? She was gone. I was getting more confused by the minute while I listened in on his brain activity.

*"Kevin, are you busy?"*

*"Nah. What's up?"*

*"I was searching Cam's brain and..."*

*"Stay away from him; he killed you in my weird dream last night."* Kevin sent, interrupting my thoughts.

*"Wait, what?"* I ask in disbelief. I know Kevin didn't trust Cam, but I think he could try to put in some effort.

*"He stabbed you in the chest."*

"Hey, class is over," Cam said as he shook my shoulder. I pulled away with fear as if he were attempting to kill me. I couldn't help my reaction. "Hey!" Cam said as he took a step back and threw his hands in the air as if he was in retreat. "You were staring off into space like you were having a stroke or something. Are you okay?"

"Shit, Cam! I'm sorry. You startled me." My behavior was ridiculous. Why would I be afraid of Cam? It was just a crazy dream. But Kevin saw the same thing I did. Oh yeah, Kevin.

*"Hey, Kevin, we'll talk some more in a few."*

I shook my head as Cam studied me. He was thinking he should be alerting Andy. I was going to end up ruining my friendship with Cam if I wasn't careful. When I reached the classroom door, David was standing with Andy.

"Hey, David. Lunch today?"

"Maybe," he answered with a grin.

During AP class, we were given some time to work on our own, so I decide to hit Kevin again.

*"Hey, could I ask you some questions about that dream you had?"*

*"I'm retaking a History test. So, make it quick."*

*"You mentioned something about Cam stabbing me."*

*"I don't remember everything, but Cam was kissing me while I was at a track meet., and then he stabbed you in the chest."*

*"That's exactly the same dream I had,"* I told him. *"Why would Cam want to hurt me?"*

*"I don't know,"* Kevin said as if he was trying to concentrate on something else. *"The more important question is, why would Cam want to kiss me? Hey, do you know the date for D day?"*

*"June 6th, 1944."*

*"Cool, thanks. What was Hitler's second in command?"*

*"Heinrich Himmler. Aren't you the least bit freaked out about this dream?"* I asked, trying to figure things out.

*"I'll think about being freaked out after I pass this test. Who was the US commander of the European Theater?"*

*"George Patton. Didn't you have time to study?"*

*"I've been busy taking care of everyone else's needs.* Kevin was right. After what I witnessed this morning, I believe every word he was telling me about not having enough time in the day to study. *"One more. What year did Russia invade Poland?"*

*"Germany invaded Poland on September 1st, 1939, and then Stalin invaded Poland on September 17th, 1939."*

*"How the hell do you remember all this shit, dude?"*

*"I never forget anything."* I reminded him. *"Now, help me figure out this dream thing."*

*"I don't know; maybe your dream subconsciously transferred to me."*

*"That's it. You're a genius!"*

I was starving when I entered the cafeteria food line. Good, we were having pizza today. Pizza was the best food on the menu at our school. The lunch lady looked at me with surprise when I ask for three pieces. Each piece was the size of my head. When I finally got to our table, I sat down and said 'hey' to everyone, including Dom, who had apparently joined us today. Dom was wearing a white t-shirt that had an F, space, and then CK. In the small print below, it said, 'all I need is u.' I couldn't believe he hadn't been sent home.

"Nice drip, dude," Zach said to Dom.

Everyone at the table was quiet; no one had even acknowledged me. When I looked around the table, my friends acted as if I was a stranger.

"So, why is everyone so quiet today?" I asked no one in particular.

"We were just discussing your sexy body before you walked up, catching us in the act." Cam's humorous answer relieved some of the tension at the table, but I couldn't come up with anything witty to say. Finally, Zach spoke up.

"Dude, it's like all of a sudden you're like, getting bigger, you know like you're on roids or something." Wow, 'like' would you 'like' to use another 'like' in there, Zach?

"Really, you've noticed my growth spurt?" I asked, rather than proving what a condescending ass I could be.

"It's not a growth spurt, dude; it's more like an explosion," Zach retorted. Cam gave me a wink as I chowed on my second piece of pizza.

"I don't take steroids. In health class, we learned that steroids make your dick shrink; I can't afford to lose any inches in that department." Everyone was almost falling off their chairs laughing; Dom accidentally spat a mouthful of grape juice across the table toward Cam.

"That almost hit me!" Cam said as he started to help Dom clean up the mess.

*"Well done,"* Kevin sent as he glanced in my direction.

*"If making fun of myself is all it takes to break the tension, it's worth it."* As I finished eating my third piece of pizza, I noticed David sitting beside me. He looked nervous. "Hey, David, where's your lunch," I asked?

"I got hungry in third-hour," he said with a meek voice.

"Hey, David, how's it going?" Cam asked as he reached across the table and gave him knucks.

*"Who invited him?"* Kevin sent.

*"I did. Is that a problem? We call it being inclusive, Kevin."* I shot back with a pissed-off response.

*"Okay, whatever,"* Kevin added, trying to diminish the importance of inclusiveness.

"Ah, why are you eyeing my food? Are you going to scarf mine too?" Cam asked, joking around with me.

"Haha, I think three pieces is enough. Don't you?" Truthfully, I could eat three more pieces if someone offered.

"How do you eat so much and stay so thin?" Dom asked. I just ignored his question, realizing that the awkwardness of David joining us was over.

"Hey, David. How's it going?" Kevin said, leaning back to see around me.

"Fine, thanks," David answered with a quick nod.

*"Thanks, man!"*I sent to Kevin.

*"You don't have to thank me. You're right; sometimes I can be a dick,"* Kevin admitted with some shame oozing from his thoughts.

*"You're forgiven,"* I answered with a reassuring smile.

When I walked into sixth-hour, I notice twelve yellow roses in a vase on Mr. Smit's desk. He seemed to be in a better mood, so I would assume everything went well with Mr. Burns's apology. Cam, on the other hand, seemed unsettled as he messed with his phone under his desk. I decided it wouldn't hurt to snoop around a little. I needed to set my mind at ease. *He needs to be at play practice at noon on Saturday,* I heard Cam think as he continued to text. What the hell? Maybe it was his Mom. No, he was texting someone who he was afraid of. Could it be his aunt or uncle? *No, it would be too suspicious if I asked him to skip practice. You're just going to have to deal with it. There's nothing I can do,* Cam punched into his phone.

"Cam, please keep your screen time to a minimum in class," I heard Mr. Smit tell him as he stood beside Cam's desk.

"Sorry," Cam apologized as he stuffed his phone into his pocket. Now I was even more confused than ever. 'Skip play practice? Suspicious?' Fear? What the hell was going on?

"Hey, Rob," David said as he tapped me on the back. When I turned around, David was smiling with those dimples in full display.

"Hey, what's up?" I asked him, trying to sound cool.

"My dad is taking me fishing out on the big lake Monday and…" David paused as if he had lost his nerve. I was reading fear of rejection in his mind, but I didn't say anything; instead waited for him to finish. I noticed his pronounced Adam's apple move up and down as he swallowed deeply. "You know, on Memorial Day, and I was wondering if you'd like to come along," he finally finished.

"I'd love to go; I'll check with my mom," I answered with a massive grin as we made our way out of Mr. Smits's classroom.

"Hello Robert, please come with me," Doctor Kelly said with a forced smile as he held the door open. My doctor seemed kind of sad.

"So, how are you today?" he asked as I sat down in his office.

"I'm doing fine," I answered with an enthusiastic tone.

"Very well. Did you enjoy your time with your father last weekend?"

"Yeah, it was fun; we attended a State Dinner at the White House." I was curious about why my doctor was so sad. I should be able to find the reason quickly without too much trouble.

"Well, I'm sure that was an exciting experience. There it is. Doctor Kelly was thinking about his son's thirty-fifth birthday. There was another door beyond the one I just entered from the corridor. This was new for me; I've never been able to see a connecting door. My curiosity propelled me into the room so I could open the next blue door. Doctor Kelly was remembering his son, who was getting married to another guy. I didn't know he had a gay son.

"Yes, the trip was fun," I answered as I twisted my dog tags around my fingers.

"I don't recall you wearing those last week," Doctor Kelly said, pointing at my tags.

"My father gave them to me as a gift. One was his, and the other belonged to my Uncle Keith."

"Well, that's an uncommon gift." *The last time Robert was here, he sought counsel regarding his sexual orientation,* I heard Doctor Kelly think.

"I told my dad I was gay," I blurted out, saving him the trouble of asking.

"And how did that go?" Doctor Kelly asked with surprise.

"Not as well as I had hoped," I answered. Without a response from Dr. Kelly, I continued. "My dad didn't take the news as well as my mom did. Unfortunately, he said he was struggling with my choices." My doctor thought that my dad may have blown an opportunity.

"And did his reaction disappoint you?"

"Yeah, quite a bit."

"Perhaps, you wouldn't mind telling me how you felt when your father reacted in this manner?" Suddenly, I felt as if I would start crying. I planned to get out of here today without shedding any tears.

"We've always been able to talk about anything, but this time he left me confused. You know, how he really feels about me being gay?" Doctor Kelly nodded as if he wanted me to spill my guts. "I guess I'm angry about him holding his values in higher regard than his own son's wellbeing. I just want to be accepted for who I am. It shouldn't be that difficult."

"Robert, let's pretend your father is sitting with us in this room," he said, pointing at an empty chair. "I'd like you, in your own words, to tell your father how angry you are with him. Please say it three times." I looked over at the empty chair, thinking about how stupid it would sound, but he was the doctor. What did I have to lose?

"Dad, I'm angry with you." He's right; speaking to the empty chair was kind of liberating. "Dad, I'm angry! Dad, I'm confused and pissed off!"

"And I just want you to accept me for who I am," the doctor added as if he wanted me to repeat what he said.

"And I just want you to accept me for who I am," I repeated just before I broke into tears.

"Your father loves you, Robert; he won't trade your well-being for his values. You're far too important to him to let something like values stand in the way of your relationship." I reached for some tissues to wipe my tears.

"I know," I was able to say between sobs. It was the truth; my dad said the same thing while we were out for dinner last weekend. Dad had said, 'You're way too important to your Mother and me; we won't let anyone or anything take you from us.' I shook my head, yes, acknowledging his statement.

Within a few seconds, I collected myself and wanted to talk about someone other than my dad. "I think I may have fallen…" Was love the right word? I shouldn't use love. "I met this kid in DC last weekend," I said instead. "I'm kinda infatuated with him; I can't seem to get him out of my mind. Can fifteen-year-old boys fall in love? Or is it just a sign of immaturity?"

"Fifteen-year-old boys can fall in love, and it's not immature. On the contrary, I believe having these feelings for another person is a good sign of maturity. It's not uncommon at your age. Love can develop quickly without having any sexual ties." Oh, believe me… There are some sexual ties in this scenario, I thought to myself.

*Why are you so sad, Doctor?* I sent him. He looked down at his tablet for a few seconds; it was as if he was trying to find the answer while silence filled the room. *What is it, Sir?* "Why are you so sad today?" I finally asked bluntly.

"What makes you believe I'm sad?" he asked.

"Doctor, you should never answer a question with a question," I said as I looked into his sad eyes.

"Well, I'm sorry you were able to detect my distraction."

"No, Sir, you aren't distracted; you're sad."

"You remind me of my son William. I haven't seen William or his new husband for six months. They have a new baby and can't travel from Germany.

*Maybe if you took some time off from work to go see them,* I sent inconspicuously. "What do you see in me that reminds you of William?" I asked, forging ahead.

"You look like William, especially your curly hair, your exceptional intellect, your shy personality, and your sexual orientation." I gave him a nod. From what I had seen in the video, I did resemble his son.

"Do you think my dad will come around and accept me for who I am? It seems as though you have accepted your son's sexual orientation."

"Your father is probably worried about the challenges you'll be faced with for the rest of your life. That's how I felt initially," my doctor admitted. I look down at the floor to gather my thoughts. I was confident that my dad knew what struggles his brother went through as a queer kid.

"Thank you for sharing your perspective," I told him as I looked back into his eyes.

"You're welcome. Unfortunately, we are out of time already. I'll be looking forward to seeing you next Thursday." I walked over to Doctor Kelly as if I planned to shake his hand but instead pulled him into a hug. He was very rigid and nervous about me hugging him. *I'm sure William misses you as well. Maybe you should go buy some flight tickets,* I sent him through a safe, green passage.

I was exhausted and hungry when I left rehearsal. Mrs. Wells had dinner warmed up when I walked through the door. While sitting at the kitchen island, finishing off my fourth piece of meatloaf, something strange happened when I saw another vision. This vision was so real it felt as if I had left my body and traveled to an unknown location. I saw a big man swing a handgun toward Kevin, striking him in the back of his head. "No!" I screamed before opening my eyes. Mrs. Wells quickly moved away from me as if I had frightened her.

"Robert? What's wrong?" Mrs. Wells asked with shock in her tone. The vision was so real, it felt as if I had teleported to the location, but I didn't recognize the man who struck Kevin. After Kevin fell to the floor, there was a lot of blood. My hands started to shake, and I felt nauseous.

"Who just screamed?" Mom said as she rounded the corner into the kitchen. "What's going on?" she asked Mrs. Wells.

"I'm not sure, Suzanne, we were sitting here talking, suddenly Robert looked as if he was about to pass out," Mrs. Wells said with a shaky voice.

Mom was standing beside me at the island, rubbing my back, asking me if I was sick, but I was too distracted by what I had just seen to answer. “Robert, you’re as white as a sheet, and you’re trembling.” I just shook my head. Damn it, I was about to be sick. I put my hands over my mouth before making a run for the restroom. I was just about to the toilet when I started creating a vomit trail. There was so much blood coming from Kevin’s head as he laid there, motionless on the white tile floor. I wasn’t even sure if he was breathing.

My mom and Mrs. Wells were busy cleaning up my puke trail as I sat on the cold floor next to the toilet. Gross, it was chewed-up meatloaf.

“Tell me what’s going on with you,” Mom said, standing over me, combing my sweaty curls with her fingers. “This is the third incident you’ve had.” I couldn’t reveal my vision of someone trying to kill Kevin, so I ignored her question.

“Could I just lie down in my bedroom for a while?”

“Sure, I’ll come up to check on you shortly,” Mom answered. My head no more than touched the pillow on my bed, and I felt myself falling asleep.

“How are you feeling?” my mom asked as she gently shook my shoulder, waking me up from a sound sleep.

“I’m fine now. What time is it?”

“Around nine. You better get ready for bed.”

“Thanks, Mom.”

“Goodnight,” she said as she left my room with worry plaguing her thoughts.

I was too keyed up to go back to sleep, so I sat down at my computer to work on my lines. I came across another song I would be expected to learn, and... damn, the lyrics would be hard to sing. I clicked on a YouTube video of a high school’s production, and wow, the kid was good! He looked a little older than me, but he had a great voice. All his animated facial expressions were spot on.

“It’s open,” I told the person who was knocking on my bedroom door. Sam stuck his head in the door to see if it was safe before entering.

“Heard you puked. Hey, is that gay porn?” Sam asked with excitement, stepping up to where he could see my screen.

"Very funny," I said as I paused to think for a few seconds. "I never look at porn on our home network. I use this," I told Sam, pulling my hotspot from my desk drawer. "You don't use our network for porn, do you?" I asked as he shook his head no and gave a nervous gulp. "It's just a song I have to sing in the play," I said, referring to the video.

"Liam told me you're a natural. He said you've done more in three days than the other kid had done in two months."

"Is he gay?"

"Who, the kid who got hit by the car?"

"No, Liam."

"Yeah, I'm pretty sure he is. Why don't you ask him? Oh, do you have the hots for him?" Sam asked with a big grin.

"No, I was just wondering," I said as my phone vibrated on my desk.

"Your boyfriend?" Sam asked, pointing at my phone.

"Haha," I answered, hoping it would be RSA.

"I saw Liam at the homecoming dance with another guy; they were doing some front-to-back grinding. So, you can come up with your own conclusion. Night, I gotta go delete some history," Sam said as he closed my door.

"Goodnight, Sam." I didn't have the heart to tell him that it was too late to delete. I immediately checked my phone, and it was RSA. A smile formed on my face after reading the text:

Hey, sexy! Wyd tonight?

Hey RSA! So, R U straight, bi, or gay?

Wow! Blunt, aren't we?

You're the one who called me sexy.

Ok… I'm bi... How about U?

Gay... Do you live in Michigan?

No. I still can't tell you too much about myself. I can tell you this, though. I have a big crush on you. BTW… My father can never find out. He'll never understand or accept my orientation.

I know how that feels. Does anyone else know about you being bi?

Only my mother and best friend, Lydia. How many know about you? RSA asked, probably referring to my sexual orientation. I'd like to ask him if he and his best friend were hooking up, but that wouldn't be fair since I didn't know who RSA was.

3... My rents and brother. I answered.

How old is your brother?

17. Almost 18. So, it's ok for me to know you're bi, but not your name?

Anyone could be bi, but you would know who I am if I told you my name. There's something different about you, Robert. You're as much of a mystery to me as my identity is to you.

Well said. Your anonymous text makes this fun and exciting anyway.

Texting you on my phone is dangerous. I have to delete our text so my father doesn't find out that I'm crushing on a boy.

Do you have a girlfriend or boyfriend?

No. How about you?

Nope. Do you go to a private school or public?

Private.

I could stay up talking with you all night, but I need some sleep.

Me too, goodnight, Robert. RSA was crushing on me! Hell yes!

*****

I suddenly woke up to find myself floating above Doctor Kelly's office. I looked through a large skylight to find Dom and Cam smashing grapes with their bare feet while standing on Doctor Kelly's desk. Just as I start to gain altitude, I saw Doctor Kelly trying to control the grape juice runoff with some tissues.

I flew around until I saw David and Kevin lying on the pole-vaulting mats at my school, sharing, what appeared to be, a meatloaf sandwich. Liam was hooking Zach to a lifting harness, so he could help him with the pole vault.

*****

I landed on my bed so hard it knocked the wind out of me for a few seconds. My elevation must have been close to the ceiling. I looked over at my phone, and it was 02:55.

# Taken Chapter 12

Friday, May 26th Taken

Halfway to the pool, I noticed that I accidentally wore soccer shorts instead of a swimsuit. The shorts didn't end up slowing me down as much as I thought they would during my forty-minute workout.

*"Hey, are you awake yet?"* I asked Kevin as I left the pool room.

*"Really? A meatloaf sandwich? Are you joking? And what was pretty boy Liam doing with Zach? Do you have a crush on David?"* Not as big of a crush as I have on you and Lukas, I thought to myself.

*"Maybe,"* I admitted as I reached the first-floor landing. *"Sorry, that leaked again. I don't know how to make it stop. Do you have a track meet tonight?* I asked, trying to change the subject.

*"Yeah, I do. But Dude, that was a messed-up dream. Please try harder to keep your love fantasies out of my mind."*

*"I know. Sorry, it's embarrassing."*

*"You think?"*

*"Hang on a second; my mom has the road blocked at the second-floor landing."*

"Good morning, honey. How are you feeling?" my mom asked.

"Much better," I answered. Uh-oh! Busted for not taking the time to dry off before leaving the pool room. Just as quickly as my mom looked down at my sopping wet soccer shorts, her eyes averted back to my face.

"Robert, I would recommend the proper swimming attire. Your shorts are a bit revealing."

I was horrified when I look down near the 'Nike swoosh,' where I could see my sparsely dark-colored hair and a clearly defined outline of my own 'swoosh' through my white shorts. I immediately left, covering my front with both hands, hoping that Kate didn't come out of her room before I made it to mine. Why did life as an adolescent have to be so damn awkward?

When Andy and I arrived at school, I saw Cam standing at the front door waiting for me. "Hey Cam," I called out as we approached.

"Hey, are we all set for tonight?" Cam asked.

"Yeah, Andy will bring me after rehearsal. Do you know what theater we'll be going to? I need to give Andy the details," I said with some annoyance in my tone.

"Why does Andy need to know where we're going?" he asked with concern.

"He plans on hanging with us at the theater," I reluctantly told Cam.

"He will?" Cam asked with surprise.

"Yeah, Andy was coming up with all kinds of excuses. He said most theaters have too many exits," I explained with an eye roll. I quickly looked back at Andy to make sure he didn't hear me dissing him.

"Okay… I'm not sure what theater it will be," Cam said with apprehension.

As we walked into first-hour, I hit Kevin's yellow corridor. I wanted to see if he was still wigged out about the dream from this morning. *"Hey, how's it going?"*

*"Dude, I'm still nervous about you going to Cams tonight. Where does he live?"* Kevin asked.

*"Check your phone; I just sent you his address, so you can call in an airstrike."*

*"Shut up. Quit being a dick. Maybe Andy or Gary could stay with you."* Kevin was right; I needed to validate his concerns.

*"Andy has a plan."*

*"That's good,"* is all Kevin sent back.

*"See you at lunch,"* I sent as I sat down at my desk.

*"Okay, but I wouldn't recommend drinking grape juice for lunch. I'm not sure those guys washed their feet,"* Kevin sent.

I spent most of first-hour and part of second-hour memorizing my lines. By the time second-hour was done, I was able to hammer everything out. Liam would be elated. I couldn't believe Liam was playing footsie with me yesterday. He was definitely getting braver.

While standing in the lunch line waiting to pay, I notice Dom behind me waiting as well. He told Zach he was jumping ship so he could sit with us again today. Dom had a build for strength. His dark hair perfectly complimented his flawless dark brown skin. I usually shied away from reading Dom since he spent a lot of time thinking about girls' anatomy.

"Whassup, bitches!" Dom shrieked as he sat down at our table and opened his grape juice.

"Hey, guys, do you want to come to my brother Kurt's graduation party tomorrow afternoon? There will be a lot of hot girls wearing bikinis at the pool party later in the afternoon," Zach said, looking at Cam and me.

"I have other plans," Cam said with disappointment.

"Sorry, me too," I told Zach before chomping into my grilled cheese sandwich that was burned on the underside. "Thanks for the invite, though," I replied as I noticed David sitting beside me, pulling a PBJ from his sack lunch.

After eating lunch, several of us were lying out in the middle of the football field, enjoying the sun during PE. Zach was busy flirting with a new girl while Kevin and I lay side-by-side, catching some rays. Kevin seemed a bit jealous of Zach's efforts, so I checked his gray corridor to confirm my speculations. What I read was incontrovertible; Kevin was in love with Zach.

*"Have you been practicing your liftoffs?"* Kevin asked.

*"Yeah, in the pool, but I'm not levitating over the solid ground without you."*

*"A lot of help I was."* We both start to giggle out loud again, thinking about our trash can crash incident.

"You two are so adorable, lying here giggling at each other," Zach said as he jumped on top of Kevin, putting some wrestling moves on him.

"A little help?" Kevin said, looking over at me. I jumped into action, laughing, as we had some fun rolling around on the ground. Mr. Dewey blew his whistle from the other side of the field, ending our playful contact.

"Dude, you're an animal," Zach said, looking at me as we headed for the showers,

We've been working on building a wind turbine/propeller in science. David, Cam, and I developed a kick-ass design with a proper chord length and the correct pitch. Cam talked us into building the balsa wood structure larger than it needed to be, but it should work fine. If we can get it connected today, we'll be able to measure the voltage produced across a resistor.

"How is the play going, guys?" Mr. Smit asked as he stood by our table, watching us try to connect the spinning axle shaft to a DC motor.

"It's going well," I told him, trying to downplay my excitement.

"Have you flown yet?" Mr. Smit asked.

"Ah, yeah, about that," I said, looking at David. "Is there a different harness I could try today?"

"What's wrong with the harness we used yesterday?" David asked.

"It's a little uncomfortable. You can't imagine how it feels when you have two snug straps crunching both sides of your… ah…" I left the last part to their imagination as I point down at my crotch. Mr. Smit covered his mouth with a loosely clenched fist to hide his amusement.

"And you wouldn't believe how surprised I was the first time you tighten that thing up," I told David with my eyebrows raised, eyes widened, and my mouth wide open. "The hoisting is only part of the discomfort. When I'm finally lowered, I'm expected to perform my lines in front of everyone without making proper adjustments." I squirmed around, pretending to do self-adjustment without touching anything.

"Oh, and don't forget about the wedgie strap," I continued as the three of them laughed. "It feels like I'm wearing a thong. Not that I've ever tried wearing one," I added quickly, feeling my face heat up. Mr. Smit was laughing so hard he had tears. David was holding his gut, almost falling off his stool.

Rehearsal flew by, and I was almost to the truck when David caught up to Andy and me. "Did you check to see if you could come with us fishing Monday?" David asked.

"Oh, yeah, my mom gave me the all-clear on that, but I'll have to bring Gary if there's enough room on the boat."

"I'm sure it won't be a problem. See ya Monday; I'll text you the details," David said as we went our separate ways in the parking lot.

"Sounds good. Bye," I said to David as I opened the truck door. Speaking of bi. I haven't checked my text since the end of sixth-hour. Yes! There was a text from RSA:

Hey there, gorgeous. How's your day going? RSA had sent the text only thirty seconds ago. Gorgeous? Was he delirious?

Absolutely incredible day! How about you?

Other than thinking about you, my day has sucked. RSA sent back immediately.

Sorry, you've had a bad day. Btw, I have no idea what you look like, but I'm trying to figure out what you see in someone like me. I wasn't looking for a compliment; I just wanted to clarify some confusion.

"You all set?" Andy asked as he started the truck.

"Yup, I'm good," I told Andy as I started to fish for a dry shirt and deodorant from my backpack. Come on, please be in here, I thought to myself. My phone kept chirping at me while I wiggled into the fresh shirt. The message RSA had sent was so long that I had to click 'View all.'

If you're referring to the gorgeous comment? That question is easy to answer. First, I love your meek, mild, shy personality. As for your looks, let me start at the top and work my way down. There's something about your exceptionally curly hair that makes me want to touch it. Those luscious, full lips and your high cheekbones complement the symmetry of your face perfectly. Let's not forget about your beautiful green eyes that I can't look into without losing my mind. Your sexy little bubble butt is to die for. And, I've never seen the rest of your well-proportioned body uncovered, but I'd like to.

I was dumbfounded and a bit aroused after reading what RSA had written. His text made the tops of my ears burn. Wait, what? I have a bubble butt? I've never had anyone describe any part of my body like that. I needed a distraction to bring myself back to reality.

*"How'd you do at your meet?"* I ask Kevin as I folded my sweaty shirt and place it in my pack.

*"I took fourth in the one hundred."*

*"That's great! Where are you now?"*

*"My dad and I went out for dinner to celebrate him landing a new job,"* he answered with excitement.

*"Please tell your dad congratulations for me,"* I said to Kevin as I tried to figure out what I was going to say in my following text to RSA. It would sound too nerdy or conceited if I said thank you.

"Do you know what movie theater you're going to this evening?" Andy asked again.

"Not yet," I said to Andy as I text RSA back:

Wow! I'm flattered, but I think you may be exaggerating just a bit. LMAO... I'm on my way to a friend's house, so I'll text you back in a couple hours; I quickly punched into my phone; all the while, Andy continued to nag me.

"I'm gonna need the name of that theater so I can call ahead to talk to the manager before you arrive," Andy said before he produced an audible sigh as if he was thinking, 'this kid is frustrating the hell out of me.'

"I'll text you the name of the theater after I ask Cam." Andy gave me a quick nod.

*"Hey man, take care; I'm almost to Cam's house,"* I told Kevin as we turned down another road that I didn't recognize.

*"Okay, see ya,"* Kevin sent back.

Cam's driveway wound through some large trees, ending where we found the house nestled in a heavily wooded area about a half-mile off the main road. There were some large blueberry fields beyond the house's back, with giant sprinklers watering the plants.

Cam came out of the house to meet me as I climbed out of the truck. "Hey, how did play practice go?" he asked. Cam seemed much more relaxed than he was in science class today; he was dressed casually, wearing only a pair of shorts. I needed to keep redirecting my eyes to where I was walking, so I didn't trip and fall.

"It was fine; we were able to get through the whole second part today."

"Are you hungry?" he asked.

"I'm starving," I replied as we stepped up onto a wrap-around porch. Cam noticed me glancing back at the circle drive where Andy was still sitting in the truck.

"How come your detail isn't leaving?"

"Ah... he decided to stay, but he'll just stay in the truck." Having Andy here was a perfect example of why I got so annoyed with being required to have my own detail. It was impossible to be a normal kid.

"Yeah, sure, he's fine," Cam lied with a nervous tone as we walk into the farmhouse-style kitchen.

"Wow, there's something familiar about this place. It's like I've been here before," I said with a light chuckle.

"Aunt Sara likes the traditional style decor," Cam said as he reached into the fridge for some chocolate milk to go with the pile of homemade chocolate chip cookies that were sitting on a cooling rack.

"Where is everyone?" I asked.

"Aunt Sara is grocery shopping, and Uncle Carl won't be home from work until six-thirty."

"And your Mom?"

"She flew out to Hawaii on Wednesday to meet up with my dad." Cam was lying about where his Mom was as well. He didn't have a clue where his mom or dad was. Why would he lie about that?

"Aunt Sara is planning to do burgers on the grill for dinner if that sounds good."

"Sure, I love burgers," I told him, realizing I shouldn't ruin my appetite.

We each grabbed four cookies and headed up to Cam's bedroom. The room didn't seem to fit his taste. There were posters of monster trucks, cars, and race bikes. This defined Cam in a way I had not expected.

When I sat down on Cam's bed, I bounce a few times while giving him a worried smile. He smiled back, but it quickly turned into a grimace. I dove into Cam's gray corridor, trying to find out what was going on with his parents. I sensed regret and sadness. Cam doubted that he would ever see his parents again. Why would they leave him? Behind a blue door, there was a video of Cam struggling to get away from an adult male. What the hell was going on?

"Hey, Cam, where are your parents?" I finally asked pointedly, looking for the truth. Cam seemed as if he were about to answer, but he was cut off.

"Cameron, are you upstairs?" someone shouted from the floor below us.

"Yeah, Rob and I are up here in my room."

"Dinner will be ready in fifteen minutes. Who's in our driveway?" the person shouted with a heavy accent.

"He's Rob's detail," Cam answered with a shaky voice while looking uneasy and worried.

"What is it, Cam? Is something wrong?"

"Nothing, why?" he answered defensively.

"You seem nervous about someone who's down there," I strongly implied with good reason.

"Nah, I'm good." Cam was lying to me again. Something in my gut told me to run, but I didn't want to be too obvious.

"Can I use your restroom?" I asked, trying to sound as calm as possible.

"Sure, it's down the hall, first door on your left." It just didn't feel right. Cam was on edge, and everything that came out of his mouth was a lie. The person downstairs was angry about Andy staying. I needed to call Andy so he could get me the hell out of here. My hands were shaking while I locked myself in the bathroom. I hardly ever called Andy, I usually texted him for everything, so I wasn't surprised when he answered on the first ring.

"What's wrong, Robert?" Andy asked with alarm in his tone.

"I'm locked in the bathroom upstairs; I need you to come and get me," I whispered with my urgent plea.

"What's going on?" Andy asked as his voice strained while he quickly stepped out of the truck.

"I don't know, something's not...... Andy? Andy!" I screamed into my phone, which was no longer working. Shit, my phone went dead. The screen showed a full battery, it had four bars earlier, and now there was nothing. I was startled when I heard several gunshots fired outside. My mind filled with dread when the shooting turned into automatic gunfire, sounding exactly like the video game Kevin and I played last week. Only this time, it wasn't a game; it was Andy's life at risk. I tried to call 911, but there was still no signal.

*"Rob, I just heard you scream Andy's name. I'm at the end of Cam's driveway."* Kevin said, surprising the hell out of me.

*"You're at Cam's house?"* I asked Kevin frantically while someone started to scream at Cam in the room next to me. Cam cried out in agony as if someone were beating him. *"Kevin! Call 911! I'm in the second-floor bathroom!"* I quickly shut off the bathroom lights and hid in the shower. The Sheriff's deputy at our school taught us to avoid-deny-defend. I've already tried to avoid, I have the door locked to deny, so I was prepared to fight when it was time to defend.

*"My cell won't work either; I'm coming for you!"* Kevin sent.

"It's not my fault; I didn't know his bodyguard was going to stay!" I heard Cam cry out while someone continued to hit him.

"Where is he?" I heard a deep calm voice ask Cam.

"He jumped out of my window." There was more screaming from Cam as he continued to be beaten. I felt as if I should try to rescue Cam, but he was the one who lured me here, so he couldn't be trusted.

*"Kevin! Don't come back here; they have guns!"*

"Where is he?" a man demanded. "I'm not going to ask you again." I closed my eyes to see where Kevin was. I could see what looked like the back of the farmhouse. I disconnected from Kevin so I could hear what Cam was saying to his fake uncle.

"He's in the bathroom. Please don't hurt him; he's my friend," Cam begged.

*"I'm hiding in the trees behind Cam's house!"* Kevin told me with urgency in his thought. A door slamming closed in the hallway made me shake with fear.

"Please don't hurt him. Please don't hurt my friend," Cam said repeatedly.

*"Kevin, run and hide, find a landline, call 911! The cells are being jammed!"*

"Open the door, Robert." I heard a man's calm voice demand from the hallway. No way in hell. Do you think I'm stupid? I thought to myself.

*"I'm on the back porch; no one knows I'm here,"* Kevin sent just as a loud crash startled me. I screamed, giving away my position.

The guy I saw in my vision last night was pointing a gun at me while I was still crouched down, trying to hide in the shower stall. This was it. This is where I fight or die. I had a sinking feeling in my gut, but I knew I needed to fight back. I needed to defend myself, but it would have to be with the element of surprise. I may be smaller and faster, but he was probably more extensive and had a gun, I contemplated.

*"Listen, Kevin, these guys have guns. You need to escape while you still can!"* Now I wished I would have told Kevin about my vision.

"Get up and don't try anything stupid," the big guy said with a thick accent. He reached down, grabbed my arm, pulling me up to my feet as if I were a feather pillow. A quick read on the bad guy revealed the truth. The FBI warnings were credible. I was being abducted.

*"I'm not leaving without you!"* Kevin said. The guy had a tight grip on the back of my shirt, so I thought that I may be able to break free if I could get my shirt to rip off.

*"Kevin, please run!"* I told him as the asshole literally pushed me out into the poorly lit hallway toward the stairs. I tried to use the element of surprise to my advantage when I quickly turned toward him with as much force as I could. My shirt ripped clean off as I took a quick step back to reach for his gun. I dropped to the floor with a thud after he slugged me in the side of the head with his free hand. My vision was blurry as I laid prone on the hardwood. Breathing was almost impossible with his knee in my back.

"Get off me, you, motherfucker!" I was able to yell after catching my breath.

*"Do you see Andy anywhere?"* I asked Kevin as the jerk grabbed a handful of my hair, pulling my head up off the floor. The asshole leaned forward, putting more pressure on my back. His face was so close to my head, I could smell his cigarette breath.

"Don't try that again, kid, or you'll be eating this barrel. Do you understand?" It was an eerie sensation with the cold, hardened steel pushed against my left cheek.

*"No, I don't see him; he must be in the front. Getting you out through the back is the only way.* Kevin sent. Cigarette breath started to drag me down the steep stairs causing searing pain in my left shoulder and back as I hit the first step and then anticipated the anguish of catching the next.

"Aargh!" I cried out. "That hurts...," I tried to say as I hit thirteen additional hardwood steps.

*"Kevin, you're the only one who can help me now. Run to get help."*

The asshole pulled me into the kitchen that I now recognized as the room in my vision. I needed to save Kevin, so it was time for drastic measures.

"Come on, get the kid; let's get the hell out of here," the guy who was holding me demanded. He talked to a woman in a different language, but I could still read them just as if they were speaking English.

The woman, who was apparently a fake Aunt Sara, entered the kitchen dragging Cam from his zip-tied wrists. Cam's eyes were telling me, sorry, as smoky breath tightened a zip-tie restraint to my wrists. The jerk holding me was now squinting his eyes as I increase the force, turning the door handle in the wrong direction. I could see the misery in his eyes, so I just kept the pressure on until he passed out less than two feet from me. "What the hell are you doing? Wake up!" another guy screamed just as I start applying pressure to his brain as well.

My concentration was broken when the back door flew open. The nightmare worsened when I saw a tall guy with long greasy hair drag Kevin into the kitchen. Kevin started to struggle and was somehow able to get loose. Kevin was much faster and stronger than the idiot expected. Kevin turned, giving greasy hair a sidekick square in the nuts.

The guy who had dragged me down the stairs had regained consciousness but seemed to be off-balance as he stood, trying to respond to greasy hair guy who was now on his knees holding his groin. Before I could find a door handle in smoke breath's gray corridor, he reached over and struck Kevin in the head with his gun. It all happened so fast; Kevin fell to the floor. Seeing blood leak from the back of Kevin's head caused every muscle in my body to tense. An explosion went off in the room when I screamed Kevin's name.

*****

When I finally woke up, two paramedics were moving me from the farmhouse on an ambulance stretcher. My head had excruciating pain, and there was a collar wrapped around my neck that was a bit restrictive.

"Where are you taking me?"

"To the hospital," one of the paramedics' answered.

"Did you see another teenage boy here?" I quickly asked, referring to Kevin.

"No, you are the last to be transported," the paramedic said. There were vehicles with flashing lights lined down the driveway as far as I could see. Just as they got ready to load me into a waiting ambulance, two black trucks came racing up between the emergency vehicles. The trucks come to a screeching halt before my dad launched from the lead truck's rear passenger door. "Hold on, it's my dad," I told the paramedics, referring to my dad's grand entrance.

"Robert! Are you all right?" my dad asked as he reached the stretcher.

"Dad, I don't need to go to the hospital in an ambulance. Can you just take me to find Kevin?"

"You need to ride in the ambulance. We'll check on Kevin when we arrive at the hospital," my dad answered as he looked at the IV bag hanging above me.

"What's wrong, Dad? You're withholding information." I could read dread in my dad's thoughts when he said Kevin's name. "If you know something about Kevin's condition, you need to tell me now," I demand.

"I'm sorry, Robert. I'm afraid I have some bad news," he said, pausing for a few seconds to gather his thoughts. "I wanted to tell you in private," my dad said with a sympathetic tone. I reach up to grab my dog tags as I become more upset by the second.

"What is it, Dad? Just tell me what's going on," I pled.

"While I was on my way here, Kevin's father called to tell me Kevin passed away from his injuries."

"No… No, someone has made a mistake," I said calmly as my dad shook his head, no. "Kevin's Dad is lying!" I yelled. I could taste bile creeping up my throat. Anger clouded my vision as I looked for a hint of untruth in my dad's mind. I closed my eyes, *"Can you hear me, Kevin? Answer me, please."* I could only see darkness. *"Kevin?"* My dad wasn't lying; I couldn't feel Kevin's energy anymore. There was nothing.

"All three of the stretcher seat belts released simultaneously when I telekinetically ask them to. I was off the stretcher within a split second, pulling the IV tubing from my arm before anyone could stop me. I could feel blood trickling down my arm, but I didn't even care anymore.

"Get back on the stretcher, Robert," my dad said with authority. "Your friend Zach is on his way to the hospital; you are going to need each other's emotional support." When I start to cry, my dad stepped up, trying to give me a hug. I pulled away, screaming at the top of my lungs, causing a bright flash to fill the sky when a transformer exploded just down the driveway. Everything was dark now, except for the truck lights and the burning transformer.

"Robert?" my dad said with a nervous tone. I looked to my left just as Gary took a step toward me, so I took a few steps back.

"He's dead, Dad! Don't you get it!" I screamed. "Kevin is dead because of you. He's dead because you chose your career over your family."

"Robert, calm down; you're behaving irrationally."

"Irrational, Dad? Do you want to see irrational? I'll show you irrational!" I only had to think about what would happen next, and it wasn't going to be pretty. One of my dad's unoccupied trucks took off like a rocket flying over the top of trees, smashing upside down in the blueberry field behind the house.

I took off running down the long driveway; I heard someone chasing after me, so I started to run faster.

"Let him go!" I heard my dad yell with authority. "Just let him go." I kept running. I didn't even know where I was running to. I just kept running in the dark. I felt the sweat running down my whole body. My shorts were soaked, but I didn't care. From time to time, I heard a helicopter hovering overhead. They probably tracked me with infrared, but I didn't let it bother me; I just kept running.

Wait, how'd I get here? I was standing in front of my school. A car parked in the nearly empty lot, with someone sitting by themselves on the vehicle. Could it be? Was that Mr. Smit?

"Kevin is dead," I told Mr. Smit bluntly as I sat down beside him on the warm hood of his car.

"I just heard," he said as his voice cracked.

"How'd you know where to find me?" I asked as I laid my head on his shoulder. My body was swamped with sweat; I was sure that I didn't smell the best, but Mr. Smit couldn't escape my snare. We were touching the way I've always wanted us to make contact. "What am I going to do without Kevin?" Mr. Smit draped his arm over my shoulders to hug me tight.

"Robert, I need you to get into my car," he said with urgency in his voice.

"Why, where are you taking me?" I asked with confusion.

"I'm taking you to the hospital. You're bleeding. If I don't get you there soon, you'll die." I looked down; both of my wrists were bleeding profusely.

"Am I dreaming?" I asked as I slipped into his front passenger seat. "Mr. Smit, I think I'm going to pass out."

*****

*****

It felt as if someone was standing on my head. Where am I? Through cloudy vision, I could see bandages on my wrists and an IV in both arms. My mom was resting in a chair adjacent to the hospital bed.

"Mom? Where am I?" I asked with a groggy voice.

"Robert? Oh, Robert, thank God you're awake!" my mom said as she stood up, throwing her arms around me.

"Where am I?" I asked her again.

"You're in the children's hospital in Grand Rapids," she said weakly.

"Why am I here?" I asked, even though I already knew the answer.

"You tried to take your own life. You cut your wrists."

"What day is it? Did I miss Kevin's funeral?" I asked while scanning the big scary hospital room.

"It's Christmas day. But I'm sorry, I don't know any, Kevin," she said with genuine concern in her tone.

"Kevin Larson? You know who Kevin is," I said adamantly as I reached for my dog tags, which were unfortunately missing.

"I don't know Kevin Larson, honey. Just a minute, I think I better go find the doctor," she said with a worried look as she turned to leave.

"Wait, Mom, please don't leave me."

"All right," she said while rubbing her hands together nervously before pushing the nurse button on my bed.

"How long have I been, you know, out?" I asked while trying to sit upright.

"Sixteen hours. They had to do several blood transfusions. I found you unconscious on your bathroom floor; you lost a lot of blood."

"Where is Dad?"

"He's on his way back from China. He couldn't find a flight, so Grandpa sent someone to fly him home. Andy is waiting at the airport to bring your Father here."

"I'm sorry, Mom."

"There's no need to apologize. We just need to help you get things back on track. You've probably figured out how all of this is going to work."

"Yeah, I got it. I'm going to be talking with Dr. Kelly."

"Who is Dr. Kelly?" she asked.

"Never mind, I'll explain later," I told her as a nurse approached my bed to change an IV bag.

"Hello, yes, he just woke up," I heard my mom say to someone after answering her cell. "He seems confused. I don't know; he's mentioning names of people I've never heard of. Could you please hurry?" she whispered into the phone. Mom must have been talking to my dad. "Room, 3376. Okay, I'll see you soon."

It was definitely a dream. I even had dreams within my dream about dreams. But they were so real, and I could fly…

"Hey, Slugger," my dad said as he rushed into the room past my mom and put me into a bear hug.

"Sorry, Dad, I know I made a poor choice," I said through sobs. Suddenly out of nowhere, a young, cute medical assistant with dark spiky hair, and sparkling brown eyes, appeared beside the bed.

"Hey, Robert, I'm Drew. I'll be changing your bandages before you go home," he said while pulling on some purple gloves. He looked a lot like the pharmacy tech in one of my dreams. "Are you having any pain?" Drew asked with a kind voice.

"No," I replied with a short answer, hoping he didn't see me blushing. When Drew took the bandages off the right wrist, I was almost afraid to look.

"What's this?" Drew said with surprise in his voice as he exposes the left as well.

"What? What's wrong?" I asked quickly.

"Erm, the lacerations are completely healed," Drew answered.

*****

Oh, man, I have a pounding headache. Where am I? Someone must've hit me in the head. The throbbing pain inside my skull felt as if my brain had a pulse of its own. Why couldn't I see? My arms felt like they weighed three hundred pounds each. Damn, I couldn't move them. My legs wouldn't work either. I could hear road noise like I may be traveling down a road. Maybe I was on my way home from the hospital.

No. I was never in the hospital. It was a messed-up dream.

*"Kevin, can you hear me?"* Nothing from Kevin. I've never connected long-distance with anyone but Kevin. Kevin could be dead; his head was bleeding badly when I saw him lying on the farmhouse's kitchen floor. I think that's the last thing I remember. Come on, you need to fight to stay awake, I told myself.

*"Kevin? Kevin, please don't leave me; I'm scared. Please answer me! I can't do this alone."*

# Dreaming Chapter 13

Monday, May 29th Dreaming

My head was throbbing. I needed something for my headache before my brain exploded. If I could only make it into my bathroom to get some Tylenol. My eyes wouldn't open, my legs wouldn't work, and I couldn't lift the blankets. Wait, I didn't have any covers. Hearing the road noise reminded me that I had been abducted. I tried to move my arms again and again, but neither would budge. When I tried to search for any close brain activity, everything was foggy and garbled. It sounded as if thousands of people were trying to talk over each... talk over... trying over others… trying to…

# Survivor Chapter 14

Tuesday, May 30th Survivor
*****

"Get away from me. Leave me alone!" I yelled as I squirmed around and kicked at a weird-looking part human, part fish-man. The gills on his neck were retracting like he was starving for oxygen. He was trying to pull me under where I wouldn't be able to breathe. His gross slimy, webbed hands slipped from my leg when I gave one final kick. "No, don't take me under! Please don't take me!" I shook my head and squint my eyes to see if the creature was gone. The last thing I saw before the green fish-man vanished into the murky water were his green webbed feet. I was safe now. Wait. I wasn't safe at all.
*****

My head pain was grinding into my temples; I must have been having another dream. Now that I was somewhat awake, I needed to figure out how long I've been missing. I hoped Andy wasn't dead; he must've made it to the truck's rear, where the security team kept the rifles. There was a distinct sound of automatic rifle fire outside the farmhouse. Andy had a wife and two young boys. He hadn't rescued me, so he was presumed dead, and his boys no longer had a father.

*"Kevin, can you hear me? Kevin, please answer me!"* Maybe Kevin was dead as well. Hell, I may even be dead. I still couldn't move, but I was able to hear road noise. I could smell urine, and my eyes felt like I hadn't taken my contacts out for days. So, I still had all my senses. I wasn't dead.

Kevin wasn't answering, so I needed to find someone who would. There wasn't anyone coming for me. It was like Ed Sheeran's song, 'Save

Myself.' It was time to do just that; I needed to save myself. Why was it that I could connect long-distance with Kevin? What made Kevin unique? I found Kevin attractive; I knew he was in love with Zach; therefore, Kevin was unobtainable. Was there anyone else who I was attracted to and was unobtaina…? Wait, what about…? *"Mr. Smit, can you hear me? This is Robert."*

*"Robert, is that you? How'd you get into my apartment?"* I heard him ask through a yellow corridor. *"Let me turn on the light so I can see you. Ouch!"* he said, tripping over something after stubbing his left big toe.

*"Mr. Smit, you can't see me. Someone took me."*

*"Hang on for a second, let me wake up; this isn't making any sense." I must be having a dream,* Mr. Smit thought to himself.

*"I can assure you; this is not a dream. I'm speaking to you through telepathy. Listen to me carefully. I need you to contact my dad, tell him that I've been kidnapped."*

*This can't be real. But I'm awake, and I can hear Robert's voice.* He thought to himself.

*"Mr. Smit, this is real; I need your help. Just think back to me; I can hear you answer."*

*"Robert?"* he sent with a high level of stress in his thoughts.

*"It's okay, Mr. Smit; I can hear everything you think or say."*

*"Umm, everything?"*

*"Yes,"* I confirmed.

*"Robert, your father knows. You've been missing for three days,"* Mr. Smit finally said as if he was starting to believe this was really happening. *"Chris, wake up; I need you to call 911! No, I'm not dreaming. Give me your phone." "Robert, where are you?"* Mr. Smit asked as he listened to the phone ring.

*"I'm not sure, but I think I'm in a vehicle."* I was surprised when I felt my fingers move. Wait, I could lift my head too. It hurt so bad. I laid my head back on the hard surface, which I would assume was the floor of a truck.

*"Hello, yes, I have some information for the police." "Shh. Chris, please be quiet; I'll explain in a second." "Yes, I'm here. I'm talking with Robert Van Stark. Yes, the Robert Van Stark, who's missing. He's one of my students. Yes, I'll stay on the phone." "Hold on, Robert. I'm on the phone with 911; they're getting us some help." "Chris, you better get up; we need to get dressed. No, Chris, I'm not losing my mind. No, just chill, don't*

*worry, I'm fine. Wait for a second! Can you hear Robert's voice? Well, I can hear his voice; he's talking to me." "Hello, yes, ma'am, I'm talking with Robert Van Stark telepathically."* Without an orange corridor, I wouldn't be able to hear what others were saying to Mr. Smit, so I would just have to work with what I had. "*All right, yes, I'll hold."* Mr. Smit told the dispatcher. *"Yes, Chris, I can hear Robert's voice. No, I don't need to sit down. I just need this damn dispatcher to talk to me."*

*"Mr. Smit, tell the dispatcher to call my dad."*

*"Hold on, Robert." "Yes, ma'am, I know this sounds impossible, but Robert Van Stark is talking to me telepathically. No, I haven't had anything to drink. Well, not in the last three hours anyway. Yes, I'll stay on the phone as long as you need me." "Robert, are you there?"*

*"Yeah, once I have a lock on your mind, you can't get rid of me unless I disconnect from you first."*

*"Have they injured you?"* Mr. Smit asked.

*"I'm not sure. I have a terrible headache, but other than that, I can't feel anything."*

*"Hang on, Robert." "No, I didn't ask to talk to the dispatch supervisor; I want to talk to the police. Umm yeah, sure, but they're welcome to come into our apartment if they wish." "Chris, the police are asking that we exit the apartment with our hands up." Holy shit, there are six Sheriffs cars in the lot. Why are they pointing rifles at us?* I heard Mr. Smit think. *"Chris, they think we have Robert here in the apartment. I don't know, but we better do exactly as they ask."*

*"I'm sorry, Mr. Smit, please tell the police about Kevin. I think they took him too."*

*"Kevin is in Grand Rapids at the trauma center."*

*"He's in the hospital?"*

*"Yes, he's been in a coma since they found him Friday afternoon unconscious."*

*"Kevin, can you hear me?"* I looked through Kevin's eyes; all I could see was darkness. Wait! I could feel his pain. Kevin's pain was even worse than my headache, but he was alive; that was all that mattered.

*"Mr. Smit, are you okay?"*

*"The Sheriff's deputies are searching through our apartment for you. They're convinced that Chris and I are holding you captive." "No, Sir, I haven't seen Robert Van Stark since Friday afternoon. Yes, I watched him at his play rehearsal, around four-thirty. No, Sir, I just enjoy watching their*

*progress. No, I don't have any pictures of the rehearsal. No, I don't have any pictures of Robert on my phone. Here look for yourself."*

*"Mr. Smit, tell them to call my dad. He'll know what to do."*

*"Robert would like you to contact his father. Yes, it's like I told you, I'm talking to him telepathically."* Hey, I felt my arm move, I think I could see as well, but everything was dark and blurry.

*"They don't believe me, Robert. I can see why, though, I'm having difficulty believing all of this myself, and I'm the one talking to you telepathically."*

*"You need to convince them; my life may depend on it."* It was true; Mr. Smit may be my only hope.

*"I'm sitting in the back seat of a police car by myself with handcuffs on; Chris is in another car."*

*"I'm sorry. I'm really sorry you're being treated like that."* I tried to pick my head up to look around, but I felt too weak to move. I thought I could hear brain activity around me. It was hard to distinguish who was thinking or talking.

*"Hello, Sergeant. Yes, I've already explained everything to your deputy. Yes, I'm communicating with Robert Van Stark. No, up until about twenty minutes ago, we had never communicated like this. Can someone take these handcuffs off, please? I need to use the restroom. No, it's like I told your deputy; I haven't seen Robert since Friday at four-thirty in the afternoon. Yes, of course I know he was abducted."*

*"Mr. Smit?"*

*"Robert, just call me Kyle."* I was surprised my teacher would offer the use of his first name, but the street traveled in both directions.

*"Okay, it's Rob then. I'm... a... I'm terrified, Kyle."*

*"We will rescue you, I promise."* I could sense the relief in Mr. Smit's thoughts, and then it dawned on me what he was doing. How could I get the cops to believe Mr. Smit? 'Communication can help to facilitate the illusion of reality,' Ms. Manning said last week during our Psychology class.

*"Hey, Kyle, are you done peeing yet?"*

*"How do you know I was..."*

*"Oh, sorry... I can read emotions as well; you were relieved while you were emptying your..."*

*"Okay, got it,"* he interrupted. *"Yes, I'm done, but this feels as if I'm in a nightmare, unable to wake up."*

*"Oh, believe me, I've been having a ton of fuc... I mean, messed-up nightmares."* I had to remember I was talking to an adult. I couldn't use the F word.

The road we were traveling on needed some repairs. I was probably somewhere in an area that contended with harsh winter conditions. The asphalt always takes a beating when the ground freezes and thaws rapidly.

*"This all seems so impossible. How long have you...?"* Kyle started to ask before I cut him off.

*"Only two weeks. Hey, I have an idea. You may be able to convince the police that we are communicating if you start repeating everything, I tell you."*

*"That may work, Rob. Hang on." "Hey, Sergeant. Robert has asked me to repeat everything he's telling me telepathically." "The Sergeant just rolled his eyes, Rob. This is going to be a tough sell."*

*"Tell them I'm in a large box truck traveling at a high rate of speed."* I didn't know the vehicle's exact speed, but by the sound of the tires whining on the road, I knew we were moving right along. I wished my stomach would settle down. I felt as if I could upchuck when I tried to move my head, even the slightest.

*"Robert said, he's riding in the back of a big box truck. The vehicle is traveling at a high rate of speed."*

*"I can't move any of my limbs, and I can't see."*

*"Robert said he's unable to move his arms or legs, and he isn't able to see anything."* I was nervous to ask the question, but I needed to know if Andy was killed during the gunfight.

*"My bodyguard, Andy. Is he dead?"* I asked while holding my breath. As if starving, my brain of oxygen would change the outcome of something that had already occurred.

*"The last I knew, Andy was still alive. He's at the same trauma center Kevin is at. I haven't heard any updates on his condition since yesterday."* Taking a deep breath to replace my depleted oxygenation felt good. *"Rob, I want you to know there are a lot of experts who are searching for you. The FBI is working with several other law enforcement agencies, including every United States military branch. We-will-find-you,"* he told me with confidence.

As I laid in a fetal position on the floor, shivering, I realized that my senses were starting to acclimate. My hearing was less distorted, and my vision was less blurry. When I heard the truck I was riding in begin to slow down, I quickly took notice. Now the truck was stopped. I could feel the vehicle turn to the right and then to the left as it moved slowly. Finally, the truck came to a stop, and the engine shut off. Men were outside of the vehicle, talking as a gas pump started. The men's voices sound as if they were talking through a long tunnel.

*"Hey, Kyle, the truck just stopped for gas. I hear the gas pump running."*

*"Sergeant, Robert said the truck just stopped for fuel,"* Kyle said with urgency. When the rear doors of the truck opened, I closed my eyes and froze.

"Have you been sleeping again?" I heard someone ask in a different language.

"I was just resting my eyes for a few minutes. Where the hell are we?" A man asked with a sleepy voice.

"Somewhere between hell and who knows where," the other guy answered with a sarcastic tone. "I got you some chips and smokes. Stay awake, and don't let those IVs run out, or there will be hell to pay," the guy said before closing the doors causing everything to go dark again. I could feel the IV taped to my left arm. The IV must have had something to do with my incapacitation. When the gas pump shut off, the truck's engine started, and we were back on the road with the smell of cigarette smoke in the air.

*"Okay, I'll tell him."* I heard Kyle say to someone. *"Rob, we've been joined by a detective and a captain from the Sheriff's Office. I think they're starting to believe me." "No, Sir, I've never talked with Robert telepathically before this evening."* When I opened my eyes again, I could see the outline of the man sitting on a bed, no more than ten feet from where I was lying on the floor. The floor was hard, wet, and reeked of urine. I could also see the orange end of a burning cigarette in the man's hand as he tore into a bag of chips. I needed to take this idiot out before he noticed that my IV had, in fact, run dry.

That was why I regained consciousness. If the guy changed the IV, the sedative would start to run through my veins again, I would go back to a terrifying dreamland. This may be the only opportunity I had to escape. I immediately closed my eyes when the guy pointed a flashlight in my direction. A loud curse came next when the guy saw that the IV bag was empty. Damn it. I was too late. *You don't need to worry about the empty IV bag. Go back to sleep, dipwad.* I sent him through a green corridor. Somehow, he was able to ignore my suggestions and started changing my IV bag anyway.

*"Are the rest of my family safe?*" I asked Kyle, trying to use my time wisely before I was knocked out again.

*"Yes, they're all at home, except your father. The media has been hush-hush about him."* Kyle answered. "*The police are taking me to the airport in a convoy of police cruisers.*

*"Kyle. I may not be able to talk with you much longer. I think they're drugging me with IV medication to keep me sleeping." "Robert just told me that he's being drugged. I don't know; let me ask him."*

*"Rob? The police want to know if the truck that you're in is still moving?"*

*"Oh yeah, without a doubt. We haven't stopped since the gas station. Is it dark outside?"* I knew it was nighttime when they stopped for fuel. The canopy lights were shining through the door, but I was able to catch a glimpse of darkness beyond the gas station lights.

*"Yes, it's three twenty-two in the morning."*

*"Mr., I mean, Kyle. There's someone in the back of the truck with me."*

*"Hang tight, Rob; I'll tell the detective."* It's time to take some action. The IV needed to come out. I was able to lift my arms high enough to reach the IV tubing with my teeth. I pulled until the first piece of tape came free, and then I took another bite. Pull... Ouch, ouch, ouch, that tape hurt coming off. One more pull. Got it. I felt the IV pull entirely free from my arm.

*"Rob, the police are ushering me to a waiting aircraft. There's an FBI agent boarding with me." "Hello Agent Loker, yes, that's correct, I'm communicating telepathically with Robert now. As we were pulling up, Robert told me he's able to see someone in the truck with him.*" I heard Kyle tell someone. *"I'll relay that to Robert." "Hey, Rob, the FBI Agent wants you to pretend that you're sleeping, don't move, or let the person see you move."*

*"Got it, play dead."*

It felt as if the truck was taking a sharp curve as we change direction or possibly transferring to a different highway before it sped back up.

*"Rob, the agent wants to know if you can talk to him directly."*

*"No, I can only talk long-distance to you and Kevin."*

*"Can you read the driver of the truck?"* Kyle sent.

*"There are several different voices I can read, and they're changing all of the time. So, I can't distinguish who is who."*

*"Robert, the agent, wants to know if you've been able to read the minds of the abductors."*

*"Yes, I did at the farmhouse, and I can read the guy who is in the back of the truck with me."*

*"Robert said, yes,"* Kyle told the agent. *"Rob, we're coming in for a landing, and then I'll be boarding a helicopter."*

*"Hey, Kyle, I can take the bad guy out. Should I do it?"*

*"Robert believes he can overtake one of the abductors. Okay, I'll tell him." "Robert, the agent said not to move for now. He's concerned they'll hurt you." "Just a second, hang on. I want to make sure I understand so I don't mess this up,"* I heard Kyle say to someone. *"He's just a boy, and his hands are tied. You want Robert to pull his IV out? How's he going... Yes, yes, he's brilliant... Okay, okay, fine, I'll tell him."* Wait, what? I'm 'just a boy?'

*"Rob, the agent wants you to carefully pull your IV out if you are able."*

*"It's already done; I feel fluid running down my arm."*

*"Did you say you've already pulled out your IV?"*

*"Yes, it's done."*

Oh man, everything hurt when I turned my head to make sure numbnuts had gone back to sleep. I finally got myself sitting upright; now, I could see a bed less than three feet away. It felt like a mattress without sheets or blankets. The agent told me not to move, but the cramps in my legs made me want to scream; besides, my dad has always taught me to be my own advocate. I needed to take this guy out so he didn't see me stand. This door will do the trick, I thought to myself as I turned the handle in the wrong direction. *"How does that feel, big tough guy? I'm just a little one-hundred-thirty-five-pound weakling, and I've just rendered you ineffective."* I knew that I shouldn't be talking to him through his yellow corridor, but something inside me wanted to make someone pay for hurting Kevin.

I heard his groans turn into screams before he started retching. I hated the smell of vomit. *"If a little pressure made you puke, let's see how a lot will affect your pea brain."* The idiot tried to stand before falling face-first, not more than six feet from where I was sitting on the floor. *"I bet lying face down in your own puke isn't very nice, is it? There's some of your own medicine for leaving me lay in my own DNA, on this hard floor without any blankets, you dick."*

Oh, it felt so wonderful to move around. When I tried to stand up, I got shaky, so I sat my ass on the bed. Ouch! It hurt when I pulled the rest of the tape from my arm.

*"Kyle, are you there?"*

*"Yes. The helicopter that we are flying on is coming in for a landing."*

*"Can we talk for a minute, or are you aha...?"*

*"No, it's fine,"* he interrupted.

*"I need to ask you some personal questions,"* I told him while trying to figure out what I was going to say and how I was going to say it.

*"It's not a problem, go ahead. We just landed on the roof of a building, I'm walking, but I can still talk. I mean, think."*

*"Did you know that I've had a big crush on you ever since last fall?"*

*"I had my suspicions."*

*"Well, I don't want this to get weird or anything, but if something happens to me. You know, if I die. I want you to know how I feel about you."* I took a deep breath to stall so I could get enough courage to get it all out there. *"I kinda fell... how do I explain this... I kinda fell in love with you."*

*"Rob, I love you like I love all of my students. But I've always kept you in a special place in my heart."* What he told me made me feel loved and accepted. But I was hoping for a little more commitment than he was willing to offer. Earlier, he had mentioned something about Chris. I wondered who Chris was. His wife? Girlfriend? Husband? Boyfriend? Whoever they were, I didn't like them much.

What the hell is that up there? I could barely make out the silhouette of another person toward the front of the truck. The person's hands were tied in front of them with plastic zip ties as well. I've already tried to break the restraints from my wrists and failed. It felt as if the plastic would cut my skin if I pull too hard. When I touched the bare chest of a boy around my age, I could feel him breathing. His face had smooth skin with no facial hair.

*"Kyle?"*

*"I'm here in FBI headquarters with hundreds of other people."*

*"I think I'm in some kind of a truck with beds. It seems big inside. The idiot who was changing my IV is now unconscious."*

*"The abductor who is in the back of the truck with Robert is now unconscious. I don't know, but it doesn't matter. And he said the truck is like a big moving truck with beds."*

*"Kyle, there's another kid in here with me. I don't know who he is for sure, but I think it may be Cam."*

*"Cameron from sixth-hour?" "Shut up! Everyone-shut-up!"* I heard Kyle shout. "*I can't concentrate on what Robert is saying when all of you are trying to talk to me."* Damn. Kyle sounded really pissed off. I've never heard him talk to anyone that way except for one time in sixth-hour when he heard Mark call Samantha the N-word. Mark's feet weren't even touching the floor as Mr. Smit removed him from the classroom.

*"I'm sorry, Rob, at least fifteen people were trying to ask me questions at the same time."*

*"Yes, Cameron from sixth-hour, he's tied up with plastic ties like I am, and he has an IV in his left arm."*

*"Robert told me there is another boy in the back of the truck with him. Yes, I'll tell him." "Rob, Cameron's IV needs to be pulled out."*

*"I think Cam lured me into this whole mess,"* I told Kyle.

*"Robert believes the other boy may have been in on the abduction. No, the other boy's name is Cameron Haas. He's one of my students as well. Yes, just a second." "Rob, the agent, still wants you to pull Cameron's IV. We need to obtain some information from him."* When I removed Cam's IV, he didn't even flinch. Now, all I needed to do was wait for him to wake up so I could ask him some pointed questions.

"*Cam's IV is pulled out."*

*"Good job. The agent told me that someone is on their way to our location, who may be able to help us."*

*"Please tell the agent that I think there may be more than one vehicle. While we were at the gas station, I heard several men outside speaking in a different language."*

*"How many is several?"* he asked.

*"At least four, maybe five."*

"Hey, Cam, wake up," I said as I gave his arm a hard shake.

"Rob, is that you?"

"Yes, it's me, Cam. But what the hell? Why did you sell me out?"

"I'm sorry, I wanted to tell you…" he said as he started to cry.

"Why couldn't you tell me? I trusted you," I demanded with anger in my tone.

"They're holding my mom and dad captive, and they'll kill them if I don't do everything they tell me to do," Cam tried to explain between sobs.

"Who are they? Who's holding your parents?"

"I don't know where they're holding my mom and dad. There were eight men and two women, but I think I saw two dead at the house. I'm so sorry, Rob," Cam said as he started to sob again.

"Stop crying! Now!" I yelled. "I need more information. There's no time for crying." Maybe, I was a bit insensitive, but this was serious shit. "Where are they from? The abductors, where are they from, and what do they want?"

"They want you. I'm not sure what County they're from," he said with an apologetic tone. I don't know what made me do it, but I put my arms around Cam and hugged him tightly. I could feel him trembling as he laid his head on my shoulder. "My head hurts really bad. What is that horrible smell?" Cam asked.

"It's our used body fluids, I think. Haas isn't your real last name, is it?" I asked.

"No, it's Dade."

"Well, Cameron Dade, your headache will get better; I've been awake for about two hours; my headache is almost gone."

"What's up with him?" Cam asked as he pointed at the silhouette of the man lying in his puke.

"He's not dead, but he probably wishes he were. We need to find a way to cut these restraints so we can get the hell out of here. Do you have any tracking devices on you?" I asked.

"I don't think so. Let's see if that guy has a cell. If he does, we'll be able to check our location and call for help," Cam suggested as he pointed at the guy on the floor.

"Great idea!" I said as I crawled slowly over to our prisoner. The unconscious guy didn't have a phone, but he had a knife and a flashlight. I was able to cut Cam's restraints before he cuts mine. "I need to talk to Mr.

Smit for a second, so don't try to talk to me." I couldn't see Cam's face, but I could read his confusion.

*"Kyle?"*

*"I'm here, and so is your father."* I don't know why, but the news of my dad being with Mr. Smit caused tears to start flowing.

*"Dad?"*

*"He's here, Rob."* I wasn't able to connect with my dad. I tried a few times, but it didn't work.

*"Please tell him that I love him."*

*"Robert said he loves you, Sir." "Your father said that he loves you too, Rob."*

*"Cam is awake. His last name isn't Haas; it's Dade. And he told me that the abductors are holding his parent's hostage, and he doesn't know where,"* I listed off for Kyle as if I wanted to get back down to business.

*"Cameron is awake now; he told Robert his parents are being held against their will in an unknown location." "Hey, Rob, there's a Special Agent Daniels here; he would like to communicate with you if he can."*

*"Thanks, that would be great; I have a few questions for Kipton. Can you relay the information? I've tried to connect with him, and it won't work."*

*"Kipton?"* Kyle asked.

*"Kipton is his first name. Tell Kipton that I don't know how to distinguish between friend and foe. Ask him how I can tell where the person is located who I'm tapping into? I'm hearing all of these thoughts of different people while we're on the road, but I can't figure out where we're located. While they were filling the truck with fuel, I heard someone ordering a Grande coffee from Starbucks. I even heard the barista ask if they want them to leave any room for cream. And that could have been anyone anywhere."*

*"Robert is asking how to distinguish between friend and foe. How can he tell where the person is located that he's tapping into? I understand." "Hey, Rob, Kipton said, it's likely the person you're hearing will be nearby. So, if you're able to focus on someone who is reading a sign, map, or their GPS, you may be able to get a lock on your location."* Damn, why didn't I think of that?

*"Please tell him, thank you, that's great advice."*

*"Kevin, please talk to me. Can you hear me?"*

*"I'm here, Rob."* I start to leak tears again. I just told Cam to quit crying, so I needed to hold it together too.

*"Thank you for not dying,"* is all I could think to say.

*"I could say the same to you,"* Kevin told me.

*"I'm in a really messed-up situation here, and there's a good chance I could die,"* I admitted.

*"Where are you? I can call the police,"* Kevin said.

*"Mr. Smit is with the FBI, and they are already trying to find me. My abductors have me locked in the back of a truck. If they end up killing me, I won't ever get a chance to...*

*"You're not going to die, and neither am I,"* he interrupted.

*"Just listen to me for a second, please. If I die, I won't ever get to tell you this, so here it goes. I love you."*

*"I love you too, Rob."* The way he sent his response came so naturally and comfortably. It was almost as if he was planning on telling me the same thing.

*"They didn't mess up your pretty face, did they?"* I asked as I closed my eyes and concentrated on what Kevin was seeing.

*"Nope, the money maker is still in good shape."*

*"When I figure out where we are, I'll call you back."*

*"We?"* he asked.

*"Yeah, it's a long story, but Cam is here with me."*

*"Don't trust that asshole."* Just as Kevin was warning me about trusting Cam, I heard someone think, 'Boulder thirty-two miles.'

*"I'm fine; I'll explain later. Talk in a bit." "Hey, Kyle?"*

*"Go ahead,"* Kyle answered immediately as if he just keyed up a two-way radio mic to start talking.

*"Someone close to us just read a sign. The sign said Boulder thirty-two miles."*

*"Got it." "Robert told me he just heard someone reading a sign that said Boulder thirty-two miles."*

"Rob, what are you doing? How come you're not talking?" I just put a finger up to Cam like I was saying to give me a minute more.

*"Hey, Rob, there are seven cities named Boulder in the US. The Air Force will be scrambling fighter jets out of four different bases. They have reason to believe you're in Colorado, so they'll be coming out of Colorado Springs as well. The jets will be there soon, and they'll be making a lot of*

*noise when they fly over. So, you'll need to let us know as soon as you hear them pass over. Once they've found you, the police will be converging on your location. There will also be several helicopters dispatched to your location. The police plan to surround the truck after it stops. The agents are asking that you and Cam lay flat on the floor of the truck."* Kyle sounded as if he was reading from a script.

*"Gross, we'll have to lay in piss, puke, and who knows what else."*

*"Rob, your father, wants me to tell you he loves you and that he's proud of you."* Damn. My dad must think I have a good chance of dying soon. Cam nudged me with his arm.

"Rob, what are you doing? How are you talking with Mr. Smit? What's going on?"

*"Cam, you're going to have to trust me; I can speak to some people with who I've made a strong connection or anyone who is nearby."*

"This is... impossible. How'd you...?"

*"There's no time to explain we're about to go into a firefight. We'll need to hit the floor as soon as we hear some low flying jets."*

"So, you and Kevin do talk to each other privately at lunch."

"Yeah, for the last two...." My voice was drowned out by three big booms. "Holy shit!"

*"Kyle, the jets just went over us."*

*"Okay, get on the floor and stay there. The next time the fighter jets come over, they'll be flying slower, so you'll need to tell me precisely the moment they go over."*

"What the hell was that?" Cam asked.

"Dude! That was three fighter jets traveling faster than the speed of sound!" Wait, did I just call Cam, dude? Kevin and Zach must be rubbing off on me. "Come on, we need to lay flat on the floor." Damn it, the guy lying next to us was starting to move around. "*Stay down if you want to live, dumbass,"* I sent. He was trying to sit up. We needed him alive so he could tell the police where to find Cam's parents. "*I warned you... here it goes; it'll be better to have a headache than dead. I hope you have a good medical insurance plan,"* I told him as I turned the door handle. The jerk immediately fell back into his vomit.

"What just happened to him?" Cam asked.

"Let's just assume he doesn't do well with pain."

*"Kyle, the fighter jets just went back over and shook the whole truck. It sounds like our truck is speeding up."*

*"Rob, the FBI agent just told me the helicopters will be at your location within five minutes."*

*"Okay... they better hurry. The jets just flew over us again. They're coming back. Holy shit, that time, they were flying really low. The whole truck felt like it was coming apart."*

*"Hang on, Rob, we have your exact location; you'll be safe in no time.* The defining jet engines sounded as if a fighter was hovering over us.

*"Kevin, can you hear me?"*

*"Yeah, I'm in a CT scanner tunnel. Has anyone ever told you how claustrophobic these things make you feel?"* I needed to give him some information, so I ignored Kevin's question.

*"The police are almost ready to stop the truck we're riding in. This could be the last time we ever talk..."*

*"Rob, you'll be fine; just hang in there,"* he said, interrupting my thoughts.

*"Goodbye, Kevin Larson; I love you." "Kyle, talk to me. Where are those choppers?"* The jet noise was gone.

*"The helicopters are at your location, waiting for the signal to move in. The police have the road blocked just ahead; the truck will be stopped soon,"* Kyle sent with confidence.

*"Don't forget about the additional vehicle,* I reminded him.

*"These guys are about to find out they messed with the wrong kid, Rob."* First, I was a boy and now a kid. He wasn't interested in waiting for three more years. He saw me as a kid. But then again, I was a kid. Mr. Smit was probably already romantically involved with that Chris guy. I mean, who wouldn't want someone like Kyle? I needed to clear my mind. I may have to use it.

Cam and I were lying on the floor, spooning each other like this may be the last human contact either of us ever have.

"I'm sorry for getting you into all of this," I heard Cam mumble through his tears.

"You were doing what you had to do; besides, if it weren't for me, they never would have had a reason to take you in the first place," I told him. Cam was terrified, too, so I needed to think of a distraction to calm our minds. "Why, Hawaii?" I asked Cam calmly.

"What?" he asked, raising his voice over the noises outside.

"Why did you choose Hawaii? You know you said your mom and dad were in Hawaii."

"Oh, I've always dreamed of going there; it's the first place that came to my mind," he said as we both trembled uncontrollably. "Have you ever been there?" he asked.

"A few times. My grandparents have a house in Lahaina, Maui."

"Tell me what it's like there," he said with a sad voice as if he may never get a chance to go. Cam had figured out my strategy to stay calm. The truck was slowing down, it felt as if we were coming to a stop, so it was challenging to remain calm.

"It's beautiful, the rainbows are so fly, and the color of the water is gorgeous. The air always seems to be a perfect temperature, and the smell of flowers is amazing. But the best part is the..." I froze, squeezing Cam with all my strength when I heard automatic gunfire.

*"Fuck! Shots fired! Shots fired, Kyle! It sounds like a war out there! I hear people yelling!"*

*"Just stay down,"* Kyle said calmly. The guns had stopped firing. There was more yelling, and then an eary silence hung in the air. A cold sweat ran down my face as I continued to hug Cam.

*"Sorry, I said the f word, Kyle."* I could tell Kyle was crying as if he was having a nervous breakdown. *"Kyle, are you okay?"* I asked through my own mental pain. Before he could answer, the doors of the truck flew open. I was ready to take someone out. If they weren't the police, I was prepared to kill someone, but all I could see were bright, blinding lights shining on us. Finally, my eyesight recovered enough to make out the large FBI and Swat labels on the officer's protective gear.

*"Kyle, it's the police; please tell my dad I'm safe."*

"Team one to Command, we've got'em!" I heard one of the swat cops say into his radio.

"Ten-four, Team one, we've got two stretchers coming your way," the radio answered back.

"Are you boys hurt?" an officer asked as he entered the truck. "Are either of you injured?"

"No," Can and I answered simultaneously as a big guy who was wearing a black "Swat" vest scooped me up and cradled me as if I was a baby in his arms. He carried me to the back of the truck before handing me off to another guy who was wearing ballistic gear as well. The early morning air was cold on my bare, wet skin, causing me to shiver. It felt so good when they laid me on a stretcher and cover me with a warm blanket. At least ten rescuers were carrying us toward the choppers that still had the engines running. Even though they had me strapped on, I felt as if I could fall off.

*"Kevin, we're safe and on our way to the hospital."*

*"Oh, man... Dude, I..."* Kevin's response caused a lump to form in my throat. "*Call me back as soon as you get to the hospital!*" Kevin sent.

*"I will,"* is all I was able to send back while trying to control my own tears.

A paramedic immediately placed hearing protection on my head after we were loaded into a medical chopper. "How's that, Robert? Can you hear me?" the paramedic asked.

"Yeah, I can hear you," I answered into a small, attached microphone.

"Do you know what day it is?" he asked. I didn't have a clue what day it was. I should probably be asking him.

"I'm not sure what day it is, Sir," I answered the twenty-something paramedic respectfully.

"Robert, do you know the name of our president?" the paramedic asked with a smirk in his expression.

"Umm... It's President Barnes. I met him last week; I think he gets spray-on tans," I answered with a smirk as he and his partner chuckled.

"My name is Troy; I'll be starting an IV on you," he said as he got things ready. I heard the turbine engines start to speed up as he tied a tourniquet around my arm. Troy was thinking about a girl, maybe his wife. *Tonight, I can tell Susie about the rescue of Robert Van Stark during my proposal.* Nope, not his wife. It was kind of cute knowing that my story may be helping him out with his romantic relationship, but how the hell did Troy know my last name. And it would be appreciated if Troy would focus a little closer on my arm before he stuck that garden hose, size IV needle in my vain. "Here comes a big poke," Troy said, warning me to hold still.

"Where are you taking us? Ouch, ouch, ouch...," I asked as Troy speared a vein in my arm.

"Hold still, Robert, I'm just about finished. We're en route to the Shock Trauma Center in Denver," he told me as he hooked up the IV tubing to the needle thing and then taped it down to my arm. I looked to my left and saw Cam getting an IV as well.

*"Kyle, we're in the air, on our way to Denver. Please tell my dad that I need to talk to him as soon as I land."*

*"Your father is on his way to meet you in Denver. He should be there within an hour."*

*"Can someone find Cam's parents, please?"*

*"They've already been located; the military has been dispatched to rescue them."*

*"Can I tell Cam?"*

*"Yes, Kipton said you can tell Cameron."*

*"Thank you Kipton, we'll talk again sometime soon,"* I said, hoping Kyle would relay.

*"Hey, Cam?"* I said, trying to get him to look at me. *"They found your mom and dad. The military is on its way to rescue them."*

*"Thank you,"* Cam sent back as tears streamed down his cheeks. I felt the tears welling up in my eyes again too.

"Hey, guys, we're coming in for a landing," Troy's partner told us.

"Good, cuz, I gotta take like a major piss!" Cam told him. Frankly, I was relieved that we were landing. On the way here, all I could think about was how Uncle Keith died in Afghanistan. The density of a chopper and how it stayed in the air was a mechanical miracle. If you thought about how it worked, it would be a bit scary. The blades beat the air into submission to gain altitude. If the engines stop working, there was no gentle gliding back to the earth. The thing would drop out of the sky like a crowbar. But it was cool when we land on the roof of the hospital; I've never experienced anything like it. First, I felt the rear tires set down on the roof, and then the chopper slowly leveled out as the front tires softly set down.

"Air ambulances are cool, don't you think?" Troy asked.

"They're badass," I answered as I tried to look out the window. It was still dark out; I had no idea what time it was. "Please tell the pilot, thank you for us," I told Troy.

"Sure will," Troy answered just before he removed my hearing protection.

*And good luck with your proposal to Susie,* I sent him through a green corridor.

Cam and I were both moved into an elevator before we were wheeled into a trauma room. I was in trauma bay 7 and Cam in 8. At least that's what it said on the walls. But why a trauma bay? We weren't traumatized. I wasn't even sure why we were here. I didn't think we had been physically injured, but the psychological trauma would be challenging for Doctor Kelly to sort through.

Several people were rushing around who seemed to be very efficient in what they were doing. An RN named Amanda asked me questions regarding the past three days of my life, which I couldn't recall. I guess I could tell Amanda about the messed-up dreams I had while they had me drugged. The webbed hand, green, slimy Aquaman would be interesting for her to hear about. Or I could tell her about totaling out one of my dad's trucks when I got pissed. Nope, not a good idea.

There was also a person standing on my left side, putting stickers and wires on my chest.

"Umm, Amanda, what time is it?" I asked.

"Two-thirty," she answered after checking her watch. I knew there was a two-hour time difference between eastern and mountain time.

"Is there anything I can get for you, Robert?" Amanda asked after hooking up a blood pressure cuff.

"A couple of cheeseburgers would be great," I told her after she removed the thermometer from my mouth. My temperature was probably low. I just couldn't seem to warm up.

"I think we can make those arrangements as soon as the doctor authorizes some food." When Amanda turned to walk away, I clearly heard her thoughts. *So, he's the cute boy the whole world has been talking about for the last three days.* My face went flush within seconds after hearing her 'cute boy' reference. My temperature was recovering.

"Hello there," I heard a friendly voice say as someone approached my bedside. "My name is Dr. Thomas; I just spoke with your father on the phone; he has given me permission to treat you. I've been hearing a lot about you on the national news, young man," Doctor Thomas said as he used his stethoscope to listen to my lungs and heart. "You've become quite a celebrity over the past few days."

"Great, that's all I need," I replied with a rhetorical tone.

"Do you have any pain?" the doctor asked as he pushed on my abdomen. I automatically tightened my muscles when he went too deep. "Try to relax those rock-hard abs," he said with a smirk as he continued to apply pressure.

"My head hurts a bit, but other than that, I'm fine," I told him.

"Do you have any blurred vision?" he asked, shining a bright light in my eyes. Not until you burned my retinas with that LED light.

"No," I told him instead, trying not to be a dick.

"Alrighty," he said with a cheerful tone as he gave my left thigh a light pat. "We'll be doing a few tests on your blood."

"I'm sorry if this sounds rude, Dr. Thomas, but I really need to get back to Michigan as soon as possible; it's already four-thirty there."

"Why is that?" he asked. "Do you miss your family?"

"Yeah, I miss them and my best friend, Kevin, too. But that's not the most pressing issue."

"What's your most pressing issue?" He asked, probably trying to humor me.

"I have a lead part in our high school play next weekend." Doctor Thomas started to chuckle. I was confused at his response; I wasn't trying to be funny.

"What's your part in the play?" he asked with a big grin he could hardly control.

"Peter Pan, Sir. But I just started to learn my lines last week. Trent Dade got hit by a car and broke his leg, so I took his place." I was sure this all seemed trivial to him, but I was serious; there were a lot of people who have worked very hard and were counting on me. Things had quickly changed. An hour ago, I was making life and death decisions. Now I was back to being a nerdy high school kid who had a minimal list of responsibilities.

"Well, Robert, I'll check you over to make sure you aren't sick or injured, so we can get you back to Michigan." *He is so damn cute, but I don't think this kid knows how close he was to death or how famous he is. Little does he know; his life has changed forever.* Oh, believe me, I didn't think I'd get out of that truck alive. But he would be correct about me being clueless concerning my future and my popularity. I laid my head back on the pillow to check in on Kevin. He was being pushed down a long hallway; all I could see were ceiling tiles. *Hey man, we're at the hospital; everything seems fine so far."* Kevin's vision became blurry as the ceiling tiles continued to pass by.

*"Love ya,"* is all he sent.

*"Love ya too,"* I said in return, thinking the 'ya' reference must be code for two guys telling each other that they love each other without sounding too gay.

*"How's it going over there, Cam? They're not sticking anything in orifices that are off-limits, are they?"* Cam turned his head toward me. He looked miserable.

*"I just heard the doctor mention something about a rape kit, so that's got me a bit worried. Have you heard any updates about my parents yet?"*

*"No, but I can check with Mr. Smit. He's in the FBI headquarters."*

*"Hey, Kyle, have you heard anything about Cam's parents yet?"*

*"No, I've been taken out of the loop. I'm on my way to the airport. Your Grandfather has offered to fly me back to Holland. Where are you now?"*

*"Cam and I are at a trauma center in Denver."*

*"Are either of you injured?"*

*"No, I think Cam and I are physically okay. The last time I checked with Kevin, he was conscious, riding on a CT scanner table."*

*"I'm so relieved you're all doing well. I need to call Chris; I'm sure she's worried.* My gut immediately sunk into the abyss when he gave me the news about Chris being female. If Chris would have been a guy, I may have had a chance someday. I swallow hard, trying not to show any emotion about the reality of the situation.

A guy wearing bright green scrubs was getting ready to stick me with another needle, so I decided it would be proper to look in his direction.

"Hey, Robert, my name is Nolan; I'm going to be drawing some blood." I just nodded and look away as I sulked about Kyle. "I feel like I've known you for quite some time," Nolan said as he filled a purple-topped tube with my blood. I was still on the part from before, so I kind of just heard something, something, something, I've known you for quite some time.

"Um… What? Why's that," I finally asked, so I didn't seem disinterested or rude.

"Your abduction story has been in the national news for the last three days," he explained. "You can't turn a TV on or read the news online without seeing your face on it." I just gave a forced smile in return. I should have been honest with myself about the probability of Kyle being straight in the first place. I guess I've kind of known all along, but I didn't want to admit it to myself. I knew it was time to grow up and deal with the fact that it will never work between Kyle and me.

*"It's Tuesday, isn't it? Are you going to miss school?"* I ask Kyle.

*"No, I'll make it in time."*

*"But you didn't get any sleep,"* I told Kyle as if I was trying to talk him into taking a sick day.

*"I'll be fine. I've worked with a lot less sleep."*

*"Thank you for saving my life again,"* I said to Kyle with sincere appreciation. If it weren't for him, I'd still be lying in piss.

*"You're an extraordinary young man. We have an exceptional bond; I think we'll be close friends for a long, long time."* Young man? I liked that. And I guess I could live with a close friendship for now.

"Is it true that your brother Sam will be going to the Naval Academy?" Nolan asked.

"Ah, what? I'm sorry, I have a lot on my mind," I told him honestly.

"Your brother Sam. Was he accepted into the Naval Academy?" he repeated.

"Erm, yeah, how do you know about my brother?" I asked with a confused tone.

"CNN calls it filler news. When they don't have anything to report, they start digging for information," he said as he tipped the tube of blood back and forth.

"Oh, ah, yeah," I said with a weak smile.

"I tried to get in but was unsuccessful," Nolan said, apparently referring to the Naval Academy. Nolan packed his tubes in a pouch and started to walk away.

"Ah, Nolan?"

"Yeah," he answered, turning back to face me.

"Thank you." He smiled and gave me a wave.

*"Hey, Cam, Mr. Smit hasn't heard anything yet. But my dad should be here soon; we'll ask him."* I no more than had my thoughts transmitted to Cam when my dad came charging through the door under heavy guard. Three guys surrounded him with hospital security in the lead as he ran up to the ER bed and threw his arms around me.

"I love you, Robert! Thank God, you're safe!" he said as he squeezed the shit out of me. Without warning, the floodgates opened; I felt as if I was a five-year-old boy being held by my daddy. I just couldn't seem to stop; they just kept flowing until his shirt was drenched.

"Congressman Van Stark, I'm Doctor Thomas; we spoke on the phone."

"Yes, Doctor, how's he doing?" I saw a woman near Cam's bed as well, but she wasn't hugging him like my dad hugged me.

"Robert's blood work will be back from the lab in a few minutes; if that checks out, he'll be free to go. We've only found minor injuries on both of the boys."

*"Who's that, Cam?*

*"She's my federally appointed guardian. But she sounds more like an interrogator when she talks."*

*"I'm getting out of here; you're coming with me."*

*"That would be great if we could stick together; I'm still freaking over here,"* he said.

"Hey, Dad, will Cam be able to come home with us?"

"Yes, that's the plan. You two have a few questions to answer that will be taking place in our house."

"Dad? Cam and I are going to need a shower before anyone wants to get on a plane with us." He laughed out loud, grabbing both sides of my head, and planting a kiss on the forehead.

"Thank God, you're safe," my dad said.

"Where are Cam's parents?" I asked my dad.

"Their location is classified, but we should be hearing back from the FBI within the hour."

"Can you tell me how Andy is doing?"

"He was shot three times. He's still listed as critical, but it looks like his chances of survival are high."

"They jammed our phone signals; we couldn't call for..." I start to explain before Dad cut me off with the drop of his head and a hand wave.

"I know, let's get you home; we'll cover all of that later. Getting you home to your worried Mother is a top priority."

We were flying home on one of grandpa's jets at 05:40 when I decide to check in with Kevin.

*"Are you going to school today?"*

*"Dude, where the hell have you been?"*

*"Medical people were poking and prodding us to make sure the aliens didn't plant any microorganisms in our brains."*

*"You probably do have frequent micro-orgasms in your brain without anyone poking you,"* Kevin said, laughing at his own play on words.

*"Haha,"* I said as I laid my head back against the seat and close my eyes. Kevin was back in the scary room, but he didn't seem to be affected by the machines beeping. I knew the time would come soon when I needed to come clean about Kevin's mind's orange corridor. I've been dreading the thought. He would be angry, but I didn't think I could put it off much longer.

*"Seriously, are you going to live?"* Kevin asked.

*"We're fine, don't worry about us; we're on our way home. The question is, did they find a brain when they did a CT scan?"* I asked, trying to get him back for the micro-orgasm comment.

*"How's Judas doing?"*

*"Cam is fine too. His parents are being rescued as we speak."*

*"What do you mean, rescued?"*

*"He was being used as a pawn to get to me. His parents are being held by terrorists. Who even knows if his parents are still alive?"*

*"Dude, I'm sorry. Tell Cam, I'm sorry."*

*"I will. You better get some rest. See ya soon."*

*"Hey, Cam, Kevin said sorry for being a dick."*

*"He's not a dick. He was just looking out for his friend. Are we still friends, or do you want to dump me?"*

*"I want to start over and get to know the real you. Like, where you live. Are you really sixteen, by the way?"*

*"My real name is Cameron Dade. I live in Clintonville, Wisconsin. I'm sixteen, both of my parents are self-employed writers.*

*"That's a good start."*

"Cameron," Dad said as he put his phone down to his side.

"Yes, Sir," Cam answered.

"I just finished speaking with the director of the FBI; he told me that both of your parents have been rescued. They're on their way to Michigan to meet with you." Cam covered his face with his hands and leaning forward to rest his head on his lap. I felt him trembling as I slide in beside him. The seat was only big enough for one full-size adult, so squeezing my skinny ass between him and the armrest was no easy task. I put my arm around Cam to comfort him as I felt my dad put his hand on my back from the seat behind us.

*"Are you doing okay?"* I ask Cam after he raised his head from his lap.

*"I'm doing better. You must have some other powers, I mean, other than telepathy.* Cam said.

*"What do you mean?"* I asked, wondering what else he may have noticed.

*"When Glad hit Kevin in the head with his gun, your whole body went rigid like you were having a seizure or something. As you screamed, every window in the room blew out, maybe even the entire house. The glass was flying everywhere; the explosion was so violent that it caused the whole house to shake. Plaster was still falling from the ceiling when they drug us out to the truck. It was all kind of scary,"* Cam said as if he suddenly realized that maybe he shouldn't be sitting so close to me.

*"I ah... I made an explosion?"* I could have killed us all. I needed to learn to control my aggression.

*"I think so because it happened when you screamed."* I was in disbelief, or maybe it was denial.

# Homecoming Chapter 15

Tuesday, May 30th Homecoming

It was 08:30 in the morning when we land at Tulip City Airport. I could see satellite trucks parked on the side streets with cameras and news reporters standing ready to talk with someone. Hopefully, that someone wouldn't be me. I looked like shit, not to mention, I was still freeballing in some light blue hospital scrubs. I could see my mom standing with Kate and Sam. It was difficult to know for sure, but it looked as if everyone had tears except Sam. Would it kill him to show some heartfelt emotion? As the jet engines were winding down, I saw another jet identical to the one we were in taxi past us. I could guess who that was.

Before the doors opened, Brad stood at the front by the cockpit to start his briefing on what we could and couldn't tell the media.

"Mr. Congressman, you and Suzanne will give a brief overview of the morning events and the condition of only Robert. Suzanne has already been briefed. We will provide the media with a chance to talk with the boys after they are cleared. *Not in this lifetime,* I sent to Brad through his green corridor. "Cameron and Robert, you'll be escorted from the aircraft by Gary. He'll give you a chance to give brief greetings to your family before you make your way to the truck." A brief greeting? Are you serious? I was just kidnapped! I thought you knew my mom better than that. It was doubtful she would let go once she got me in her clutches. "After you're secured in the truck, you will be driven home by Gary." I felt as if we were back on the campaign trail again, where every word and minute was scrutinized.

The door opened slowly, so security could disembark first. I wasn't even sure who the security guys were; I've never seen them before. My dad was the next one off the plane, followed closely by Brad and Cam's escort.

"Okay, here we go," I said to Cam as I moved toward the door. "Are you ready for this?"

"Nope, how would I ever prepare myself for anything like this," he answered with a nervous tone.

"Come on, we'll get off together," I recommend and then quickly realized I should have phrased my recommendation differently. Cam was grinning uncontrollably as we made our way out the door.

When we walked down the steps, the crowd of media started asking questions. They sounded more like a swarm of bees. My parents hugged each other until my mom saw me and abruptly let go of my dad to grab me. Cam was standing beside me when my Grandma noticed him without hugs. Grandma pulled Cam into a hug as well; he looked kind of funny towering over her, but Cam was smiling. Before I knew it, we were being rushed to the truck by Gary, just as Brad had instructed. I couldn't believe my mom released me from her death grip.

Sam turned to smile from the front seat as we pulled off the tarmac.

"You really know how to bring attention to yourself, don't you?" Sam said as he pointed at the news trucks. "That's nothing compared to our front yard. There are so many people at our house; they've had to bring in porta-potties and tents," he said as we passed the line of satellite trucks.

"Hey, Gary?"

"What is it, Robert?" he answered while looking in the rearview mirror.

"Cam and I are starving; can you please drive through Mickey D's?"

"Sure, I'll just have to make some arrangements," he said as he picked up his phone.

"You know Mrs. Wells will be crushed when she finds out you've already eaten," Sam said with another smile.

"Don't worry, we'll eat whatever she makes us. We had a snack at the hospital three hours ago, but that didn't do much for us," I explained to Sam, speaking for Cam as well, who hadn't said a word since we climbed into the vehicle.

"I don't have any money," Cam finally said as we pulled into the drive-through.

“Neither do I. Sam is buying,” I told him.

“I’ll pay you back,” Cam said emphatically.

“Don’t worry about it,” Sam said.

“Okay then, I’ll take three bacon, egg and cheese biscuits, three hash browns, and a cup of black coffee,” Cam said.

“Ditto,” I added with a big grin. Sam was looking at us as if we were freaks.

“Don’t give me that look, Sam; I watched you eat six corn dogs two weeks ago down at the Grand Haven boardwalk.”

*“Hey, Kevin, how are you feeling?”*

*“Dude, how do you do it?”*

*“Do what?”*

*“How is it? You always know when I’m in the shower? It almost seems like you wait until I have all of my clothes off before you call me.”*

“Why are you smiling?” Sam asked. “Do you think it’s funny that I’m spending $28 bucks of my hard-earned cash on your breakfast?”

“No, I was just thinking about something Kevin told me.”

“Do you want to use my cell to call him?” he asked.

“No, thanks, we already talked on the way home.”

*“I didn’t know you were showering. It was just lucky timing on my part.”*

*“Where are you?”* Kevin asked.

*“In the drive-through at McDonald's in Holland.”*

*“I knew you were back in Holland. They just interrupted Good Morning America with breaking news. It was you coming down the steps of a kick-ass jet. You look cute in those hospital scrubs, by the way.”*

*“Haha,”* I respond as we pulled up to the pay window.

“Are they with you?” the food window guy asked, pointing at the truck in front and behind us. Gary shook his head, yes. I still wasn’t sure why my grandpa bought black vehicles. Another unanswered Rob question. Like the question that comes to mind right now. Where do people who are at a nude beach carry their cell phones? Hmm.

*“My dad said the Hospital here in GR has a bunch of TV trucks waiting to hear how Andy and I are doing. I’ve never felt so important.”*

*“I’ll be there to see you as soon as we’re done being interrogated.”*

“Thank you, Sam,” I said as I chowed down my second breakfast of the day.

"Anything for my prodigal brother who decided to return. But don't expect me to kill the fatted calf for dinner," he said with sarcasm.

Our driveway was packed with media vehicles. Thankfully, Gary immediately pulled into the garage and closed the door behind us. "Sam, do you have some jeans, and a shirt Cam can borrow?"

"Sure, no problem, they may be a little baggy, but at least you won't have to wear scrubs," he said to Cam. We walked through the mudroom door, where Mrs. Wells was waiting. Petey kept doing laps around us until Cam knelt down to pet him.

"Mrs. Wells, this is Cam," I said as she loosened her hold on me.

"I've heard so much about you, Cam," she said as she pulled him into a hug as well. "I'm making you boys some breakfast. I hope you're hungry," she said as Sam scooted by, clearing his throat loudly.

"I had no idea you were so well off," Cam said with amazement as he entered the central room of our house.

"Ah... yeah, my dad comes from a lot of money."

"Hence the private jet we flew back on. I figured your family must have a lot of money, but I never would have dreamed you live in a place like this," he said, continuing to look around.

After our third breakfast and reciting or past events to the FBI, we were free to leave so we could visit Kevin. According to my dad, I couldn't see Andy because he still wasn't up for having visitors. When we entered the children's hospital lobby, several people looked at us and even pointed as if we were famous. It was a bit unnerving and embarrassing to be seen like this. I could tell Cam was feeling uneasy as well.

*"We're here,"* I announced to Kevin.

*"You're not expecting a kiss or anything, are you?"* he asked.

*"Shut up. A hug would be nice."*

Kevin was sitting in a chair beside his bed, talking with his dad when we walk in. Our smiles were hidden as we bury our faces in each other's shoulders.

"Thank you for not dying," is all I was able to whisper.

I looked over at my dad, who was introducing himself to Devon. "Dad, this is my friend Kevin," I announced as my dad stepped up next to Kevin and me.

"Thank you for trying to rescue Robert; that took a lot of courage," my dad said as he shook Kevin's hand.

"And Mr. Larson, this is Cameron," I said as I turned to find no one standing behind me. "Where'd he go?" I gave Kevin an awkward look as I turned to go find Cam. Just as I suspected. As I rounded the corner in the hallway, I found Cam with his head down, looking at me out the corner of his eye. "What are you doing?"

"Waiting," Cam answered.

"For what, an invitation?"

"I thought…"

"You thought what, Cam?" I whispered, stepping back to give him the 'you first' hand gesture. He reluctantly made his long legs move toward Kevin's room. "Mr. Larson, this is my friend Cameron." "Cam, this is Kevin's father, Devon."

"Nice to meet you, Sir," Cam said before looking over at Kevin, who was still tethered by his IV tubing.

"I don't bite, Cam," Kevin said.

"I'm sorry," Cam started to say before Kevin reached out, dragging him into an embracing clinch.

"Dude, there's no reason to apologize. I would have done the same for my dad. When do you get to see your parents?"

"Um… I'm not… I'm not sure," Cam was finally able to say. I looked over at my dad to gauge his discomfort level on the awkward scale. He and Devon both had proud smiles.

"I just need to know one thing," Kevin said.

"Sure, what is it?" Cam answered.

"Are you really sixteen?" All three of us started to laugh.

When we left the children's hospital's lobby, the entrance was littered with reporters and TV cameras. I was getting more anxious by the second as we made our way to where Brad was standing with the media.

"Hey Robert, how are you feeling?" Brad asked as he gave me a side-by-side hug.

"I'm fine," I answered matter-of-factly.

"The media would like to have a quick interview with your Father. And if you're willing to stand next to him, it will be comforting for many who care about your wellbeing," he said.

"Sure, no problem," I said bravely, even though I didn't understand why strangers would care.

Three days ago, there were only a handful of people on this earth who even knew I existed. There was another stupid phrase that I frequently use. How many people could I actually fit in my hand? I guess Doctor Thomas was right. My life, as I knew it, had changed.

Our arrival at school was just before, sixth-hour ended, and wouldn't you know it, the end of period tone went off before making it to the media center. The hallways were flooded with students looking at me as if I were Daniel Radcliffe, who decided to visit our school unexpectedly. It was like the parting of the 'great sea' as we made our way down the hall.

Finally, we entered the media center, where my eye caught Liam first. His emotions went into high alert as he ran to meet us. "Thank you for coming back alive; I haven't slept for three days," Liam said as my feet left the floor when he hugged me.

*"Quit smiling, Cam,"* I sent to him while looking over Liam's shoulder.

*"I think he's in love."* Cam teased.

"You were so brave, Robert," Ms. Hukins said while taking her turn to hug me. "I can't believe you came to rehearsal after being through everything that..." She trailed off just as David came through the door. David stopped dead in his tracks, stared at me for a second before turning on a heel, and off he went back out the door. Shit! What was up with David?

"Let's all get to work," Ms. Hukins recommended as she dabbed her tears with a tissue. "We have a long way to go before opening night on Friday. Everyone will start with scene one, while Peter and Hook work on scene five." "You will be staying, won't you?" Ms. Hukins asked. I give her a nod.

"Are you ready?" I asked as I gently placed my hand on Liam's shoulder.

"Sure, if you are," Liem said as he led me backstage to where they had a table and chairs set up for us to work at.

“It kinda stinks like dirty socks back here, don’t you think?” I asked, wrinkling up my nose while pressing the back of my hand against my nostrils.

“I just can’t believe you’re here. You seem unfazed by this whole thing,” Liam told me before taking a deep dramatic breath.

We were able to get through scene five, but Liam seemed distracted and kept forgetting his lines. Finally, he stopped abruptly and looked at me as if he was frustrated.

“You don’t get it. Do you?” Liam finally asked, throwing his arms out in front of him.

“Get what?” I asked defensively as I quickly straighten up from my relaxed sitting position and turn toward him. After all, Liam was the one messing up his lines, not me.

“You don’t realize how this whole thing has affected our school, our town, hell, our whole damn Nation,” he said, raising his arms above his head, moving them in a circular motion. Liam took a big cleansing breath as if he was trying to get his emotions in check. “The story about your abduction was running nonstop on every news network in the world. My mother and I were sitting up watching Fox News at four this morning because I was too much of a wreck to be on my own all weekend. The news had been running updates on you every twenty minutes. Finally, there you were. Breaking News,” Liam said as he moved his hands dramatically in front of us. “Several rescuers were loading you onto a medical helicopter. There were so many conflicting stories on the news, we didn’t know if you were alive or...” Liam said before pausing to brush some tears from his cheeks.

“Dead?” I finished for him. I was in disbelief, not knowing what else to say. I really didn’t think about how any of this had affected our nation. I guess I was in survival mode, so I didn’t think beyond my own little world.

“News flash, Robert Van Stark, you’re the son of a United States Congressman. You were kidnapped by terrorists. The media made the whole thing sound hopeless. The picture they were painting was bleak. The likelihood of you being rescued was nil-to-none. I was hardly able to eat anything all weekend.”

“I guess I didn’t realize how this had affected everyone... I… ah… I’m sorry,” I stammered, searching for the right words as I held my dog tags in my hand.

"Holy crap, Robert, are you serious? There's nothing for you to be sorry about. You were the one they took. I'm only attempting to help you understand the totality of this whole thing. I've been beating myself up all weekend," he said, swallowing deeply and hesitating for a few seconds. "I was too gutless to tell you how I really felt about you." Oh, shit, I could read Liam clearly now.

"Umm… you can tell me now if you'd like," I said, looking around to make sure we were still alone because I knew what Liam was thinking about doing next. I felt his left hand on my arm while he leaned in so close that I could smell his cologne.

"Ever since I met you in the freshman hallway, you know the day I asked you for your phone number? I've had this thing for you, but there's a bit of an age difference. I didn't want to come off as a creeper," he explained as he looked into my eyes with a hint of lust in his mind.

"I have serious issues. How can you be attracted to someone like me?" I asked. Oh shit, he's going to... Before I could prepare myself for what was coming next, Liam had his lips pressed onto mine; they were soft, wet, and I could taste mint. I had never been kissed before, but I kind of liked it. I had to admit, my first kiss was a bit awkward.

"Was that okay?" Liam asked quickly, trying to gauge my reaction.

"Erm… it was better than okay," I finally admitted.

"I'm only going to be sixteen for two more days, so we don't have much time."

"Time for what?"

"Ah… you're fifteen, right?"

"Okay, I see your point. But there's someone else." Liam looked at me with apparent confusion. Damn, I shouldn't have said anything.

"You mean like there's another guy?"

"I'm sorry this is kinda awkward," I told him, looking away slightly.

"No… It's fine, I thought you… were… Is he the tall blonde kid who came in with you?" Liam asked, slowly removing his hand from my arm. "He's adorable; I don't blame you."

"No. You 'thought' right, I don't have a boyfriend. And no, the tall guy... he isn't who I'm… into."

"Well, who is he, then?" I stared at Liam as if I was unwilling to give up any other information. "It's not Kevin Larson, is it?" Liam guessed for his second attempt as he puts his hand over his mouth for the dramatic effect.

"I've seen you two hanging out together. I was wondering if... He's sizzling," Liam said as he stared at the table as if he were dreaming.

"No... Yes... No..." I said, stammering while I searched for the correct phrase.

"Use your words, Robert," Liam teased as if he had just recovered from his temporary trance and was now able to be witty again.

"I mean... I like Kevin, but he's not into me that way." I couldn't tell Liam about the feelings I had for the First Son, Lukas Barnes. I'd sound like a lovesick groupie who was off his rocker. The reality was, I hadn't heard anything from Lukas since I saw him at the State Dinner. "It's a secret; besides, the guy I like may be straight," I tried to explain before Liam took it too far.

"Well, let the best man win!" Liam said with a confident smile. "I know this may sound a bit juvenile, but I was hoping we could... you know, go out within the next two days," he said with a slightly embarrassed expression. I wasn't sure about his overly aggressive approach. Again, I was lost for words, but he had a lot more than just kissing in mind when I read him. I gave Liam a shrug because I was too caught off guard to say anything.

"Tell you what, lover boy," Liam said as he lightly slaps me on the back. "It hardly ever works out when you have a crush on a straight guy. There's almost always heartbreak involved while the drama plays out." Suddenly I saw the curtain move slightly before Kyle stepped into our smelly space.

"Sorry to interrupt, guys," Kyle said, pretending he hadn't heard our conversation.

"Kyle!" I shouted. Without thinking about what I was doing, I jumped up before throwing my arms around Kyle with full frontal body contact. Kyle felt solid like Kevin does. Not a stitch of fat on that body. "Thank you for saving me," I whispered. Kyle hugged me back for a few seconds before awkwardly separating us.

"Can we talk in private for a minute?" Kyle asked, looking into my eyes, still holding me out at arm's length. I've never noticed before, but Kyle's eyes were the same color as mine.

"I can leave," Liam said after picking his jaw up off the table.

"No, Liam. You stay here; I'll have Robert back to you in five minutes." Kyle led me out into a well-lit hallway, smiling broadly as he turned toward me. "How are you doing?" he asked.

"Other than not being able to get enough food in my stomach, I'm fine. Sorry about the hug in front of Liam. It's just that… you know... seeing you for the first time since we went through the ordeal and…"

"There's no reason to apologize, but that's what we need to talk about." Somehow, I knew this subject would come up.

"I know how important your career is to you; I promise, it will never happen again," I whispered, so Gary, who had moved in close, wouldn't hear us.

"Our bond is stronger now than it was before all of this happened, but you have to always call me Mr. Smit while we're here at school and no hugging in public. I have a girlfriend who will soon be my wife, so it will never work between you and me," he said half-jokingly with a hint of seriousness in his voice.

"I know, it's kinda childish of me to have this schoolboy crush on you, but…"

"No, I'm flattered; you're a handsome boy, but you're…" It seemed like we were both looking for the right words to use.

"Just a boy," I finished for him as I dropped my gaze to the floor. I felt his fingers lift my chin. "You're an extraordinary boy, and I'm honored to be your mentor. You better get back in there. I'm sure you have a lot of work to do. We'll talk more tomorrow in class."

*"I'll forever love you, and I'll always be in your debt. Can we still talk like this?"*

*"Only when we're in school. Your parents may not appreciate you talking to an adult when you're... um, never mind."* Kyle smiled again as I walk away.

My mind was still swimming when I returned to find Liam sitting where we left him. I knew the consequences were going to suck, but I needed to wipe Liam's memory. I couldn't risk Kyle losing his job.

"What was that all about with Mr. S? Is he the mystery guy… Oh, my God. Do you two have a thing going?" Liam asked, tilting his head like a puppy. *"Liam, you didn't see me hug, Mr. Smit. I did not call him by his first name."* I was immediately introduced into Liam's mind, and now I was a twelve-year-old boy in the Jr. High locker room where some boys were teasing me. "Hey, you little queer, come here. You know you want this," one of the boys said as he pulled down his gym shorts.

"Hey, Robert! Wake up. What happened? Did you pass out?" Liam asked as he knelt beside me shaking my shoulder.

"Sure, I'm fine. I just felt dizzy." I did my best to focus on Liam's blue eyes. And little by little, it was true. I was feeling fine. I should learn to sit my ass down before entering any red corridors to avoid bashing my head into an immovable object.

"Do you need to go back to the hospital? Here, let me call my dad; he'll be able to help," Liam recommended as he pulled his phone out.

"No! Please don't tell anyone. I'll be fine," I pled as Liam helped me to my feet.

"If you're sure," he said with concern as we joined the others. I was thankful that we got through the rest of the production without having any more personal, dramatic encounters.

"Hey, Rob," I heard someone call out from behind me as Cam and I neared the front exit of the school. I stopped quickly, turning to see David approaching. "How are you feeling?" David asked.

"Hey, David, I'm doing fine. Sorry, I missed the fishing trip." It was awkward as we stood looking at each other. I could read that he wanted to tell me he was happy to see me come home safely.

"It's all right. We didn't end up going after… Ah… I just wanted to let you know that…" David said before hesitating. David looked at the floor as he burrowed his hands into his pockets. His jeans were definitely going to his ankles if David didn't stop pushing. "I'm glad you're safe, and you too, Cam," David quickly added as if Cam was an afterthought.

"Thank you, David," Cam responded. I felt terrible for David; he wouldn't even look up at me.

"Yeah, I'm glad... Umm, you know… that you're both safe," David said, trying again.

"I'll see you tomorrow, then?" I said, so our awkward conversation could end.

"Bet, yeah, sure, see you tomorrow morning," David answered as he turned to leave. He was gone in a flash.

*"What do you think was going on with him?"* I ask Cam.

*"I think he likes you."*

*"You think so?"* I said with excitement.

*"Yup."*

As we made our way to the truck, we were mobbed by the press. But there were several County Deputies who made it impossible for the media to affect our exit. After we quickly piled into the vehicle, Gary received a call from my dad. We needed to hurry back. Cam's parents would be arriving within the hour.

We were finishing dinner when I heard a commotion coming from the front foyer area. "I think your parents may be here," I told Cam. He quickly slid his chair back and ran for the front door. When I rounded the corner in the foyer, I saw Cam embraced with two tall people. Well, that was one thing Cam was truthful about.

"Honey, we haven't had a chance to talk since you arrived home," my mom said as she came up behind me and draped her arm over my shoulder. "Do you think I could have a moment?" Wow, everyone wants to talk; I wasn't sure I liked all the attention.

Mom closed the door behind us in the study and smiled.

"Okay, what can I fill you in on?" I asked.

"First of all, I just want to tell you how proud I am of you."

"Thank you," I said with a blush.

"Second, I need to know why you chose not to tell anyone about your special gift."

"I ah… I connected with Kevin first. It was kinda scary for us both. So, I figured it would be best to keep it on the down-low until I had a better handle on things. But most of all, I didn't want you and Dad to know there was another thing wrong with me. I just want to be a normal kid," I tried to explain as we stood face to face.

"Normal is a setting on my washing machine, honey. There is no such thing as a normal person," she replied. I looked at her with confusion as she continued. "Normal is much like beauty," she said as she reached up with her protective, loving hand and moved some curls out of my eyes. "It's in the eye of the beholder. No one is normal; we are all different, with different gifts. I don't want you to be like the other boys. What I want for you is to be your own beautiful self. How long have you been telepathic?"

"*Three weeks*." She looked at me as if she just found out she has a fourth child.

"Have you discovered any other gifts you would like to tell me about?" my mom asked, trying to be brave.

"I think we should take this slow," I recommend.

"I'm sure I can manage," my mom assured me as she dropped her chin and raised her eyebrows. I lifted my hand toward a book sitting on a nearby desk. She turned just as the hard-cover time-travel book started to float toward us. I instinctively held my arms out to catch my mom as she fainted.

"Holy shit, Mom! If you can't handle it, don't pressure me," I told her limp body, knowing that she wasn't able to hear me. I carefully lowered her to the floor and placed a pillow under her legs. "Good, you're waking up," I said to my mom as she started to open her eyes. "Are you okay? I think you passed out."

"I'm fine; that was apparently just a bit more shocking than… I mean, I should have been sitting down. I can't believe my own son can do these things. How many others know about these gifts?" she asked as I helped steady her on the way to the sofa.

"Just Kevin, Mr. Smit, and Cam, and obviously the Feds know."

"Very well, don't share this information, please."

"Okay…, why?"

"We'll talk it over with your Father before you share this with anyone else. I don't want you to be exploited." Damn it, now my mom was crying. "I feel like you've grown up over the past few weeks, and…"

"Mom, I'll be fine. I survived; we all did. Speaking of us all, would it be okay if I went to visit Kevin this evening?"

"You haven't slept; you've been nonstop since you were rescued this morning. Maybe it would be best if you called Kevin rather than traveling to Grand Rapids."

We stopped talking when we saw the door open. "There's someone in the front room who would like to meet you," my dad announced.

Cam and his parents were sitting on the sofa when we entered the room. I offered my hand to Cam's dad, but I was surprised when he grabbed me and hugged me as if we were long-lost army buddies. Cam's Mom took her turn to squish the shit out of me as well. "You're not taking my friend away from me, are you?" I asked.

"Not until tomorrow; our flight doesn't leave until three in the afternoon. And your Father has offered to let us stay here with you until then," Cam's mom said.

After spending at least an hour getting to know Cam's parents, we headed off to bed. "Can we talk?" I asked Cam as we transcend the stairs toward my room.

"Sure, your Mom has already sent someone out to buy me and my parents' clothes. So, I need to try them on before I go to bed."

"You can meet me in my room as soon as you're ready; I gotta take another shower. I stink again, or maybe I still stink, I'm not sure," I said as I stepped into my bedroom, chuckling at my half-hearted humor.

My third shower of the day felt good as I wet my hair. If I could just stand here long enough to wash off the traumatic, messed-up worry I have. Or was it fear that I was experiencing? I couldn't seem to get the events that occurred at the farmhouse out of my mind.

"Come in, Cam," I told him as I slipped a shirt over my head.

"You wanted to see me, Sir," he joked as he stepped in and walked toward me.

"Yes, it's about the trip you'll be taking tomorrow," I joked as well. Cam flashed me a smile that stretched the entire width of his face. "Seriously, I'm going to miss you," I told him as I deliberately stuck out my lower lip as far as it would go.

"How'd you know it was me at the door?" I tapped my head with my index finger and smiled. "I'll miss you too," he said, copying my lower lip maneuver.

"Do you think you could talk your mom and dad into moving to Holland?"

"I don't think so; they love Wisconsin for some reason." There was an awkward silence between us as if we weren't sure who should speak next. "You're an amazing person, you know that?" Cam said as he turned his head toward me.

"Nah, just a small-town gay nerd."

"What does that matter?" Cam asked with an irritated tone. "My friend Thomas is gay, and he's awesome. Sexual orientation doesn't define a person."

"It's just that we've never talked about this, and…"

"What is there to talk about," he interrupted. "You like boys; I like girls. It's as simple as that." I nodded to validate Cam's brilliant, straightforward assessment. "I gotta take my new stuff down for your Mom to wash. She said something about dangerous chemicals and insisted on washing them." I just smiled.

"I'm gonna crash out then. Goodnight."

"Night, man," Cam said as he left my room.

*"Are you awake, Kevin?"*

*"Yeah, just trying to find something to watch on TV that's not about us,"* he sent with evidence of frustration.

*"I can't come and see you again until tomorrow after school."*

*"Are you too tired to tell me how you were rescued? I mean the real story, not the one you've been telling everyone else."*

*"I'm fine,"* I said as I climbed into bed. "It's open," I said to whoever was knocking on my door.

"Hey," Sam said as he stepped into my room.

"Hey," I answered as I turned toward him.

"I just wanted to check in on you before I went to bed. How are you feeling?" Sam asked as he sat on the edge of my bed.

*"Just a minute, Sam just barged into my bedroom, and now he wants to have a brotherly conversation,"* I sent Kevin.

*"No big deal, I'm not going anywhere."*

"I'm just a little tired," I told Sam.

"That's okay; you can tell me your story another time."

"Yeah, it's kinda long, and I'm exhausted."

"Bet. Get some sleep, little brother," he said as he leaned over and gave me a hug.

"I don't think I've ever been hugged by you before," I said sarcastically.

"Yeah, don't get used to it, you little dickhead," Sam said before standing. *I love you, Sam,* I sent him as he left my room.

After I shared my story with Kevin, I knew that it was time to come clean with him about his orange corridor stuff. I started by saying, *"I've been doing something friends should never do. So, before we go to sleep, I need to have a difficult discussion with you."*

*"This sounds serious,"* Kevin said.

*"I... Ah... This is... I don't know how to tell you without making you angry."*

*"Why would I be angry?"* Kevin asked.

*"I wasn't honest with you. But I didn't want to lose my friend, so I've been putting off telling you. I realized that the longer I kept this from you, the more difficult it would be to say and would just keep snowballing."*

*"You weren't honest, like how? What are you talking about?"*Kevin sent back.

*"I can see what you see,"* I finally admitted.

*"I don't understand,"* he said.

*"If I close my eyes and focus on you. I can see what you see, what you're saying, touching, smelling, even tasting. Everything."*

*"So, what are you saying,"* he thought with anger. *"Are you saying that you've been spying on me? Like when I'm naked and stuff?"*

*"No, I would never do that!"*

*"Why should I believe you? You've been lying to me for... How long has it been? How long have you been lying to me?"*

*"I'm sorry, Kevin. I'm telling you the truth now. I promise it will never happen again without you knowing."*

*"How long, Robert?"* he demanded, ignoring my plea.

*"Since the day we met in the coffee shop."* I reluctantly admitted.

*"How could you?...* There was nothing but dead silence. Maybe I shouldn't have told him.

*"Kevin?*

*"Leave me alone, Robert, just go to sleep; I'm done talking with you,"* he said with more anger.

*"I'm sorry I hurt you, Kevin."*

*"Go to sleep, Robert."* I knew our conversation was over. Hell, our friendship may have been over. Who could blame him, though? I'd be pissed, too, if I were him. I was so angry at myself that I couldn't keep the audible sobs from escaping anymore.

"Robert?" I heard my mom say through my door that Sam had carelessly left open. "Can I come in?" she asked.

"Sure," I said as I wipe my tears on the sheets, pretending I hadn't been crying. "What's up?" I asked as if nothing was wrong. Who was I trying to fool? She could tell.

"Do you want me to stay in your room with you tonight?" Mom asked after sitting on my bed. As comforting as the offer sounded, there was no way she would be sleeping with me; talk about awkward.

"No, thanks. Did I wake you?"

"No, I haven't slept the past few nights. You'd think I'd be able to sleep now that I know you're safe. But, I'm worried about how you'll get through… Through everything." Mom was probably referring to the emotional scarring that a traumatic event can leave.

"I'll be fine," I tried to reassure her. "Did Dad leave for DC yet?" I asked, trying to change the subject.

"An hour ago. Would you like to tell me why you're upset?" I wasn't sure why, but the way she asked the question caused me to start crying again. I couldn't seem to control my emotions. "Honey, what is it?"

"Kevin and I were… I really messed up," I told her through my sobs.

"We're human, and sometimes we mess up," she said, trying to comfort me.

"I broke our trust... I had to tell him... It's been eating at..." I couldn't seem to finish a sentence.

"I know, honey, it will be alright," she assured me.

"I had so much guilt I couldn't… I couldn't withhold the truth any longer."

"Kevin is your friend; he just needs some time to process everything." She didn't even know what everything was. I was afraid if I told her, she'd be disappointed in me too. I couldn't stomach any more disappointment.

"He's furious. I could read his anger and disgust."

"Let him sleep on it. After you both get some rest, the significance of this will dissipate." 'The significance will dissipate?' No wonder I talk the way I do. I've always wanted to believe that it was my dad who I mirrored. But it wasn't Dad; it was my mom; it has always been her. I was more like my mom than I want to admit. But what's wrong with being like her? She was cool as long as she didn't buy KY warming jelly while I was with her.

"You're right, Mom; I need some sleep." She leaned over to kiss me on my cheek before she stood.

"Goodnight," she said as she shut my lamp off.

"You too," I told her.

*"Goodnight, Kevin."*

*"Goodnight, Rob. Now go to sleep."* I smiled and drifted off.

*****

The thirty-foot fishing boat bounced around like a bobber in Lake Michigan while our captain maneuvered the four-foot waves. David was standing behind me, helping hold onto the fishing pole as a Coho fought the line. We danced around on the back of the boat, trying not to lose our balance or, worse, let the fish get away. "Slow down just a bit, Dad," David yelled to our captain.

The reel spun backward, making a zeeeeeeee sound. "Just keep tension on the line! Keep the tip up!" David said as he pushed into my back, extending his arms around me to pull the pole back.

"It's hard," I said as I looked back, expecting to see David. Instead, I saw Glad. He had a gun pointing at my head. I heard the gun go off with a deafening blast in my left ear.

*****

My glasses were around here somewhere, I thought to myself as I felt for them on my nightstand. Ouch, bad headache. It was only 02:29. I needed headache meds. Never mind, I was too tired.

# Close Call Chapter 16

Wednesday, May 31st Close Call

My alarm went off at 05:30, so I dragged myself out of bed and headed down to the pool. Hey, my headache was gone, or was that part of my dream? Nope, that was after Glad shot his gun less than two inches from my left ear.

When I walked through the pool room doors, I heard Sam moving through the water. While filling my water bottle, I had the urge to go back to bed, but I knew some vigorous exercise would wake me up. After my fifth lap, I start to feel alive again. Sam seemed to be moving along fast, but I lapped him during our fifty minutes.

My emotions were running ramped this morning. I just couldn't quit thinking about how angry Kevin was with me last evening. Why was I out fishing with David and his dad? That never really happened on Memorial weekend. Instead, I was lying in a pool of piss on a hard truck floor. Our rescue seemed like it was more than a week ago, but it had been less than twenty-four hours since we left Denver. I needed to find time to visit Kevin today so we could talk face to face.

"You're getting stronger," Sam said as he dried himself off. See, that's why Mom liked him better; he's a rule follower and didn't make a habit of walking through the house soaking wet. It just didn't make much sense to use a towel to dry off and then step back into the shower so I could do it all over again.

"Oh, come on, you weren't even trying," I told him as I stood on the deck, dripping, wet, devising a plan on how to make it all the way to my room without Mom catching me.

"Ah, yeah, I was. I could hardly keep up. Are you taking roids or something? Look at how your chest and arms are developing. And look at those abs," he said, giving me a soft punch in the gut.

"It's because I have superpowers," I told him while displaying a big smirk.

"Shut up and just accept the compliment."

"Thanks," I told him as he turned to leave.

When I finally made it to my shower without Mom seeing me dripping on the steps, I jumped in and called Kevin.

*"Are you awake yet?"* Dead silence. *"I'm sorry. I won't talk to you if you're not ready."*

*"Help! I'm dying!"* I heard Kevin say through groggy thought.

*"Shut up. You're not dying. I'm sorry okay?"* I said, squeezing the body wash bottle.

*"I'm serious. I can't open my eyes or move. I can't call for help."* I quickly looked through Kevin's eyes; everything was blurry until his eyesight went dark.

*"Kevin!"* I screamed. Who do I call? Should I call 911? Stop panicking and think, I told myself. I didn't have a phone! Kevin was in a hospital; 911 wouldn't work. I quickly got out of the shower, and without even drying off, I slipped on a pair of shorts before running for the stairs. "Mom! Mom, I need help!" I screamed as I ran down the stairs.

"What is it? What's wrong," my mom answered with alarm as she turned the corner into the hallway leading to the kitchen.

"Mom, it's Kevin; he needs help. I don't know who to call." Out of my peripheral vision, I saw security come crashing through the door.

"Honey, slow down, take a deep breath and tell me what's going on with Kevin," she said calmly, placing her hands on my shoulders.

"Suzanne? Is everything all right?" the new security guy asked.

"It's fine," my mom told him.

"No, Mom! It's not fine; Kevin is dying! He asked me to call for help just before he became unconscious. Now he won't answer me!" Cam came flying around the corner and asked why I was yelling.

"Robert, you're not making any sense; Kevin is in the hospital; there are people there with him," my mom said with a calm, convincing tone. She wasn't getting the urgency here! Abandon plan!

*"Kyle, help me!"*

*"What's wrong?"* Kyle asked as if I had startled him.

*"It's Kevin! Kevin is dying! He's in the hospital, unconscious, and he can't call for help. Please help!"* Mom shook me, telling me to focus as the new security guy looked at us with confusion.

*"I'll call the nurses station. Do you know what room he's in?"* Kyle asked.

*"Room, 6346!"*

"Robert, talk to me; what's wrong with Kevin?" my mom asked, looking directly into my eyes. I glanced to my left and noticed Sam standing beside me, only wearing shorts.

"Listen up, all of you," I said with a commanding voice. "Kevin needs our help. Kyle is calling the nurses station."

"Who is Kyle?" Mom asked.

"It doesn't matter, Mom. Call Devon, please; tell him to get to the hospital. Sam, call the Children's Hospital Security Department, Kevin, is in room 6346. Tell them Kevin can't call for help himself. Cam, go get dressed. We're going to the hospital." Sam, Mom, and the new security guy were all on their phones when I headed for the stairs.

*"Kevin? Kevin, can you hear me? Please answer me."* I repeated over and over again as Cam and I ran back up the stairs.

"What's wrong with Kevin?" Cam asked as he entered my room.

"I don't know. Kevin said it felt like he was dying, and then he went silent."

We rushed back down the stairs, and Mom was waiting for me at the bottom. Her face was telling me things were bad. I refused to open any doors at first, but I knew I need to.

"Robert, come here and sit down so I can explain what's going on," Mom said as she pointed into our living room. I didn't like her tone, so I searched to find confirmation that Kevin was in trouble.

"Mom, just tell me what's going on," I demand as I sat on the sofa. Oh no, he's not breathing! I start to cry instinctively, pulling on my hair as I curled forward.

"Robert, listen to me." I could feel her hand on my back as I rocked back and forth. "I'll take you to the hospital, but first, I need to explain what's going on with Kevin," she said as I started shaking my head, no. I couldn't hold it in; I felt like I was going to explode. "Robert," she said calmly. "I just spoke with Kevin's father. He told me he's on his way to the hospital. The hospital staff saw some changes in Kevin's monitors, and when they went in to check on him, they found him not breathing." I still had my head buried in my lap when I let go of my hair, pulling my arms behind my head, and screamed.

"Robert, get a hold of yourself and listen to me," my mom said calmly, pulling up on my arms to expose my wet face. Why was there shattered glass on the sofa next to me? What just happened? Did the lamp break? "They're preparing Kevin for emergency surgery. The doctor believes Kevin may have some pressure on his brain." I shook my head, yes, thinking that there was a chance he may survive. "Let's all say a prayer for Kevin before we leave," Mom recommended as she bowed her head.

"Mom, please don't take offense to this, but I think our time would be better spent driving to the hospital. We can pray in the truck if you think it'll help."

When we arrived at the hospital, my gut was turning. I felt like I may vomit any second. We hadn't taken time to eat anything yet, but I didn't think I could eat anyway. Now I know how Liam must have felt when I was missing or presumed dead. He said he hadn't felt like eating for three days.

We were directed into a large open surgical waiting room with several large TVs hanging on the wall. I saw Devon, Zach, and two adults who were were having a conversation. When Zach saw me, he ran toward the door and threw his arms around me. I could feel his shoulders moving as we both tried to get ahold of our emotions. When I picked my head up from Zach's shoulder, there wasn't a dry eye in the room.

"Oh," Zach said, wiping his tears away. "Rob, this is my mom and dad," I had no idea Zach came from a biracial family. I wasn't surprised by the appearance of Mr. Scott. Zach looked exactly like him, but his Mom was white. Zach didn't resemble his Mom at all. I guess my narrow mind just assumed his Mom would have black skin as well. My mom was introducing herself to Kevin's dad as I was introduced to Zach's parents. I remembered

Zach telling me that his Mom was a Gynecologist. Well, he actually told me she was a baby doctor. 'You know the kind of doctors who deliver babies,' he said. Zach's dad is the Superintendent of our school.

When I turned to look for my new detail, I saw Derek standing guard just inside the doorway, watching as more people enter the room. His short, brown hair was cut flat across the top, and his tailored, black suit fit his solid, six-foot frame perfectly. Derek's dark brown eyes continually scanned the room for possible threats, ready to take action if anything should present itself. *I think we'll be safe here, 'new guy,'* I sent him through his green corridor.

"Have there been any updates," I asked Devon with a shaky voice.

"No, they took him into surgery before I arrived," Devon started to explain before someone from across the room called his name.

"Mr. Larson."

"Yes?" Kevin's dad replied as we approached the reception desk.

"Dr. Davis would like to meet with you for a moment, please."

"Very well," he said to the woman. I could hear the dread in Devon's voice.

"Would it be possible for Zach and me to come with you," I asked?

"Sure, guys, that would be welcomed," Devon said nervously, looking at our parents for approval. I could read Devon. He was reliving a day just last year when Kevin's Mom died during surgery.

Zach and I were sitting together on the sofa as Devon paced the floor of a tiny private waiting room. We almost jumped out of our skin when someone knocked at the door just before they entered.

"Hello, Mr. Larson, my name is William Davis; I'm the neurosurgeon who just finished a procedure on your son. He has responded well to the surgery and is now breathing on his own. I believe we were able to relieve the pressure between his occipital region and his cerebrum before any irreversible brain injury had time to occur. Kevin will be moved to the critical care unit for the next twelve to twenty-four hours. Do you have any questions for me?"

"How are the rest of his vitals, Doctor?" Devon asked with concern.

"They're all fine."

"And are his pupils both equal and reactive?"

“Yes, before and after the procedure. Kevin remains unresponsive, but everything looks promising.”

“When will I be able to talk to him?” I asked abruptly.

“He’s sleeping, so you won’t be able to talk with him until he wakes up,” Doctor Davis answered.

“Thank you, Doctor; I know what unresponsive means,” I wasn’t sure why I responded with a nasty, disrespectful tone. I was so angry, I wanted to slug something. Swimming and not eating afterward may have dropped my blood sugar a bit.

“I’m sorry if I’ve offended you,” Doctor Davis said, pausing to wait for my name.

“Robert, Sir, Robert Van Stark.”

“Oh sure, you’re Congressman Van Stark’s son, who was kidnapped last weekend?”

“Yes, Sir. And Kevin is here because of the jerks who abducted me.”

“Robert, it’s difficult to say how long Kevin will be unresponsive.”

“Doctor, you mentioned something about a brain injury. What are the chances of him having any injury at all?” Zach asked with a shaky voice.

“Slim,” the doctor answered. “And your name is?”

“Zach Scott.”

“And were you the other boy who was taken?”

“No, that was Cam; he’s like, right out there,” Zach said as he pointed at the closed door.

“Very well, Zach. I believe your friend will come out of this without any neuro deficit, so he’ll be just fine. This unfortunate incident has affected us all in one way or another. My son is a junior who goes to the same school as you boys. He didn’t eat or sleep at all last weekend.”

“I know; we even canceled my brother’s graduation party,” Zach said as his eyes wandered toward an abstract painting on the wall.

*“Kevin, can you hear me?”* There was no reply, so I closed my eyes and saw nothing but darkness.

“Robert?” Zach said as he shook my shoulder. I looked up to find all three of them staring at me as if I had a head injury of my own. Yup, the doctor was convinced that I needed to be re-evaluated.

“Oh, sorry, I guess I zoned out thinking about Kevin.”

All three of us returned to the large waiting room to find our parents and Cam drinking coffee. I wasn’t sure when it happened, but the waiting room had filled with other people who were probably waiting for their loved one to come out of surgery. When the traumatic event started this morning, it felt as if time had stopped; everything became surreal. It was as if the time should stall out and wait for me to catch up. But time marched on at the same pace, one second, one minute, one hour at a time, whether I was willing to jump on, to travel along, or not.

When my mom stood to hug me, the tears start to flow from my eyes again. I wondered when I would grow out of this crying thing; it felt awkward when I couldn't control my emotions. It was like, I wanted to be all grown up and take care of everything on my own, but a hug from my mom made me feel safe. I guess it didn't matter anyway; Zach had tears as well. I still had my face buried in my mom's shoulder when I heard my name mentioned on a nearby TV.

Almost everyone in the room was watching CNN at seven fifty in the morning. They had a host and his co-host sitting in front of a large screen with video streaming of Cam and me being carried to the medical chopper. Then they flash to the video of Cam and me leaving the school last night.

"The lost boy from Neverland has returned, Alisyn. There have been reports from his school in Holland, Michigan, confirming that Robert Van Stark still plans to perform tomorrow evening in his high school production." The host used my name as if it was a household name.

"He is one brave boy, Chris. What part will the young man be playing in the composition?" the co-host asked as if she actually cared.

"The Congressman's son will be playing a lead part of Peter Pan himself," Chris answered.

"Wow, that was a witty play on words," I said before producing a nervous laugh.

"CNN will have live coverage as he is on the run from Captain Hook Friday evening at seven o'clock eastern time. He is one popular lost boy, Alisyn. Our producer has been receiving tweets here at the studio nonstop from young ladies who would like to learn more about this interesting young man who has apparently been sprinkled with pixie dust," the co-host said with a wink to the host. Cam reached over and gave my shoulder a slight push. "We have a live interview with Congressman Van Stark coming up next. Kathy, let's go to you live in Washington, DC." Damn it.

"Thank you, Chris," the reporter said as she adjusted her earpiece before shoving a microphone in my dad's face. "Mr. Congressman, how are you and your family adjusting after the dramatic rescue of your youngest son yesterday morning?"

"Everyone is returning to school today, trying to get back into their routine." Good, my dad is keeping his answers short.

"You mentioned routine, Mr. Congressman. I understand Robert has been given the green light to participate in his high school production tomorrow evening."

"Yes, Robert's mother and I have agreed to allow him to perform tomorrow evening," my dad said with a million-dollar smile. When the reporter asked the following question, I could hardly believe my ears.

"Congressman Van Stark, have you noticed any signs of emotional trauma in your son since his return?" The TV had a full-screen picture of my freshman school picture. I had a tone of zits on my face. It must have been a bad skin day.

"Oh, for the love of God!" my mom said dramatically. The look on my dad's face gave the reporter the only answer she would be receiving. I dropped my head back to my mom's shoulder with embarrassment.

Devon must have seen my discomfort and said, "Are you boys hungry? You have time to grab some breakfast, Kevin will be in recovery for at least an hour, so I'll stay here and let you know the minute he wakes up." All three of us shook our heads, yes.

"That's a good idea. You boys need to get some food in you. A car will be here to pick me up in a few minutes," my mom said. "After Kevin gets out of recovery, Derek will take you to school."

"Girls want you," Zach teased as he coaxed Cam for help. Cam snorted out a laugh as we headed for the cafeteria. Now that we knew Kevin would recover, we were letting our humor guide the way to our recovery as well.

"Haha. I guess we all know there will be nothing reciprocated by me," I said with as much humor as I could muster.

Zach, Cam, and I spent almost an hour having a feeding frenzy before Devon called to let us know we could see Kevin.

When we reached the recovery unit, the nursing staff stopped us at the door, but Kevin's dad was able to get us in.

"Hey, Kev, the guys are here," Devon announced, trying to wake Kevin.

"Hey, guys. Someone drilled a hole through my skull," he said with sleepy, slurred speech. I grinned for a few seconds until suddenly, I was overrun with some more unwanted emotions that caused me to become a blubbering idiot again. How many tears could a body produce in one day? It seemed as if I'd have run out by now.

"Come here," Kevin said with a groggy voice, holding his hands up for a hug.

*"I promise I'll never look through your eyes again without your permission."*

*"I know."* he sent through a yellow corridor.

Cam and I were riding side by side as Derek drove us back toward Holland. Apparently, Cam's parents would be meeting us at the school to take my new friend back to Wisconsin.

*"You look really sad,"* I sent to Cam. I knew he didn't want to leave. I could read some conflicting thoughts. He was homesick and wanted to go home, but he didn't want to leave his new friends.

*"Yeah, I'll be fine,"* Cam answered as he continued to look out the window of the truck.

*"It'll all work out. Our friendship will survive even though we're separated by Lake Michigan."*

*"I know it will."* Cam transmitted back.

*"Do you have a lot of friends?"* I asked, looking into his eyes.

*"Just two, back home. Thomas and Kellen. I talked to both of them on the phone last night. Well, I mean, we cried more than we talked."* I gave my head a nod as we were pulling into our High School parking lot.

"Here we are, guys," Derek announced as he parked in his designated spot. I saw Gary standing by his truck with Cam's parents as we approached the front entrance.

*"Well, I guess this is it, man. I'm really going to miss you,"* I sent Cam as we stood in the middle of the driveway holding each other in a tight hug.

"I promise we'll bring him back to visit as soon as we can," Cam's dad said as he rested his hand on my left shoulder.

“Take care; I’ll give you a call when I get home,” Cam whispered in my ear.

“Okay, I’ll ask my Grandma if she’ll take us to Maui,” I said as I felt him shake his head yes. I thought that the time Cam and I spent saying our last goodbyes in the abductor’s truck had created an inseparable bond between us that will never break. I waved goodbye as Cam pulled away, leaving me standing in the driveway, riding my emotional rollercoaster that just took a one-hundred-foot plunge.

“We better get you inside,” Derek said as he motioned me to move my ass out of the driveway before someone ran me down.

“Could you give me a couple of minutes to ah?…”

“Sure, he said,” cutting me off, understanding that I needed a few minutes to get my shit together before I went inside. I sat down on a bench by the front door with my head tipped back and taking deep breaths, trying to keep from crying. A quick read on Derek revealed his mind was going one hundred miles per hour. His tactical thought process was fascinating. When I looked at him, the corners of his mouth turn up just a bit. “You’re a courageous young man. Did you know that?”

“Thank you, but I don’t feel courageous at the moment.”

“I’ve served with full-grown men and women who have nowhere near the same level of courage you have.” It just dawned on me, other than Derek’s notable handsome features that his Latino ethnicity gave him; I really didn’t know anything about him.

“You served?” I asked.

“Eight years in the Marines, until I went to work for your grandpa two years ago.

“Thanks,” I told him, referring to serving our country.

“Proud to serve. Are you ready?” Derek asked. He and I both knew what I was about to step into.

Every head turned when I walked into third-hour, causing me to come to a sudden halt and not knowing what to do next. Mr. Bennett quickly walked toward me, holding his hand out for the pass that was stuck in my grip. As I looked around the room, I could see that several of my classmates had been crying. Apparently, someone started a rumor that Kevin died this morning. Mr. Bennett wanted me to set the record straight. I guess the rumor was close to being true. After all, Kevin did stop breathing.

After I recited the morning's events and tried to clear up the rumors, I headed off to the cafeteria. There was no one sitting at our table. Even though there were hundreds of kids in the cafeteria, the room felt empty. I couldn't even imagine going back to the old days of eating alone. Cam will be boarding a plane within the next two hours, and Zach wasn't here yet. David startled me when he sat down next to me.

"Hey, David," I said as he opened his sack lunch.

"Hey, Rob, I heard about Kevin," he said as he looked out the window before looking back toward me. "Is he a....?"

"Yeah, he's doing better," I explained as I saw Zach walk into the cafeteria.

"Hey, David, how are you?" Zach asked, taking a deep breath as he sat down.

"I'm fine," David said before tearing into his PBJ.

"Did you just get here?" I asked Zach.

"Yeah," Zach said as he rubbed his head with both hands.

"Just wait until you get to your next class; everyone will be asking you to confirm that Kevin is still alive. There's a rumor going around school that he's dead."

"Can't wait for that!" Zach said as Kimberly and Rebecca approached our table with three other girls.

On my way to PE, I bump Kevin. *"How are you feeling?"*

*"I'll live. Just a bit of a headache. Damn, someone is here to draw my blood for the third time today."*

*"I'll leave you to your anguish. Oh, I'll text you when I get my new phone this afternoon."*

*"Do you think you could visit me tonight?"*

*"Sure, I'll ask Derek to bring me."*

"Hey," Liam said with an eager smile as I entered the media room after sixth-hour. "How is your friend Kevin doing? I heard he had a close call this morning."

"Yeah, he did. Who did you hear the news from?"

"It's been all over the school, but your brother told me in first-hour. Sam said you were upset this morning when you were leaving for the hospital."

"Yeah, a neurosurgeon told us we were close to losing him."

"Really? what was the surgeon's name."

"William Davis, I think. Why?" I knew it was William Davis. I needed to stop trying to hide my memory abilities. I was tired of hiding who I really was. If people couldn't deal with the real me, it was their problem.

"He's my father!"

"Wait, what?" I asked with confusion.

Liam extended his hand as if he wanted me to shake his hand and said, "Hello, my name is Liam Davis; it's short for William." Of course, the doctor said his son was upset about my abduction last weekend. I really needed to start processing more thoroughly.

"Wow, it's a small world, Liam Davis," I said, taking his hand and shaking it as if we had never met.

"How are you doing now that he's out of danger?" Liam asked.

"Other than wanting to cry every ten minutes, I'm doing well." Liam gave me a warm smile and a nod.

"Okay, everyone, we only have fifty-one hours until opening and a long way to go before we're ready. I'm not sure if you've all heard, but the tickets have sold out for the Friday night opening," Ms. Hukins announced as she walked into the media room. "This is the first time in the school's history of anything like this happening," she said with a giddy tone.

I would have never guessed how good it made me feel to belong. It was probably why my parents have encouraged me to join a sport or school activity. Participating in a function like this helped me feel wanted and needed. It even gave me some sort of purpose. Who would have thought a stupid school play could make such a big difference in my attitude?

After a two-hour rehearsal, I felt more confident with our progress, but I was tired and hungry. Convincing Derek to drive me back to the Grand Rapids hospital was easier than I thought it would be. Kevin and I needed to get everything out on the table. We should have had the difficult conversation face to face last night instead of initiating the disaster from thirty miles away. I had a feeling that there was some information we both needed to divulge.

Derek handed me my new phone as I climbed into the truck. I couldn't wait to see if RSA had texted me since the day I was taken. Yup, there's one from twenty minutes ago:

Hey, Robert, I'm glad to hear you're back home...

It's good to hear from you, RSA!

We pulled into the hospital parking ramp, and I got out of the truck. Derek grabbed my arm forcefully, pulling me between our vehicle and a parked car. I peeked up over Derek's broad shoulders as three men went running by as if they were in a hurry. When I looked down at Derek's waist, he had his hand on his gun.

"Sorry, Robert, they looked like they could have been a threat," Derek said as he straightened out my shirt sleeve. Everyone was still on high alert. I wondered how long this would last?

"It's fine; they did look kinda scary," I said, validating his actions, even though I thought he was overreacting.

Kevin had a big bulky bandage around his head when I entered his room. "Hey," he whispered. You seem distraught."

*"Distraught? You're starting to sound nerdier than me. Maybe my nerdisms are rubbing off on you,"* I sent him.

*"Shut up, dude. I thought your play practice would go later. I mean rehearsal."*

"Yeah, it went well," I whispered so I wouldn't wake Devon, who was sleeping in a chair less than five feet from Kevin's bed.

"Hey, Robert!" Devon said as he stood and stretched his arms above his head.

"Hey, Devon, how are you holding up?"

"I'm fine, just catching up on some z's," he said.

"Hey, Dad, do you think Rob and I could have a minute in private?"

"Sure, boys, I can tell when I'm not wanted," Devon said jokingly as he picked up his phone and left.

"Some attorneys from your grandparent's company visited me today."

"Yeah?" I said with confusion.

"They dropped off a check to my dad for my hospital bills. Your grandma found out that we won't have medical insurance until my dad has been at his new job for two weeks."

“Was your dad okay with that?” I recalled Kevin telling me he didn’t take handouts. Especially from rich people. Kevin gave me a nod while I attempted to find the right words to start my apology conversation.

“I wanted to apologize in person, for… umm… Withholding the truth until last night,” I blurted out as I looked at the door to make sure we were still alone.

“It’s cool dude, I’m over it; besides, you promised to never do it again.”

“Have you ever told Zach? … Erm, you know? … How you feel about him?”

“Never going to happen.”

“So, you’re planning to go through life pretending?” I asked.

“Says the gay kid living in the closet.” I tip my head, giving him a don’t mess with me look. “You’re right; I’ll talk with Zach when the timing is right,” Kevin said, hoping that I would change the subject.

“I promised my mom I’d only stay for a few minutes, so…”

“Yeah, I know. Please tell your grandma, thank you,” Kevin said as I gave him a hug goodbye.

Before I left the medical campus, I was going to try to visit Andy. I knew I shouldn’t feel responsible for his injuries, but for some reason, I did. Even though I knew Andy would say it was his duty to keep me safe, and he wasn’t able to pull it off.

I’ve checked my phone ten times since I text RSA, and there was nothing new by the time I knocked at Andy’s partially closed door.

“Hi, Andy, how are you feeling?” I asked as I peeked in after opening the door.

“Hey, Robert, come in,” Andy said, stretching his arms out for a hug. “This is my wife, Kathy, and my son Zenn and Amery.”

“Hi, Kathy,” I said as I shook her hand. I walked over to the boys and shook their hands as well. I’ve always hated being ignored when I was a little kid, so I made an effort to recognize younger children’s existence. “How is your dad doing?”

“My daddy is a hero. He got hurt, saving an important kid.” Andy gave me a broad smile.

“Kathy, would you mind taking the boys down for some dinner?” Andy asked.

After Andy's family left the room, he patted the side of his bed for me to sit down.

"I heard you took three bullets."

"It turns out I'm hard to kill." I gave Andy a weak smile.

"I'm sorry," I said as I looked down at my lap.

"Why would you be sorry? You've done nothing wrong," he said as I felt my new phone buzzing three times in a row.

"You almost got killed protecting me."

"I knew what I was signing up for when your grandpa hired me. I've grown quite fond of you; I would put my life on the line for you again."

"Thank you, Andy, please get well soon and come back to work; I really miss you," I said as I brush away some more tears.

"I will," Andy promised.

After leaving Andy's room, I quickly pulled the new phone from my pocket. There were three texts in a row from RSA. The first text said:

Robert!

The second text said, Is that really you?

And the third said, Answer quick… I have to go down to dinner in 5 min.

Who else calls you RSA? I sent back.

I'm so glad you're safe. I have 100 questions, but I'm late for a mandatory dinner with the fam. I'll text again as soon as I'm freed from my parental prison. I couldn't stop smiling. It was kind of weird. I didn't even know who this guy was, but I felt so close to him.

At ten-thirty, I finally sank down on my bed and placed my glasses on my nightstand. I was feeling a bit sad about not hearing back from RSA. Wait, my phone just chirped. I fumbled around to find my glasses and retrieved the phone from its charger. It was David:

Hey, Rob, how is Kevin doing?

He's doing well; he may get to come home tomorrow.

Great news. Goodnight.

David?

Yeah?

Is everything good with you?

I'm fine. See you tomorrow.

Cool! C u tomorrow.

******

We stood hand-in-hand, David on my right and Zach on my left, as we peered down into a deep hole in the ground. We were focused on a casket that was sitting in a concrete vault. "Who died?" I asked David as I tossed some loose soil into the hole.

"What do you mean, who died?" Zach asked with concern.

"Are you feeling alright?" David asked.

"I asked a simple question. Why are you guys acting so strangely?" I shot back.

"Come on, let's go sit down," David said, grabbing my hand and turning me toward three empty chairs that were lined up in front of a bunch of people who were standing behind them.

"Devon, there's something wrong with Rob," David said with an alarming tone.

"What's wrong?" Devon asked, standing quickly.

"Rob started asking bizarre questions. He's not making any sense," David said.

"Robert, do you know where you are?" Devon asked, lifting my eyelids open and looking into my eyes carefully.

"No," I said with confusion.

"You're at Kevin's funeral," Devon said.

"No, that can't be true," I said calmly.

"Robert, Kevin died three days ago," Devon said.

"No!" I screamed as I pull away. "You're lying," I yelled as I started to run. I couldn't move away from the casket; I was stuck in quicksand and was getting sucked into the ground.

*****

"Robert?" I thought I heard Sam say calmly.

"No, Kevin can't be dead!" I yelled.

"Robert, wake up; you're having a nightmare," Sam said, shaking my shoulder.

"What? Oh... Bad dream," I muttered, trying to recover. I looked at my phone, and it was 01:04. Damn, that sucked. There was a text on my phone, but I didn't take the time to check who it was from.

"Slide over," Sam said as he pulled my covers back before climbing into bed with me. Sam was warm and comforting as he draped his safe arm over me. Man, I was glad I started wearing shorts to bed, I thought to myself as I drifted back to sleep.

# Healing Chapter 17

Thursday, June 1st Healing

Sam woke up when I reach over the top of him to retrieve my noisy phone. He gave me a weak smile as he fluffed my matted hair.

"You okay?" Sam asked.

"Yeah, I'm fine. Thanks for saving me from my messed-up dream this morning," I told Sam with sincere appreciation.

"No problem, but don't get used to me spooning you. Let's go for a run," Sam offered as he flung the covers. "Oops," he said, using both hands to cover his prominent morning issue. We both started to laugh as we climbed out of bed.

"I don't have permission to leave the house," I warned Sam as I moved toward my bathroom.

"Screw the rules. You never follow them anyway," Sam said as he left my room.

When I checked my phone, I was excited to see a text from RSA:

I need to apologize for my late text. The damn dinner went until ten-thirty. I couldn't escape Alcatraz.

No prob. Going for a run. I'll text you back on my way to school.

We immediately got into a nice, even pace. "Looks like we have a storm moving in," Sam said with minimal effort as if he were relaxing on the sofa. He was right; the dark clouds were coming in heavy. There were some lightning striking out over the water as well. "Race you back," Sam recommended as we turned around twenty-five minutes into our run. When it started to rain, Sam peeled off his wet shirt, so I followed suit. The thunder was deafening, but the rain felt refreshing on my hot skin.

As we approached the house, I saw a small car parked in the driveway, with Derek closing in on the car fast. Oops, busted. The car sped off before Derek could make contact, but not before someone in the vehicle took several pictures of Sam and me. "Good job keeping up," Sam said as we kicked our wet, sandy shoes off in the mudroom.

"Thanks. How much trouble do you think we'll be in?"

"I think you'll be fine. By the way, you're always welcome to sleep in my room if you..." Sam trailed off. He wasn't sure if he should bring up the dream.

"Thanks, I hope I never have another one like that," I told him.

"Put some meat on those bones," he said as he lightly slaps my chest with the back of his hand before turning to leave.

After a much-needed shower and a great breakfast, I met Derek at the truck. "Hey, Derek, I have a law question. And you have a law degree, am I correct?"

"I'm not an attorney; I have a Criminal Justice degree," he said as he pulled out onto the road.

"Liam is my friend and...."

"And he turns seventeen today," Derek finished. "You are wondering where that leaves you and him with a relationship," he explained, using air quotes with one hand over his head.

"Wow! You're good," I said as a compliment.

"Answering your question bluntly is probably the best approach," he said with little emotion. "Liam turning seventeen today changes nothing." Now I was confused. "It's a common misconception that a minor cannot consent to sexual activity until they are seventeen. Michigan law states that a sixteen-year-old is considered a consenting minor. You are, in fact, fifteen, so you are not a consenting minor; therefore, if you like Liam, you should keep your distance." I processed Derek's information as fast as I could.

"If you'd like, I can explain how a felony conviction could negatively impact Liam's future." Derek was right about me, not knowing the consent laws. I always thought seventeen was the magic number.

"No, thanks. I'm getting the general message. I think Liam has a firm understanding of what boundaries can't be crossed. Are you planning to tell my mom about catching me out of the house this morning without supervision?"

"No," he said, smiling at me in the mirror.

It was time to text Liam:

Happy 17th!

Thank you. I got a new car for my birthday. Do you want to go for a ride when we finish rehearsal today?

I'd love to go for a ride, but today I'm going to see Kevin at his house immediately after...

Sounds good.

See you at school.

My phone chirped again as Derek pulled into his spot. There was a text from RSA:

Good morning, Robert! I saw a sexy pic of you running in the rain shirtless;-)

Really? Where did you see that?

It's posted on your local newspaper's Facebook page. RSA's following text was a picture of Sam and me running this morning. Damn it. "Oh, sorry," I said to some poor girl who I just ran into while looking down at my phone.

Suck! My class is starting; I gotta go, I sent RSA.

Ok, my class is starting as well. See ya, man.

"Are you ready for tonight's dress rehearsal," I asked David as we stood to leave first-hour.

"We're ready, but I'm really nervous that I'll screw something up," David answered.

"You'll do great; see ya at lunch," I told him as we exited the classroom together. David stopped when he noticed Orin standing at the opposite side of the hallway. I stopped as well when David put his arm out as if he was a crossing guard. I looked around for Derek and saw him standing halfway down the hall, talking with a ParaPro. But Derek was looking in our direction, so he was keenly aware that Orin was somewhere he shouldn't be.

"Hey, you little bitch! I see you brought your little celebrity boyfriend for protection. That would mean you'll have to take turns blowing me," Orin said from the other side of the hall.

"Hey, Orin, how's your hand?" David asked, showing his bravery. Orin took a few steps toward us, so I gave him a confident smile to show him I wasn't intimidated either.

"You just need to mind your own business," I told Orin emphatically. Damn, that sounded nerdy. *"Okay, let's try this again,"* I said after entering Orin's red corridor. "*Listen up, you idiot. You will never bully kids in this school again. If you do, your headache will be ten times worse than the one you are about to experience. And when you get home from school today, you'll ask your Mom to take you to a counselor for some therapy."*

Orin looked confused before showing signs of becoming ill as I turn the door handle in the wrong direction. I knew that I didn't have much time before I experienced one of Orin's memories. Orin's eyes went closed first before putting his left hand up to his mouth, trying to prevent the inevitable eruption of vomit. Quickly, he turned to run for the restroom, only five steps from where we stood. Damn it, that's the restroom I was going to use. "See you at lunch," I told David quickly as I followed Orin through the restroom door. There would be hell to pay for me, so I needed a place to hide until the torture was over.

"You can go to your next class, David; I've got this," I heard Derek say as he entered the restroom behind me.

I heard Orin retching in the first stall as I stood in another. His memory trespassed through the red corridor just as I took hold of the grab bars by the toilet. I was thrust into the body of a nine-year-old Orin who was being beaten by an adult male. I looked up at the shirtless man who was slurring his words and reeked of booze. The adult kicked me in the back repeatedly as I laid in a fetal position on a kitchen floor, covering my head. A woman was screaming for the man to stop as she frantically pulled at his arms. "I told you to take the trash out!" the man yelled.

The pain was excruciating, causing me to finally pass out. I was back in my own brain. The memory was over, but now it was my turn to start retching. Nothing but saliva would come up. How could anyone treat a child like that?

"You alright in there," Derek asked me.

"I'll be fine; just give me a minute," I answered, wiping my mouth with some toilet paper that felt like cardboard.

"How about you, kid?" Derek asked who I would assume was Orin.

"Fine," I heard Orin answer as the sink faucet turned on. I didn't want to come out of the stall until my back stopped hurting or Orin left the restroom. I just couldn't face him. What Orin had gone through or could still be going through is… was… agonizing.

While sitting in third-hour, all I could think about was how horrible it felt to be kicked. It was the only domestic violence I had ever personally witnessed, and it was the worst pain I had ever felt. It was even worse than Glad dragging me down the steps at the farmhouse. I felt sorry for Orin. How could a small child endure so much physiological, emotional, and physical trauma in his life without…? Without lashing out at others? Damn it.

My brain was still in a funk when I made it to lunch. David and Zach were already eating. I could see David smiling as Zach talked. There was someone else sitting with them as well, who was wearing a black hoodie. Zach looked in my direction and gave me a wave. By the time I got to our table, they were red-faced from laughing.

Adam Johnson was sitting at our table; he was smiling at whatever Zach had just said as well. Some of the kids at school called Adam 'Smokey Joe,' but I knew what it was like to be called names, so I didn't partake. Kids could be mean; that was probably why I've never seen Adam eat lunch in the cafeteria.

Adam kind of reminded me of myself, minus the smoke smell and his less than desirable wardrobe. He wore the same black hoodie every day. I guess Adam may have several identical hoodies, but I doubted it. Adam looked older than us, even though I knew he was the same age. His hair was close to the same color as mine but much straighter and looked like it could use proper washing.

"Hey Adam," I said as I sat between Zach and him.

"Hey Robert," Adam answered meekly.

"How are you feeling?" David asked me.

"I'm fine. What'd I miss?"

"Zach was just telling us about a time when he was in seventh grade; he dared Kevin to take his shorts off and wear his boxers into their English class," David said with a giggle.

"They looked just like tight shorts," Zach continued.

"I remember that. It was in Mrs. Wheat's class," Adam said as he turned toward Zach. He talks! I've never heard Adam link more than 3 words together.

"Oh yeah, you were in that class, too," Zach said.

I was elated that Adam felt comfortable enough to join us at our table. He and I shared some of the same traits. I often saw Adam walking with his head down just as I did. I've never seen him with friends, and like me, I believed he liked to read. Last week I saw him sitting outside by himself, reading a novel called '13 Reasons Why.'

"Anyway," Zach continued. "We thought no one had noticed until Kevin's mom got an email explaining that Mrs. Wheat would be happy to provide proper attire if they couldn't afford clothing for their son. She also took the opportunity to explain how distracting it can be for other students when the outline of her son's anatomy could be seen through his clothing." The way Zach told the story was hilarious. I could hardly breathe as I continued to laugh. "I'm not sure that last part is true, but that's what Kevin told me. Kevin ended up having to write an apology letter for allowing his dick to be seen in class." I almost choked on my orange juice when Zach mentioned Kevin's dick.

"Are you guys, friends?" Zach asked, pointing at David and then Adam.

"Newly acquainted," David said, smiling at Adam. I wasn't sure, but I think Adam almost cracked a smile.

*"Hey, are you home yet?"* I asked Kevin as I left lunch.

*"Just arrived,"* Kevin answered.

*"Can I come over after rehearsal?"*

*"Sure, I should be up. What time will you be here?"* Kevin asked.

*"Around seven. I have a dress rehearsal today."*

*"Knock 'em dead."*

When I arrived at the dress rehearsal, everything was ready. I couldn't believe tomorrow was opening. David gave me a big smile as I walked over to wish Liam a happy birthday. Getting our makeup applied and dressing for the part took a lot longer than I had intended. But we were able to move through the whole production within the time frame we were supposed to be in.

I was nervous about my songs, but everyone gave me high fives at each set's end. At one point, Derek gave me a standing ovation after Kimberly, and I sang the song 'What Happens When You're Grown Up.' I won't admit it to anyone else, but I'm really starting to enjoy singing. I've become that stereotypical gay kid singing in the high school play. Oh well, that's fine. I am who I am. If people don't like it, they can bite me. Don't get me wrong, most of the kids in our production are straight. I thought they were straight anyway; it was tough to know for sure. It wasn't like we all wore name tags that said, 'Hi, My Name is Robert, I'm Gay.'

It was five thirty-five when I checked my phone. I didn't know how all these kids could go without eating for so long. Just as I thought I may perish from starvation, my mom walked through the door with a stack of pizzas. Three weeks ago, I was at the point of despising my mom, and now I appreciated her more than anyone.

"Thank you, thank you, thank you," I repeatedly said as I walked up to take the pizzas from her.

"Oh, honey, your costume is so cute," my mom said as she handed me the food.

"Thanks, Mom." That was just what a fifteen-year-old boy wanted to hear from their mother while he was wearing green tights and makeup.

"I didn't know how late practice would go, so I thought you may get hungry. I put a couple of pizzas in Derek's truck so you can take them with you to Kevin's when you're finished here," she said with a supportive expression. My mom was suddenly the most beloved mother in the world, with everyone thanking her. Kevin was right; I was fortunate to still have both parents who loved me. Why couldn't I see that back in January? They haven't changed, so that could only mean one thing. I was the one who had matured.

*"Hey, if you haven't eaten dinner yet, my mom is sending pizza with me when I come over in twenty minutes."*

*"Starving! Hurry up!"* Kevin answered.

When we arrived at Kevin's house, Derek followed me up to the front door. A lot had changed over the last six days, including the close presence of security. I wondered how everything would play out at Liam's party on Saturday. If only I could figure out how to tell Liam to pump the brakes if he made sexual advances. We needed to discuss the fifteen-year-old thing so he could hook up with someone in his age group.

Zach opened the door, holding his arms out as if he wanted a hug. "Come to daddy," he announced as he grabbed the pizza and took them to the family room.

"Hey, Kevin," I said with excitement in my voice.

"Hey, thanks for dinner. My dad won't be home from work until eight, and apparently, Zach doesn't know how to cook."

"Hey, I can cook!" Zach said defensively, holding a piece of pizza in each hand. "I'm a superb mac and cheese chef, but you don't have any in the house." Kevin looked so much better sitting in his own house than lying in a scary hospital room.

It was already six-fifty when I arrived home; I knew I needed to take a shower. Believe it or not, flying caused an extraordinary amount of stinky perspiration. As I climbed the stairs, I meet Kate coming down with her friend Sara.

"Hey, Kate, Sara, how are you?" I asked as I approached.

"Hey, Robert," Sara said as she passed. Oh no, I could tell that Sara had a thing for me. She was picturing me standing next to my dad during our media interview.

After I was done showering, I pulled on some soccer shorts and sat down at my computer to find someone singing the 'Come Away' song. I just couldn't seem to get the song right, no matter how hard I tried.

"Hey, Robert?" Kate said as she wandered into my room, uninvited.

"Yeah?" I answered, not bothering to look up from my computer screen and trying not to sound annoyed.

"Sara is staying over tonight, and we were wondering if you wanna join us for chocolate malts? Mrs. Wells is making them for us."

"I'll be down in a sec," I told them as I walked over to my closet and pulled a t-shirt over my head. Maybe it was time to break the news to Kate that I was gay. Sara and Kate looked in my direction when I walked into the kitchen. Sara was apparently dissatisfied with the attire I had added to the top of my body.

By the time I arrived at my quiet place overlooking the beach, it was already eight-fifteen. It would be dark within a half-hour, so I wouldn't be able to stay long. Sara and Kate saw me sneaking out, so I may have to dip into my savings to help them remember how to keep a secret.

As the daylight started to give way to darkness, the familiar warm, euphoric feeling flowed through my whole body. I was convinced that my spot was the most beautiful place on earth, and I didn't want to leave, but I knew I needed to get back before someone noticed I was missing.

I was regretting not bringing a flashlight as I started to navigate the dark foot trail. While trying to find the flashlight app on my phone, I tripped, falling forward into a tree less than a foot from the one-hundred-foot embankment. After doing an impressive face plant into a tree, I felt myself starting to fall from the edge of the steep bank. I felt myself stop in mid-air within milliseconds until I hovered back toward the top of the dune. Thankfully, the touchdown was smooth when I firmly plant my feet on the trail.

*"What the hell is going on, dude?* Kevin said, surprising me as he talked to me through his orange corridor.

*"I almost fell off the side of the dune just now."* I transmit back without having to open any corridors.

*"Ahh... yeah! I know. And I thought you were going to plummet to your death,"* he answered. I wouldn't have died from the fall. I would have done some dramatic tumbling and rolling down the side of the dune, but it was unlikely that I would have been injured. Suddenly, I felt something wet on my face, so I reached up to confirm my suspicions that my left cheek was...

*"Damn it! I'm bleeding!"*

*"Umm... dude, you have a big cut under your left eye."*

*"How do you know that?"* I asked Kevin.

*"Because I can feel it on my own face."*

*"What do you mean, you can feel it?"*

*"What I mean is; I feel the cut just as if it were on my own face. I saw us go over the side of the embankment and float back up to the top,"* Kevin said with a bit of excitement.

*"How do you think it happened?"* I sent him.

*"I think you must have tripped over something."* Kevin sent back as if I didn't already know that.

*"No, I mean, how are you able to see all of this? I didn't connect to your orange corridor. You connected to mine."*

*"I don't know, dude, but you better get something on that gash. I feel warm blood running down my face, dripping onto my chest."* Kevin was right; I had some significant bleeding.

I finally found my glasses and phone in the tall dune grass after getting down on all fours. My bloody finger slid over the screen to turn the light on. After I put my glasses on, I turned my camera to selfie mode.

*"I didn't know you wore glasses,"* Kevin sent.

*"Yeah, since I was twelve."*

*"Dude, that cut looks bad,"* I heard Kevin think.

*"Wait! You can still see what I'm seeing?"*

*"Yeah... kind of creepy. Don't you think?"*

I peeled my white t-shirt off and used it to apply pressure to my bleeding laceration. The shirt was ruined anyway.

*"Oh, no! I have the play tomorrow. I hope I won't need stitches."*

*"It's definitely going to need stitches, dude,"* Kevin said as I walked back toward the house, still holding my t-shirt to my face. The Shawn Mendes song about the needle and thread kept going through my mind.

*"This is going to take some creative explaining when I ask my mom to take me to the ER. I didn't have permission to be out of the house independently, so she will probably freak just a bit. Do you think makeup will cover stitches?"*

*"I don't do much makeup, dude, but I don't think it will. You can just say Captain Hook hacked you up with his sword."*

*"Nice."*

When I opened the door to the mudroom, Kate and Petey were looking back at me. Petey immediately circled me a few times before licking my leg as if he knew I was injured. I was still holding my blood-soaked shirt over my wound so Kate couldn't see how bad it was.

"What happened to your face?" Kate asked. I put my left index finger up to my lips as I kicked my shoes off.

"She was a lot bigger than me, so don't judge," I whispered with a smirk. Sara came around the corner to find me shirtless again. Only this time, all she could do was point her finger at the copious amount of blood.

"Where did all of the blood come from?" Sara asked as she cupped her hands over her mouth.

"Shush. It's just a little scratch." "Where's Mom?" I asked Kate.

"I think she's in her office," she whispered back. Petey continued to dance around me with his nails, clicking on the tile floor.

If I could make it to my room without my mom seeing me, I would clean the blood off so she wouldn't freak out. I had some superglue and bandage supplies in my first aid kit that I kept in my camping backpack. I stealthily moved up the steps toward my bedroom with Petey on my heels.

"Robert, is that you?" my mom asked as I tried to get past her partially closed door.

"I'm heading for the shower," I told her, hoping she wouldn't call me back.

"All right, honey," is all she said. Apparently, my mom didn't want a stinky boy sitting on her office furniture.

Damn, all I could see was blood when I looked into the bathroom mirror.

*"Dude, that's a lot of blood."*

*"I know. Have you figured out how you're able to see this?"* I asked as I wet a washcloth and started to wipe the blood from my face.

*"You're the brilliant one; you figure it out. Wow, the cut seemed to be a lot bigger when you first did it,"* Kevin said.

*"I agree. It looks like the bleeding is controlled. Erm... do you think I'll be able to jump in the shower by myself so I can wash this blood off?"*

*"Dude, you're always jumping in with me. How do you like it?"* Kevin teased.

*"Please? Having you in there with me will be embarrassing if... you know... if things happen to me."*

*"Your brain is making me see this, so you'll have to be the one who shuts it off."* Kevin was right; I needed to find the open door.

*"Here it is. Can you see anything?"* I asked, concentrating on shutting every door in the orange corridor and only communicating with Kevin through the yellow.

*"Nope, I can only hear you now. Your powers seem to be getting stronger every day,"* he said as I lathered up with soap. *"By the end of the week, you'll be shooting lasers from your eyes."*

*"Haha... I have to really focus on making it so you can't see what I'm seeing. It's like I have to hold the door closed so it won't open."*

After I was dried off, I stepped back in front of the mirror. Wait, what? I couldn't believe my own eyes. I must have let go of the door I was holding closed because suddenly I heard Kevin gasp.

*"Dude! It's healed! Your cut is completely healed!"* He was correct; I could only see a small red line under my left eye. "*Do you think you could maybe put some underwear on? I can see everything in the mirror."* I quickly closed the door, but it was as if the access lock was broken with a strong spring trying to hold it open. I walked into my closet to find some shorts to slip on. Standing naked in front of Kevin reminded me of the dream I had with Kipton and George watching me in that Pentagon office. Only this time, it wasn't a dream. At least I didn't think it was a dream. I slapped my face a few times to make sure and...

*"Ouch, dude, I can feel that."*

*"Nope, not dreaming."*

*"You are so weird. I really need to get some rest; do you think you could find a way to shut this off?"*

*"Sure. I'll just go ahead and Google it, or maybe I'll be able to find something on YouTube to explain how to do that,"* I sent with sarcasm while trying to find a plastic trash bag to hide my bloody shirt.

*"No need to be so salty."*

*"I'm sorry, all of this kinda pushed me over the edge. No pun intended. Try to get some sleep. I'll start working on a fix,"* I told Kevin as I stuff the bagged shirt in my trash before turning out the lights.

It felt good to lie down on my bed. When I close my eyes, I was able to find the broken door again. My mind rewired the primary grid that operated the broken door. When I opened my eyes, I was back in my room. Petey was curled up by my head. He was kind of purring like a cat. I knew it was impossible, but sometimes I thought Petey might be part feline. When I sat up, Petey jumped down off the bed and stood by my bedroom door as if he wanted to leave. I opened the door telekinetically; he was gone in a flash.

As I plugged my phone into the charger, I noticed there was a text from a number I didn't recognize:

Hey Rob, this is Cam… my actual number... Text me back when you get a chance.

Hey, Cam.

How'd practice go? Cam text back.

It was okay, I'm getting nervous about a song I can't seem to get right.

What's it called?

Come Away.

LMAO… Come away, sounds like you're giving your friend a handy.

Shut up. Does everything have to be about sex?

Are you seriously asking a sixteen-year-old guy that question? Of course, it does.

How are you adjusting? Any nightmares? I sent back after securing my bedroom door. I lifted my nightstand, causing my lamp to fall off onto the carpeted floor.

It's great to be home, but yeah, a few nightmares.

I retrieved my lamp from the floor before floating it over, where it met up with the nightstand that was still hovering above my bed. It was kind of like juggling balls in the air. The practice was making it, so I didn't have to concentrate as much anymore.

Oh, by the way, my friend Thomas wants to meet you. He saw you on TV. He thinks you're cute...

Really? Your friend Thomas must be high. Haha. I gotta get some sleep, it's gonna be a long day tomorrow. Text me a pic of Thomas.

Okay, cool, I will. Call me tomorrow.

I felt my phone vibrate. Cam was texting again:

This is Thomas…

Oh, man Thomas was handsome, in a rugged hot kind of way. I was getting so tired I could hardly keep my eyes open anymore.

*****

"Wow, this is great," I screamed to the person who was steering the tandem bicycle we were riding together! The bike was at top speed, racing down a big hill on the streets of Mackinac Island.

Lukas turned around and screamed, "This is so fun!" Wait, what! Lukas was steering our bike? Oh well, we were having fun in the summer sun, so I was going to relish the moment. We kept riding until we came to a secluded beach.

"Let's go for a swim," Lukas recommended as we dumped the bike in the sand.

"I'm not sure that's a good idea; we don't have bathing suits," I explained while standing in the soft sand, looking out over the water at the five-mile-long Mackinac Bridge. "Oh, what the hell," I said. We both started to giggle like a couple of little kids as we stripped down to our underwear before running out into Lake Huron. The water was very refreshing as we played around, jumping in the rolling waves. I tried to think of when I had this much fun, but I couldn't come up with any.

"Take me flying," Lukas begged.

"Fine, but I have to warn you, I'm not that good." The view was spectacular from two-hundred feet as I flew around the island, carrying Lukas piggyback.

As we came in for a landing in the middle of the main street, I realized that I had set us down in the pile of fresh horse crap. My feet slipped on the shit, and over we went, crashing into a stack of trash cans. As Lukas and I tried to get up off our asses, I heard someone laughing. When I looked in the direction where laughter came from, I saw Kevin and Zach sitting at an outdoor restaurant table eating pizza. I wasn't sure if they were laughing about the horse crap thing or the fact that we were tangled up with some trash cans, or maybe it was because we were only wearing briefs.

*****

I woke up and looked at the clock. It was only 03:47. Wow, that was fun! I won't mind remembering that one in the morning.

# Opening Night Chapter 18

Friday, June 2nd Opening Night

It was hard to believe how fast the opening day had arrived. I would be working with Mr. Scott today, so I'd have to miss second and third-hour. Cam was such an idiot; every time I sang that damn song, I would be reminded of what he said about helping out a friend.

I was only ten minutes into my swimming workout when I saw Sam come into the pool room. I quickly shut the colorful door in his mind because he was thinking about having sex with his girlfriend. I didn't need any lunch lady video recurrences.

A few minutes after, Sam joined me in the pool. I stopped at the end of my lane for a quick drink. Rather than getting out to retrieve my water bottle at least ten feet out of reach, I telekinetically floated the container over to my hand. As I took my first swig, Sam stopped in his lane next to me. "What the hell was that?" Sam asked.

"What the hell was what?" I answered with labored breathing.

"Do you have a string attached to your water bottle?" I've been planning on telling Sam about my gifts; now seemed like a good time; besides, if I couldn't trust my own brother, who the hell could I trust?

"I have telekinetic powers," I told him while trying to gauge his reaction.

"Don't mess with me, little bro. How did you do it? I saw your water bottle move with my own eyes." We were both hanging onto the edge of the pool, mostly submerged with our goggles on our foreheads. I was sure I looked as ridiculous as he did. Sam's water bottle was three lanes over, so

I lifted it from the deck. Sam let out a slight scream as his bottle floated over to him. I let go so he could grab it from mid-air.

"That was outstanding; when did you learn magic?" Come on, Sam. Try to fire up a few brain cells. See, that's what I mean about being condescending. I just needed to stop.

"It wasn't magic; it was telekinesis," I said instead.

"Whatever. Are you trying to tell me that you can…?"

"That's not all I can do, but I caused Mom to pass out when I showed her," I explained, interrupting Sam.

"Stop stalling and tell me what else you can do."

*"Okay, but I warned you, so don't freak out on me."*

"My God, you just… you just..." he stammered, holding his head with a hand on each side.

*"It's called telepathy."*

"Can I think back to you? I mean, can you hear me without me saying anything?"

*"Sure, give it a try."*

*"Okay, are you getting this, you little twerp?"*

*"I'm not a little twerp. I should warn you that I've become very effective in the art of causing one hell of a headache for people who deserve it."*

"This is hard to wrap my head around. We better get back to our workout, so I can try to process all of this… Whatever this is," Sam said, as he pulled his goggles back over his eyes. It was difficult to believe that I thought Sam hated me two months ago, and now, I realized that he may like me.

*"Hey, are you awake?"* I asked Kevin after I was out of the shower. Since the scary morning we had on Wednesday, I felt as if I needed to check in early.

*"I am now,"* Kevin answered.

*"Did you sleep well?"*

*"Right up to the point when I had an unfortunate dream about you and a mystery dude frolicking in the water, like a couple of idiots."* I was mortified when it clicked in my brain that Kevin saw my dream again.

*"Um… I'm sorry that leaked. The mystery dude was Lukas."*

*"You mean, as in Lukas Barnes?"*

*"Yeah, I'm not sure how he ended up in my dreams."*

*"I do. You're obviously in love with him. By the way, your landings still need some work before I go up with you."* I laughed, remembering the horse crap/trash can incident.

*"Text me if you need anything,"* I sent back.

I kept on messing up on the song 'Come Away' during our special rehearsal this morning. Unfortunately, I had to start over several times.

"Just slow down and don't get so nervous," Liam recommended with a confident tone.

"Yeah, it's just… You know, we'll be at the opening in less than ten hours; I still can't sing this song."

"Let's not panic," Ms. Hukins said with a calming voice. "Windy, would you go find David, please? I believe he's backstage."

"Did you need me, Ms. Hukins?" David asked, returning with Kimberly.

"Yes, David, would you please sing this song with Robert? Just grab that headset over there," she said, pointed at a shelf that was loaded with equipment.

"Umm… sure, but…"

"It's okay, David; I know you can help Robert get started with 'Come Away' tonight at the opening," she said as I felt my cheeks flush. "Lost boy David and Peter, from the top," She said.

The piano started playing while David and I stood together. His voice was significantly lower than mine, but our voices complemented each other nicely. When we were finished singing the whole song, I gave him a high five. "You're an amazing singer," I told David.

"Thank you," he said while removing his headset.

"Okay brilliant," Ms. Hukins said! "I believe a duet will be a nice rendition to enhance the storyline."

"Thank you," I told David feeling much more confident.

Lunch couldn't come soon enough. I was so hungry I could have eaten anything they put in front of me. Except that! Holy shit, whoever's idea it was to cook hamburger, kidney beans, and tomato sauce in a big pot must have been delirious—I hatted chili. Thankfully, the Perk, where the food was sometimes more tolerable, had a pasta dish that looked better.

When we arrived at our table, I asked Zach if he had talked with Kevin this morning.

"Bet, I like, texted him, like on my way down here," Zach said with a mouth full of food. Oh man, that was disgusting. Now I knew why my Mom insisted I not speak with my mouth full.

"Hey Adam," Dom said as he sat down beside him.

"Hey," is all Adam verbalized.

"What's up with the big grin, Dom?" Zach asked.

"I just asked Stacey to go to the play with me tonight, but she told me everything was sold out yesterday. So, I was wondering if you can pull some strings?" Dom asked, looking directly at me.

"My mom has four extra tickets; just show up; I'll ask her to meet up with you."

"Bruh, I have a hard time talking to your Mom," Dom said, still looking down at his phone. "She was my teacher in sixth grade at Christian, and I had a big crush on her."

"Gross! Shut up," I told Dom as he looked up at me with a smile.

"Hey guys," David said with excitement as he sat down with his PBJ sack lunch.

"Hey, David!" Dom answered before anyone else could say anything.

"Do you think your Mom would sell me a ticket too?" Adam asked without lifting his head.

"Sure, but it wouldn't be any cost. Or do you need two?"

"Just one," Adam answered.

"Give me your cell number so my mom can text you," I told Adam.

The tone sounded, ending lunch, so I stood to leave, literally bumping into Adam, who was standing beside David.

"Thanks for the ticket, Robert," Adam said quietly.

"My friends call me Rob," I offered Adam as I studied his turquoise, ocean-colored eyes. Adam gave me a hooded nod before walking away with David.

While leaving sixth-hour, my phone beeped, so I took a quick look. There were two texts. One from Cam and one from RSA:

Good luck tonight. Cam sent.

Thanks, man! I'm nervous.

No answer from Cam. The one from RSA was interesting:

Hello there... I heard that you're going to play Peter Pan in a production tonight. Unfortunately, I can't attend, but apparently, they will have some highlights on CNN.

Hey there. Sorry, you can't make it.

Yeah, I've been grounded anyway.

Why R U grounded?

I got caught doing something...

Something?

Yeah, I got caught sneaking out. Haha

The pic of Sam and me running this morning was a result of us sneaking out. Haha.

Good luck with the play tonight.

Thanks. See ya.

It was only twenty minutes before curtain; the butterflies in my stomach were doing backflips. After briefing me on post play etiquette regarding the reporters lined across the theater's back, Brad left the stage area. The satellite trucks in front of our school weren't helping my unsettled stomach.

"Oh, there you are! Did you see all of the news cameras out there?" Ms. Hukins asked with excitement.

"Yeah," is all I could think to say as she ran both of her hands down her dress to straighten a few wrinkles. *I hope this doesn't make me look fat,* I heard Ms. Hukins think. "You look stunning, Ms. Hukins."

"Thank you, Robert. My boyfriend flew in from Germany to see our play; we haven't seen each other for several months," she explained as she fussed with her hair.

"Ms. Hukins?" David said as he approached us from stage left.

"Yes, David."

"The cable lift keeps getting jammed, so during Robert's high flight, I need to be up there to make sure it doesn't malfunction again."

"Brilliant, David, but do be careful up there; it's extremely high." I loved her fake British accent.

"It's only forty-five feet; I'll be fine," he said confidently.

"Keep me safe up there," I told David as I give him a wink. He blushed bright red after doing so. Wait, what? Was that a... David blushed when I winked. *I hope I have the guts to introduce Rob to Mom and Dad tonight.* I heard David think.

I peeked out the front curtain and holy shit. The place was packed, but I didn't see my dad. His flight only landed twenty minutes ago. Hopefully, he wasn't heavily guarded tonight. Extra security always made everything so awkward. Grandma and Grandpa were in the front row with Mom. Grandma was sitting next to Adam. She and Adam appeared to be having a conversation as if they've known each other for years. Dom and Stacey scored on some good seats beside Adam.

*"Are you here yet?"* I sent to Kevin, scanning the crowd for anyone I may have recognized.

*"Yup, we're all nestled in the nosebleed section. I'm sitting with Zach and my dad."*

*"Thank you for being here. I'm so nervous you may get to see me puke."*

*"You'll do fine, dude."*

*"Thanks for the pep talk. I have to go find Liam."*

*"Be good,"* Kevin sent with a chuckle.

"Hey, Liam, are you ready?" I asked as I approached from stage left.

"Yeah, but I've got Tyce down there in the orchestra pit who keeps blowing me kisses," Liam said, pointing at a cute blonde kid who was playing the drums.

"He's a senior, right?" I asked, smiling down at Tyce.

"Yeah, I think he likes me," Liam said, rubbing his forehead as if he was trying to figure out what he was going to do next.

"Well, good luck with that one," I said as I gave him a nudge.

"Places everyone," Ms. Hukins said with a nervous tone.

Okay, get ahold of yourself, Rob; your first part won't be starting for thirteen minutes, I told myself. The curtains opened, and here we go. Wait, that was one of my lines, haha.

*"Can you even see the stage from way up there?"* I asked Kevin.

*"Yeah, we're good. What's your first part?"*

*"The bedroom scene with Windy."* Damn it, that was the problem with telepathy; the first thing I thought was automatically sent.

*"Wow, I can't wait to see you fake that one!"* Kevin sent with sarcasm.

"Hey, can you come over here? We need to hook up," David said, blushing after he realized what he had just said. I walked over to David with a big grin on my face and turned around so he could hook the cable to my back.

*"Okay, coming out in two minutes."*

*"To everyone?"* Kevin joked.

*"You know what I mean. I'll be flying out onto the stage. I need to focus now, so shut up."*

My first scene had come off without a hitch, and everyone had remembered their parts. I realized I didn't suck as bad as I thought I did after my first song.

*"How was that?"*

*"Dude, you were awesome,"* Kevin answered.

We were finally nearing the part toward the end of the play when Hook was trying to kill me with his plastic sword. As I floated upward, I could see David was having some trouble with the cable. The railing David was standing on didn't give him much support. As he reached out to grab the line, it suddenly un-jammed from the pulley; he lost his balance and started to fall.

He had only dropped six to eight feet before I stop his accelerated descent. David was just like my lamp floating above my bed, but I didn't even have to raise my hand this time. My brain stopped him from falling as soon as the thought had crossed my mind.

David barely had time for a slight scream before I had him safely standing back on the catwalk. He looked over at me with shock as he sat down to prevent himself from passing out. Matt walked over to check on David as I started to float down, where Liam was waiting for me to finish him off with my tiny plastic knife. David, who seemed fine, was talking to Matt when I look back up at the catwalk.

The last scene had been finished for two minutes; we were all standing behind the curtains backstage congratulating each other when I suddenly caught a glimpse of David, who was now running toward me. I thought he was going to congratulate me too, but he didn't. He threw his arms around me and planted his lips on mine. Everyone who had witnessed the encounter was still staring.

"Lineup for bows, please," Ms. Hukins shouted. David was still standing only a foot away, looking at me, trying to determine if I was upset about the kiss.

"You saved my life!" he said only loud enough for me to hear. Captain Hook was standing beside us; he appeared to be crushed. "Great job, Peter!" Liam said.

"And you as well, Captain, sorry I had to kill you and all." David turned on a heal, and off he went to the lineup.

"What was that all about?" Liam asked as we stood, waiting for the curtain to reopen. I gave an exaggerated shrug.

"If you two are a couple, I won't interfere," he said as we were motioned onto the stage for our bow. I could see Kevin. He was on his feet, along with everyone else in the place. I saw my dad standing near the exit with TV cameras pointing at him. But he wasn't talking to anyone. Instead, he was clapping and yelling bravo. I could also see Mom and Grandma standing down in front with Grandpa on one side and Adam on the other, as Hook, Wendy, and I step out in front to take our final bow.

I was immediately surrounded by family and friends when I made it out to the large foyer. Mom gave me a big hug, and then it was my dad's turn to lift me up off the floor. The camera flashes were blinding; however, I could still see David and his parents standing by themselves near the exit. Dad lowered me, and I was immediately hugged by Sam.

"Great job, little brother; I'm proud of you!"

"Thank you, Sam." "Can everyone excuse me for just a second, please? I need to meet someone; I'll be back in a jiffy." I snuck my way through the crowd, past the TV cameras to where David was standing with his parents. David looked shocked as I stood by him, waiting for him to introduce me. David smiled and mouthed the words, 'thank you.' There was a camera not more than two feet away, pointing at our faces. Out of the corner of my eye, I saw Derek step between the camera and us.

"Mother and Father, this is my friend Robert."

"It's a pleasure to meet you both. Did you hear David and I sing 'Come Away' together?" I ask with a bit of a blush. Damn it, Cam.

"That was you, David?" his mother asked, placing both of her hands over her mouth. "You boys sang beautifully together," she said, with a muffled tone. David beamed and shook his head, yes.

"I'm proud of you, David. How long have you two been practicing the song?" David's father asked.

"Only once this afternoon," I declared as I gave David a side-by-side hug. "I literally couldn't have done it without him." David's parents were glowing with pride. Of course, some more news media had found a way around Derek and seemed overjoyed with me hugging David. This media stuff was starting to get on my nerves, but they had a job to do, so I needed to stop whining.

"Good job, guys," Adam said with a barely audible voice as he approached us.

"Thanks, Adam," David and I answered in unison, just as if we were still singing Come Away.

"I better get back over there," I said, pointing at my family.

David was introducing Adam to his parents as I begin to make my way past the news cameras. My parents had been joined by Kyle, and someone who I would assume was Chris.

"Congratulations, Robert," Kyle said as I returned to the group.

"Thank you, Mr. Smit."

"Robert, this is my fiancée Chris..."

*"She's beautiful,"* I sent through a yellow corridor. Kyle grinned. I hated Chris a lot less once I had connected the kind person to the name.

"It's nice to finally meet you, Robert," Chris said as she handed me a small bouquet of flowers. I handed them off to Kate and Sara, who had been designated flower carriers. Kyle may have been pushing the whole too personal thing a bit too far by getting me flowers, but he was a better judge on that stuff than I was.

"It's nice to meet you as well," I said to Chris, shaking her hand respectfully.

I was finally backstage in the dressing room, getting undressed when I was approached by a humble-looking David.

"Hey, thank you for allowing me to introduce my parents," he said after taking a knee in front of my chair.

"I wish I could have gotten you close enough to my parents to meet them as well. Tomorrow night, things won't be as crazy." David nodded and dropped his gaze to my chest.

"I'm sorry I kissed you in front of everyone; I was just caught up in the moment."

"Why are you, sorry? I'm definitely not." David hesitated for a second to study my face and then smiled after confirming that I was serious.

"Thank you for what you did up there tonight," David said as he pointed up at the catwalk. "I had a dream about you being a superhero last night, and come to find out, you really are one."

"I'm no superhero," I told him with a squinted eye.

"I'll need to have you explain how you did the ah... you know... sometime soon. I assume you're keeping this stuff a secret," David said as I gave him a nod.

"Maybe I could explain everything at the after-production party tomorrow night. If you'll go with me?"

"Are you serious? I'd love to go with you!" David said as he slapped my bare thigh and then disappeared. Man, David, was great at disappearing.

I saw Matt talking to Brittany on my way out of the dressing room, so I quickly read him to see if he was thinking about what he may have seen on the catwalk. Nope, shut it off; he's trying to work his magic with Brittany.

There was a text from RSA when I check my phone:

Great job! Congratulations!

Thank you! I need a hint.

Hint for what. RSA sent back immediately.

Your identity.

Okay. We have a lot in common.

Other than not being straight. What else?

We're both annoyed by having security follow every step we take.

Wow! That is a commonality.

When I left the media area, I saw my dad standing in the hall waiting for me. Derek headed off in another direction. It was like the changing of the guards.

"Hey, slugger," he said, draping his arm over my shoulder as we walked toward the truck.

"Hey, Dad, thanks for waiting."

"You did well. Your Mother and I are proud of you," he said as he jumped into the driver's seat. My dad driving the truck with security following in separate trucks could only mean one thing. He wanted to get me alone so we could talk.

"Thanks, everyone put in a lot of hard work," I answered in agreement as I twisted his dog tags on my chest, thinking about David kissing me tonight.

"Yes, I'm sure you all did; the production was evident of that; however, that's not what I was referring to."

"What?" I asked, turning toward him.

"Being inclusive is the most incredible act of kindness anyone can ever gift to another person. More than fifty people wanted to talk with you after the play, and you chose to acknowledge your friend who didn't have a lead role in the play. Who is the boy? The one who introduced you to his parents after the play."

"His name is David Blanch."

"Are you and David close friends?"

"We are planning to go to Liam's party together tomorrow evening if that's what you're asking?" I casually mentioned my planes, trying to test the uncharted waters.

"And will there be alcohol at this party?"

"I don't think so. But to tell you the truth, I hadn't even given alcohol any thought. Do you think there will be?"

"Yes, but I trust you won't partake."

"Nope, not even interested in that stuff after seeing how it has affected Kevin's dad."

"Very well, then. So, do we need to have a sex talk?" Dad asked.

"Dad!" I gasped in disbelief.

"What? I'm just asking. You're fifteen now, and I know what fifteen-year-old boys think about doing. I was fifteen just a few years back."

"This is the most awkward conversation we've ever had," I tried to explain as I looked out into the dark of the night.

"Just work with me here, so I can tell your Mother we had this conversation... So, condoms?"

"Dad, please, can we do this when I'm older?"

"You won't need this talk when you're older; you need it now."

"Yes, I'll use a condom if it ever gets to that point. But I don't have any intention of doing anything for a few years that would require a condom."

"Believe me, teen boys never need to have any intentions when it comes to sex. Sometimes it just happens without any intent. Always remember, a hard cock has no conscience and is always willing to lead the way, whether you have intentions or not."

"Dad!" I gasped again.

"It's scientifically proven that a boy who is sexually aroused is depriving his frontal cortex of oxygen. Blood is being rerouted to his... To other parts of his body. If you check your closet under the tall stack of shorts, you'll find what you need. But please try to wait for a year or two before you get to the stage of needing condoms. My dad took a deep breath before letting it out slowly as if he were trying to relieve some stress.

"When you left DC last week on your birthday, I felt…" Dad took a pause, but I didn't say anything. "I felt like I had blown it."

"It's fine, Dad."

"No, it's not. The way I behaved was…" My dad was never lost for words; it was so weird to hear him struggle. "My behavior was unacceptable," he said, continuing to navigate those rough seas he had earlier referred to. "I beat myself up over the next five days, and then you were taken. I was afraid I'd never get a chance to apologize." I heard him gulp as if he were trying to control his emotions. I wanted to give my dad a hug, but he was still driving, so I reached over and took his free hand that was resting on the center council. "For the next three days, I couldn't live with myself; I couldn't come to terms with how I would be able to go on without you." I knew what he meant. There were a few days last winter when I felt the same. It was hard to describe the feeling I was having at the time, but it wasn't pleasant.

The truck was utterly silent as my dad drove up our driveway and parked in the garage. "Your Uncle Keith struggled his entire life," my dad said, breaking the silence. "In the mid-eighties, when Keith was in high school, things were much different than they are now. The public was terrified when people started dying from sexually transmitted diseases. The gay community was blamed for the epidemic, which forced gay people like Uncle Keith to stay in the closet," Dad explained as the garage door light automatically turned off. I felt my phone buzzing in my pocket, but I ignored it. "I saw how much pain Keith had to go through, and I knew that you would have to go through the same unfair treatment and turmoil he did." I gave my dad's hand a squeeze letting him know that I understood. He squeezed back, signaling the same.

"When you told me you were gay last week, all those memories of your Uncle came rushing back, flooding my mind with dread. I'm not trying to make excuses for my behavior; I just want you to know that I couldn't process things fast enough, and once I realized how insensitive and unfair I was being, you were gone." I heard him snuff some snot up into his nostrils to prevent it from leak out. I knew I needed to say something, but I was afraid I would start crying, so I stayed quiet.

"I'm sorry I was unfair and insensitive. You're one of the bravest young men I have ever known; I don't want you to live your life in the closet as Keith did. I want you to be out and proud when you're ready." He chuckled, probably realizing it sounded funny when he said the 'out and proud' phrase.

"I love you, Dad; I'm sorry you lost your only brother. You won't lose me. I'm staying here with you."

"I know you are," he answered as he rubbed the small scar on the underside of my wrist. "If you ever want to talk, I'll be here for you." My dad had figured out what happened last December, but he didn't mention the event.

"Thank you, I promise I will." We both exited the truck at the same time and made our way into the mudroom. He gave me a hug before we left in different directions.

*"Are you home yet?"* I asked, checking in with Kevin when I made it up to my room.

*"Yeah, my dad made me come straight home to lie down because I have a killer headache."*

*"Hey, maybe I could fix it."*

*"Dude, I don't know. I still have a tube in there."*

*"Just let me try,"* I told him as I close my eyes.

*"Okay, go for it. How could it hurt more than it already does?"* I entered Kevin's orange corridor and opened the first door I came to. There was a red, pulsating wall to my left. When I put my hand on the wall, it turned yellow like the rest of the walls in the room. I could already tell he had less pain after I left.

*"How's that?"*

*"Wow, I think it's getting better! So, you and David?"* Kevin said, changing the subject.

*"Who told you?"*

*"Kimberly saw him give you a full-frontal hug and a kiss like he wanted you. It's the word on the street. What does Hook think about you and pretty boy David's display of public affection?"*

*"I think Liam has kinda given up. I had a very awkward sex talk with my dad on the way home tonight,"* I sent to Kevin.

*"Dope! How'd that go?"*

*"Embarrassing. I'll give you the whole play-by-play tomorrow after you've had some rest."*

*"Okay, night, man. Thanks for fixing my headache."*

*"Goodnight."*

There was a text from Cam when I checked my phone:

Hey man... Give me a call if you're still awake.

"Hey there, superstar!" Cam said when he answered on the first ring. "Thomas and I just saw you on the national news. By the way, Thomas has the hots for you." "Ouch, that hurt," I heard Cam say to someone who I would assume was Thomas. *You had it coming, dumbass.* Wait, this was new. I could read what Cam was comprehending as Thomas talked to him. Wow! This unique gift would definitely be helpful.

"Quit trying to embarrass him," I told Cam.

"He has a pic on his phone of you and your brother out running with your shirt off." *Shut up,* I heard Cam comprehend from Thomas.

"Leave him alone, Cam," I said, trying to save Thomas from embarrassment.

"I'm just saying that he had to wipe the drool from his mouth a few times." "Ouch, stop. That was my tit, you just twisted!" Cam said. "Thomas is staying over tonight; he'll probably need a cold shower before he goes to bed," Cam teased. I locked my door telekinetically before I slowly and carefully start to levitate from my bed. I loved the feeling of hovering; it made me feel free.

"I better get some sleep, man," I told Cam.

"That's cool." *Tell him congrats,* Thomas said to Cam. "Thomas sends his congratulations on the play."

“Tell Thomas, thank you,” I told Cam as I pushed the end button.

*****

“Get away from me. Leave me alone!” I yelled as I squirmed around, kicking at a weird-looking part human, part fish-man. The gills on his neck were retracting as if he was starving for oxygen. His gross slimy, webbed hand slipped from my leg when I kicked at it from the watercraft. He was trying to pull me under where I wouldn’t be able to breathe. “No, don’t take me under! Please don’t take me!” I screamed. The creature was gone, but now I noticed Lukas Barnes sitting on a watercraft, not more than one foot from mine.

“Don’t worry, I won’t let anyone take you away from me,” Lukas said.

*****

Effing Aquaman dream. Why was Lukas Barnes in my dream again? I took my phone from my nightstand and ventured down the hallway toward Sam’s bedroom at 02:02. Using the phone’s screen light to navigate Sam’s floor’s minefield was my only hope of not tripping. After climbing into Sam’s bed, I immediately drift off to sleep.

# After Production Chapter 19

Saturday, June 3, After Production

It was 09:00 when I woke up; Sam had already left for work. I had to be at the school for play review by nine-thirty, so I took a quick shower before finding some food. Mrs. Wells had the day off; therefore, I would have to fend for myself.

Derek was waiting for me in the security garage when I arrived with a raspberry pop tart in hand.

"You did well last night," Derek told me as I approached the truck. "I saw the commotion backstage just after the play ended."

"Thanks," I answered with a tinge of awkwardness. I wasn't sure if Derek was referring to the kiss from David or the levitation. "Are you going to get stuck staying late again tonight?" I asked, hoping to change the subject.

"I'll be driving you to the party, but I'll be staged outside while you're there," he answered, making eye contact through the mirror.

*"Did you get any sleep last night?"* I asked Kevin as we pulled into the nearly empty school parking lot.

*"Yeah, I slept well. But dude, that green fish thing was effed-up,"* Kevin answered.

*"Yes, it's disturbing. I'm off to rehearsal; see you tonight at the party."*

*"Only if my dad lets me go,"* Kevin sent back.

David was sitting on the lawn under a small flowering tree, waiting for me to arrive at the school. "Hey, David!" I said as I walked toward the front doors.

"Good morning!" he said with excitement as he jumped up to meet me. "I just wanted to confirm that we're going to the party together tonight. I woke up in a panic this morning when I thought I may have dreamed that you had recommended we go together." I just smiled for a few seconds because he was so damn cute.

"I asked you, and you said sure, but I wouldn't be opposed to being in your dreams as well." We both start to laugh as we walk toward the doors.

Our second production went off without any near-death experiences this evening. When the final curtain fell, I was relieved that it was over for the night, but I felt I needed more. I loved being on stage; now, I would have to wait until next weekend to feel the exhilaration of performing again.

As I made my way out to the foyer, I saw David standing alone, wearing his Lost Boy costume. Ms. Hukins had changed the scene so David could stand with me on stage while we sang Come Away.

"Come on, I want to introduce you to my family," I told David as I grabbed his hand. I could feel his excitement as we continued down the narrow hallway leading to the lobby. It was challenging to let go of David's hand before re-entering the judgmental public eye, but I knew it was necessary. Contrary to what my dad told me last night, I didn't believe our conservative community was ready yet.

As I introduced my awesome family to David, I felt someone small squeeze between David and me. Before I could see who it was, I felt a small child's hand holding mine. I looked down to find Ahmad looking up at me with a big grin. He was wearing a cute little black suit with a bow tie.

"Who is this handsome boy?" my mom asked as she got down on one knee to shake Ahmad's free hand.

"Mom, this is Ahmad; I met him on my way home from DC last week."

"It's nice to meet you, Ahmad," my mom said.

"Do you know magic too?" Ahmad asked David as he reached up, grabbing onto David's left hand.

"Sorry, I don't know any magic," David answered with a smile.

"I saw you on TV, Robert. It was scary," Ahmad said as his voice started to crack. He was so cute not being able to pronounce his R's.

"Hello, I'm Aliya." Ahmad's mother said, introducing herself to my mom. "I had to bring him tonight to see Robert. Ahmad has been talking nonstop about Robert since he met him on a flight. Would you mind if I got a picture of you together?" Aliya asked.

"Sure, no problem," I said as I took a knee with one arm around Ahmad. I guess you never know how much impact you can have on someone if you simply share some kindness. "Thank you for coming to the show, Ahmad," I told him as I stood. Before I knew what had happened, Ahmad wrapped his arms around my waist.

"Apparently, you've made quite an impression," my dad said.

"Come along, Ahmad, we better be on our way," Aliya said as she pried Ahmad's hands from my waist.

"Goodbye, Ahmad," I told him.

I had some time to kill while Derek was driving me to the party, so I checked my phone to see if I had any text from RSA. It was as if I couldn't wait. The excitement of the unknown was driving me insane. Yup, there was one from RSA eleven minutes ago:

How did night 2 go???

Hey RSA. It went great! I'm on my way to an after-production party.

With whom? RSA had sent it immediately, so he must have been bored or waiting for me to answer.

Why are you asking? Do you want to come along?

Your boyfriend won't mind?

I've told you. I don't have a boyfriend.

JK, I'm still grounded anyway, haha. But the level playing field sounds promising.

Sure does… If I only knew who you were. I gotta go.

I hope you enjoy the party… Wait, what? I've recently heard someone use that exact phrase. I quickly searched my memory banks, and… There was no way it could be him!

"Please clip this to your belt," Derek said, handing me a small device as he parked the truck on the street in front of Liam's house. "If you have any trouble, push the button. No one can jam the device." A week ago, I would have bitched about wearing the thing, but tonight, I was okay with the extra protection.

As I stepped out onto the street, I saw David arriving as well. I gave him a wave as he stepped out of his dad's vehicle. I wish I'd learn the manly wave. It seemed like every time I tried to do something masculine, it felt awkward. David, on the other hand, had accomplished masculinity. His wave and walk conclusively placed him in the macho category.

"Hey," I said to David with both hands now safely placed in my pockets. I didn't know why I felt so nervous as we walked toward the front door, but I was sweating bullets. Wait, what? How could someone sweat bullets?

"Robert Van Stark, how are you this evening?" Liam's dad said with a big smile as he greeted us at the front entry.

"I'm fine, thank you."

"And you're the lost boy who sang so well," Liam's dad said, shaking David's hand.

"Thank you, Sir. I'm David Blanch."

"I won't have to search either of you for weapons or alcohol, will I?" Doctor Davis asked as he gave us a wink. We both shook our heads, no innocently.

After making entry into the house, I caught a glimpse of Liam on the other side of a large room filled with people just before he and Tyce snuck through a sliding door.

"Would you like something to drink?" I asked, pointing at an open kitchen island area.

"Sure, I have to admit; this is the first party like this I've ever been to," David said with a slight blush.

"Yeah, me too," I told him as we made our way to a makeshift bar where they were serving drinks in some cool-looking Peter Pan glasses. I noticed David's eyes light up as we both took a sip.

"Wow, this is delicious! I think it's the best drink I've ever tasted," David said.

"Hey, Peter and David," Ms. Hukins said as she approached. "Your duet was a brilliant performance again, even better than last evening's. You two may want to consider exploring a partnership."

"Thank you," we replied simultaneously and then grinned at each other.

"Oh, there you are," Ms. Hukins said as she walked away, trying to catch Kimberly.

“Let’s find a quiet place to talk,” David recommended with a bright smile. A quick read revealed David’s plan to ask me about levitating him. Who would have guessed that?

“Okay, spill it; the suspense is killing me,” David said as we sat side-by-side on a bright yellow loveseat in a small music room. David studied me as I swallowed deeply, trying to figure out why I was so nervous.

“Erm, maybe if I give you the shortened version.”

“Sounds good,” David said as he took a sip of his tropical drink through a straw.

“I have some gifts. You saw one gift last night. I’m telepathic, telekinetic, and I can read emotion too.”

“How long...?”

“Three weeks,” I answered before he could finish. “The telepathy started first.”

“Can you do it to me?”

*“Oh, believe me; I would love to do it to you.”* We both start to giggle as if we were playing with a shiny new toy.

*“So, am I able to tell you how hot you are without anyone hearing me?”* David sent as he slowly leaned in toward me. Just before our lips had a chance to make contact, I stopped and looked to my left when I sensed the presence of someone in the room with us. Sam and his girlfriend were standing in the doorway, grinning.

“Hey, guys, what’s going on in here?” Sam asked with a sly tone.

“Nothing,” David and I answered simultaneously as Sam made his way into the music room.

“Dad just called and said he’s on his way here to pick us up.”

“But why? We just got…”

“Samuel and Robert?” Derek said with a commanding voice, interrupting my whining.

“Yes, Sir?” Sam answered, turning toward Derek.

“Come with me immediately. It’s crucial we move you both to a secure location.”

# Epilogue Chapter 20

Tuesday, August 20 Epilogue

August was a beautiful time of the year to visit Mackinac Island. My parents stayed with Governor Malone in his vacation house on the island, and the rest of us were guests at the iconic Grand Hotel. When we moved to 'Number One Observatory Circle,' everything changed. We had to move again two weeks later, so I hadn't been able to spend much time with Kevin. Thankfully, Mom allowed Kevin to come along on our family vacation. After everyone went to sleep tonight, we were going to give my security detail the slip so we could go flying.

The End

# Acknowledgments

I just wanted to say thank you to all who helped me make my first book a reality. To my wonderful family who believed in me (Derek, Shalee, Joel, Toni, Jill, Ryan, Lydia, Trae, Thomas, Elizabeth, Eleanor, and Oliver). Also Troy Jones, Jonah Nelson, Blake DeVerney, Toni Gerencer, Mark Gerencer, Elliot Hasty, Brody D., Drew Gerencer, Rick Gregory, Sam Pascoe, James Mitchell, Theo M., Faith R., Anthony N., Suzanne Proksa, Kristi Walsh, and finally to my wonderful wife, Laurie who has offered her patience, support, and love while I spent thousands of hours staring at a computer screen.



Dreaming To Live



ISBN-9781696205337

Cover design by Jenna Simmons

# About the Author

Davis T. Gerencer (*Thomas Gerencer*) began his quest to help prevent teen suicide in late 2016, hoping to reach teens by writing young adult fiction. His stories include funny, exciting, adventurous, emotional, and educational experiences. Thomas became a Firefighter/Paramedic in the early 1980s and is now a retired Fire Chief in West Michigan, where he lives with his wife, Laurie. Forty years of Fire/EMS has given him firsthand experience of the gut-wrenching effects depression and suicide can have on teens, their families, friends, and EMS providers.

As a teen, Thomas experienced the loss of his friend. His teen friend chose suicide, leaving Thomas with devastating grief, contemplating and attempting suicide himself. He believes reading his books will offer other teens an opportunity to learn skills about coping with depression and entice them to treat others with kindness, acceptance, and inclusion. After all, a straightforward act of kindness may save a teen from choosing suicide.

Dreaming To Live (*book one of the Embracing Life Series*) was written in memory of all teens who have taken their own life. Please, never give up. There is always hope for you. Your life will get better like it did for Robert. Always remember that the moment of feeling suicidal will pass. But most of all, know that you have a support group that cares deeply about you. We will always accept you just the way you are, and we will always love you. 'Living To Dream' (*the sequel, book two of the Embracing Life Series*) will be released in late 2021.

Ten percent of the profits from this book's sale will be donated to 'The Trevor Project,' and 'It Gets Better' organizations, which strive to save our youth's lives.

Visit. www.trevorsproject.com

Visit. www.itgetsbetter.org

# Teen suicide prevention

Teen suicide is at epidemic levels across our Nation. Many parents believe suicide won't affect their son or daughter. But in reality, suicide affects us all in one way or another. According to the National Youth Risk Behavior Survey, 17.2 percent of American high school students reported they have seriously considered attempting suicide in the past year (*Trevor Project 2019*).

This book was written to help teach general acceptance, tolerance, and coping skills to help save our youth's life. The book's main character is a gay fourteen-year-old boy who lives with his wealthy, conservative, religious family. I chose this life for Robert because recent studies have shown that boys are twice as likely to succeed at suicide than girls. LGBTQ teens are five times more likely to attempt suicide than straight kids. And teens who live in a conservative community are more likely to choose suicide than those who live in a moderate or liberal community.

The book's suicide prevention message is not meant to take a political or religious stance. Robert struggles with his faith because so many choose not to accept those who are different from themselves. The author wanted to add some reality to Robert's life, so the readers may relate to the challenges of being gay in some settings.

Scientific facts have proven that a teen's sexuality is a basic human fundamental that drives their thoughts, feelings, behaviors, and pleasure-seeking. Teens are thrust into a midfield of sexual unknowns that are driven by the need for biological reproduction. Their brains come pre-wired at birth, allowing them to orient themselves to the attraction of others.

A teen's sexuality is part of being human. However, the stigmas associated with sexuality are often driven by society's expectations for teens to be straight. These expectations often put added pressure on our teens, causing unthinkable consequences, including suicide. Please always remember that fundamental sexual attraction drives a person's sexual orientation, and one's sexual orientation does not define the person.

Made in the USA
Monee, IL
26 March 2022